Nicole Alexander is a fourth-generation grazier. She returned to her family's property in the early 1990s and is currently the business manager there. She has a Master of Letters in creative writing and her novels, poetry, travel and genealogy articles have been published in Australia, Germany, America and Singapore.

She is the author of eight previous novels: *The Bark Cutters*, *A Changing Land*, *Absolution Creek*, *Sunset Ridge*, *The Great Plains*, *Wild Lands*, *River Run* and *An Uncommon Woman*.

Also by Nicole Alexander

NICOLE ALEXANDER

Stone Country

PENGUIN BOOKS

PENGUIN BOOKS

UK | USA | Canada | Ireland | Australia
India | New Zealand | South Africa | China

Penguin Books is part of the Penguin Random House group of companies
whose addresses can be found at global.penguinrandomhouse.com

Penguin
Random House
Australia

First published by Bantam Australia in 2019

This edition published by Penguin Books in 2020

Cover images by Shutterstock
Cover design by Adam Laszczuk and Cathie Glassby © Penguin Random House Australia Pty Ltd
Typeset in Fairfield LT by Midland Typesetters, Australia
Printed and bound in Australia by Griffin Press, part of Ovato, an accredited
ISO AS/NZS 14001 Environmental Management Systems printer

A catalogue record for this
book is available from the
National Library of Australia

ISBN 978 0 14378 683 2

penguin.com.au

MIX
Paper from
responsible sources
FSC® C009448

For rarely are sons similar to their fathers: most are worse, and a few are better.

Homer, *The Odyssey*

⤜ Part One ⤛

1901–1919

⋘ Chapter 1 ⋙

Adelaide, South Australia, 1901

The two brothers darted back and forth across the wide thoroughfare, dodging carts, carriages and horse-trams. They skipped and jumped over the piles of horse dung, some fresh and steaming, others hard enough for a person to trip on. When a motorcar chugged past they ran after it, calling to the driver to give them a ride. Each time a horse-drawn vehicle approached them, the elder boy, Alastair, would wait on the edge of the footpath until it was almost too late to cross and then he would dash out in front, startling the horses and drivers, before running to the other side of the road.

'One, two, three. Go!' cheered his younger brother, Ross.

Alastair sidestepped two carriages. One of the horses baulked and the driver drew back on the reins before letting the animal have its head again. By the time the horse was under control Alastair had already crossed the street and was waving at Ross to hurry up. From down the road a tram approached. Two horses, one grey and the other the shade of burnt biscuits, pulling the load. As the vehicle grew closer Ross could see the travellers through the saloon glass. On the top deck, ladies sat at the rear holding parasols where

3

the canvas awning didn't quite screen them from the sun. Ross felt the familiar rush of excitement. His chest rose and fell. The horses drew almost level. He dropped his head and ran.

'Get out of the way!' a man on a penny-farthing yelled.

Ross hadn't seen the bicycle on the other side of the horse-tram. The high-wheeler wobbled left and right as it struggled to veer out of his path, then the tall front wheel struck something on the road and its rider was pitched headfirst over the handlebars. The man's hat soared upwards while the owner landed heavily, sprawling on the road. The traffic slowed as the riderless bike clattered across the street to fall on its side.

Ross stared at the unconscious man, whose limbs were splayed like a paper cut-out figure, a fine dribble of blood seeping from parted lips. People began running towards the injured rider. They were calling for a doctor, asking what had caused the accident.

'Come on, Ross.' Alastair dragged him through the gathering crowd.

Women reached for lacy handkerchiefs, grimy hemlines ruffled the dirt, men scratched at whiskery faces as a voice called out for a clear passage to be made. A black bag with a shiny metal clasp skimmed Ross's shoulder. Alastair kept Ross's wrist grip-locked until they reached the footpath.

'It's a stupid contraption anyway,' said Alastair. 'No one rides those old things anymore. Come on.'

'But what if he's hurt?' asked Ross. 'Or worse?'

'Then we don't want to be hanging around, do we? Let's split up for a bit. I'll meet you outside the hospital in ten minutes.' Before Ross had a chance to reply Alastair was gone. He couldn't help looking back at the chaos. Two men were lifting the twisted penny-farthing. What if the bicycle man had been killed? Ross's hand went to his neck. They hanged murderers.

He stuck around, waiting to see if the man had survived but the crowd still clung to the place of the accident and Ross knew that it was best to leave and find his brother. He began to walk towards the hospital, gradually moving faster, rushing past the paperboy and finally breaking into a run, not slowing until he reached the wrought-iron enclosure of the Royal Adelaide Hospital.

'Where have you been?' his brother asked, barely out of breath.

Alastair was waiting outside the hospital gates, a foot propped up behind him as he leant against the fence. He was smoking a cigarette, the thin tube of paper dangling precariously from his mouth. He took a deep puff and then carefully stubbed it out. Wetting the tip with a glob of spittle, he slid the smoke into a pocket.

'Where did you get that from?' asked Ross.

'It's a free country.' Alastair beckoned him to the fence. Three nurses dressed in their walking-out clothes, long black capes, and caps with floppy bows tied under their chins, stopped to help a sobbing woman who spoke with the same German accent as their housekeeper.

'Another one for the dead house,' said Alastair. 'You know when they chop someone's leg or arm off, they bury it in a big hole behind the hospital.'

'They do not,' said Ross, trying to match his brother's stride.

'Do so. Where else are they going to put them?'

'I think I killed that man,' admitted Ross, trying to stop tears from filling his eyes. 'He fell on his head. And there was blood and everything.'

Alastair's face lit up. 'I didn't see the blood.'

'It was there. Lots of it,' said Ross solemnly. 'They hang you for killing people, Alastair.'

'You were just crossing the road.' His older brother pushed him forwards and together they followed on the heels of an elderly man with a slight limp, Alastair dragging his left foot as he mimicked him. 'Even if you did kill him it wasn't your fault, and if it was, the police would be after you, wouldn't they?'

Ross wasn't convinced. 'I suppose so.'

'And can you see any police?'

The street was busy with traffic and the people riding normal bicycles rang tinny bells so you'd know when they were overtaking.

Maybe his brother was right. The problem with being eight years old was that you didn't know everything. It was a very bad age. Alastair said that there was all manner of things that only became knowable and interesting once you turned the magical age of twelve. Which was, Ross thought, rather convenient for his older brother.

'When I'm your age do you think Father will let us go north to visit Waybell Station?'

'If you still want to go,' said Alastair.

'Don't you?'

'It's a long way. Father's not even been there.'

'That's why we should,' said Ross. 'One day I'll be just like McDouall Stuart. The most famous Scotsman in the world. I'll cross the desert, explore country no white man's ever seen and float down alligator-infested rivers.'

'They're called crocodiles, Ross!' Alastair picked up a stick and began using it like a sword, wheeling it back and forth, stabbing at the air.

'We can dive for pearls and go back to the property at night,' Ross continued. 'You have to come with me, Alastair. Promise?'

Without answering, his brother ran ahead. When they stopped a few minutes later it was outside a stone wall. They stared through an open side gate at the long two-storey building that sat atop a rise. Wings extended from the main doorway, which was flanked by gabled windows, and a vine crawled across the face of the structure.

'I'm not going in there,' said Ross. 'It's full of mad people.'

'That's why we *have* to go, Ross.'

'But if we get caught . . .'

'One look. Promise.'

They loitered near the gate as a gardener loaded clippings and branches into a horse-drawn dray. He worked methodically, shovelling shrub trimmings and leaves in first before throwing the longer lengths of brushwood on top so that the smaller, finer rubbish wouldn't blow away.

Alastair sat on the ground and took off his shoe. While the gardener worked, he removed the laces and then slowly rethreaded them through the punched leather holes, making a show of checking the length before tying a neat bow. 'We'll be here all night if he doesn't hurry up.'

It was cold in the lee of the wall. The air pricked Ross's bare legs as he hoped for the dray to break down or for the horse to go lame. The asylum was on Alastair's list of 'things to be done', which meant that sooner or later they would have to go inside, but he'd always hoped it wouldn't happen. At least not while he was still a boy. Alastair's list was comprised of a series of tests he devised after reading about the feats given to the Greek god Hercules. Ross blamed their tutor, Mr Storey. The four-eyed teacher was more obsessed with the Greeks than Alastair was.

Overhead, the boughs of a tree reached across the wall. Shapes seemed to nestle in the leaves above. Ross imagined nine-headed monsters and enormous bulls, for his brother had taught him to see Greek stories in everything. But the problem with Alastair's myths was that they were all make-believe. A place of gods and mortals without an inch of truth to any of the tales. Ross would choose *King Solomon's Mines* over Hercules any day. A lost world it might be but at least Africa existed, and exploring was much better than fighting monsters.

The gardener gave them a friendly wave as Alastair impatiently tugged the second set of laces from the other shoe. 'Sit down, Ross. He'll think we're up to something.'

Ross kicked at a newspaper in the gutter, sneaking his fingers into a pocket where he'd placed a handful of boiled lollies. Alastair's tests of manhood were becoming riskier and riskier. The smoking of their father's pipe and the drinking of a glass of whisky had already been accomplished, although the stealing of sweets from the Rundle Street confectioner hadn't been quite as success-ful. Ross may have managed to whisk away some candy from an unattended open jar, however the shop owner had seen him. The problem was that he didn't *want* to take anything from the store. He liked watching Mr Johnston unscrew the lid on the glass jars and with deliberate slowness count the candy into a paper bag, a long-nailed finger sliding each lolly across the glass counter as if he was counting out Ross's weight in gold.

There were other things in his brother's notebook. The kissing of a certain girl who didn't have a name. And the construction of wings that would allow Alastair to float down from the upper branches of the camphor laurel tree. But the lunatic asylum, well, that was his brother's biggest test.

The gardener turned his back to the boys and finished loading the dray. Alastair waited for just a second before catching Ross by the sleeve and dragging him to his side as they slid through the gate. Inside, they levelled their bodies against the wall, listening as the gardener closed the gate behind them, then they crouched behind a hedge.

'I don't think this is a very good idea,' Ross whispered.

Alastair lifted a finger to his lips. 'Quiet,' he warned. They crept slowly towards the front of the building, keeping clear of the open veranda, their bodies crouched low and tight within the manicured vegetation.

'If anything happens, Ross, head straight for the Botanical Gardens.'

'What's going to h-happen?' he stammered, anxiously scanning the wide gravel path. There didn't seem to be anyone around, but he could hear noises coming from inside the asylum.

'Shush,' his brother warned again. 'I don't know. We might get chased by a mad person.'

Ross took a step back. 'But I don't want to –'

'Come on,' Alastair enticed. 'It will be dark in a couple of hours. All the patients will be inside now. Tied up for the night.'

'They tie them up?' gasped Ross.

'Straitjackets.' Alastair made a moaning noise as he wrapped his arms around his body.

The younger boy felt a tingling sensation on the back of his neck. The sun was dipping behind the stone wall, patches of darkness already obscuring the flowerbeds and bushes that led to the gardener's gate.

'Let's go.'

Ross watched Alastair as he ducked, running towards the building. At the jutting bay window he held onto the lattice that was securing a trailing vine, put a foot on the ledge and shimmied up onto the gable-shaped canopy. He squatted on the roof and beckoned to his brother.

Ross gritted his teeth and rushed across the lawn, wedged his shoe on the trellis and began to climb. He was too short to step straight across to the window shelf, so he climbed a little further. The framework creaked under his weight.

'Hurry up,' Alastair hissed.

Ross managed to get one foot on the window sill as the timber frame gave an ominous crack and started to bend.

Alastair knelt on the roof above. 'Stand on the sill. Reach up and grab the ledge.'

'They'll see me,' said Ross.

'No they won't. The curtains are drawn.'

Ross tried to pull himself higher by gripping the edge of the canopy but there was nothing to rest his feet on and he wasn't strong enough. 'Help me.'

Alastair heaved him up by his shirt as Ross pushed the soles of his shoes against the glass. Inch by inch, he wormed his way towards his groaning brother.

'I can't do it!'

'Yes you can, try harder,' puffed Alastair.

With a final burst of energy Ross kicked out. There was the sound of breaking glass as he fell on the roof.

'Now you've done it,' scolded Alastair. The boys squatted on the small sloping space, holding their breath as people called out from inside the asylum. Ross braced his shoes on the rolled iron edging. Below, curtains were tugged open and a woman called for help. Alastair pointed to an open window a few feet above them. 'I'll go in and then I'll help you.'

The trellis was lurching out over the flowerbed. It was a good ten-foot drop to the ground. Ross found himself agreeing.

Alastair reached up to take hold of the sill and hurled himself inside the building. A few moments later his head popped up. He was grinning.

'Come on. It's easy.'

Ross moved gingerly across the canopy. Reaching out one hand and then the other, his fingers grasped the protruding brickwork. The weight of his body pulled him forwards and he slipped, his chin hitting warm brick as his arms stretched from their sockets. 'Alastair?'

His brother had him instantly and pulled him inside. They landed with a thud on the floor.

The room was in semi-darkness. When Ross grew accustomed to the light he saw two people sitting quietly by their beds. He waited for one of the men to call out or to complain but their eyes remained fixed on a picture of a sailing ship.

'Don't worry about them,' said Alastair. 'They don't know we're here. I've already checked.'

'Are they sleeping?' asked Ross quietly, getting to his feet.

Alastair waved a hand in front of the men's faces. 'With their eyes open.'

They'd seen their first mad people and they weren't scary at all. Except that when Ross got a little closer he discovered that the men were strapped to their chairs, wrists and ankles bound tight. One of them was drooling. A thin line of wetness had attached itself to the man's shirt, forming a damp patch on his chest.

'I don't like it here,' admitted Ross.

'I bet they've been given special drugs like heroin or opium, or maybe he's been sitting in a freezing cold bath for days. It makes a person into a turnip. Look at them.'

Ross waved a hand in front of the unseeing patient and stuck out his tongue. 'But why do they want to turn them into a turnip?'

'They don't. They're trying to make them normal again. But when they're as mad as a hatter you can't make anyone normal again. You can only lock them up and feed them. They don't feel anything, you know. They don't know if it's summer or winter. If it's hot or cold. Nothing.'

Alastair went to the door and turned the handle. It opened easily. 'Guess they don't have to lock them in when they're tied up.' Outside in the corridor he began checking the wards. He slid bolts across to reveal empty rooms. Only one was padlocked. 'That's probably where they keep the really mad lunatics.'

'Won't someone come looking for us?' asked Ross, thinking of the broken window pane.

'Doesn't seem like it. I bet they're searching the garden. Let's try this one.' Inside the ward sat four children on narrow cots. They looked younger than Ross. A battered teddy bear lay abandoned on the floor, and a little girl started to cry. Alastair held a finger to his lips to shush her, and they quietly left the room.

'Are they mad too?' asked Ross once they were back in the hallway.

'Maybe they're orphans,' answered his brother. Downstairs they could hear people moving about. 'We'd better hide. Just until things quieten down.'

A key sat in the padlock of the last door and without hesitating they unlocked it and entered. A man in a white jacket with long sleeves wrapped tight around his body shuffled in a circle across the empty room. 'If they let me go I won't do it again. If they let me go I won't do it again,' he repeated.

Alastair reached a protective arm across Ross and, very slowly, they edged to the door.

'I said I wouldn't do it again. I said I wouldn't do it again.' The man rushed towards them.

Ross screamed as they ran into the hall and straight into the path of a young boy clutching a teddy bear. 'Hello,' he said, with a timid smile.

'We need to get out of here,' said Alastair to the child. 'Is there a way?'

The boy nodded and they followed him to the landing. Sitting on the top step, the bear in one hand, the boy began to push himself down the flight of stairs on his bottom.

'We'll be here all day,' complained Alastair as they watched the little boy's progress. 'I'm going to carry you,' he whispered to the child. He swept the boy up into his arms and ran down the rest of the stairs. At the bottom the child pointed to an alcove under the stairs, and the three of them squeezed into the small space. Concealed by a table crammed with books, they hid in the gloom as doors slammed and people called out for any intruders to show themselves. Ross's fingers closed around the sweets in his pocket and he gave one to the boy. A swatch of dark skirt swished past them. The little boy pressed closer to Ross, the teddy bear wedged between them. The stairs creaked.

When they eventually crawled out from under the steps the boy led them to the back entrance of the building, pointing to a set of keys hanging from a hook on the wall. 'A way out,' said Alastair, as he began trying each key in the lock.

'Hurry up,' urged Ross. The keys tinkled in Alastair's fingers. On the floor above doors were being banged as rooms were searched. Next to him the little boy jigged up and down on one leg, clutching the bear by its neck. He tugged on Alastair's sleeve.

'I'm going as fast as I can,' Alastair replied.

After what seemed like an eternity, the key turned in the lock and they pushed through the door. Alastair shouted his thanks to the boy and then he took off, skirting the hedges, calling to Ross to keep up.

Ross concentrated on Alastair's heels as they hurdled flowerbeds and weaved past blossom-drooping trees, out a gate and towards the expanse of the Botanical Gardens. He glimpsed the child once. A small shape quickly consumed by deepening shades of green.

≼ Chapter 2 ≽

As his father paced the drawing room, a tobacco pipe wedged firmly between his teeth, Ross wished that his grandfather had never left Scotland. For, at this very moment, he was in dire need of the clan's help. As he waited with Alastair for judgement to be passed, Ross stared at the Grant family crest hanging above the fireplace. The image represented a burning beacon atop Craig Elachie, a hill that was the assembly point for the Grants. He'd been told by his grandmother that there was a fine view down the length of the Upper Strathspey from this hill, and that if you lit a fire on its summit members of the clan would come from miles around to help you. It didn't matter if you were about to attack your enemy or needed help to defend yourself and your home, the clan would come to your aid. Although Ross Grant had never seen Scotland – his family had left their homeland for Australia two generations earlier – he knew his people were fighters. They'd battled red-coated Englishmen and upstart clans from across the mountains for many years, striking down their opponents with a broadsword in one hand and a shield in the other. Ross stole a glance at his father and pictured himself running up the steep hill, his boots slipping in damp heather, the torch he held aloft flecking the night sky with trails of burning ash.

Barely half an hour had passed after their return from the asylum before the police had arrived, and Ross's torn shirt and grazed chin provided immediate cause for interrogation. The mistake they'd made was to stop in the kitchen for a glass of water instead of going straight upstairs to wash and change. Miserably, Ross understood how they must have looked to the constable: guilty. They had no excuse. Now the police were gone but, considering his father's expression, Ross rather suspected that it may have been safer if the uniformed men had remained.

Morgan Grant turned at the end of the room. Lamp glow threw smudges of pooling light on the mantelpiece and tables. Their mother was present, a rare occurrence. Only exceptional occasions drew her down to a family gathering. Like when one of the old great-aunts fell ill, which they seemed to be in the habit of doing. If Ross moved his neck very carefully he could see her. Her ostrich-plume fan fluttered like a bird, her dull coin eyes staring at nothing. 'Your father's gout is back. The warmer weather does not agree with him.'

And then in swept their grandmother, who settled in a chair, smoothing her blush-pink gown. 'What have I missed?'

'Where to start?' countered their father.

Next to Ross, Alastair made a noise like a whoosh of air. With their grandfather's deteriorating health keeping him bedridden, their grandmother's presence was always prized. Punishments were never quite as severe when she was around, although Ross guessed that tonight he and Alastair would both feel the sting of the thick leather strap stored in the second drawer of their father's desk. It was all right for Alastair, he didn't have an already sore backside, but this would be Ross's third lashing in a week. One of the maids had found Alastair's sketches for the camphor laurel wings under Ross's bed, his brother having decided they were safer there than in his own room. Then Alastair had blamed Ross for leaving the stable gate open, explaining he'd receive a lighter punishment as he was younger. It never turned out that way. Ross spent more afternoons grasping the edges of his father's wooden desk than he cared to recall. Quite often, as Ross tugged up his britches, he caught sight of Alastair through the window, running around the garden tossing a ball to the dogs.

The only good thing about getting a whipping was that his nose spent time hovering inches above his father's desk, where letters and maps were always strewn about. Last week there'd been a telegram from Pine Creek. One of the stockmen on Waybell Station, up in the Northern Territory, had been bitten by a crocodile. He'd survived the attack but eventually died.

Ross searched in his pocket for a boiled lolly and quickly put it in his mouth before anyone noticed. He pushed at the sweet with his tongue and realised too late it was one that required a great deal of sucking. It stuck between his teeth.

Their father started at the end not the beginning, telling his grandmother about the policeman who'd come to the house and the newspaper reporter who waited outside for an interview, refusing to leave. They were in serious trouble, he said for the second time.

The ball of sugar finally came free. Ross let it rest on the middle of his tongue.

Their mother sighed dramatically. 'I think I'll go upstairs. This is all far too tiring.'

'Aye, you do that, Mary,' responded their grandmother. 'I'm sure you've had an extraordinarily busy day.' Grandmother Bridget flicked the fan in her lap impatiently as their mother left the room. 'Now that Mary's gone perhaps you could refrain from wearing the last of the pile from the rug, Morgan, and for heaven's sake stop masticating that infernal pipe.'

'The doctor says it's good for my health,' he replied. 'It expands the lungs.'

'Aye, right, well, I dinnae require my lungs expanded too,' she snapped.

Ross moved a little closer to his brother. Alastair risked a glance at him. If things were bad enough to draw their mother down from her room, they were made even worse when she didn't stay. The inexplicable boundary that kept Mary Grant apart from her family could at times be crossed, like this evening, but their mother was never quite one of them.

A knock sounded on the front door. The boys' grandmother and father exchanged a cautious glance as the housekeeper, Mrs Blum, went to see who it was.

As his father and grandmother waited for the visitor to be announced, Ross looked at the portraits on the wall. At the tartan and swords. There was an Englishman across the waters who'd saved a Grant once and to whom the family owed a life. It was a very old story. Ross thought it make-believe, and yet every New Year's Day a glass was raised to Captain Thomas of the West Indies.

This was it then, Ross thought. If it all went bad, their father would choose either Alastair or him. One of them would have to go.

They heard what sounded like the caller complaining at being kept waiting and then lumbering footsteps and a tapping noise carried along the marble hallway towards them. They all knew who it was and their faces fell. If Ross could have hidden he would have.

'Who is it?' his father called out of habit.

'Who do you think? Your aunt,' came the reply from just outside the drawing room. Supported by two walking canes, the oldest member of the Grant family shuffled into the room. She acknowledged her sister-in-law and nephew with a curt nod, the familiar scent of lavender and old age trailing the black taffeta gown she wore.

'Stand fast, stand sure,' Alastair whispered the Grant family motto.

Nothing was worse than a visit from Great-Aunt Fiona. Everyone knew she didn't like children. Children were meant to stay out of sight until they were fully grown. They were to be fed and watered in closed confines and only let out in the sun twice a day for limb-growing exercise. And they were never meant to speak. *Ever.* Ross heard her once say that children's brains were not fully developed enough to comprehend common sense and, accordingly, it was a waste of time listening to them. Her two surviving children were proof of these beliefs, for even in late adulthood they rarely talked unless spoken to first and when outside they followed daylight like sunflowers.

'It's unlike you to come out at night, Aunt,' commented their father.

'And it's unlike you to query my coming, Morgan,' she replied. Halting before Ross she gave a brief grunt. 'Did I not tell you this would happen?' She brushed aside her nephew's offer of help as she lowered herself into the chair next to Ross's grandmother, the blackness of her skirt creasing into glossy folds. Ross almost expected cobwebs and dust to puff out all around her. Trying not to stare, he fixed his gaze instead on the mantelpiece, where a picture of the dead Queen Victoria was displayed. Great-Aunt Fiona looked like her, very grumpy, and they wore the same clothes, down to the white handkerchief on her head.

'You have been far too lenient, Morgan. And before you offer up one of your paltry excuses I should tell you that there is a newspaper man loitering in the garden. I jabbed him with my stick but he refused to leave. Were the Lord to grant me another ten years I hope never again to witness such an assault on this family's reputation.'

Ross rolled the sweet around his tongue as their great-aunt leant forward. Holding up her spectacles, she wedged the circles of glass under gappy eye bones and squinted. Little by little she examined them until, inspection completed, she gave a shudder. Ross felt like one of his grandfather's butterflies mounted under glass.

'And look at their clothes. They are a disgrace,' she finished.

'I am aware of the reporter.' Their father checked the squat gold carriage clock above the fireplace against the fob watch on its chain. 'We have a gentleman in hospital with a crack to his skull, a broken penny-farthing and damage at the lunatic asylum.' Pipe smoke streamed from his mouth. 'And did I mention that there is a man in a straitjacket out wandering in the Botanical Gardens somewhere?'

Ross turned to Alastair.

'Do you think this is funny, sir?' Their father looked at Ross. 'You have been named as the cause of the bicycle accident on North Terrace. You were seen by Mrs Johnston.'

Grandmother Bridget gave a polite cough. 'I dinnae think the confectioner's wife can be trusted. Not after the recent troubles.'

'What troubles?' asked Great-Aunt Fiona, inwardly pulling what remained of her lips.

'What about the paperboy?' Their father drew on the pipe. 'The police have his statement.'

Ross pushed the candy to the side of his mouth. 'It was an accident, Father.'

'An accident? And was it also an accident that led to you breaking into the lunatic asylum, destroying their property and unlocking wards so that inmates could wander around unsupervised? Did you not hear what I said? There is currently a lunatic in the Botanical Gardens.'

'Oh dear.' Great-Aunt Fiona waved a black fan and took on the aspect of someone about to faint.

Please, God, Ross said silently, let her faint.

'He was wearing a straitjacket, Father,' said Alastair earnestly. 'He can't do any harm.'

Their father's cheeks grew mottled. He gave a short cough that developed into a convulsion that shook the length of his thick frame. Sitting his pipe on a table he went straight to the decanters on the trolley, where he poured a good measure of whisky and skolled it.

'Well, well, well.' Their grandmother patted the arm of the chair. 'You've both had a busy day.'

'But it wasn't my fault, Grams,' said Alastair. 'It was Ross's.'

Ross opened his mouth to protest, shocked that Alastair would blame him when it had been his idea and things had gone so terribly wrong.

'Alastair, dinnae tell your grandmother to suck eggs.'

Ross sighed, relieved that Grams knew it wasn't all his fault.

18

'That is not the least of it, Mother,' said their father. 'There is a child missing. An orphan.'

'What?' Great-Aunt Fiona's handkerchief dropped to the floor.

'The little boy?' Ross exclaimed, and the hard piece of sugar shot from his mouth, hitting his great-aunt's skirt. It quivered for the slightest of moments and held fast. Everyone looked at the white blob of saliva-coated candy stuck on the mourning black taffeta. No one said anything. The clock ticked. His great-aunt drew back as if she'd been struck and then with the utmost reluctance she poked at it with a finger.

'Confectionery,' Great-Aunt Fiona said, as if it were poison, before flicking the sweet to the floor. Her bent figure pointed at him. 'I always said this one would be trouble. From the very beginning. Now we have these, these murky doings to contend with. A multitude of sins to be inked on paper for posterity come the morning. Perhaps if you'd told him of his less-than-fortunate entry into this world, Morgan, he would have been more aware of his shortcomings. Then something could have been done before this.'

'Fiona,' their grandmother said loudly, 'dinnae say another word.'

'You were one of two, Ross Grant,' she spat. 'But you ate your brother in the womb. There should have been another boy here, a finer boy. One that deserved to be a Grant.'

'Aunt Fiona, stop it please,' pleaded their father.

Another brother? One that he'd eaten? Ross didn't understand.

'Aye, that's quite enough,' Grandmother Bridget agreed.

'Instead your twin, our William, died before he lived while you scrambled from dark to light in a heartbeat, thriving from the very first day.' Leveraging her body up on the canes, she moved towards him. 'Our William was born without arms or legs. Half the size of you. A battered body. Mauled before the poor lad had a chance. I've asked myself every day since, even as your poor mother sank slowly into oblivion, why you're here and he isn't. You've done this family no favours today, my lad.' She tapped Ross in the chest with one of the canes. 'And to think I used to wonder if the one God chose to take was not the finer.'

'Fiona!' Grandmother Bridget was at the older woman's side, knocking the cane away from Ross's body and forcefully dragging her backwards. 'That is quite enough.'

'Yes, it is,' their great-aunt agreed. 'It is not my place to judge you, Ross. There is no need. When they weigh your soul it's not heaven you'll be going to. It's hell.'

Ross fled the room, flung himself up the wide staircase, ran to his bedroom and positioned a chair under the doorknob. He crouched in a corner. How had he not known that he'd done such a terrible deed?

One that his family hated him for.

❖ Chapter 3 ❖

Ross listened to Alastair calling to him through the panelled wood, a chink of light showing beneath the door. His brother had been knocking quietly for the last few minutes and, knowing Alastair, he wasn't going away. Reluctantly, Ross moved the chair that was wedging the door shut and allowed his brother to enter the room. Ross crawled back to the space he'd been inhabiting on the floor at the end of the bed and scowled.

'What do you want?' he asked.

'I came to tell you what happened after you left,' said Alastair. He set the candle down and crawled under the bed to retrieve the biscuit tin that held Ross's most special possessions.

Ross reached for the container. 'Hey. What are you doing? Give it back.'

'Shush,' said Alastair. 'I only wanted to see your marbles.' He held the tin out of reach.

Ross tried to grab it. 'If they find you here with me you'll only say it was my fault and then I'll get into more trouble.'

'You will not,' said Alastair.

'Will so,' answered Ross, finally snatching the case and hugging it to his chest.

They stared sullenly at the candle.

'I want to play cricket tomorrow and if they thought it was my idea to break into the asylum then I'd be the one being locked in my room for a week and not you,' explained Alastair. 'Anyway, if you hadn't have spat that lolly at Great-Aunt Fiona she wouldn't have gotten so angry.'

'A whole week?' repeated Ross.

'It won't be so bad,' said Alastair. 'It could be worse.'

'How's that?'

'Well, they decided against giving you the strap again and they did send me to my room too.'

That was something, Ross supposed, Alastair getting sent to his room too. 'Did you know about the other baby, Alastair?'

His brother wet a finger and began waving it through the yellow candle flame. 'Not really. I'd heard stories about why Mother is the way she is and I knew it had something to do with another baby but I didn't know it was you. Do *you* remember the other baby, Ross?'

'No,' he replied.

'You're sure?'

'I don't know anything.' Ross squeezed closer to the cold wall.

'All right, don't start being a girl. I'm only asking.' Alastair picked up the candle and tipped it so that the wax dripped onto the saucer-shaped holder, forming a silky puddle that quickly dried, creamy and smooth.

It had scared Ross, what his great-aunt had said. He didn't want to believe her but he was just a boy and she was a grown-up, and neither his father nor grandmother had said it wasn't right. And Ross couldn't remember anything. He couldn't even recall being a baby.

'Do you think it's true, Alastair? What Great-Aunt Fiona said about me eating the baby?'

Alastair lifted the candle so that his face went white and then made a noise as if he was a ghost. 'Wooooooo!'

'Stop it,' begged Ross.

'Okay. Okay.' Alastair sat the candle back down, screwing the base of it into the hardened wax. 'Maybe the other baby was bad and that's why you ate it, to save the family,' he suggested. 'Or maybe he attacked you when you were inside Mother and you had to fight back. You know some of the Greek gods ate their children.'

Ross's stomach was beginning to churn. If it was true – if he'd eaten a little brother – then he was a cannibal and a murderer. A murderer twice over if the man on the penny-farthing happened to die. It was turning into a very bad day. 'They hate me, you know. Mother and Father and Great-Aunt Fiona,' said Ross.

'Great-Aunt Fiona doesn't like anyone,' Alastair told him. 'Least of all children. It wouldn't surprise me if she'd eaten some of her own.'

'I don't want to talk about it anymore,' said Ross. 'Go away.'

'I'm starving. We won't get any supper, you know, so let's sneak down to the kitchen and steal something to eat while Mrs Blum isn't looking,' suggested Alastair.

'No,' said Ross.

'Come on,' coaxed Alastair. 'You're going to be locked in here for a week. Probably with only bread and water to eat. A whole week! You'll be starving by the end of it. You'll be like Robinson Crusoe. You'll get so hungry you'll have to eat the mice and you'll have no one to talk to. You'll be a prisoner. Like the people in the asylum. You might even go mad. Neither of us have ever been locked away for that long before.'

'Stop it.'

It was true. Last year Ross had spent two days in his room for breaking an expensive vase after playing chase in the house with Alastair. By the end of it he'd felt like one of the animals at the zoo, but he didn't think he'd go mad.

'I'll make sure there's no one about and then you see what you can find us to eat,' said Alastair.

'Why do I have to be the one to do it?' asked Ross, placing the special box on the bed.

'You're smaller than me so there's less chance of you being seen, and secondly, I'm faster so if I hear someone I can run into the kitchen and tell you to hide.'

'I don't know, Alastair, it doesn't sound like a very good plan,' said Ross.

Alastair removed the pillowcase from Ross's cushion on the bed. 'There, now you have something to put the food in.' He pulled Ross up from the floor and, handing him the bag, blew out the candle and opened the door. 'They're still in the parlour and then they'll go to the dining room. They won't even know we're downstairs.'

'I really don't want to get into any more trouble,' said Ross.

'Wait!' Alastair ran back to the bed, opened the tin and snatched up a couple of the marbles.

'What are you doing? Give those back!'

Alastair opened his palm. 'They're only a couple of boring cat's eyes. You can have them back when we're finished.' He pulled Ross into the hallway, flattening himself against the wall. 'I'll be Achilles. You can be Ajax. We're storming Troy and stealing food for the army before we attack at dawn.' Alastair ran along the hall. At the top of the stairs he beckoned to Ross. 'They're sneaky, those Trojans, so be ready.'

'Oh boy,' muttered Ross, but he kept pace with Alastair as they crept downstairs, crawling past the dining room as their great-aunt complained that her place setting was not square with the edges of the table. At the kitchen entrance they peered through the door.

Mrs Blum was carving meat for supper. Slabs of cold mutton were being arranged on a large platter, while other plates held piles of steaming potatoes, beans and carrots.

Alastair tapped Ross's shoulder. 'Go,' he whispered.

'No,' said Ross. There was no possibility of entering the kitchen without being seen.

Alastair took the marbles from his pocket and rolled them across the kitchen floor so that the round balls hit the skirting board with a clatter. Mrs Blum stopped her preparations and, laying down the knife, went to investigate the noise. Alastair pushed Ross into the kitchen and he grabbed at the potatoes, stuffing them into the pillowslip.

'You just can't help yourself, can you, Ross?'

24

Alastair was gone. In his place their father blocked the exit.

'Ross, what are you doing?' Mrs Blum took the pillowcase from him.

'But it wasn't my fault,' said Ross. 'It was Alastair's idea.'

'It's always your brother's idea,' said his father. Taking his son by the ear he led him upstairs, refusing to let go until Ross was back in his bedroom. 'You're an embarrassment to this family. I'd send you to boarding school except I couldn't be sure you'd behave, so instead I've decided to separate you two boys. No more shared lessons or playing together. All that ends today. It's time to grow up, Ross. If that's possible.'

His father slammed the door and Ross fell on his bed, kicking his heels on the cover. After a little while he lit a candle and stared out the window to where the rest of the world readied for the night. He shouldn't have followed Alastair or done what he'd said. Alastair always made a mess of things and *he* was the one who suffered the consequences.

≪ Chapter 4 ≫

Adelaide, 1910

The garden party was their grandmother's idea. An opportunity for Alastair to be paraded before a selection of Adelaide's finest on the occasion of reaching twenty-one. Ross selected a glass of champagne from a tray and then quietly manoeuvred back through the guests to the corner of the marquee. He winced at the taste of the alcohol, emptying the glass on the lawn. The liquid foamed before evaporating into the ground. He stared briefly at the grass then lifted his gaze to follow a young woman. The hem of her white gown trailed across the turf and was slightly dirty. She was tiny about the waist and she toyed with a blue-tasselled sash, her face concealed by a large hat. Beneath the brim her coiled hair was a masterpiece and Ross found himself wondering about the thickness and length that was twisted and curled into such clever proportions. She stood slightly apart, her spine straight, shoulders pulled back so that from where he watched the stretch of material across her chest verged on the undignified.

Ross waited for the girl to move so that he might better see her features. If she proved pretty he thought of introducing himself, but beauty could also mean an inclination towards waspishness, which he'd encountered in the past. While he deliberated on whether to approach the young woman, his friend Drummond emerged from the mass of partygoers to speak to her and then, one after another, three other companions joined in so that the girl was encircled by admirers and Ross realised he was most definitely on the outside looking in. She laughed, accepted the champagne offered and as she sipped from the flute he saw her unobstructed profile and berated his caution.

Connor Andrews arrived to stand slightly behind him. He was bearded and stunted to a mere five foot five inches and his Scottish accent remained strong despite over a decade in Australia. Had Connor been alive in the 1700s, Ross had no doubt he would have helped mobilise the clan for war. The man excelled at taking and giving orders, which made his official position as head of stables a poor description for someone who was often sent inland to their other holdings to check on the management of those properties.

'So which filly will catch your brother's eye, do you think?' asked Connor.

'All of them, I'd imagine,' replied Ross. The girls flocked to his brother like seagulls searching for a morsel of bread. Alastair's leanness of youth was gone, replaced with a broadness that matched his impressive height, and he exuded a confidence that Ross admired.

'Aye, well, you're not helping your chances hanging back here,' said Connor.

'*I'm* not looking for a bride,' countered Ross, as the girl was gradually absorbed by other guests forming tight rings of conversation.

'Neither's your brother,' said Connor with a wink. 'He's playing the field as you should be doing. Not that he was ever lacking with the ladies. University's done Alastair some good.'

Ross doubted that studying the classics and French was going to be of help in the real world. 'And what's he going to do with all that learning, Connor?'

'Alastair's born to be a laird. The Much Honoured Alastair Grant. Has a nice sound to it,' said Connor.

'It might if we were still in Scotland,' complained Ross.

'Aye, right. I dinnae see your father complaining about keeping to some of the old ways.'

'As if he would.'

'Come now, lad. He's been tough on you boys but didnae you come out of it fine. The both of you have. If you have the chance, tell your father I fired McKinley. The man's a useless manager,' Connor told him. 'How are things at Gleneagle Station? Have they made a grazier out of you yet?'

'Hot and dry,' replied Ross. 'And yes, I'm learning.'

'Good, and how long are you staying in Adelaide?'

'One or two nights. Enough to appease my father and spend a little time with Alastair.'

'Aye, well, your father won't take kindly to your one-foot-in-the-stirrup visit,' said Connor. 'Neither will I. We've two new mares in the stables that could do with some work.'

'I don't think he'll mind, as long as the Grants are united for the occasion. Besides, it's all about Alastair, and with the house filled with visiting relatives it's hardly a homecoming when the younger son has accommodation in the city.'

'Aye, family can be strange at times. Do you think he'll take the car or one of the sheep properties?' Connor asked, referring to Alastair's choice of birthday gifts.

'I know what I'd take,' said Ross. A bell rang. 'Speeches.'

'And my cue to leave,' said Connor.

Ross moved out from behind the marquee and leant against the timber support. They were lined up on the lawn, his grandmother and parents, his mother managing a shaky wave in his direction. Alastair, skolling a glass of champagne to the accompanying laughter of friends, strolled casually through the guests, stopping to say hello to various people before joining the family. He appeared so relaxed, so suited to the role of elder son. His hair shone. His teeth were straight and white. His face was tanned in the way of

28

those who received just enough sun. Even Alastair's clothes were perfect. It was not that Ross had dressed any less fashionably for the celebration, his father had made sure of that, but rather if the two of them were in the same smelly attire of a bagman Alastair would still appear the better dressed. It had little to do with quality of cloth or expense, but the way Alastair presented to the world an air of acceptance for what had already been his due and what might be forthcoming.

Someone called out to Ross and he gave a vague sign of acknowledgement, raising the empty glass but not moving. His father was quick to commence one of his lengthy discourses, a well-practised fable on the importance of family and duty often heard by Ross over previous years. On this occasion, Alastair's name was frequently inserted along with an inventory of the history of the Grants in South Australia. A necessary inclusion, Ross supposed, when his brother was yet to distinguish himself, and Morgan Grant had rarely shied from the public. Some of the guests began to talk softly. Ross felt his mind slowly close off from the festivity of Alastair's life, until the family and their friends and relatives became boxed and lidded.

Even the opportunity of seeing his brother was not quite enough to draw Ross from Gleneagle Station without feeling irritated by his family's demands. He'd been more than pleased when his father had agreed to his request to work on a holding in the mid-north of the state, forty miles northeast of Burra, and since leaving he'd not missed any of them. Ross's great-aunt was long dead, however the seed she'd planted with those cruel words in his childhood had taken root within him.

It was strange how the memory of that day lingered. Ross still recalled the accusatory looks and the hopeless feeling of dread, which had trailed him for months as if it had human form. The horror of his malformed dead twin and the implication that the fault somehow lay with him far outweighed the shock of discovering the existence of another brother.

Ross knew that the antics of that long-ago afternoon contributed only somewhat to his penance. Although the wandering inmate and the little boy were eventually located, it seemed to Ross that it was the revelation of the details of his birth that had led to their lives changing. He and Alastair rarely spent another afternoon alone together. Alastair was sent away to school and Ross's childhood was filled with allocated hours with tutors, his free time with friends limited.

Soon after that day, he began to have the dream. Even now, when it came massing at the edges of his subconscious, Ross was only aware of a darkness, an impenetrable thickness that at times threatened to choke him. There was always a feather and a set of scales in the dream, and although he placed no belief in the Victorian conviction that entry to heaven depended on the outcome of one's soul weighed against a feather, Ross couldn't shake the feeling that his chances of spiritual acceptance were shaky.

He grew up with the knowledge that his birth came with a mark against it. That was part of the reason he'd ended up at Gleneagle, on a property with few visitors, a tight-knit group of wiry men and an honest manager whose wife was cook and mother to them all. The other reasons were varied and more complicated and Ross was still trying to untangle them, like knots in a rope, trying to figure out how he'd been led astray as a child, cast out by his family and then, on willingly choosing exile, how he'd come to love where he now lived more than home.

Later that afternoon, Alastair found Ross napping on one of the garden benches, far from the gathering that was making merry noise on the opposite side of the house.

'This is lovely.' Alastair kicked at the seat and Ross jolted awake. 'We've barely spent any time together and you're passed out at the back of the garden.'

'Over, is it?' asked Ross.

'Hardly. There's another crate of champagne to finish.' Alastair pushed Ross further along and sat down. 'It'll be some time before the old man puts his hands in his pockets like this again. Come and help me make the most of it.'

'No thanks,' said Ross. 'I'll wait until the crowd leaves.'

Alastair took a cigarette from a silver case. He offered one to Ross, who refused, and then lit his and took a long inhalation. 'I chose the motorcar, if you're wondering.'

'Really? Why?' asked Ross.

'I can't exactly use a property. At least, not right now and the thing is, Ross, it's all going to be ours in the future anyway. A motorcar is far more useful. Especially at university. The girls will love it.'

'I suppose they will,' replied Ross. He wasn't surprised by his brother's choice, but he knew what he would have selected.

'How are things at Gleneagle?'

'Fine. University?' asked Ross.

'Swell.' Alastair took another puff of the cigarette and flicked the ash from the end. 'Has Father asked you about further study? You'd enjoy university.'

'Gleneagle suits me fine.'

'You're happy being there?'

'For the moment, yes. If I stick it out until I'm twenty-one, Father's agreed to let us both go north to Waybell Station,' said Ross.

Alastair stubbed out the cigarette. 'It's years since we talked about Waybell. You still want to go up there?'

'Of course. We can follow the overland telegraph straight up to Darwin, spend a week or so exploring and then catch the train south part of the way. It's a few days horse ride from there.' Ross studied his brother's expression. 'You don't look very keen.'

'It's a long way,' said Alastair.

'You do still want to go, don't you?'

'I hadn't thought of it,' admitted Alastair. 'That's four years away and Father's already said that after university I'll have to do a stint with an accountancy firm. Get some hands-on experience for the family business. He's making me take bookkeeping as an extra subject.'

Ross rather suspected their father's requirements of Alastair would become weightier. 'Waybell is perfect then, Alastair. What better way to escape a dingy office.'

His brother tapped the bench's wooden slats thoughtfully.

'If you don't come, I doubt Father will let me go, either,' Ross persisted. 'You know what he's like. He'll send me to another property instead. Anyway, we decided years ago we'd visit the Territory.'

Alastair flipped the lid of the cigarette case open and closed. 'It's not really on the agenda now, Ross. I mean, I know you rambled on as a child about seeing Australia, following in the footsteps of the great explorers and all that, but Waybell is *so remote*.'

'Exactly. Imagine having the opportunity to live up there.'

'Yes. Imagine,' replied Alastair.

'You can't spend your life reading Greek stories and courting women, Alastair.'

'Oh, I see. So now the little brother is giving me life instruction?' They locked eyes for a few seconds and then Alastair laughed.

'You owe me,' said Ross.

His brother lit another cigarette, the smoke curling upwards. 'You always were too quick to listen to me. I was just a boy as well, you know.'

'Older than me.'

'Oh no, I'll not take the blame for our father's harshness,' replied Alastair.

'So it was my fault, the asylum? And whose idea was it to raid the kitchen? It seems to me I was the scapegoat for your adventures on more than one occasion.' Ross wondered if today would mark a turning point. If Alastair would finally admit his childhood mistakes and say sorry. 'You owe me,' he repeated.

Alastair considered the ultimatum. 'I'm not saying yes because of what happened.' He took a few more puffs of the cigarette and then tapped the end on the edge of the bench. Embers and unsmoked tobacco fell from the tip.

'Will you come with me or not?'

'Fine, I'll come,' said Alastair.

They clasped hands and shook.

Ross grinned. 'When I turn twenty-one. That's when we'll leave. The day after. Not a moment later.'

'I hope I don't regret this.' Alastair stood, looking back to the house in the direction of the celebration going on in his absence. 'I need a drink. This will be the last of the partying for a week or so. We've got the athletics carnival on soon and I'm expected to at the very least place in the mile.'

'It must be strenuous, university life,' said Ross.

Alastair pointed a finger. 'You had your chance, Ross. And now I'm off to pursue a young lady.'

'Which one?'

'Emily Prior. Large hat, white gown, blue belt.'

Ross wished Alastair luck as requested, and when his brother left he thought of Emily Prior with her curled hair and sashed waist and wished that he didn't know about the law of probability. Even with some random variables, probabilities and axioms thrown in that might skew the results – Drummond and his friends, parental interference and other enticing women – the outcome was inevitable. Alastair would get what he wanted.

⫷ Chapter 5 ⫸

Gleneagle Station, South Australia, 1919

Ross removed the wrench from his saddlebag and gave the barely moving pump-rod a mighty whack. The rod shuddered, as a metallic ring vibrated up the shaft towards the windmill. With a reluctant groan the rod began to rise and fall at an increasing pace, driving the piston. Overhead, the sails rotated and water spurted into the trough. Sheep began to gather, taking tentative steps towards the watering point. Ross threw the wrench against the side of the windmill and sat in the dirt under the moving shadow of the windmill's sails.

Alastair had gone to war and he was still missing, three years on.

The reports were confusing. Ross's childhood friend Drummond said that he'd been blown up somewhere on the Somme, in a battle where the armies of Britain and France had bled to death. The other version, the one that carried more weight, came from Alastair's commanding officer. His correspondence confirmed that Alastair had indeed been wounded and was not expected to survive. But eventually word came that he'd been classified as a deserter, having fled the hospital as soon as he was able to walk.

No one had heard or seen anything of Lieutenant Alastair Grant since September 1916.

There were times when Ross believed that, had he been allowed to join up, Alastair would never have disappeared. They would have watched out for each other, as brothers should. However when war broke out, their father refused to place both boys in the hands of the British. As he told the family at dinner one night, he had his own legacy to be thinking of and trusting the English never came easily to Morgan Grant. At first, Ross questioned why he'd not been chosen, the expendable younger son, but he'd assumed his father thought he'd make a botch of going to war while Alastair would make a fine officer.

The series of telegrams received by Ross's parents following Alastair's wounding until his disappearance had been abbreviated for him into a single page written in his father's hand. Ross burnt it on receipt. It was bad enough knowing the contents without driving himself mad by trying to decipher more from this final account. It was also impossible to believe the various stories of Alastair's wounding and vanishing. None of it made sense.

The last letter his brother wrote to him in early 1916 briefly mentioned a girl he'd met in London. He called her a fine filly, the sort their parents would like. The war was referred to only in vague terms, and he warned Ross not to take it on at any rate. There were descriptions of Westminster Abbey and a sketch of an Australian digger with bulging pockets and rakish slouch hat, however Alastair was more interested in other things.

Agitated that he wasn't stationed in Mesopotamia, despite the British army having surrendered to the Turks at Kut, he filled the remaining pages with a lengthy explanation of the region located between the Tigris and Euphrates river system, excited at being so close to the fabled city of Babylon. The placenames had leapt from the paper and the envy Ross tried to keep buried rose anew. He couldn't help it. Alastair was living the life of adventure Ross had aspired to.

In the weeks following Alastair's disappearance, Ross's father had remained quietly confident that their eldest would be found. That some military bungle lay at the centre of it all and that his commanding officer would in the future be obliged to apologise for ever having the temerity to call their boy an absconder. But too much time had passed and Ross, who'd hoped for the impossible, that Alastair was still alive, perhaps suffering amnesia, his identity lost, was forced to admit that his brother was almost certainly never coming home.

He pictured Alastair the last time they were together. They were lying on the lawn in Adelaide staring at the stars, their stomachs filled with Christmas food. Alastair was smoking, endlessly smoking, flicking the used butts into the hot night air. There was a hip flask of whisky lying between them, another empty one somewhere in the wilted flowers.

'I don't want to miss it,' he said. 'Not that I have much choice. But I want to go.' He turned towards the house. 'Not for them,' he admitted, 'for me.'

'Are you scared?' asked Ross.

Alastair considered the question, lighting another cigarette from the one almost finished. 'I don't know what to fear, Ross. I know people are dying over there. But it's all numbers to me. Words in a newspaper ironed every morning so we don't get print on our hands. Besides, our boys are in Egypt having a fine old time. Imagine standing where Napoleon used the Sphinx as target practice. Having a splash in the Nile.' He lifted a finger to the half-moon, moving his thumb back and forth as he made the crescent shape appear and disappear. 'There's always the possibility that King Constantine of Greece might change his mind and join the Allies. He can't stay neutral forever. And if that happened, we might be sent there.'

'You and your myths,' said Ross.

Alastair turned on his side. 'I can't help it. They've always interested me. Those stories go so far back no one can remember the beginnings of them. We only study the scraps. A morsel that has fallen from the table, like Homer.'

'Well, if that morsel fell on my foot it would probably break it,' answered Ross.

Alastair threw a cigarette into the night, the embers glowing. They'd not seen much of each other in the four years since Alastair's twenty-first birthday celebrations. His brother, having elected to travel to Sydney after completing his studies, with the ruse of preferring to work in a well-known accountancy firm in that city, had followed a girl there. Emily Prior. The relationship ended when the young lady began to hint at marriage. Alastair had come home only to be confronted with war.

That Christmas Day Ross had been aware of the fragility of the time left before Alastair sailed for the Australian Imperial Force training camp at Salisbury Plain in England. A feeling of anticipation moved with his brother and it remained unstated that few things would be the same in the future, even when Alastair did finally return. Alastair the dreamer, the romantic, the unrealistic Don Quixote of the family, the boy who fought imaginary monsters, never saw the world for what it was and yet he was about to be thrown into it.

'I wish I was going with you,' said Ross.

'So do I. You'll be missed,' said Alastair.

'I still think about my twin. How different things might have been if he'd lived,' said Ross.

'Children die all the time. They still do,' said Alastair. 'Anyway it was a long time ago. Do me a favour, Ross. Try and get on with Mother and Father while I'm away, they do care about you.'

'When the war's over we'll still go north to Waybell Station,' Ross insisted.

'The point of owning a property in the wilds that barely turns a profit defeats me. But as you've had your mind set on it since we were boys I guess I have little choice,' answered Alastair.

'So it's agreed?' said Ross.

'Sure. We'll go north. When I get back,' replied Alastair.

'Keep your head down, brother. Keep your mind on the job.' It was the thing Ross feared most: losing him when they were now old enough to push aside the mistakes of youth. To forgive.

Closing his mind to that long-ago Christmas, Ross knuckled tears from his eyes, and let out an almighty scream. The sheep scattered, bolting away along veiny tracks that eased into the earth. Finally the air stilled. He wiped the dirt on his trousers and slipped the wrench back inside the saddlebag. The horse gave a gentle whinny as Ross swung a leg over the saddle, his boot finding the metal stirrup.

'Come on,' he said. Drawing on the reins, he directed the mare back towards the homestead. A sense of finality had struck him over the previous days. As if a phase of his life was about to conclude, and with it would disappear all possibility of his brother ever returning. It couldn't be expected after all this time. Ross had to let go of the possibility. Had to throw away the boyish plans they'd made. He had to move on.

☙ Chapter 6 ❧

Ross anchored his boots in the soil as he was buffeted by the wind. The grit from the westerly stung his face and neck as he stared at tufts of grey-green woody shrubs spreading out from the road across treeless plains. Had the mail announcing his parents' arrival been one day later Ross would have already left to go mustering with the other men. Alastair once told him that timing and opportunity often fortuitously conspired to arrive together. But not today.

Mrs Toth joined Ross where he waited near the road that forked towards the homestead and outbuildings. The dwellings stood in the centre of the property. Stone structures dropped like garden pavers in an area not larger than a quarter mile. And stretching beyond, red dirt and the crooked stubs of saltbush, relieved only by the odd outcrop of rock, a glimpse of hills and an undulation of countryside.

The manager's wife was anxious at the arrival of Ross's father. There'd been much fussing over accommodation and more than a passing interest in the reason for the visit. Three times the woman mentioned that Ross would be glad of his father's coming.

Ross's mouth dried at the thought. Mrs Toth was not a busybody, she was a caring woman whose lack of children seemed to have made her more attuned to everyone's needs. She wasn't caught up by responsibility, curtailed by belief or hobbled by disappointment. She simply existed in her own right and she smiled a lot. Ross liked that about her the most.

A sweep of dust against blue sky marked the snaking progress of the travellers. Mrs Toth, dressed for the occasion in a pale blouse and skirt that showed off dusty lace-up boots, looked up at him enquiringly. The question was the same. The woman hoped all was well. Ross replied that everything was fine.

'And your mother, you haven't seen her for a long time?' she asked carefully, a hand clamped to a hat as the wind strengthened.

Ross thought of Mary Grant with her strawberry-blonde hair and hazel eyes. A children's picture book character who demanded love. Ross liked to think that they had both tried their best, but the reality was very different. She was lost to him at birth. Apart from his father's yearly visits to the property, Christmas 1914 was the last time he'd been with all the family. Months after that holiday, Alastair had left for the war.

'I remember the day you arrived here, Ross. You were so tall with that curly dark hair of yours. Tall and proud. My husband thought you haughty and aloof, coming from the family that you do, but I saw through all that. You were always cautious, never one to jump in or speak out of turn but you were also thoughtful. Carrying things for me if you were about. Always stopping for a chat. It was a pleasure to have you around in those early years before the war. Before everything turned inside out and your brother disappeared.'

Ross gave a quizzical smile. 'And now I'm not so pleasant to have around?'

'You've changed. We all have, I suppose. But you've become too quiet, Ross. The other men, well, I expect that of them. Years of being alone in a lonely place does that to a person. But you're a young man. You should be out enjoying yourself when you can.

What happened to that nice girl in Burra you were seen with a few times, Mrs Watson's daughter?'

'That was years ago. Anyway, there was nothing to it. We were only friends.'

The travellers were growing closer.

'Mr Toth and I know the hard time you've had, Ross. People can be cruel. Sometimes it takes more strength to stay behind and bear the insults than to lift up a gun and follow orders. Remember that, for things will get better now the war's over.'

He took a step away, concentrating on the road. Mrs Toth patted Ross's arm and returned to the low-slung homestead where a house-girl swept the dirt floor of the veranda. He was grateful that her husband's departure with the men that morning coincided with the arrival of these uninvited guests. He imagined the Toths suspected another family tragedy, the sort of event that warranted a journey of over 125 miles from Adelaide. To some extent, it was.

The wagon grew steadily in size as Ross waited in the harsh afternoon light. The rest of the men were long gone, riding twenty miles westwards in search of sheep. By dusk they would be camped beneath a rocky outcrop amidst clumps of saltbush and bluegrass. Stars emerging overhead, the red plains cooling as they unrolled swags and waited for the quart pot to boil. And here he was, anticipating, readying for an argument. In some ways it was amazing they hadn't come for him sooner. Alastair had been the hinge upon which the rest of the family swung.

'Are you going to say anything?' demanded his father, slapping a hand on his thigh.

Ross had expected his father to be tired from the journey north. Having refused to take the coach service to Burra for fear the last of the influenza epidemic might strike were they to mix too freely with the public, they'd travelled with few rests. Not that the journey caused him any undue hardship; he'd been talking for a good half-hour.

'No.' Ross turned from the window. He felt as if sacred ground had been violated.

His father's tone grew impatient. 'No, you're not going to answer me or . . .'

Ross looked to where his mother sat. She was toying with a teaspoon, which rattled on the dainty saucer. Her fair hair was now grey. He'd been surprised at her coming too.

'No, I'm not going to do what you want.'

Morgan Grant placed hands on hips and glanced about the space that served as both kitchen and sitting room.

'It's far too early to be drinking,' his wife stated simply, as if in response to a question. She looked at Ross, her eyes tired. 'You're a long way from home, son.'

It wasn't far enough, it seemed.

The first of their demanding letters had arrived three months ago. The contents were not what he'd expected. None of this was.

'The understanding was that you would come here to be educated, Ross. That's what you wanted,' began his father. 'You needed toughening up, we all knew that. And when the time was right, you and your brother were to go north to check on my interests. We had no choice but to delay things once war broke out, but now –'

'But now Alastair isn't here you expect me to forget about everything I want?' Ross finished.

The teaspoon clattered.

His father placed a hand briefly on his wife's shoulder. 'Your brother is an utter disgrace. He was in the papers, you know. *Honour extinguished* was the headline, if you require reminding.'

'So you prefer the fact that he's most likely dead.'

'Don't, Ross, please don't.' His mother cried quietly into a handkerchief.

'Son, it's been three years. If Alastair was still alive he would have made contact with us. He would have come home.'

'But we don't know he's dead,' argued Ross.

'Not formally,' agreed his father. 'Do *you* think he's still alive?'

Ross didn't reply. His head told him that Alastair was certainly gone. That was the bitter conclusion he woke to every morning, but until they received some sort of official statement, a document that spelt out the end of hope, Ross still clung to the possibility of his brother being found.

'You have to come back with us,' his father said.

'I don't believe this.' Ross had done his best to atone for his messy beginnings by leaving home, and here he was being asked to uphold the family honour by returning. He should have guessed there would be a final reckoning.

'So you're telling me that, after all these years, all that talk about wanting to visit Waybell Station, now when you have that opportunity you don't want to go anymore?' His father scratched at a broad, craggy forehead.

'Not on the terms offered.' Alastair had once warned Ross not to underestimate their father. He was a canny man. 'I'll not sacrifice myself for the right to manage one of our properties.'

'You should be grateful it's come to this. That the proposal's been accepted. You're stepping into your older brother's shoes. You will be head of the family one day.'

'I don't want to step into anyone's shoes.' Ross's horse was in the stables. It wouldn't take much to be on his way. A bit of flour and salted mutton. His rifle and swag. He wondered what made his parents think that they could make such demands of him, as if they'd always been the proud parents and he the obliging child.

'I understand it's daunting for you, lad. You're not like your brother, but things will work out.'

Wasn't that just like his father? Approval and criticism in the same breath.

'I didn't make the offer, Father. So I'm not bound by it.'

'You'd rather be a sheep- or cattle-herder?' his father spluttered. 'For that's what will become of you.'

'But isn't that what we've always been?' argued Ross. 'Farmers? Haven't I heard since I was knee-high that's how it was for the family back in the Highlands? And now you criticise me for doing what's in my blood.'

'I want you to start managing, lad. I want you to be giving the orders, not taking them.' The spittle from his father's rage reached Ross from across the table. 'But you must do this one thing first. You're twenty-six years of age. It's time to grow up.'

'That's the thing, Father. I've been growing up for a long time. The trouble is that neither of you ever took the time to notice.'

Were Morgan younger, Ross thought it highly likely that he would have throttled him. His father had been fast when he and Alastair were boys. Quick enough to catch them and give them a thrashing.

'You have gall, speaking to me that way. If it wasn't for your mother and me –'

'I don't want to hear you two argue. Scotland has changed,' interrupted his mother. 'And were it for the better we'd have never left our kin to be wrenched from hearth and home and stranded here in this place.'

Father and son looked at her. She was playing with the teaspoon, feeling the concave surface. Ross chose not to remind his mother that it was a good seventy years since any of their line had set foot in Scotland. They were about as far removed in place and time from the old country as they could be.

'All your old friends have done well.' Walking the length of the small room, his hands clasped behind his back, Morgan Grant set a smile on his face. 'George is a lawyer, Drummond has shown an interest in public office. A fine lad, Drummond. I can see why you chose him as a friend. A good choice. A very good choice indeed. And his family. Top drawer. They were both wounded. George lost a leg, but he's doing well.'

'I haven't spoken to either of them since they joined up,' replied Ross.

'Well, you must make more of an effort to keep in contact, Ross.'

'Right. Yes. Of course, Father. And what do you think we're going to talk about? The friends we lost while standing knee-deep in slush in the trenches? I can just see George and me sharing a beer, him with his trouser leg pinned up, and me in my prime, untouched by the war that killed thousands. It was George who christened me a mama's boy when he learnt I wasn't going to enlist. Did you know that? And Drummond. Yes, dear old Drummond. He wrote to me when Alastair disappeared. He wanted to know if, considering what had happened to my brother, I really didn't feel some moral obligation to join up. He was prepared to forgive me for my spineless behaviour if I did what was expected of any decent, able-bodied man. If I didn't, he doubted he could continue calling me a friend.'

His father nodded. 'There'll be time to mend friendships.'

'And reputation? My honour? What of that, Father?'

'If you'd shown such pluck in 1914 I may well have let you go too. Perhaps –'

'Perhaps what? Perhaps I would have been the one killed and Alastair would have been returned to you?'

His father looked at him with empty eyes. 'Once you're home –'

'I'm not coming home.'

His mother emitted a tiny 'Oh'.

'Your friends understand the importance of hard work, of representing their families. But not you. You'd rather walk from your family, as you have always done. You would wither away in the middle of nowhere sooner than doing what's right. Or do you fancy yourself an adventurer like in all those books you read as a child? A great explorer. The likes of Stuart? Are you going to set off on foot and go westwards to the desert, lad? If so, I can tell you that such aspirations are better left to those who have ability.'

Ross left the cottage, slamming the door on the way out, and trudged the short distance to the stables where he found Connor. The Scotsman had travelled with the Grants from Adelaide and waited with one eye on the cottage, the other on the deserted road, as if even here in the reddened depths of South Australia there might be an attack. Such was the Highland blood that ran through his marrow.

Connor stood on his approach, a pipe sticking out from a mat of whiskers.

'It's not going well, then?' he asked, the pipe barely moving as he spoke.

Ross clutched the wooden tethering rail. 'Did you even try and stop them from coming?'

'Me, try and stop a descendant of a chief of your clan? Your father will always be a laird, like his father, and his father before him.'

'This isn't Scotland,' Ross pointed out.

Connor tapped out the pipe on the railing. 'Aye, you're right. It's not. But some things still stand firm, Ross. Like duty and loyalty, and let's not be forgetting,' he picked at the bowl of the pipe with a pocketknife, 'it was your father who took me in when I first arrived in South Australia. It's one thing to be feisty when you're a lad but I'm forty-five years of age now.'

'It seems to me that half the world is bound to the old man,' said Ross.

'Anyway,' continued Connor, 'it's not your father who I'd have had the problem stopping.'

He was right. The arrival of his parents had been made more unnerving by the appearance of Ross's grandmother along with them. It had taken the efforts of Connor, Ross and his father to help the old widow down from the wagonette. On finding solid ground beneath her feet, Bridget Grant had surveyed the dusty surroundings and commented loudly on having travelled a long way for so very little. While Mrs Toth's welcoming smile barely altered, Ross knew she would not have appreciated Grams' pithy condemnation.

'You know why they're here, don't you?' asked Ross.

'I may be an ignorant Highlander but it doesn't take much between the ears to guess.' Connor pulled tobacco from a pouch and began filling his pipe. 'I recognise a perfumed peach when I see one. The poor lass has been in Adelaide for over two years, Ross.' He struck a match and drew heavily until the tobacco lit. 'I'm surprised they didn't drag her out here as well, dangle the girl in front of you. Were we in Scotland I'd warn you to keep clear of the Sassenach; that an English woman and a Scotsman bound together will end up like two thistles in a bag. But she's a good lass.' Connor nodded towards the manager's house where a woman in black stood out against the whitewashed stone walls of the building. 'It looks like Herself is ready for you.' He brushed imaginary dirt from Ross's shirt. 'Off you go now and don't upset her.' Ross raised an eyebrow as Connor clasped his shoulder. 'Good luck.'

Halfway across the wind-rippled dirt, Ross met his grand-mother's gaze. She looked older than her eighty years and he suspected there was some truth to the rumour that Bridget Grant had lied about her age on meeting his grandfather, there being no birth certificate to prove otherwise.

'Ross.'

'Grandmother.' Joining her in the shade of the veranda, he kissed a cool, lined cheek. 'You've had a long journey.'

She scowled. 'Your father was determined to be here today.'

'I'm surprised at your coming,' admitted Ross. He wondered if her presence was his father's doing or if they were all here at her bidding.

'Aye, and I'm surprised you've grown, for the land you've planted yourself on looks as dry and arid as me,' she replied.

'It's a fine property. The wool is first class.'

'I wonder at that when a place can't even grow a tree.' She tapped stumpy fingers on the arm of the rattan chair. 'And the men are away, Mrs Toth tells me.'

'Yes.'

'A pity. I was quite prepared to take stock of the younger lads.' She gave a wink and Ross sat by her side. 'You like this farming life, eh? The dust and lack of society.'

'I do,' he confessed.

'Space and air and none of the fiddling pastimes that city life demands. So you dinnae like people then?'

'I like people well enough, Grams,' Ross replied. 'It's what they talk about that doesn't always interest me.'

Her grey hair was pulled tightly from its centre part to a thin bun on the nape of her neck. She patted one side, and as she did so a sprinkle of dead skin fell to a shoulder. 'Wool and weather are also discussed in Adelaide, my lad, by men who know what they are talking about. You might learn something.' She peered across at him. 'You were always a fidgety child. Desperate to be outdoors, by yourself.'

'I wonder why, when I've been practically chaperoned since I was eight.' Ross concentrated on the silver haze blurring the horizon.

'Well, there's something to be said for being a loner. But you don't fool me. You shun your family, not society. You creep into the bush because you're more comfortable here. Away from us. Away from your father and mother.'

'And you know why. Anyway, this is my job.'

'I'd not expected you to still be so angry.' The chair squeaked as she leant back. 'The gentlemen's lounges are full of talk of what the pastoralists are up to. Buying and selling, arguing over Goyder's imaginary line. This property is clearly on the right side, if there is a right side. I can't imagine a crop surviving here. At least that is what Connor tells me.'

'And what else does he tell you, Grandmother?' Ross was curious.

'That this will be my first and last trip out of Adelaide. I came for you of course, my boy, but an old woman has to see what all the fuss is about.' Her mouth puckered as if she'd already passed judgement. 'I've been reading and hearing about this great state and the men who've been attempting to open it up for many years. It seems a pity to die and not to have travelled past the boundaries of Adelaide. To never know why so many have been willing to strike out on a horse to try and discover what's beyond the beyond.' She turned to Ross. 'It's not pretty, you know, what I've gleaned from our brief histories. Most die, although there's plenty of options when it comes to death.' She counted off on her fingers. 'Attacked by spear throwers, madness, dead of thirst or lack of food or stupidity, many get lost. Even your Stuart ended up blind and in very poor health. Besides, the place is all desert.'

'Not north it isn't.'

Her eyes narrowed. She lifted a finger, waggling it at him. 'So, you do still want to go there.'

Ross frowned. 'Of course I do. Haven't I sat here and waited like the dutiful son? I've complained only once – when war was declared and it was decided that Alastair should go and I would not. I never should have agreed to that. Never.'

She patted his arm. 'You were sensible.'

'I was an idiot, Grams.'

'War is for fools. Only generals die in bed.'

'Maybe, but I've had to live with the consequences.' Ross had eventually stopped going into Burra to collect supplies. It was one thing to be considered a shirker for not doing one's duty when so many were dying, quite another to be branded a coward. Especially when Alastair was mentioned twice in despatches for bravery. Ross carried mended bones as proof of the contempt in which he was held, thanks to those who showed their anger with their fists.

'It will pass. People are quick to forget.' She placed a finger on his elbow. 'It's not even a decade since the north was separated from South Australia. It's an untamed place, Ross. Uninhabitable, uncivilised. We were all intrigued by the idea of a great central state, but it's too unwieldy and too distant to control. That's why we handed it over to the government, washed our hands of it. And now we're left with a property in this so-called land that I never should have allowed your father to invest in. If you must prove yourself, do it some other way, for if you go north I can't see you prospering. Few do from what I've heard.'

'Thanks, Grams.'

'There's no point pouting, lad. I could be selfish and tell you that if you go I won't see you again, but a young man doesn't want to hear that. Don't romanticise, Ross. Don't imagine that you'll live some grand, adventurous life. You've been stuck out here for too long. Do you even have any idea what's been going on up there?'

'There's always something going on somewhere, Grams. It's called civilisation,' he argued.

'Dinnae be wise with me, Ross. Darwin's Government House was stormed last year. The Administrator Gilruth and his family were virtually prisoners in their own home and a gunboat was sent to protect them. Why, the rebellion was the nearest thing to a revolution since that uprising at Eureka.' His grandmother's look was steady. 'In running further away you'll lose yourself. As you have here, except this time you'll be ignoring your family's need for help. You must see that what you want cannot be done, not at this time.'

It was all he'd thought about, heading northwards. Seeing first-hand what the pioneers saw. Ross worried about the new, wild country he'd read about in his younger years disappearing. That the taming of the land and the enlightening of its natural inhab-itants would be completed. The last great Australian wilderness conquered and fully populated before his arrival there. He'd only delayed so long in the hope of his brother's return.

'Surely you've had enough of this place at least,' said his grandmother.

Ross *was* weary of working with sheep, of feeling the greasy wool between his fingers, of the stench of it on his clothes. At first the property was an escape and then, in lieu of active service, it transformed into Ross's only contribution to the war effort, the industry partially succeeding in pacifying his guilt. But now when he thought of sheep, Ross only saw the blood on the uniforms that he'd helped create.

'I came on this trip to ensure that you would do your father's bidding.' His grandmother folded and refolded her hands in her lap. 'Ross, you must come home. If you dinnae do what is asked you won't be welcome on any of your father's stations in the future.'

'It's blackmail, then,' said Ross.

'Call it what you will. The result is all that matters.'

He'd be alone. Cut off. With no claim on his father's associates for help. No chance to prove his ability by managing one of the family's assets. 'Why is the opportunity to go north conditional on her?'

'Her name is Miss Darcey Thomas, and you know why.'

Ross moved away to the edge of the veranda, the heat of the sun striking his face like a slap. 'It's archaic, ridiculous. I told Father the same. I told him I wouldn't do it.'

His grandmother slapped at a fly. 'Sit down, Ross. I said *sit*.'

Ross did as he was told.

'Dinnae think I haven't given this a great deal of thought. I've wondered at the sense of it. Of the point of serving up two young people on a platter to protect the Grant reputation. I myself would prefer you settled down with a good Scots wife. However as Alastair is no longer with us, this falls to you, Ross. There is no one else. You must see the sense in this, lad. You'll not find a suitable wife out here and your lack of service as well as your brother's dishonour can't have endeared you to the fairer sex. In a few years' time attitudes will have changed, of course. The families snubbing their noses at us now will be wishing they'd paid more attention to Ross Grant once the full extent of the war's losses strike home. But it will be too late. You will have struck a good match. This is not some small favour that I ask of you. This is simply something that must be done. Alastair asked the Englishwoman to marry him and in good faith she travelled here to us in the hope that he would come home.'

'Then Alastair should return and claim her.'

'Is it possible that my grandson is sitting here arguing with an old woman instead of listening to sense?' She spoke to the veranda rafters as if conversing with some ancient god.

'Grams, I –'

'*Let me finish*. Your brother is dead. There, I've said it. It's been far too long without word, and most of our boys have already returned home from the war.' Spindly fingers grasped at his arm. 'There is honour in doing this and you, Ross, having lost much of yours through circumstance, should be glad of having it restored.'

51

They stared at each other. 'You mean I now have to pay for the family's decision not to send me to war?' said Ross.

'Because it's you that must live with the consequences,' replied his grandmother. 'However unfair.'

'Why is she still here, Grams? Why didn't you send her back? It's nearly twelve months since armistice. Why on earth did you let her stay?'

His grandmother took a sip of the water at her side. 'In the beginning, Miss Thomas refused to go home. Absolutely refused. She remained convinced that the circumstances around Alastair's disappearance were proof he was still alive. She was adamant he would be found and that eventually he'd return to Adelaide and to her. That's how much she believed in your brother. In the sanctity of the promise made. I admired her for that and it was I who told your father not to force her to leave. I kept thinking how she'd risked her own life to get here. How certain she was that Alastair would eventually make his way home. God only knows what happened to your brother. War produces a variety of different wounds, Ross, but for some families death is not the very worst that can occur.'

Ross squeezed his grandmother's hand. Alastair's shame was a humiliation on a grand scale. Their father, having ensured Alastair's entry into the war as an officer, was left with the dishonourable legacy of his eldest abandoning his regiment.

'Were he English, your brother would doubtless have been shot on sight if he'd been found, and if he had returned to Australia he'd have been court-martialled. Alastair was a public disgrace,' she finished.

'And I'm expected to pick up where Alastair left off?' said Ross. 'To carry his burdens, ease my family's embarrassment and marry his fiancée. To sacrifice my own desires to restore the family name. I can't do it. Don't you see? It will be like it's happening all over again. Ross Grant, the poor replacement for another lost brother.'

'I didnae want to hear you say that, Ross,' his grandmother said quietly. 'My sister-in-law Fiona was a woman of strong opinions and she did wrong speaking that way to you all those years ago. It was not your fault. That baby was malformed.'

And the rest of it? Ross wanted to ask. What of the rest of it? It was possible his grandmother wasn't aware of what transpired in his childhood. The passing of her husband, his grandfather, occurred when he was fourteen. It was a long illness over many years and a slow death. So perhaps his grandmother hadn't noticed how loveless his life had been.

'Here.' She passed him an envelope.

Ross held it briefly, wondering at the contents before breaking the seal. The edges of the photograph were slightly curled, the heart-shaped face faded. To have the woman presented to him by way of a gummy envelope was strange to say the least. 'This is Miss Thomas?'

'That photograph warmed Alastair's pocket. The field hospital forwarded it after he disappeared, along with his last letter to her.' She looked towards the setting sun as if she could find some answer in the light. 'If you'd bothered coming home for Christmas that wouldn't be needed. She's thirty years of age, Ross, living far from home and she has no one except the family of the fiancé who deserted her, and very little money.'

'Much to recommend,' replied Ross. 'I'm surprised she would even consent to this.'

'And what should we do? Send her back to the north of England to sit and sew with her father when all the young men from that area are either dead or missing? This family has a responsibility to the girl. And you have a duty to fulfil. The Grants need an heir, Ross, and only you can provide one.'

'An heir? This is too much,' said Ross.

'There is nothing we can do about Alastair now. But we can salvage something from his life.'

Ross left the veranda and walked a few feet away from the homestead. The sun was casting the last of its heat across the plains. His grandmother came to his side, crooking her arm through his.

'There is some good news. The Commonwealth is compiling a war record. Your brother's name will be included. Unlike other deserters, he did fight. And I'm pleased to say that the mentions in despatches Alastair received will also be entered in the document.'

'And?' said Ross.

'Many young men have been left mutilated by this damned war, most of them beyond repair. I like to think that you were saved for greater things, Ross. Marooned out here, growing strong, readying yourself for a future you had no knowledge of. Well, this is it, lad. At least come home and meet the girl. One day you'll be head of this family and a very wealthy man.'

They didn't understand. None of them did, thought Ross. It wasn't about the money.

'You *will* come home, Ross.'

'And what will I tell the Toths? They're like family to me.'

'Tell them whatever you must.' She tugged at his shirtsleeve. 'But don't forget, they work for us.'

⋘ Chapter 7 ⋙

Ross was in no hurry to leave Gleneagle, electing to wait a few weeks before heading south to the city. He carried little when he set out, except for saddlebags and a rifle. His possessions were rolled inside a blanket and strapped to his horse.

He rode past decaying farmhouses with gaping windows and tumbled roofs fracturing the red dirt. The remnants of lives conquered by weather. The land in the north was no place for the plough. At every mile the dusty road narrowed a bit more, almost as if he were being reeled in, inch by inch. It was a tedious journey made untenable by what lay ahead. His grandmother had been his undoing. If she'd not come, he never would have agreed to meet Darcey Thomas.

At the beginning of the Mallee woodlands that marked the transition into more fertile country Ross took to the scrub, riding at night to avoid the increasing heat. At least that's how he justified it. The weather was only part of the reason. Closer settlements increased the chance of meeting people and he didn't want to speak to anyone. It was easier out here. Ross liked the quiet of the brush. The scurry of tiny creatures over and under leaves.

The snap of a twig as a kangaroo darted into the trees. Through the branches a sliver of moon hung against a pattern of stars. It trailed Ross through the timber. He took comfort in seeing the distant brightness. In the rhythmic plodding of the horse.

In the darkness he sensed Alastair. Alive somewhere in Europe, running from all those things Ross once thought his brother held dear. He knew it was the last strings of hope that made him imagine that Alastair still lived, that and an anger towards his brother that he couldn't deny. During the war years he'd received only five letters from him. Two of which spoke fleetingly of Darcey. Their first meeting when his brother was on leave in London was explained simply as being quite unexpected. They'd taken afternoon tea together and quite hit it off, and enjoyed five days together. He described Darcey as being a good sort. Delightful.

Delightful. Alastair could have been talking about a decent meal, a fine day, an afternoon stroll. Which made sense, as the likelihood of his older brother caring for a woman he'd spent less than a week with was absurd. Except that a few months later he'd written, telling Ross that he'd proposed marriage and Darcey had accepted. It made Ross wonder what happened in the intervening months when his older brother was away from this woman. Alastair once wrote of the monotony of war. Of the endless waiting between engagements, of the mind-dulling weeks in the trenches and then the screaming whistle, which hurtled many of his friends up and over sandbags to their deaths. Either boredom or horror drove him towards her. And so it was equally possible that injury had given him time to rethink his position. Maybe that was why Alastair ran away from the hospital, to be free of Darcey Thomas.

So why then was he, Ross, riding towards her?

In an hour or so it would be broad daylight. Ross needed to find a cool spot to camp. There were the odd outbuildings, derelict dwellings and farmers who occasionally offered shelter if they caught sight of him, however these Ross tended to avoid, choosing instead the multi-stemmed eucalypts in the scrub as cover. To his left there was a road through the trees, surrounded by patches of dirt and the brown-green of leaves gaining colour as the sun rose. Branches and twigs crackled underfoot. Yesterday he'd chewed on the last of Mrs Toth's tack-hard damper while scratching pictures in the dirt with a stick. There was little food left. Soon he'd exist on water and butchered kangaroo.

His horse whinnied in complaint. Ross patted its warm hair, riding reluctantly towards the road. There was a fence on the other side. A windmill.

'There you go, old mate,' he said to the horse. 'Water.' The trough was on the fence boundary and there was no gate nearby. Dismounting, Ross cut through the fence's sagging top wires. The animal drank greedily, pushing against the remaining metal strands as Ross climbed over and cupped the water to his mouth before splashing his face.

He recalled that in their youth Alastair wasn't one to chase class or money. A pretty face and an eager smile was enough to spur his brother on. By the time Ross had caught him behind the hedge at the back of the garden, rutting like a ram, the age difference between them seemed like a chasm. At sixteen, Alastair was tall and broad. When he'd stood, buttoning his trousers and stroking his neck in satisfaction, the red-haired girl turning away as she tidied herself, Ross understood how much they'd grown apart. He'd lingered until after his brother had departed, Alastair first giving the girl instructions to wait a few minutes before leaving as well.

'He won't marry you, you know,' he'd called out from the foliage.

The girl ran away.

Ross kept a lookout as he filled his waterbag. He returned to his horse, and rested his arms over the saddle. The wind blew whirligigs into the air as the horse continued drinking.

'Good on yah, cobber.' A farmer appeared a little way off with an armful of wood.

There was a neat house nearby and, through the trees, Ross caught a glimpse of a washing line full to bursting. Damn. Why hadn't he seen it?

'I'm sorry,' replied Ross. 'My horse needed a drink and I didn't see a gate. I'll fix it for you.'

'Don't you worry about that, young fella. Come in and have a cup of tea. The kettle's on. My boy's here. Lost most of his mates over there, so he'd be pleased to see a friendly face. You know, someone who's seen what he's seen. He won't talk to me or Mum about it. Won't talk much at all. Just sits out the back, smoking and playing with the dog. I'd be real obliged.'

'That would be good. Thanks.' Ross waved to the man.

'There's a gate a quarter mile down the road.'

Ross twisted the wires together and rode on. Most of the serving men who were able had been shipped back from Europe by now. The welcome-home banners strung up in homes and towns had been put away and the returning soldiers were trying to get on with their lives. It was everywhere, the war. The remnants of it. Glory and sacrifice. Death and honour. He steered from the road and back to the cover of the bush. The tea was tempting. The thought of explaining himself was not.

A few miles on, Ross set up a rough camp under a straggly clump of trees. He lay down in the shadows as his horse grazed. There was flour and a twist of sugar sitting in a saddlebag, but the effort of mixing up a lumpy dough and making a fire didn't appeal. He wasn't that hungry. Shuffling onto his side, he wedged a hip in the dirt and rested his hat over his eyes.

Sleep was limited to periods of exhaustion, for Ross preferred being awake. With sleep, his mind wandered. From the teasing black mass that stalked him, across distant battlefields in an unknown country, to a twin brother never known. The dream always ended the same way, with Alastair walking away.

On the city's outskirts, Ross halted. He watered his horse and turned to stare along the road travelled. Turning back was an option. There was nothing to stop him from pulling the reins in a different direction and watching the miles unfurl. Nothing, except for the simple fact that he loved and respected his grandmother and, with Alastair's disappearance, Ross was effectively an only child.

The phrase carried a hollowness to it. A certainty of loneliness. Church bells were ringing out across the city, he could smell freshly baked bread and roasting meat. Until now he'd not thought what day it was. Across the street two men were fighting. Legs staggering, the opponents lurched at each other. Some punches found their marks, others hit air.

'Those two have been brawling ever since they got back.'

Ross turned to find a man leaning on the railing outside the smithy.

'Didn't know each other until they got home,' the man continued. 'And I bet they hadn't touched a drink up till when they went over there. Bad business that, unless you own a hotel, of course. The publicans are making a fortune.'

One of the combatants staggered, falling to the ground.

'You from Adelaide then?' the man asked.

'Yes. A long time ago,' replied Ross.

'That's what all you young fellas say. Things haven't changed that much, but on the other hand, everything has. Well, good luck.' He gave a salute. 'And thanks.'

Ross rode on. After this visit he did not expect to return to Adelaide for a very long time.

⊸ Chapter 8 ⊸

Adelaide

Trees ran along the perimeter of the boundary fence enclosing the six acres in which Ross's childhood home was nestled. Although Ross remembered every space inside and outside the brick and lime-stone building, he felt no attachment to the house or grounds.

Connor greeted him at the stables. 'So you've come. They were starting to worry. Herself was convinced that you'd show, but your parents, well, it's been a good place to keep clear of the last few weeks.' He nodded towards the rear of the two-storey house. 'Any day now I've been expecting to be sent to fetch you. Willing or not. As it is, you look like you've been dragged by the ankle the whole way back to Adelaide.'

Once dismounted, he shook Connor's hand. 'Nothing's changed.'

'Maybe not here. The city, though.' Connor grimaced. 'Cars and electric trams and outspoken women.' A church bell chimed. 'You look like you've had a hard ride.' He sniffed. 'And a bath wouldn't hurt you.'

Ross patted his shirtsleeves and clouds of dust rose in the air.

'It was no easy decision then?' asked Connor.

'Would it be for any man?'

'I dinnae rightly know. I've not been presented with a perfumed peach for the taking. Usually,' Connor winked, 'they've been unripe pears and quite expensive ones for the quality of the fruit.' He led Ross's horse into the stables.

'Have you ever thought of marrying, Connor?'

Connor undid the surcingle, lifted the saddle clear of the horse, and set it down. 'I have. Once. She was a wee lass from the village where I grew up. I was seventeen years of age. Her father said no the day I asked him for her hand. She was already promised to another.' He removed the saddle blanket and began to brush the animal's sweaty hide. 'I should have seen it coming. A few years later I placed a stone on one of the cairns on a hill near our farm. It was a crumbling pile not used as a landmark for anything that I knew of. Some said there was an old chieftain buried there. Others reckoned it was a lookout for when the English attacked. All I knew was that moorlands and mountaintops lay beyond it and that on a clear day when there was only a middling fog in the valley you could see another cairn in the distance. That's when I wondered what was on the other side. I left a few years later. It was hard to say goodbye to my father, but harder still to stay and see that girl every day for the rest of my life.' Connor patted the horse, tweaking the animal's ears. 'What I'm trying to say, Ross, is that you have to get married at some stage and it's better this way. To have the thing done for you. It's the hope that wears away at a man. Waiting for the right one to appear is like expecting a star to fall from the heavens. I don't think it happens.'

'What if it does?' asked Ross.

'Ah, then, that's another matter. Not that you need to worry about that. Your life's been mapped out,' he told him.

'I said I'd meet the girl, nothing else,' insisted Ross.

'Aye, right. You've ridden all this way to say hello. I've not heard anything so daft.'

'It's not daft.'

'Just go and get it over with, Ross.'

Ross kicked at a rake leaning on the wall. It fell, knocking down a makeshift shelf holding tins of nails and other bits and pieces.

'Steady on,' said Connor.

'Why does everyone think they have the right to tell me what to do?' said Ross.

61

'Perhaps it's because you're acting like a fool,' answered Connor. 'The family's been through enough without you behaving like a spoilt wee boy.'

'I won't be bothering to count on you for support,' said Ross, his voice rising.

'If you want to yell at someone, yell at me. Dinnae take your anger inside to them.' Connor rested the currycomb on the railing and with deliberate slowness walked from the stall. 'You've always been a stubborn one. Come on then, lad, let's show me what you've got.'

'I don't want to fight you, Connor.'

'Better me than fighting yourself,' he replied.

The anger that started building the day the first of his father's letters had arrived at Gleneagle now goaded Ross. He tried to recall the location of the nearest church, for shortly he was going to have to find a pew near the back, under a stained-glass window, and ask for absolution. At this point he needed more than Presbyterian stoic conservatism, because he was seriously thinking of punching Connor in the face.

'Didnae your brother give you enough floggings when you were young?' Connor squared up to him. 'Or your father?'

Ross's first punch missed. He should have known Connor would be quick, the small ones always were.

'Well, well. And here was I thinking you'd go meekly to your fate. It seems I was wrong. And you're angry about it. Good. It's good to be angry. That's it. Get those fists up and have a go, lad. It's been a year since I gave someone a good belting.'

Ross stepped straight into Connor's left jab.

'Forgot I was a lefty, didnae you? Come on.' He beckoned. 'You can do better than that.'

They moved across the dirt of the stables, Ross throwing punches as Connor ducked and twisted out of reach.

'A pretty boy like you should be married, you know.'

Ross slammed his fist into Connor's jaw and received a winding blow to the stomach in return. He staggered backwards into the stable wall, gasping for air.

Connor rubbed his jaw. 'Enough?' he asked.

Ross nodded. 'Enough.'

They sat on a bale of hay catching their breaths. 'If you didnae come back for her, why are you here?' asked Connor.

'My grandmother,' admitted Ross. 'I agreed to meet Miss Thomas. Nothing more.'

'Ah, aye, it's important to know where the real power lies in a family. But seriously, Ross, there will be hell waiting at the gate if you dinnae do this. If you refuse to marry her.'

Ross turned to his friend. 'I said I'd meet her and I will. Then I'm off. I need you to buy me two tickets on the next steamer out of Adelaide. Cargo, passenger, mail, any kind will do. As long as it's leaving soon and heading north. I'd always thought I'd take the inland route, meet up with the cameleers, follow the telegraph line, but that won't be happening now.'

'Are you going north then? To the Territory? To Waybell?' asked Connor, his interest clear.

'Yes. About time, I think.'

'Why two tickets?'

Ross prodded his injured right eye. 'One for you and one for me. If you're up to it.'

'Aye, I'm up to it, lad.' Connor's smile disappeared. 'What of your father? I don't expect he'll let you run off, or me.'

'I'm not letting him stop me. Anyway, I'd be surprised if he said no now that I'm here and prepared to meet Miss Thomas. But I doubt they'd let me leave without a chaperone,' said Ross, placing a hand on Connor's shoulder. 'Who else would he send? You've been with us for years. And now the war's over it shouldn't be too diffi-cult to find a man to take over from you while you're away.'

'I dinnae know.' Connor shook his head doubtfully. 'It's not that easy a position. We couldn't get just anyone. They'd have to be experienced.'

'You mean old like you?' said Ross.

Connor gave Ross a shove and he fell from the bale to the dirt. 'Careful, lad. I'm in my prime.'

❈ Chapter 9 ❈

They were assembled in the drawing room, each of them arranged carefully like players on a stage. Had Alastair been present he would have theorised on the archetypes in the room. Tyrant that their father was, he would certainly be the ruler, Zeus. Hera, the now insubstantial caregiver who took the form of his mother, and the indomitable sage Isis, his grandmother. Which made him, Ross supposed, Hermes. The wanderer and fool.

After the pleased but restrained greeting Ross received from his parents and grandmother, his request to meet Darcey Thomas alone was grudgingly approved. He knew his parents wanted to be present, to ensure it went smoothly and that the result they sought was guaranteed. They didn't trust him and they were right not to. His father even went so far to say that Darcey needed a chaperone, which was, to Ross's mind, a ridiculous idea considering the circumstances.

'We all know why I'm here,' he told them. 'Let's not stand on pretence.' It was this suggestion of compliance that Ross hoped would win the argument.

'Quite right.' His grandmother sat hunched at a card table, a game of patience spread out before her, liver spots on veiny hands. 'It's not like he's courting Darcey. You took your time, Ross,' she stated. 'We expected you two weeks ago. Alastair would have –'

Ross rested an elbow on the mantelpiece. 'I'm not Alastair.'

His grandmother slapped a card down on the table. 'What's wrong with your eye?'

'I fell from my horse,' he replied.

'Really?' She gave a huff of disbelief. 'The one thing you can do is ride, my boy. Sit a horse like a brush in a gluepot.'

'You've lost weight,' commented his mother.

'Leave the lad alone,' said his father.

The housekeeper entered with glasses of lemon cordial. 'It's a pleasure to have you back here, Mr Ross. It's been such a long time.'

'Thank you, Mrs Blum. I'm pleased to see you're still here.'

The woman sat the tray on a table. 'Only just returned, sir.'

'How is your family?' asked Ross.

'They placed my two boys under house arrest during the war. They said we were agitators. Things have only recently begun to return to normal.'

'I'm sorry to hear that, Mrs Blum.'

'Mrs Blum,' his grandmother interrupted, 'can you please tell Miss Thomas that Ross is here and to wait in the sitting room. It's quieter in there, Ross,' she told him, as the housekeeper left the room. 'I never expected to re-employ Mrs Blum, especially at her age. But it's simply impossible to find anyone willing to work in a big house these days and with your return we needed someone capable.' She gathered up the deck of cards. 'Think of all those boys they killed. You do know that they changed many of the German place names back to English. Hahndorf is now Ambleside. As it should be.'

The drawing room was just as Ross remembered. The large bay windows offered a perfect view of the circular gravel drive and fountain. The camphor laurel tree still stood in the very centre and under it the wrought iron bench. Long ago, Alastair had dragged it there so it would be easier for Ross to reach the lower branches. He'd stared out the window at this scene the morning after their disastrous expedition, learning from their father that the wandering lunatic and the little boy had been found. The asylum was given a substantial donation and the injured rider was presented with a new penny-farthing bicycle. His father righted their wrongs with generous bequests and was applauded for it.

'Well, Ross, you'll want to change before the big moment.' His father broke into his thoughts.

'Yes, you look like you've been riding for weeks,' his grandmother added. 'There are fresh clothes for you in your room.'

'Off you go then,' his father ordered cheerily. 'After it's done come back here and you and I will have a celebratory dram.'

❧ Chapter 10 ❧

Ross rubbed at freshly shaven skin and then at the eye that was swollen and sore. A slight discoloration was already beginning to appear. He ran fingers through damp hair, turning from the mirror's reflection. The room was unchanged, full of schoolbooks and sporting ribbons. The same grey blanket folded at the foot of the bed. The travelling trunk with the bent latch. Inside was his cricket bat, the willow stamped with an old property brand used to burn numbers into stud ram's horns, and his marble collection secreted in the biscuit tin.

Ross opened the tin and rolled the spheres in his palm. He thought of Drummond and George. His two closest friends from childhood. The sons of his father's business acquaintances. The three of them had traded marbles, arguing about the weight of an aggie or the quality of a jasper, whether it was the colour of the sea on a swimmable day. Ross poked at the balls in his hand. There were old alabaster ones from Germany, some fine two-coloured glass ones from America and others with steel ball-bearings, which the boys complained about because Ross used them as shooters. He smiled at the memory, thinking of impromptu cricket matches, summer visits to the beach, sticky hands and chocolate faces. These sunlit days were strange to think on as they'd rarely been spent in Alastair's company and yet Ross had enjoyed these happy moments and remembered them fondly.

Replacing the tin, Ross looked out the window to the circle of plane trees planted by his grandfather. He sighed, and sighed again, aware of his procrastination. Then he walked downstairs and into the sitting room.

A woman was silhouetted by the window. She pushed back the damask curtains, the light revealing a brocade chair, a large vase of flowers with sagging greenery, and thick carpets scattered across the floor. Ross wondered if she'd heard him enter, for this woman who once belonged to his brother continued to gaze out the window. Did she still think of Alastair? Did she even care?

Darcey Thomas was dressed in emerald and cream. Strange, but he had expected her to be in black, in mourning and respectful, not bright, colourful and modern. The silk blouse she wore was loose-fitting, the fashionable skirt short like the women in the city streets he saw as he rode into town. It had been some time since Ross had been alone with a woman close to his own age. The niceties of polite society were hardly needed on a sheep property, and avoiding the town of Burra meant there was little opportunity for socialising. Maybe there was such a thing as being tongue-tied, for he silently stumbled over his prepared words, and in that moment the clearest of pictures came to him of his brother and Darcey together on a busy London road.

She turned around fully and faced him and offered him a smile. Soft and welcoming. 'It's easier for getting in and out of cars and the tram.'

'I'm sorry?' asked Ross.

'The length of women's skirts.'

He'd been staring at her ankles. 'Yes, of course it is.'

They met in the centre of the room. She was a foot shorter than he was. Pretty, in a plain English way. Her skin was lightly powdered and her lips reddened. At a loss as to how he should greet her, Ross eventually held out a hand. Hers was small and slightly moist. She was nervous. He felt somehow pleased by the fact, because, despite his family's cajoling, their marriage was not the fait accompli that everyone thought it was.

'I'm Ross.'

'Darcey,' she replied.

'Should we . . .' He gestured to the small grouping of chairs and they sat stiffly, she on the chintz sofa and he in an armchair. A gleaming solid silver teapot, flowery cups and shortbread biscuits waited for consumption on the table between them. Ross wished to be anywhere but here.

'Shall I pour?' she asked, lifting the teapot from the spirit burner.

'Not for me,' Ross answered.

Replacing the pot, Darcey fidgeted with a cup and saucer. Turned the plate of biscuits on the salver.

There were any number of comments Ross could have begun with. 'You don't resemble your photograph.'

Darcey looked up. 'I didn't know you had one.'

He fumbled in a pocket, holding up the image given to him by his grandmother.

'Oh,' was all she said.

Ross wondered what Alastair saw in the woman opposite him. If it weren't for the expensive clothes provided to her by his family, he rather thought she would have blended in with the cream walls. He was more used to women like Mrs Toth. Women who worked the land, darkened and creased by an outdoor life.

'It's just that I gave that to your brother. I wrote on it.' A blotch of red coloured her cheeks. She lowered her chin. On her wedding finger she wore a ring, a blood-red ruby surrounded by diamonds. It was vaguely familiar.

Ross turned the photo over. On the back of the image, towards the bottom in small, neat cursive, were the words, *I love you.* He stared at the message, so intimate in its admission, wondering how he hadn't noticed it before. 'And did you love him?'

'Of course.' There was a defiant edge to her voice.

'Of course,' he repeated, placing the photo on the table between them. His intention had always been to return it to her. Ross didn't want it. It was given to another.

'You don't believe me,' stated Darcey. 'I wouldn't have agreed to marry him if I didn't love him.'

'Really? How long did you know him? A week?'

The knuckles on her hand turned white. 'We wrote to each other for twelve months.'

'I see.'

'Do you?' she challenged.

Darcey wasn't timid. Maybe his brother liked that about her. Ross didn't. Boldness belonged to the likes of his grandmother. She'd earnt the right. Ross wanted to remind Darcey that she was a guest in his home. Except that the walls and ceilings, stone and timber that he'd returned to didn't belong to him, nor he to it. He couldn't tell Darcey that he was unprepared for this, for her. That he didn't want a wife or the obligation that came with being the only remaining Grant child. He was stifled by this life. Hemmed in by buildings and people and expectation, and the sense of alien-ation went beyond the years away, the many miles apart. There was really only one person Ross looked forward to seeing on returning to Adelaide – his grandmother – but even his feelings towards her had changed. What occurred to him was that, of all the people who populated his life, it was perhaps Connor who knew him the best.

Darcey poured tea into a gold-rimmed cup and sipped. 'I know this is very difficult, for both of us, and I do appreciate –'

Ross walked to his mother's mahogany writing desk. A gold fountain pen rested on the blotter. In one of the corners a capital $\mathcal{A}$ had been written in his mother's hand. A for Alastair. 'This meeting is based on everyone else's assumption.'

'I'm sorry,' replied Darcey. The cup rattled on the saucer. 'I was under the impression that it was all arranged.'

How had he allowed himself to be coerced into meeting this woman? Ross lifted a glass paperweight in his hand. 'You have no family, other than your father?'

'My brother died at Fromelles, my sister on the hospital ship *Britannic*.'

When he didn't enquire about the details she talked on regardless, as if the distance between them could be filled by words.

'Anne-Louise was so excited the day she was assigned. It was a sister ship to the *Titanic*. The closest she imagined she'd ever get to luxury.'

Ross sat the glass dome on the desk. 'What happened?'

'A naval mine exploded near the Greek island of Kea in the November of 1916. Nearly everyone managed to escape but Anne-Louise was on one of the lower decks. The nurses had opened most of the portholes on those levels to air the wards.'

November 1916. Only a few months after Alastair's disappearance. 'I'm sorry,' he said and then, curious about her part during the conflict, added, 'And you didn't share her interest in serving abroad?'

'Everyone wanted to enlist and serve overseas, which created a huge shortage of nurses in London when war broke out. St Thomas' Hospital in central London provided a three-month training course for VADs. Unqualified voluntary aid detachments,' she clarified. 'And I stayed on there. It allowed me to contribute to the war effort while also keeping my father happy. He couldn't bear the thought of us all leaving England.'

Now Ross knew why Connor liked her. Loyalty and duty. Simple words that could be relied upon and might possibly act as a bond between them if they were to marry. He expected that, at that moment, Connor was heading to the Adelaide Steamship Company offices. If they didn't have a passenger vessel leaving soon, there would be another company with a steamer heading up the coast carrying cargo or mail to Sydney, Brisbane or Townsville. Any port would do as long as he was transported further towards his destination.

Ross returned to the armchair. 'What did his letter say? The last letter Alastair sent you along with the photograph. Did he mention anything about where he was going or what his intentions were?'

71

'No. Nothing at all. Only that he was sorry.'

'Are you sure there wasn't something else? Think back to when you first met.'

'I have, and your father's already interrogated me numerous times,' she explained.

'He mentioned Mesopotamia to me, Greece, the Tigris,' said Ross. 'Alastair was fascinated by antiquity. I used to think that perhaps he'd joined the Geographical Society and gone adventuring.'

'Alastair thought that was something *you'd* do. He said you'd always been interested in the great Australian explorers while –'

'Alastair was a dreamer,' interrupted Ross. 'He'd think up these ideas, most of them impractical, occasionally dangerous, and anything old fascinated him.'

'You don't think I really knew your brother, but I did. Greek myths, Hercules, the asylum.' She counted on her fingers. 'I could go on, but I don't need to justify my relationship with Alastair to anyone. I loved him and I lost him. We all did. No one has any idea what happened to him, least of all me.' She wasn't pale anymore, but flushed as if she'd been out playing tennis. 'And that last letter, the final words, they were *I'm sorry.*'

Ross heard the catch in her throat. An audible click of sorrow.

'Followed by his name, of course, in that careful flourish,' she said.

He thought of Alastair penning those two words. An abdication of duty. He wouldn't have expected that of his brother. 'And your father, what does he think of this?'

'He understands the difficulties,' answered Darcey cautiously.

'You could return home.'

'Yes, that is an option.'

'Then why are you still here?'

'You are direct, aren't you?'

Ross realised he was making this meeting very difficult for her. Somehow he couldn't bring himself to be kinder, gentler. He was being intolerant of her, of the situation, of his family and yet it felt right to claim that ground. It was a position he could defend.

'The doctor's report said Alastair had injuries to his legs and arms. That he'd been buried alive in a bombardment. I assumed that was what he was apologising for in his note. The wounds he'd sustained. And I'd seen enough amputees in London to presume the worst. Your brother wasn't the kind of man to be a burden to anyone, Ross, and trauma affects people in many ways. Then he disappeared. The details were so unclear as to what happened. I thought perhaps there was a mix-up with identification, but if there wasn't and Alastair did simply leave the hospital without proper medical attention then his chances of survival were slight. But I still hoped. I knew that if he was found the AIF would send him back home,' Darcey explained, 'so I took a position as a nurse's aide on a returning troopship and came to Adelaide to wait for your brother. I'm still here because your grandmother asked me to stay and, if I'm honest, very little waits for me in England. My father is no longer alone. He has taken in lodgers. A widow and her two children.'

'So you stayed because you had nothing better,' said Ross.

'I remained here after I lost hope, Ross, because Alastair said if anything ever happened you would help me.'

Ross leant back in the chair. Every ounce of him wanted to accuse Darcey of seeking sympathy, of hoping to gain favour by concocting a fanciful lie. Instead he recognised the candour in her voice. He didn't doubt that Alastair would have said those very words. Ross would have done the same in his place. 'Did you tell my parents what Alastair said?'

'No,' she admitted.

It was something only between them, this sharing of Alastair's request. Darcey waited. And Ross made her wait. It was as if Alastair was standing in the room with them. Surely his brother hadn't expected him to *marry* her.

'Well, there is very little I can do that my parents haven't done already, Darcey. And as for this expectation of marriage, we don't know each other,' said Ross. The woman seated before him belonged to another time and place. To another man. And she still wore his brother's ring. 'I think this whole thing is absurd.'

Darcey observed him from the middle of the sofa. Her fingers began smoothing the material of her skirt across a knee. They were like two playthings tossed into the air by fate. The wind buffeting them back and forth until the breeze stilled and they landed with a thud. Ross waited for a response, half-expecting her to voice similar thoughts. Then he realised with renewed clarity that Darcey really was desperate. She'd elected to travel out to Australia before the war's end to wait for her fiancé when he'd already disappeared. The trip itself was extremely risky. The vessel could have been attacked. Why would a woman do that? Was it for love or for money?

Ross's thoughts gathered speed. It was not inconceivable that it may have been in the back of Darcey's mind that if Alastair didn't return from France there was another brother at home. A brother who'd spent years on a property in the middle of nowhere, safe from harm. He imagined the woman was very used to the comforts provided by his family. And although it was unlikely they would send Darcey back to England, at this stage a marriage offered security, a permanent connection to the Grant name and money. He circled the sofa. 'Why do you think my brother loved you? If he did indeed feel that way. I don't want to offend, but you were put together in rather odd circumstances.'

There was a tilt to her chin as she followed his movements. 'As we are now.'

'Can you answer me?'

'Why? Am I so lacking in attributes that you must dig for reasons?' She twisted the ring on her finger. 'Would you like to go out?' she offered. 'It's very warm inside. We could sit under the camphor laurel tree. Alastair said that you and he –'

'No,' he replied curtly. How could she even presume to know anything about his relationship with his brother? 'Do you want this to happen? To marry me? Someone you don't know? For that's what my parents expect.' When he frowned his injured eye stung. Ross moved closer. 'I'm sure my father would ensure you were financially secure. You could go back to England.'

'Ross, if you don't want me, say so, but this is not about money,' she interrupted. 'Your family have been very kind to me and I was led to believe that a marriage between us would help ease the pain caused by the last few years.'

'Pain for some, embarrassment for others,' said Ross.

Her eyelids fluttered but she didn't lower her gaze. Ross wondered what she was really thinking as she sat there offering herself to him. She was so precise in the way she spoke. So assured and yet brittle. He'd not been brought up to be discourteous to anyone, least of all a woman, yet here he was thinking of the very worst things that he could say to her. Anything to discourage her, so that it was she who made the decision to step away.

'Your grandmother said that war can do terrible things to a man,' said Darcey. 'Things that we could never understand. That it can change a person. I've seen that at St Thomas'. I understand what she means. I could never blame Alastair for what's happened.'

'I hate war,' said Ross. 'Wars have uncertain endings.'

'How would you know?' countered Darcey.

She cut him as surely as if she'd wielded a knife. 'I've lost a brother, Darcey, and I'm here today because of a war and the mess it's created. I think I know what wars can do.'

'I'm sorry, I didn't mean to upset you.'

'This was a ridiculous idea. I shouldn't have agreed to come here,' said Ross.

'As I said before, Ross, if you don't want me, say so. But I will not be the one to throw away this, this –'

'Opportunity?'

'That was unkind. You're unkind. You're nothing like Alastair.'

Ross laughed. 'Now you speak the truth.'

From a table Darcey retrieved a cardboard box. 'Your brother asked me to post this, but I kept thinking it would be safer to give it to you personally. Now I know it may as well have been thrown into the ocean on my journey here. It won't mean anything to you. The only person you really care about is yourself.' She dropped the parcel on the sofa and marched angrily from the room.

⊰ Chapter 11 ⊱

Ross shook the gift curiously and contemplated what Alastair might have wanted him to have. He worried that if he opened the parcel he would be reminded of lost youth and brotherly adventures. And he wasn't sure he could cope with returning to that place of grief after so many months of doggedly crawling from it. So he left the parcel untouched, staring at it as he rolled up his shirtsleeves.

He already missed the endless nothingness of Gleneagle. The long days of work, the pre-dawn starts and early evenings. The remoteness of living there. Being back in Adelaide only reminded him of how removed he now was from this world. He looked again at the parcel, knowing it had to be opened. Inside were layers of fine paper, within which was a piece of carefully folded rough cloth. It was old, stained and tattered. The colours were barely recognisable.

'Ross?'

He could keep the door closed to anyone but his grandmother. Reluctantly, Ross let her in. 'Hello, Grams. Have you come to give me a talking to? If so, it won't help.'

'Locked yourself in, eh? You used to do that when you were young.' She held a decanter of whisky in one hand and leant on a duck-headed walking stick. 'Get some glasses from the sideboard.'

Ross returned with the tumblers as she sat on the sofa, waving irritably at him to sit down. His grandmother seemed to have taken on the proportions of Great-Aunt Fiona. She was stunted by the curve in her shoulders, something he'd not noticed at Gleneagle, and her face had adopted a squareness of jaw that bagged around the edges. She thumped the decanter on the table. 'Pour.'

They skolled the whisky together. Ross helped himself to another. This time he poured a good four fingers' worth into the whisky glass. The liquid was still burning when it hit his stomach.

'So, I gather she's not to your liking.' She ran a finger around the rim of the empty glass. 'I'll admit Darcey is no great beauty but she's not plain either. She's pretty enough.'

'Grams, this isn't about what she looks like,' Ross protested.

'We women aren't silly enough to think looks dinnae count. They're what attracts a man in the first place. It's having the skill to keep him, that's where you separate the sheep from the lambs. Darcey's older.' She wagged a finger. 'And intelligent enough to make a good wife. No bad thing for a young buck. You, on the other hand, look worn out. What would you have us think, arriving home unkempt and filthy? And you've been in a fight by the looks of that bruise. Look at you. Sitting here in a state of undress. Half your shirt buttons undone. You'll be lucky if Darcey wants you at all, and then where will we be?'

'Saved,' he muttered.

She cupped a hand around an ear. 'What's that?'

'Nothing.'

'Take another,' commanded his grandmother.

Ross scowled and poured a splash into the glass, wishing he'd eaten something. He handed her the box.

The old woman turned the container over before lifting the lid. 'So, she gave it to you. Darcey brought that over from England.

Your brother visited the Clan Grant lands and that piece of tartan was given to him by one of the lairds who swore it'd come down from Culloden itself.'

Culloden. A battle fought on boggy ground that ended in disaster. 'It couldn't have survived that long,' said Ross, studying the cloth with renewed interest.

'Could it not?' asked his grandmother. 'It was a very bad day for the Highlanders. A poorly chosen site,' she tutted. 'The road to Inverness had to be defended.'

'Grams, you'll upset yourself.'

'Upset myself? I was born distressed. Unsettled. And why not? Look where I ended up.'

'I thought you liked Adelaide?'

'What's there to like? There are more churches than people and everything makes a clamour these days. I didnae mind the place twenty years ago. It was more like the capital of a small principality with parks and gardens and its little court society. Yes, I liked it then, before the time of conspicuous industrialism.' She leant on the cane, shuffling forwards on the seat. 'I might rant at you, Ross, but I know why you cleared off. It wasn't because you felt unjustly treated. It's in us, this need for air and space. It's in our blood.' She raised her glass. 'Stand fast, stand sure.'

'Stand fast, stand sure,' repeated Ross, lifting his own.

'The pattern is one I've not seen.' His grandmother held the cloth close to her eyes. 'But then clans didnae all wear the same setts and colours back then. The colours people wore came from the area where they lived.'

'You honestly believe . . .' Ross took the tartan from her.

'Darcey seems certain because your brother was.'

'Grams, Alastair was a dreamer,' said Ross.

'And that's no bad thing. Sometimes I do it myself. I'm always dreaming for another day. My husband, your dear grandfather, used to comment in his youth that he'd be pleased to reach seventy, but when you get there, you always want more.'

Ross held the cloth. A remnant from antiquity. Maybe it was the whisky or the long journey and lack of food, for the briefest of moments he found himself wanting to believe as well.

'A Scot whose ancestors fought at Culloden could hardly not be stirred by that piece of cloth. Alastair recognised its significance enough to pass it on to you for safekeeping. That's what allows me to sleep at night, knowing that your brother wasn't completely disinterested in our heritage or our family. That piece of tartan is proof of that,' said his grandmother. 'It is evidence of a bond that can never be broken even in death. Alastair was your only brother. Darcey was to be his wife. Go and speak to her, Ross. Both you and this family need an honourable conclusion to move forwards.'

'I can't.' He placed the material back in the box. 'She still wears Alastair's ring and, anyway, I don't want to marry her.'

'It's my ring. Take it off and put your own on her. You *have* to do this. You've been absent from this family for too many years. You must step up, lad. You know this, otherwise you wouldn't have come back.'

'I came home for you, Grams,' he found himself admitting.

'Rubbish. You came for fear of being cut off. It's a hard thing for a grandmother to say but sometimes a person has to die to make space for another. Your twin William is dead. Alastair is undoubtedly gone. You and I both know that this is your time. That's why you returned.'

'And if I don't marry Darcey?'

'No one can make you do the right thing, Ross. Only you can do that.' She got carefully to her feet, brushing away his offer of assistance. At each piece of furniture in the room she stopped, tapping at the item with her stick and pointing out the object's history as if she were discussing the pedigree of a relative. At the writing desk she revealed it once belonged to her grandmother and was carted from Edinburgh by ship to the colony of New South Wales with her family.

'I'm amazed it wasn't damaged by the final journey to Adelaide.' She returned to the sofa and sat down, hands resting on the brass-headed duck. 'I'd never disown you, Ross, for I've lost too many grandsons already, but I would ensure that your inheritance goes to one of your cousins. Someone who deserved and appreciated all that being a Grant entails. Other than that, you will always be welcome to visit,' she finished with a sweet smile.

'Father would never allow it,' Ross countered furiously.

'He's my son,' she answered fiercely. 'Try me.'

Ross broke from her stare. He knew his grandmother. The house and land may have passed to his father on his grandfather's death, but Connor was right. Bridget Grant exerted her influence across everything. She was the matriarch, the true head of the family.

'Well?' She was waiting for an answer.

Ross had never once requested money from the moment he'd left home. So why did he want it now? Because it was to be given away to another? He stared at the scrap of tartan in the box, thinking of the legacy woven into the pattern. The people, the sheep, the vegetable dyes. The women who used their own urine to set the pigments. The singing of waulking songs as they beat the cloth to soften it. At that moment he hated Alastair. They'd won. His grandmother's satisfied expression said it all. But there was still one card left to play. 'I'll do it, but only on my terms.'

His grandmother's face crinkled in annoyance. She wasn't expecting this. She'd assumed he would forget any notion of travel and take up his place in Adelaide as a married man.

'I still go north,' he said. The rest of his life depended on his grandmother's agreement to this final phrase: 'For as long as I like.'

There was no more bartering to be had and they both knew it.

'Very well,' the old woman muttered. The stick struck the floor loudly. 'Done.'

⋘ Chapter 12 ⋙

Waiting until morning may have been more polite, however Ross knew his limitations. One night spent pondering his fate would have had him on his horse before daylight. Instead, he went directly upstairs. He stopped outside the large bedroom that had been the focal point for all manner of family milestones. It was here that his mother and father had spent their wedding night. Later, the same room had played host to his mother when she spent months recovering from the trauma of his birth. It was the same bedroom where his grandfather was laid out, a stream of visitors trailing down the hall and staircase to pay their respects. This was also the room of escape. The place where he and Alastair came, climbing out the window to the eucalypt and down to freedom. It was a room of special occasions, tragedy and, as of today, farce.

Pushing open the door he strode through the mauve-wallpapered sitting area and into the bedroom. Darcey was laying on a chaise lounge in the corner, her back to the room. Her shoes were discarded on the floor.

She sat up abruptly. 'Ross.'

Her blouse was partially undone, revealing a chemise and her hair was loose. Ross spun around so that he couldn't see her, realising the rudeness of arriving unannounced. She clutched at the edges of the material, a mirror reflecting her movements as she hurried to dress. She caught him watching.

'I wasn't expecting you,' stammered Darcey. 'Could you wait outside?'

In the adjoining room there were books on every surface, hatboxes stacked neatly in a corner and on the writing desk letters tied with a ribbon. In one of the drawers there would be saved mail from his brother. He was sure of it. Once he would have liked to have seen their correspondence, to learn the truth of their relationship. Now he wanted no detail of that past life. In a corner of the room a suitcase sat open on the floor, with a pile of clothes in a heap beside it.

'You wanted to see me?' Darcey's voice was thick with formality.

Her clothes were righted but her hair remained loose. It made her appear younger, less severe. Ross could tell she'd been crying. He wouldn't have anticipated that. She'd been so forthright earlier, so confident.

She came over to face him. 'I can go home,' she said, when he didn't speak immediately. 'I should have given more thought to what you might want. I'm sorry. It was foolish of me.'

Ross looked at the open suitcase.

'I'll make my own way,' replied Darcey.

'How, by pawning my grandmother's ring?'

Darcey tugged at the ring, twisting it around her finger. 'I didn't ask for it. Grandmother Bridget gave it to me as an engagement ring when I arrived here. She said she intended for Alastair to have it.'

'Well, you're not marrying Alastair,' Ross found himself saying, calmly. 'You're marrying me. And I'll be supplying my own ring.'

Darcey's arms fell to her side. He lifted her left hand and tried to remove the ring. When it couldn't be freed he placed the ring finger in his mouth, moistening her skin. He could feel the heat of her body. There were beads of perspiration on her top lip. The ruby slid off into his hand and Ross placed the ring on the writing desk. 'The wedding will be tomorrow.'

He expected her to be pleased, to at the very least thank him. Instead, she looked as if she hadn't understood what he'd said. 'Tomorrow?' she repeated.

'There's no point waiting and there won't be a fuss, so don't expect it,' Ross told her. 'I'll be leaving soon after to go north. I don't know how long I'll be away. A few years, I expect.'

A fine line appeared at the midpoint between Darcey's eyes. 'But why? I don't understand. You're marrying me and then you're leaving?'

'Yes. You have what you want.'

'I could go with you.'

Ross wondered what she was thinking. She was a woman, and a female was expected to stay within the boundaries that her sex dictated, unless they were his grandmother. 'That won't be possible. It's not the place for you. Best you stay here.'

'Why?' she asked.

'I just told you,' he replied irritably.

'I mean, after everything you said to me, why are you marrying me?'

He looked at the woman standing opposite him with her incredulous expression and thought of his brother. 'Because I have to,' he replied.

⪻ Chapter 13 ⪼

'There's no point delaying it, Ross, you've married her, now it's time to do your duty.' Connor elbowed him. 'The wedding bed, man. You can be assured you won't be turned down and you dinnae have to pay for it.'

Ross poured another dram and took a sip, ignoring his friend. They were in his father's study, going through the files concerning the Territory property. At least, he was reading the records, while Connor was busy scrutinising the portraits on the wall and examining the leather-tooled spines of the bookcase's contents.

'Your father has a fine collection,' said Connor. 'I've only ever stood in front of this desk.'

'Well, if you can draw yourself away from my father's literary tastes perhaps you could sit down and start helping me,' suggested Ross.

Connor flipped the curtain, studied the sky. 'Aye, you're probably right. It's a bit early for bed. A man cannae look too keen.' He sat down on one of the leather chairs near the desk.

Ross frowned at the remark. A cable had been forwarded, advising the manager up north that a Grant was finally coming to visit. Ross imagined the flurry of activity it would create after the staff had been left to their own devices for well over two decades. Morgan Grant liked the idea of sitting on a large parcel of land in an area yet to be considered truly conquered by men. And he wasn't alone. The north of Australia had been carved up by wealthy investors. For many years great chunks of the country had been left in the hands of managers, with few owners bothering to take a step onto the soil they owned.

'So it's straight to business, is it?' asked Connor. 'Right. I know you would have liked to have gone by the Afghan Express, but it's too unreliable and besides it will only get us to Oodnadatta. It's camels after that, and I don't think this Scottish arse was built for such travel.'

Oodnadatta, 540 miles north of Adelaide, placed Ross in proximity to the Simpson Desert, a path his childhood hero Stuart once took. 'I would have gone that way if I'd had the time.'

'Aye, well thank the Lord there's a steamer. Anyway, it's just as well we're leaving. What with the general ruckus your decision's made. I thought Herself would be your stumbling block but if it's as you say, I'm none too shy on leaving tomorrow. There's going to be a fair skirmish here over the next few days.'

The family was barely speaking to Ross or to each other. They'd been denied their society wedding which, it seemed, formed part of their restoration plans, and his grandmother agreeing to Ross's unrestricted journey north when his place was in Adelaide with his new wife was not greeted favourably at all.

'I hope you're not in a rush to come back here, Connor,' said Ross.

Connor flipped his pipe from side to side in the palm of his hand. 'You'll return in a couple of years, Ross. Once the wanderlust is out of you.'

'Care to wager on that?'

Connor hunched his shoulders and began stuffing the pipe with tobacco.

Laid out on the desk among maps and ledgers and daily newspapers was a stack of letters which, over the preceding years, had been sent monthly from up north. Ross was doing his best to read what he could before they left, hopeful of gaining a general idea of where they were headed and what to expect. The correspondence from the manager, Bill Sowden, was much the same and Ross imagined that if he were to match months and years an almost identical cycle of content would appear, rhythmic and scarcely altering like variations on a song handed down through the ages. Too hot for growth, too wet to move. Too much rain. Too little. And circling above each verse would be the refrain, the coming and eventual leaving of the monsoon.

'Listen to this, Connor. Two hundred missing cows in 1910.' Ross ran a finger over a ledger page. 'One hundred and eighty-five in 1915. One hundred and ninety last year. Absentee owners.' Ross searched under more papers, retrieving a copy of *The Register*. 'Here.' He tapped at a page. 'The editor talks about it. That's what's ruined the Territory. People like my father buying up land and then sitting on it. Do you know that we've spent no money on improvements up there? Ever.'

'Cheap to run then, eh?'

'Connor,' warned Ross.

'I'm just saying, your father's not stupid. Besides, it sounds like he's not the only one biding his time. I'm betting the property is worth a small fortune by now.'

'More cattle. We need to buy more.' Ross was barely concentrating on what Connor was saying. 'There's a meatworks up there run by Vesty's. The prices for beef went sky-high during the war and everything I've read suggests that cattle and mining still offer the best prospects for success.'

'They've been searching for reefs of gold there for years, Ross. I'd stick to cattle.' Connor lit the pipe, his cheeks hollowing as he inhaled. 'You've got some learning to do, being the shepherd in the family.'

'Thanks.'

'I'm not denying this is an opportunity for the both of us, but have you not thought that your father knows what he's doing? He's as shrewd as the next businessman *and* he's a Scot.'

86

'And he won't be there with us,' replied Ross. Up there he would be safe from any family interference, while his father concentrated on the three sheep properties he owned in the South and the grape-growing enterprise on the Adelaide Plains that he'd purchased from a German family during the war. Ross recalled the phrase 'the tyranny of distance', first heard in the schoolroom to explain the pitfalls of the early colonisation of Australia. But there was a clear benefit to distance, one that his teacher would never have foreseen.

'And what about the vacant lots in Darwin your father owns?' asked Connor.

'He wants those sold. I'm wondering why someone hasn't made an offer already,' said Ross.

'I'll tell you why, because a big cyclone is just as likely to come in and blow anything that's built there flat.'

'You're full of good news, aren't you?'

'Excitement of the day,' replied Connor. 'I'm beginning to think that I'm far more enthusiastic about your wedding night than you are.'

'That wouldn't be hard,' said Ross.

'You do know what to do, dinnae you?' asked Connor. He puffed out smoke when Ross hesitated. 'Dinnae tell me you've not been with a woman.' He tapped his skull. 'It's my fault. I should have asked you before this.'

'I've been with a woman.'

Connor raised an eyebrow. 'As only a man can be with a woman?'

'Yes,' Ross lied.

'Who?'

'You don't know her.'

'Does she exist?'

'Of course she exists.'

'I'm only asking because I dinnae recall you stepping out with many girls before you left Adelaide.'

'There wasn't much of an opportunity then,' replied Ross.

'So who was this woman?'

'A girl in Burra, but nothing came of it.' Isobelle Watson had been partial to kissing him the year Alastair sailed for England but she would let him go no further than a hand on her breast and would have nothing more to do with him after war broke out and he didn't enlist. Meg Carr was another Burra beauty but on the day he'd mustered the courage to ask her out she'd handed him a white feather. Ross avoided Burra and women after that. 'I know enough.'

Connor's eyes widened. 'She'll be expecting more than that, for she won't know anything.' He lifted the whisky decanter and refilled their tumblers. 'You best have another. The thing is,' he said in a confidential tone, 'women like romance. They like,' he screwed up his nose, 'kissing. Yes,' he leant back contemplatively, 'kissing. It's daft I know but that's what they expect. You'll need to remember that for later when you try again, for she won't always be so willing. Tonight, though, well, you can drop your strides and –'

'Connor.' Ross really doubted if Darcey would ever be willing. He certainly wasn't. 'The thing is, if I sleep with her then it's done.'

'Of course it's done. That's the whole point.' Connor rubbed his palms together.

'I mean there's no going back.'

His friend shook his head. 'I hate to tell you this, Ross, but you're already married. There is no going back.'

Ross swirled the whisky, drinking the remains of it. He didn't see things that way. Married he might be, but his father was in agreement that the Territory was no place for Mrs Darcey Grant. His new wife was to stay behind. Time and distance could alter many things. Ross was counting on it. He began shuffling the papers into a pile. His father was forwarding a telegram of introduction to the Territory Director tomorrow. The rest of the details regarding their arrival and travel to the property was to be arranged once they reached Darwin. Closing the ledger, Ross rolled the map and sat it on top.

'Do you think your brother might have already, you know, had a poke?' asked Connor.

Ross hadn't thought of the possibility but the question gnawed at him. In response he gave his friend a shrug, as if it didn't matter to him. But it did. It mattered more than Ross cared to acknowledge.

'It's not something a woman would admit to,' continued Connor. 'Especially one as proud as she is.'

'Proud?' asked Ross. 'Actually, I think she's desperate.'

Connor gave Ross a querying stare. 'It's a bumpy track you've started on. I should let you attend to your duties before you think some more with that brain of yours. I'll be waking you before the birds flap a wing, so dinnae be up all night.'

Once Connor was gone, Ross lay down on the leather sofa. It was a warm evening and the slight breeze barely stirred the air. The rest of the household had long retired and as the building cooled after the day's heat, Ross lay quite still listening to the soft tread of someone walking. The footsteps stopped near the door before moving on and he wondered if it was Darcey seeking her husband on their wedding night. She'd worn a rather loose-fitting ivory gown and had spoken little, except to repeat the wedding vows. They'd held hands at the end but he'd not kissed her. Ross had fulfilled his side of the bargain and couldn't see the need for unnecessary affection, although his grandmother rebuked him, saying he was puffed up with anger. It was Connor, the best man, who noted that the silver wedding horseshoe the bride carried was hanging the wrong way, upside down.

Ross was leaving Adelaide with hardly anything. A change of clothes, a swag, a revolver and rifle. Having arrived with even fewer possessions than those, he'd examined the items on his bed and then for some inexplicable reason searched through Alastair's collection of books, selecting a half-dozen of his brother's favourites.

'Start with Homer and Hesiod,' Alastair had told him, the day before he sailed. 'You'll have plenty of time at Gleneagle to read and don't stop there, nearly everyone does. Move on to Pythagoras and Plato, Mithras and the Mysteries, and don't forget your near Eastern and Egyptian studies.'

'And what will I do with all this knowledge?' Ross had asked.

'We'll talk about it, you and me, as brothers should,' Alastair had replied. 'When I get home.'

In the early hours of the next morning a gust of wind rustled the papers on the desk, waking Ross from a mostly sleepless night. When he had managed to sleep he'd been drawn into a room where his brother and Darcey lay entwined on a bed. In the dream he'd been desperate to know if Darcey was indeed a virgin or not, if she'd lain with his brother out of wedlock. But in the blush of daylight Ross contented himself with the thought that it didn't matter. He was leaving and she was staying put. The union was doomed to fail.

❧ Part Two ❧

1919–1921

❧ Chapter 14 ❧

Darwin, Northern Territory, 1919

Ross and Connor walked the long strip of road that extended across the low bluff on which the settlement was built. The dirt sent up eddies of heat as they moved past the mix of buildings on Cavenagh Street. Dilapidated lean-to shops of galvanised iron and wood nestled alongside considerable stone buildings and within each of these stores a variety of trade was on offer. Tailors, bakers, builders, herbalists, jewellers and stonemasons were tucked in between restaurants, grocers and laundries. Outside one washing place, women were stringing up clothes from never-ending bins and as Ross and Connor passed by, a blast of debilitating hot air struck them forcefully from the doorway.

'We could go back to the harbour,' suggested Connor.

'You should have been a sailor,' replied Ross.

Connor gave a chuckle. 'I cannae swim. Just as well.'

They'd already been advised that there was every chance a person would be attacked either by sharks or crocodiles if they were foolhardy enough to risk the ocean. Earlier they'd stopped at the northern end of Chinatown where the headland dropped to the blue sea and watched a steamer approach the wharf, the same creaking jetty that had greeted them on their arrival in Darwin nearly a week ago. The anticipated breeze was non-existent and Ross had been struck by the mass of water before them and what lay inland. He was pleased to be off the briny pond with its pitching waves and sudden squalls, while in Connor he detected a wistfulness. It was many years since the little Scotsman's crossing to this new continent and Ross wondered if the memories of that long-ago voyage were stirred by their recent travels.

'You'd think they could give a man some peace,' protested Connor, as a shrill whistle punctuated the air. He'd already visited the docks to complain about the noisy locomotive that moved railway construction materials between the jetty and yards, puffing its way past the mangroves. 'I know why they call it Sandfly, it's blasted annoying. Ross, are you not going to say anything? You've barely spoken these last few days. I'm beginning to wonder if you even want to be here. Maybe you're having second thoughts. Perhaps missing that young wife of yours, eh?'

'I'm thinking,' answered Ross. 'And looking.'

'Aye, there's plenty to see. You won't mind if I take a wander this evening and try my luck with the ladies. I'd ask you to join me but you being a married man and all I dinnae want to be the one to place temptation in your way.' He tipped his hat at a passing woman, spinning on his heel to watch as she walked away.

Crossing the road, they made their way past old men in tunics carrying baskets of fruit and vegetables balanced on poles slung across shoulders. Outside an emporium Ross admired the carved pearl shell and embroidered silk in the window as Connor commenced a monologue on the many races the community was home to. While his friend could spend hours watching the arrival and the departure of the mail steamers in the harbour or the pearling luggers drifting on the tide, it was the mix of cultures that most intrigued him.

'Japanese,' Connor pointed. 'See. Look at her feet. Chinese, Greek, Chinese, English,' he said as the pedestrians passed. 'Chinese, two of those people from the islands, a blackfella. Take a look at his breastplate, will you. He's a regular king. Well, he must be, dinnae you think?'

Ross entered the emporium and purchased a small camphor box for his grandmother. When he caught up with his friend again Connor was bent forward, hands on knees, studying a book with brush lettering in a shopfront window.

'Did you get her something then?' asked Connor.

'For my grandmother, yes,' answered Ross. He caught the flattening of his friend's mouth. They'd been in Darwin long enough to do some sightseeing, purchase a few supplies and make contact with Bill Sowden, the manager of Waybell Station, but Connor somehow managed to mention Darcey nearly every day.

'You should write to her,' persisted Connor.

'I sent my father a telegram when we arrived. He knows not to expect to hear from us for a while,' said Ross.

'Playing hard to get, eh? Good for you. It's important to keep a woman on her toes. I dinnae let on too much myself as to what I think or where I'm going. I tell them that nothing's certain until I've said as much. It's that hint of mystery that keeps them interested.'

At the end of the street their horses waited, left in the shade near the Terminus Hotel. The animals were on loan to them from a local stable. Ross and Connor headed towards them.

'I dinnae think mine will go much further.' Placing his hands firmly on the horse's rump, Connor made a show of trying to push his ride forward. The mare didn't budge.

A large banyan tree stood nearby and beneath it three young women chatted in the shade. One of the girls was small and slight, her dark hair plaited and curled into a bun that exposed a long neck. Ross made a fuss of checking the length of his stirrups as he examined her profile. It could almost have been described as a patrician silhouette although her cheeks billowed with youth. The girl was dark-skinned with Chinese characteristics, a longish face and small button nose, but her eyes were large and almond-shaped, her mouth full. Each feature complimented the other, so as a whole she appeared perfectly symmetrical, beautiful.

'A pretty girl. Young but pretty.'

Drawn from his observations by Connor's remark, Ross sprang up into the saddle. He felt like he was back in the confectionery shop in Rundle Street with Mr Johnston's hand reaching for Ross's smaller one as he'd made a grab for the sweets sitting atop the glass display. 'Unusual looking,' he replied, quickly dismissing her.

'Where to now?' asked Connor.

They rode on to the Botanical Gardens, passing the British cemetery. Slowing, they gaped at the freshly dug graves waiting for occupants. A man was riding towards them and they drew up by his side, Connor asking what terrible tragedy had occurred to warrant so many burials.

'Nothing but the weather,' the rider told them. 'Try leaving a loved one for a day or two in this heat. Best to be prepared.'

'Seen enough?' asked Ross as they turned right towards the gardens.

'No, I haven't seen enough,' retorted Connor. 'I like Darwin. Apart from that train. There's no trams or buses. No trussed-up women dashing here and there. When we arrived I thought to myself, well, there's not much to it, this place on the edge of nowhere. But I was wrong. There's a bit of everything here and not too much of the other things that can ruin a place. I didnae mind the steamer either. Seeing clear to the horizon every day.'

An unobstructed skyline. Ross missed that too. Not the seascape, where a person was captured and dwarfed by expanse, but rather the ruddy flush of windblown land that extended onwards to a vanishing point that could never be reached. Very soon he hoped that feeling would be with him again.

Their days of exploring Darwin had led Ross and Connor along many streets, past the cool verandas and gables of Government House to more modest homes with their neat fences and shaded verandas. Ross knew he'd searched for something on their arrival and he found it now on approaching the gardens. Although the grounds were unkempt in places, coloured flowers filled the park, flashing their brightness against a background of lush greenery. Birds flitted among the foliage. Splashes of yellow, white and green feathers fluttering from one branch to another. In the stippled sunlight Connor picked out hibiscus, jasmine and honeysuckle, however the names of many hundreds of other plants in the grounds eluded them.

They rested the horses briefly in the shade. At last Ross felt that their new surrounds were meeting expectation. Here was the tropical outpost he'd imagined. 'This is what I thought it would be like, Connor.'

'And me, Ross. And me.'

It was late afternoon by the time they reached Smith Street. A block away from Chinatown, the white area of the settlement was quieter and they were soon nearing the Hotel Victoria, where they were staying. The two-storey building of multicoloured stone resembled unglazed porcelain, and one of the highlights of Ross's day was sitting on the upstairs veranda, willing a gentle wind.

Leaving their horses at the stables, they entered the lounge to find the Director, Henry Carey, whose new post temporarily replaced the position of Administrator, saying his goodbyes. Having made their presence known to the Director on their arrival in Darwin, it was he who'd suggested their lodgings at the hotel.

'Ross, Connor. Introduce yourselves to those two fine young gents,' said Henry, shaking their hands and focusing on a table around which a crowd gathered. 'Keith and Ross Smith. The first men to fly from England to Australia. Twenty-eight days, it took. Twenty-eight days. They won't be able to call us an ungovernable backwater now. Very soon Darwin will be the first stopping point for everyone coming to Australia.'

Ross and Connor greeted the aviators, and after offering their congratulations, took a table on the opposite side of the room, away from the commotion. They settled in chairs near the window, their backs to the crowd. Outside, an old man walked beside a buffalo pulling a wagon. Ross tugged at his shirt where it stuck to his skin. The air was dense with heat and didn't seem to vary greatly, regardless of whether it was day or night.

The bartender, Archie, greeted them, sitting a glass of beer in front of Connor and handing Ross a cordial. 'Are you sure you want to stick with something soft?' He was a slight man with a veil of thick hair that hung across his brow.

'Yes, thanks. I've never been much of a drinker.'

'You put a few back in Adelaide,' said Connor.

'I needed it in Adelaide.'

Archie returned to the bar and Ross scribbled a quick note to his grandmother, placing it inside the recently purchased box.

'I'll organise for it to be posted if you like,' offered Connor. 'I've a letter home to send as well.'

'Thanks.' Ross slid the box across to his friend as Archie returned to their table to talk.

'I think our Director's a bit hopeful,' said the barman. 'It will take more than an aeroplane to entice people here.' From a side table he selected a newspaper from the pile, showing them the headline in a November edition of the *Northern Territory Times and Gazette*.

No lighting, no power, no water, no sewerage, it read.

The list could be added to the growing number of things that served to emphasise Darwin's remoteness and the lack of interest from the federal government. For, while some businesses did have power, they were sitting feet away from aviation pioneers in a public space that didn't have electricity. However there was ice, which Ross was grateful for. He crunched on it as Archie sat at their table, keeping one eye on the bar and the young Japanese beer-puller behind it.

'You're still set on leaving then?' he asked.

'On the morning train,' replied Ross.

'Slow and unreliable. Especially at this time of year.' He tossed his head, flicking the hair back from his eyes. "Course, if the weather comes in she won't move. I'd be waiting a few months, biding your time, but you know the general opinion by now.'

Connor gave the slightest bow of his head. 'Aye, everyone has one, that's for sure.'

It was as if their arrival in the north of Australia had been predicted and discussed before Ross had even made the decision to leave Adelaide. A mixture of cattlemen, prospectors, overlanders and buffalo hunters all made their presence known during their short stay at the hotel. It was not an inquisition into the first member of the Grant family visiting their Top End holding, rather a general interest in the affairs of the Territory's governing body of old, South Australia. Although there was plenty of willingness to discover the extent of the Grant wealth and whether Ross intended on staying. He would have retreated to his room were it not for Connor, his friend reminding him that while he understood that Ross had been isolated at Gleneagle, talking to sheep didn't pass for conversation and that it was best he get used to company again.

'Darwin's not like it used to be,' said Archie. 'Especially Chinatown. It was cleaned up a few years ago. At one point there were more of them than us. And you can't have that.' He lowered his voice. 'The government's White Australia policy and all those Asians helped the union cause, which hasn't done us much good.'

'You need someone to do the laundry.' Connor lit his pipe. 'There'd be a bit of it what with this heat.'

The weather was topmost in people's minds and to Ross it seemed as if the subject was debated with all the unregulated passion and knowledge of a politician giving his views to an already weary audience. But it wasn't just the climate under deliberation. It seemed the Hotel Victoria was a major meeting place and a centre for discussion. There, government debate and general complaints, most of which were driven by members of the workers union, dominated the conversation. That and which poor soul had come to grief beyond the edges of the settlement.

As Connor began spruiking his recently acquired knowledge to the patient bartender regarding dry monsoons, wet seasons, northwest monsoons and southwest trade winds, Ross considered the telegram that was waiting in Darwin on their arrival.

If you must come bring potatoes. Jam. Tea.

Ross had scrunched the slip of paper into a ball, immediately replying to the manager of Waybell Station that they needed horses and a guide to meet them on Friday. It was clear that their coming wasn't welcome, which made Ross all the more anxious to get to the property. The man may have been managing Waybell for over a decade, however he didn't own it and Sowden, Ross decided, would do well to remember that.

'Think of it this way, Connor,' said Archie. 'The year is divided into six months of dry and six months of wet. Sometimes the rain comes early and sometimes late. But it does eventually come. And when it does, neither man nor beast can move.'

Attempting to argue the obvious – that the sky was blue and the town hot and withering dry – was useless. Listening and nodding proved Ross's best defence.

'Hugh Carment,' a burly older man announced, pulling up a chair.

'Mr Carment,' said Archie, deferentially leaving the three men alone.

Ross caught a whiff of rum and sweat as they introduced themselves to Hugh, who was tall, slightly stooped and with a short beard. He spread large palms on the scrubbed tabletop.

'You're new to the country, I hear. Wetbacks from down south, Adelaide.'

'Yes,' replied Ross, instantly deciding he didn't like the man.

'I'm not new. Been here three lifetimes. At least, that's how it feels.' He draped long brown arms on either side of the chair like a large bird drying its feathers. 'Been here since Darwin was known as Palmerston. Been here since before the big cyclone of 1897. That near wiped us out. By my reckoning this will be the fifth or maybe the sixth try at a settlement up here. Anyway, welcome. How do you like our little town?'

'It's more like a gateway to the East,' Connor remarked.

'You've been reading too many posters,' chuckled Hugh. 'But you're right, Connor, take a walk down the street and you'll see Malays, Manilamen, Portuguese and Japanese. ''Course it ain't like it was twenty years ago. Even the Canton coolies are down in numbers, thanks to the government and the white merchants. Still, it's worth remembering that there's no more Australia north beyond Darwin.' Archie sat a beer in front of Hugh and he slurped the liquid up with a gurgle. 'So here we are on a flat patch of land covered with woodlands, a few patches of rainforest and an abundance of anthills. All in all, it's not a bad spot if you forget the blacks and the hundreds of miles of scrub at your doorstep and the Asians across the water.'

'And what do you know of the inland?' asked Ross.

'It should have been left to the blacks but us Europeans like a bit of a challenge. Tell a man that you don't know what lies in the distance and he'll get on his horse and ride until he falls off dead. It's a bit different these days. Reasonably civilised compared to what it was. But there's still the odd black who'll steal your cattle and put a spear in your back. Frankly if I was them I'd do the same. It's a place for a man to be tested. And if he's found wanting, well . . . one would hope only the tough ones stay, for that's what the Territory needs.'

Ross wondered if Hugh Carment knew of Alastair's dishonour or his own inaction. His brother's ignoble disappearance had made Adelaide's newspapers, and word was always quick to circulate when disaster was involved.

Hugh finished his beer, wiping at the trail of moisture on his chin with the back of a hand. 'I heard you're going to Waybell Station.'

'We are,' said Ross.

'Those plots your family owns on the edge of town, I'll give you a fair price.' He called to the bartender for another beer.

Across the room, the Smith brothers were being toasted again. Ross listened to the cheers as he contemplated the offer. His father wanted the town real estate sold, however Ross thought it too soon to start selling off assets, especially now. Darwin was not destined to be an unruly and remote town forever. If Connor thought him quiet since they'd set foot here, it was because Ross was still weighing up the possibilities that the North could offer. As of this afternoon, they'd expanded considerably.

'They're not on the market.'

Hugh crossed his legs, rattling the table. 'And Waybell?'

'Not for sale.'

'We'll see. You should have a look at it, I suppose, before you decide,' said Hugh, his tone friendly but firm. 'You're not the first to sit on a piece of dirt thinking it's a solid investment but the big runs aren't worth much now. How long are you staying?' He barely acknowledged the beer the bartender had placed on the table.

'Who knows?' replied Ross. Even if he knew the answer to the question he wasn't willing to reveal his thoughts to anyone, particularly this man who was ready to buy whatever he offered.

'Don't tell Sowden that,' advised Hugh. 'He does a fair job of things from what I hear, considering.'

'Considering what?' asked Ross.

Hugh took a sip that half-emptied the glass.

When an answer wasn't forthcoming Ross said, 'You mean, apart from the cattle we seem to be missing every year?'

'He's not expecting you to stay,' Hugh answered, avoiding the question.

'You've spoken to him then?' asked Ross.

'Word gets around when there's a newcomer. Also, he's not one for company.'

Ross gave a wry smile. 'Neither am I.'

'He's a sheep man,' added Connor, nodding at Ross.

'You won't find any lice-feeders up here,' said Hugh flatly, before finishing the beer. 'I best state my business. I've got a mate who's on his last legs and we were partners. There's papers that need to be signed. But there's also a maid that's due at Holder's Run. At least, that's what they're calling her at the moment. Anyway, I said I'd deliver the girl. The ones that aren't black are as hard to come by as feathered frogs. Not that I'm against the blacks. Rather have them than the orientals. Plenty of fine people among the Larrakia and there's more than one gin that's suckled a white child and put 'em to bed of a night. Holder's place is near your station, so I figured I could leave her with you, and Marcus Holder could collect her from Waybell when he's able, or you can take her to him. I'd do it myself but I don't think old Hatty will last the distance if I make the detour.'

'A woman?' said Ross. 'I'm sorry, but I don't want to be responsible for a woman.'

'For any woman,' stated Connor, who'd been listening intently.

Ross flattened his lips together in annoyance.

'Up here we help each other, Ross. We put up with owners who appear out of the South with their gripes and fancy ideas.' Hugh's fingers tapped the table. 'And we never turn anyone away from our door. Or knock back a bloke if he needs a hand. So I'll be on the train Friday with the girl, and I'll get word to Holder that she's in your care.'

Ross tried to interrupt.

'And make sure you've got enough quinine and chlorodyne for dysentery. Plenty of men have died from a rush of the bowels.' Shoving the chair against the table, Hugh left.

'It looks like you've got a woman to look after,' Connor said smugly, arms crossed.

'We,' corrected Ross. '*We* have a woman to look after.'

≪ Chapter 15 ≫

They kept to the carriage, only stretching their legs once when the train halted with a squeal of steam and clanging metal. The driver called for assistance and, along with other passengers, Ross and Connor helped move a tangle of branches that the wind had scattered across the tracks. The men milled around to briefly talk of the weather and markets, a few of them warning the newcomers of what may be waiting for them come the rain.

'Nineteen sixteen was a tragedy,' a whale-sized man told them. 'Eleven inches in a day, thirty-five inches in a week. The water was four feet deep down the centre of Katherine. Men died. In railway camps, on rivers, from starvation and beri-beri. There was no word from some stations for months. I'm just saying,' he concluded, leaving Ross and Connor standing under a duck-egg sky.

Every so often the train rumbled across a bridge or a flood opening, all the while the whistle sounded to warn off birds and other wildlife. Nearly everyone was heading to Pine Creek, while Ross and Connor were to be dropped like unwanted packages somewhere along the line. The conductor explained that they too should have made the town their destination, in case the weather came in. Instead they were to risk the track used in the dry to get to Waybell. Safe enough, the man conceded, when Mick was in charge.

'Anyway, you'll see a bit of the country,' he told them with a smirk.

'And who's Mick?' asked Ross.

'The head stockman,' replied the conductor.

There was no sign of Hugh Carment or the girl. Connor thought to investigate the carriages, however Ross told him not to bother searching. There was enough on his mind without worrying about another man's troubles. Now that his escape was behind him, and with it the entanglements of family and wife, the departure from Darwin had jolted Ross out of the languid state he'd felt on arrival in the North and back to the sense of adventure he'd experienced on first stepping aboard the steamer in Adelaide.

Connor slept, his tongue protruding through his beard with each gentle snore, the green-brown of the bush blurring through the window. There was talk of the British-owned Vesty's meatworks in Darwin closing down. Ross gathered it was a combination of the unions continually striking for higher pay and lack of management. Which meant there was an opportunity for another privately owned abattoir in the town.

'What are you planning, Ross Grant?' Connor opened one eye. 'I can hear the mice spinning wee wheels in that mind of yours.'

'Nothing. Just thinking.'

'That's what worries me. You've said nought since we arrived in Darwin. You've the look of a man fairly bursting with knowledge.'

'Cattle. I was thinking about cattle,' admitted Ross. 'And money.'

'Well, as long as it's something worthwhile I'll leave you alone,' said his friend with a grin.

'Don't go cracking your hide with plans.' A man in the next seat tipped his hat. 'Gilruth, the last administrator, and the unions have buggered the place. Vesty's big outfit at Bullocky Point will be overrun with goats and white ants in a matter of months. All this

105

land and no industry. There's barely a man on a station south of here and hardly a coin to rub between your fingers among us all. Even some of the mining companies have pulled out.'

'Great,' said Connor. 'And I was worried about the steamer we came here on sinking.'

'I thought you were sleeping?' Ross asked him.

'Who can do that with the prospect of so much opportunity waiting for us,' lamented Connor. 'To think I was daft enough to want to leave Adelaide.'

Adelaide. Ross had done his best not to think of the place, for the moment he did, Darcey entered his mind. Not that she was confined to his thoughts of home. His mind settled on her as soon as he placed his head on the pillow at night. The steamer with its quoits and cards had provided distraction, especially after the rush of events leading to their departure. However, dry land brought reality with it. Ross found it impossible not to think of the woman. She crept into his mind at the most unexpected moments, teasing him to recall their marriage. To remember. In his harsher musings, Ross saw Darcey for what he believed her to be. A manipulator. A woman prepared to ensnare him to ensure a comfortable existence. And yet she was also a bargaining tool exploited by him and his family so that both parties could settle their differences and receive a form of compensation for the mess they'd found themselves in.

He imagined Darcey happy and content. Her momentary distress at his departure and her offer to accompany him north-wards was a measured response to a situation already decided. And if she wasn't happy, well, neither was he. In doing what they'd all wanted, Ross had offered himself up like coin on a church plate. He couldn't help but be angry at all of them, including himself. He should have refused the marriage and walked away, discarded the family that expected so much of him. But he couldn't. Ross wanted this future, and to move forward he needed to make amends for the past – both his and Alastair's. That was done. Ten times over. Now all Ross wanted was his freedom, and for that simple pleasure he could never return to Adelaide again.

The conductor who'd spent the journey chatting to the other travellers jumped out briefly as the train slowed. He plucked a hessian bag from a tree before nimbly climbing back on board the moving steam engine. 'Mail,' he announced when he noticed Ross's interest.

Timber made thick by pale-barked trees spun by as Ross sank back in the hard leather seat. Isolation meant freedom. As the air grew heavy, he felt freer. It was as if he'd not taken a proper breath since leaving Gleneagle.

When the locomotive slowed again the conductor approached them. This was their stop, he announced. They were to stay put and not go wandering about because no one would ever find them again, or if they did they'd be a pile of bones only needing a shallow grave. No matter how long they waited, they were to keep on waiting. Someone would eventually appear, but if something happened they were to wait by the tracks for the returning train. The train would come, he promised, as long as it didn't rain and the line wasn't washed out. And if it was washed out? Ross asked. Can't much help you there, he replied.

Connor hunched a shoulder, his moustache twisting up in one corner as he looked at the trees and thick scrub on either side of the line visible through the windows. 'Good spot to be abandoned. Middle of nowhere.'

Four hessian bags held provisions and personal items and these they divided equally, hoisting their load over a shoulder along with rifles and swags before stepping off the train. The whistle blew sharply and a blast of steam pooled out from beneath the engine as it rattled forwards, the carriages slowly pulling away.

Connor dumped the bags and rifle at his feet. 'I hope that's not the last of progress that we ever see.'

'So much for the wet season.' Perspiration trickled down Ross's spine.

Some of the passengers waved at them as the remaining carriages, two empty cattle crates and a goods section trundled past. The air was so damp Ross could feel his skin grow slippery.

'Well, then,' said Connor, 'that's that. And now we wait and hope that somebody shows.'

Ross barely heard Connor speak, for on the other side of the tracks stood a girl. She too stared after the departing train and then very slowly turned towards them. Dressed in a beige dress, she held a tawny carpet bag in one hand, an overly large straw hat on her head.

'This is a pretty mess,' complained Connor, seeing her for the first time. 'What if nobody comes for us?'

Ross looked to the left and right out of habit and crossed the tracks. His hello was not answered. The lack of response gave Ross time to place her, for he knew he'd seen her before. Then it struck him.

'I saw you outside the Terminus Hotel with your friends.'

She wasn't as young as she appeared. Maybe eighteen. He was taken once again by the symmetry of her features, by the calmness of her gaze. The dark almond eyes that studied him suggested a certain maturity. Her nationality was impossible to pick. Ross saw characteristics in her features that on another face would have appeared out of place and unattractive. Why he thought of Darcey at the moment he couldn't decipher. Perhaps it was because contact with young women had been scarce since the outbreak of the war and now in the space of weeks he'd found himself thrust into the company of two of them.

'Ahem,' said Connor.

'I'm Ross Grant and this is Connor Andrews,' Ross blurted. 'We were told to take you to Waybell Station. After that, someone will escort you to Mr Holder's Run.'

The girl appeared almost disinterested. Had he really needed to speak that quickly?

'Now what?' asked Connor. He leaned in to Ross. 'Is she mute?'

'We saw her talking the other day,' responded Ross.

The Scotsman slapped his thigh in recognition. 'The pretty one from the banyan tree.'

'Tree of Knowledge,' the girl corrected softly.

'The tree of what?' said Ross.

'It's called the Tree of Knowledge.' The girl looked at the bruised clouds above them and then walked to the timber that fringed the tracks. A few seconds later lightning crackled and it began to rain.

'No wet season, eh?' complained Connor as they sought shelter with the girl. 'Blue sky and hot, eh?'

Rain burst through the leaves. They huddled against a tree, the water sliding down the bark and drenching their clothes. Ross knew they must stay put, but as the hours passed and the rain continued, he wondered if they should build a shelter.

'Eleven inches in one day. Thirty-five in a week,' mumbled Connor. 'Isn't that what he said? Cripes.'

The girl sat hunched between them, sombre in her quietness. She still hadn't given her name. Connor tried to draw her into conversation, although it was almost impossible to hear over the storm.

'How long should we wait?' Connor asked.

Ross didn't know. He began to wonder why Bill Sowden was sending this man called Mick to meet them, instead of coming himself. If anyone was indeed coming. It would be easy to leave them by the railway tracks, to concoct some excuse. And if the train didn't return? Miles to the north lay Darwin and in between the scrub closed in, throbbing under the force of the rain.

'Have you got a map, Ross?' asked Connor. 'Maybe we should see what direction we should be going in?'

'Not yet. We'll wait a bit,' replied Ross. 'Let's face it, we won't die from a lack of water.'

⪻ Chapter 16 ⪼

Through the cascade of liquid that fell from the brim of his hat, Ross finally saw movement across the railway line. He stood up, reaching for his rifle as the foliage trembled violently. A full-bearded black man rode across the tracks leading two horses. He stopped where they sheltered and slid from his mount, leaving the reins to dangle free. Tall and well-made, he was not one to single out for a fight. He eyeballed each of them in turn, taking in their small party and Ross's lifted gun.

'I'm Mick. Head man.' He shook their hands.

'Headhunter, more likely,' whispered Connor.

'Not before tea,' said Mick, with a show of white teeth. 'Which one of you is the Boss fella?'

'I am,' said Ross. 'And this is Connor. We didn't think you were coming.'

'Why? It's good fine weather,' replied Mick.

They stared at each other through the bucketing rain, the uncomfortable silence brief but obvious. Ross gestured to the girl, explaining her circumstances, as the downpour lifted up the mud, splattering their trousers.

Accepting the girl's presence without a change of expression, Mick split the swags and supplies between the three horses. When they were ready to leave he sat the girl behind Connor. She straddled the horse with ease. They rode for three hours, the weather unchanging as they twisted through the trees. Reddish ant mounds, some small and conical in shape and others cathedral-like, were scattered through the bush.

'They look like tombstones,' said Connor. 'Great lumpy monstrosities.'

Water was beginning to gather in soaks and the ground became boggier. Then the sun came out and the steam rose from their bodies. Mick stopped up ahead, hesitating before veering off on an angle.

'Do you think we're heading in the right direction?' asked Connor.

'Of course,' said Ross.

'But dinnae you think we should check that map you're lugging about?'

'He'll let us know when we're on Waybell,' replied Ross.

'We'll camp soon,' announced Mick.

They snaked through the timber and came to a muddy river. At the bank, Mick waited as his horse sniffed the water and settled before taking a tentative step. The other two animals walked steadily forwards. Ross felt the draw of the current beneath the river's surface and urged the chestnut gelding onwards against the flow. Next to him, Connor did the same. The girl seemed entranced by the water as it rose to the horses' bellies. Then the muddy bottom grew firmer as the riverbed gradually eased upwards to the dry bank.

'Good crossing,' Mick remarked, as they left the watercourse and rode on through the stringy bush. 'No crocs. You're lucky you've come now. We haven't had much wet. Near Waybell it's a bit wetter. A big storm went through there last night. *Gudjewg* coming now.'

'And *Gudjewg* is the wet season?' stated Ross.

'Yes, Boss. The water apple's flowering.'

They continued until the sun was low, a dim orb masked by clouds. Up ahead, a cluster of paperbark huts, which Ross knew were referred to as wurlies, were shadowed by trees. Flat grassland extended to the bottom of low brown cliffs. They came into a clearing where a campfire was burning. Two Aboriginal women dressed in men's clothing prodded something in a fire and a couple of Aboriginal men squatted around it, smoking. They jumped up on their arrival, greeting Mick with a smile while cautiously observing Ross and Connor.

'You the Boss?' one of them asked.

'Yes,' said Ross, and they all shook hands enthusiastically, Mick making jokes about the train running to time and Waybell's owner getting baptised by a brief shower on the first day. The men, whose names were Toby and JJ, unsaddled the horses and carried the gear into one of the lean-tos.

Ross looked for the girl. She'd already retreated to the shade where she fixed her gaze on the clouds rising in the east. Rummaging through a sodden hessian bag, Ross pulled out his brother's books and carried them to the campfire to dry. He watched as one of the women, who had a pockmarked face, broke a turtle's neck and sat it on the coals still in its shell. There was another turtle already cooking, and this one she lifted from the ashes. Deftly cutting the neck, she stuck her fingers down the windpipe, pulled out the intestines and then placed it back on the fire.

'Dinner?' Connor didn't look impressed. He smacked at his arms and the side of his neck, mosquitoes rising from his body.

Toby poured tea from a worn teapot and handed around full pannikins. 'It's a good feed.'

Along with the turtle there was fish and waterfowl, a feast compared to what they'd been served at the hotel in Darwin.

'Come on. Sit.' At Mick's bidding, they arranged themselves in a semicircle while the Aboriginal women and the two other stockmen ate their meals a short distance away. The girl sat slightly apart from the group, yet close enough to receive food when it was passed around on tin plates. She watched to see the quantities Ross selected before choosing for herself, and he'd been aware of her attention on him earlier when he'd been setting each book on the ground to dry.

One of the women called out to Mick and pointed at the books, clearly waiting for an explanation.

'She wants to know if you make the words,' said Mick.

'I read them.' Ross poked at the strip of turtle flesh. 'I didn't write them.'

Mick translated using a mix of English and local dialect. The woman nodded, satisfied. 'So how come you're here?' he asked.

'None of my family have ever visited Waybell,' replied Ross, as he chewed a piece of turtle.

'So why now?' repeated Mick.

There was no answer Ross could think of that would reassure the stockman, although it was clear by Mick's studied concern that he was intrigued by the visit after so many years. 'It was time, I guess. None of us have ever been here. What about you, Mick? Have you been working on Waybell for long?'

'Long time. Since I was young.' Mick cupped the pannikin in his hands. 'No better person to work for than Mr Sowden. He's always been good to us. To my people.'

'And how far is it to the property?' Ross was eager to reach the station and meet the hostile Bill Sowden.

Mick opened his arms, encompassing the land. 'You're on it now.'

'What? You could have said so earlier.' Ross felt foolish.

'You didn't ask,' replied Mick. 'Besides, you whitefellas always seem to have a map.'

Connor made a snorting sound. 'What did I tell you?'

Ross wiped the plate with a crust of damper, swirling the bread around until the dish was dry.

'There are nets in the lean-tos,' explained Mick. 'Wrap them around your swags. That will keep most of the mosquitoes out. And don't leave them books laying around, Boss. It takes no time at all to get white-anted out here.'

The women began tidying and Mick wandered off. Unasked, Connor gathered up the books, reading each of the titles. Then he flicked through a volume and, noticing Alastair's name written inside them in a schoolboy's scrawl, walked to Ross's side. 'I thought they were his. Best take care of them.'

'Something to read,' replied Ross, 'when the wet sets in. You'll check on the girl? Make sure she's got some bedding?'

'Sure. Night, mate,' said Connor.

Ross returned to the wurley and repacked the books. Among his belongings was the pastoral lease map he'd carried from Adelaide. He unfolded it on the ground and placed a compass on the top right-hand corner. The needle quivered and then settled on North. The top half of Australia was apportioned off into hundreds of irregular-shaped parcels of leased land, of which the Grant name was written within one. There were rivers, creeks and hills traversing the 700-odd square miles of country they owned, delicate pencillings on parchment noting down surface shapes and features. From the named waterways on the property Ross concluded they were somewhere between the Mary and South Alligator rivers. He thought of what they'd ridden through, the miles traversed, and hazarded they'd travelled in a northeast direction. Within the areas marked as flat country, grassed plains, lagoons and low gravelly hills, Ross placed a cross on where he believed they were.

A mist of rain carried across on the breeze. Ross sat in the opening of the wurley, the map hanging between his knees. Birds flew low across the grasslands, stark white plumage against a darkening sky, and the honk of geese was rhythmic and loud as if someone was hitting a hollow log.

Ross remembered when he'd first learned of Waybell Station. He'd rushed to Alastair's bedroom after dark, keeping his brother awake with his whisperings of their going into the unknown, of befriending the Aboriginal people who could spear a man on sight, of becoming great cattle barons.

Now Ross was on the property he'd dreamt of visiting for so many years, and he'd not even known when he'd taken that first stirring stride onto Grant land. Perching his elbows on his knees, Ross gazed out at the land of his imaginings. After everything that had occurred, it was a bittersweet moment.

≪ Chapter 17 ≫

Waybell Station, Northern Territory

They rode through moist hot air over rocky ground, stopping at midday to make camp and swallow tea and day-old damper before setting off again. For an hour or more they travelled across a floodplain covered with a foot of water, where ghostly groves of willowy white paperbarks rose a hundred feet into the sky. The travellers were short on conversation. Stringing out behind them came the women, then Toby and JJ, with the packhorses bringing up the rear. Their chatter and spurts of laughter were loud enough to send birds from the trees.

'At least some are enjoying themselves,' said Connor.

The girl looked at Ross, her slight body moving rhythmically with the gait of the horse. The dress had been replaced with calico pants and a tunic top. There was a guardedness in the way she viewed everything, and yet she'd settled into this newness with little fuss. Quick to tend the fire and help with the preparation of meals if the other women allowed, she'd proved her usefulness. The fact that she'd travelled from Darwin not initially outfitted for horse travel suggested that she too lacked any idea of where she was heading. That created something of a bond between them,

Ross supposed. Even if they were strangers to each other, they were both outsiders in a new world.

'What's being burnt?' Ross asked Mick. Pillars of smoke smudged the sky as if a number of fires had been lit, one after another, some distance apart.

'They say you're coming.' Mick nodded. 'A few more days and you finish crossing their country.'

'You mean Grant country,' corrected Connor.

'Sure,' answered Mick, turning his head away slightly.

'Tell me about the property, the workings of it,' said Ross.

'Big team on Waybell. Maybe eighty men for muster-up. Hundred and thirty horses. Not so many here now with rain coming. This sit-down time.'

'How are we managing to lose so many head of cattle each year?' asked Ross.

The stockman pointed to the northeast, where a dark bulge of cloud threatened. Towering columns of cumulus bridged the gap between earth and sky.

'The cattle?' repeated Ross.

'Ask Bill,' said Mick.

'I'm asking you.'

'Better you ask Bill,' said Mick.

'Why?'

Mick swivelled in the saddle. 'Because Bill's in charge.'

'You're the head stockman and you don't have an opinion?' persisted Ross.

'Best you talk to Bill. Soon you know plenty.'

Ross gave up trying to press the reticent stockman. He wanted to believe Mick's reluctance to speak was a matter of hierarchy, and yet sensed it wasn't. Slowing his horse, he drew level with Connor. 'I'm not learning much,' he said.

'Aye. The only harm that could be caused by speaking were if there were things needing to be kept hidden,' replied Connor.

In the late afternoon of the fourth day, they reached the house paddock fence. Two hours later, they crossed a creek and saw a house in the distance. It was dwarfed by a sheer escarpment that loomed craggy and brown in the dimming light. The riders skirted a wide billabong covered with lotus pads and, winding their way along the track, were confronted with an oblong dwelling of corrugated iron and timber. The roof pitched downwards to rest on sturdy tree-trunks and a veranda encircled the modest house. The entire building was enclosed with chicken wire from ground to roof, with sheets of iron forming a rough door.

Ross scanned the outer buildings, wondering if there was another home nearby, but quickly concluded that the legendary Waybell of his childhood was starkly different in reality. Mick pointed out the Aboriginal workers' camp. One hundred yards away, numerous wurlies were perched close to the billabong. Sitting midpoint between the camp and the house was the men's quarters and stables, which appeared in fair condition compared to the dwelling ahead.

'Not much to it.' Connor chewed on the stem of the unlit pipe.

Compared to Gleneagle, with its neatly fenced paddocks and tidy farmhouse and outbuildings, Waybell Station resembled the last outpost on the edge of a frontier. The only other fencing Ross noted on their journey came in the form of two sets of cattle yards, ten miles apart. The last structure located near the track they'd rode in on and only a mile from the house. His father had clearly kept a close eye on the chequebook and it showed.

'I don't like it here.' The girl broke her silence.

'She speaks!' said Connor.

Ross drew level to where she sat behind Connor, her delicate fingers grasping his friend's shirt-tail. 'What's your name?'

'Maria,' she replied.

'Maria. Your parents named you well,' he told her, for want of anything better to say.

'They didn't name me, I gave it to myself.'

Connor cleared his throat. 'Now I've heard everything.'

Toby and JJ led the horses to the stables as Ross, Connor and the girl followed Mick to the house. A number of Aboriginal people ambled across from the camp to study the newcomers. There was no front garden or proper fence. Several dogs raised their heads disinterestedly as they passed. Chickens scratched in the dirt. Beneath the tin awning a white man sat in a rocking chair, a blanket over his knees and a rifle leaning against the wall. A dark woman waved a fan, stirring the air. There was a washstand further along, with a cast-iron bucket and a scrap of towel hanging from a nail above it.

'Ross Grant?' the man said curtly through the mesh, nodding pleasantly to Mick.

'Yes,' replied Ross. 'And this is Connor Andrews and Maria.' He stepped through the doorway. The chicken-wire outer walls were attached to a low fence made from two-foot-high iron sheeting, which stuck out from the ground and bordered the house.

'Keeps the snakes and goannas out.' The manager was jowly, with hair that grew in irregular tufts out of a shiny red skull. 'Bill Sowden.' He reluctantly shook hands. 'And the girl?'

'Belongs to Marcus Holder,' said Mick.

Sowden examined her. 'He always did like the shiny ones. Well, we'll worry about her in a day or two. You can dump your gear on the back veranda and then we'll have something to eat. Did you bring the potatoes, jam and tea?'

Ross held up one of the bags and the manager told the woman next to him, whose name was Annie, to take it to the kitchen, a separate building at the rear of the house.

'A place can never have too much tea,' he informed them. 'Especially in the wet season. Make yourselves comfortable.'

Ross walked inside and across the dirt floor with its covering of threadbare half-chewed hides. In the centre of the room, cheesecloth netting hung from the iron ceiling, falling to a heap in the middle of a table. The house was divided into three rooms. One area served as a dining room and study, with a storeroom attached, the other a bedroom partially concealed by a hessian curtain. The tin walls were adorned with old newspaper pictures and for airflow, shutters had been cut into the iron, held up by lengths of wood. A corner table and a tin trunk appeared to be the sturdiest pieces of furniture in the house. Next to the desk sat a couple of makeshift chairs with cattle-hide seats, and on the opposite wall an empty sideboard.

'No expense spared,' muttered Connor.

At the rear of the narrow building they stepped out onto the veranda. The sleep-out held a row of five beds each with a cheese-cloth net suspended from the sloping ceiling. There was nowhere separate for Maria to sleep, and she waited until Ross dumped his swag on a bunk before selecting a rusty-wired contraption next to his. He considered choosing another bed. The last thing he wanted was a woman next to him. Ross had some idea of what they could be like – pleasing one instant and scornful the next – but the thought he might appear prudish kept him from moving.

The bunk squeaked as Maria sat down. And for a moment Ross thought she resembled a fox, her fingers gripping the shabby edge of the bed, her eyes darting left and right.

Connor stuck his fingers through the wire mesh. 'I wouldn't be begrudging Sowden's lack of welcome. I can't say that I'd be having guests if I lived here. The man exists on the smell of an oily rag.'

'I've never seen country so green,' said Ross. Beyond the wire, emerald grass extended outwards to a vegetable garden and a rather dejected-looking structure that he surmised was the long-drop.

'Aye, it's green,' agreed Connor. He shook the wire. 'But what's this for? To keep us in, or someone out?'

⋙ Chapter 18 ⋘

Bill Sowden was already seated when they arrived at the table for dinner. They joined him, sitting on rickety chairs made from packing cases. There was fish, duck and crunchy damper as well as red jelly for dessert, washed down with scalding black tea. Annie placed everything on the table at once, arranging the platters around a kerosene lantern and then drew the netting over them before departing. Cocooned within the cheesecloth, moths, mosquitoes and other insects gradually massed on the outside of the netting as the night drew on and the lantern was lit.

Sowden didn't stand on ceremony. Ross, Connor and Maria passed the platters among themselves as Bill ate, quickly chewing large mouthfuls of food. Bread and meat were rolled around his mouth as he talked, each piece circulating for show until finally swallowed.

'I ain't moving out of my bedroom and Annie ain't leaving the house. It's important I make that plain to the both of you in case you be getting ideas. I'm sure you understand. She's my woman. De facto. And there not being enough time to build another room, well, not that there's a carpenter around to do the job, there isn't anywhere else for us to go. I built this place with my own two hands, battling cyclonic winds and white ants along the way. It's not perfect, but I figured Mr Grant Senior wouldn't care, as he ain't the one who has to live here.'

Annie hovered at the doorway that led to the separate kitchen. It was strange having an Aboriginal woman in the house. Ross wasn't used to it. The Aboriginal stockmen were different, he'd worked with them at Gleneagle and respected their abilities, but a black woman sleeping under the same roof was another thing entirely. Ross was seized by a compulsion to ask her to leave immediately. Cooking and waiting on tables was one thing but this arrangement was unacceptable.

'It's worth remembering that there are more of them than us,' said Sowden.

Annie glowered, as if they'd already told her to leave, and then stormed off.

'The conventions you men are used to don't exist up here. So you best accept things as they are,' Sowden told them. 'Black, white or brindle. It's all the same when it comes to relations and there's no point letting pride get in the way, for you'll be guzzling it down like the rest of us eventually. Mark my words, in a few months the two of you might be partial to a bit of black velvet.' He took a slug of tea. 'Begging your pardon, girl.'

'I'd appreciate it, Mr Sowden, if you didn't speak that way in the presence of a lady,' said Ross.

'No harm intended,' replied the manager.

Ross felt the pressure of Connor's boot on his own. A warning to not provoke their host.

'Have you finished eating, Maria?' he asked. The girl ducked under the netting and was gone in an instant.

'Don't be worried about the likes of her,' said Sowden. 'I'm betting she's crossed some dry creek beds to get to where she is today.'

It was strange how Sowden's features miniaturised the more Ross scrutinised the man. His eyes and mouth, even his nostrils, which flared widely when a subject stirred him, were small and nondescript, more suiting a woman.

'You want to know about the chicken wire, don't you?' asked Sowden, when he'd finished skinning the meat from the spine of the duck. 'There were wild buggers around here in the beginning. I don't know about the first few years your father owned the place. There was only a shanty by the creek when I arrived and I never met the first manager. The story was he got the fever and died but I'm more inclined to think he was run through. The first twelve months I was here they'd loom out of the bush and pitch a spear. I lost my first stockman that way. Got one in the gizzards during the dry season when we were out rounding up. Asleep he was in his swag. We never slept much after that when we were away.' He took a mouthful, holding a knife in mid-air. 'The wire went up soon after Jim died, and though I'd be unlucky if a spear found me now, after all these years, I'm happier having it. Call it an insurance policy. It requires a bit of bargaining, living here the way we do. On their country. Most of the time the tribe's happy. We give 'em a few head of cattle every year, especially at corroboree time, flour, sugar and tea and let 'em wander wherever they like and they give us a hand during round-up.

'Don't be thinking it's like down South, where the blacks are grateful for the bits you people throw their way. That's the first advice I can give a newcomer. They still own this country. They move across it on a whim and some take what they need when they choose to. Get along with 'em, I say. Strike a deal and everyone wins.'

When Sowden finally took a breath, Ross asked how far away the closest neighbour was.

'If you want people, head north or south. Waybell is the last cattle place to the northeast. After that, you're in stone country and then the big floodplains, where there's almost as many buffalo as crocs. But five days' ride south, that would be Holder's Run. Got himself a right looker with that girl. That's the thing when a man's got money. Options. You can never have too many of them, eh? But you'd know about that, Ross?'

'I represent my father,' he replied tersely.

Sowden scratched thoughtfully at his chin. 'You're the only one left, aren't you? I mean, with your brother gone and disappeared. So when the time comes,' he extended his arms, 'all this will be yours.'

Word travelled quickly, it seemed. Connor sent Ross a steadying gaze while plugging tobacco into his pipe with a jerky action.

'You know there were folk up here who didn't even know there was a war on until they walked out of the bush a few years after it started. Never saw a newspaper.' Sowden pushed a grubby thumb inside his mouth, massaging his gum. 'You didn't fight, Connor?'

'Too old. Not that age should be a guide point for ability.'

'I'd agree with that,' said Sowden. 'People come up here to lose themselves,' he continued pointedly, his head cocked to one side as if he were trying to sum Ross up. 'Others try to make their mark in some way. The losing bit is fairly easy.'

Annie returned to clear the table, bobbing under the netting and sweeping the plates and cutlery onto a wooden tray. When she was gone, Sowden produced a quart pot from under his chair and Ross and Connor received a good measure of liquid in their pannikins.

'What is it?' asked Connor, smelling the concoction apprehensively.

'Sunset rum. It's the only grog we've got at the moment. The unions didn't unload the last ship in time. Best to drink it in one go. Here's to you.'

Not wanting to appear unsociable, Ross took a gulp. He spat it back into the cup. Connor drank and winced.

'Come on, boy,' Sowden said to Ross. 'If you're going to own a man-sized slice of the Territory then you'd better be able to act like one, even if you are still a lad.'

Ross once again raised it to his lips, and this time drained the contents. Every part of his insides began to burn.

The manager slapped the tabletop and gave a raucous laugh. 'Good, good. You'll fit in here real well. And don't worry, I'll keep an eye on you, young Ross Grant. You won't go drinking me out of house and home or imbibing so much that you're in need of the deadhouse. No, we can't have that.'

'What's in it?' asked Connor.

'It's an old goldfields brew handed down to me by a prospector at Pine Creek. Methylated spirit and kerosene mixed with Worcestershire sauce and a bit of brown sugar. Gives it a nice colour, don't you think, the sugar? But keep it to yourselves. I don't need the camp getting whiff of it, not when the wet season's only just begun.'

Ross filled his pannikin with tea, swirling the cleansing taste around his mouth.

'It'll be a bit slow for you boys, coming as you have before the big wet. It's only the blacks and me who stay to sit it out. It's true, it can be a wily place but you can scratch a living out of it. Tomorrow Mick will show you around. Best horseman there is in these parts. He'd give some of those fancy southerners a run, I tell you. Come on. Let's have another drink.'

⤖ Chapter 19 ⤗

Ross fell from his bed in the middle of the night, his stomach churning. He wanted to run but was tangled in something, something that was pinning him, constricting his movements. He kicked violently, and then finally scrabbled free and crawled across the ground. The smell of dirt filled his nostrils. His head hit something hard as he reached out, grappling with a wall that bent under his touch. He pulled at the barrier, swaying uncontrollably until he was upright. In the pitch black someone snored and muttered. He edged along the wall with difficulty, certain he would fall over if he let go. Dark shapes swirled in his head as he stumbled forwards, a shard of jagged whiteness splitting the night.

He woke on the ground, head pounding and abdomen paining. It was raining heavily. Hard sheets of water pricked his skin.

'It's nearly dawn.' Maria was next to him, water running in tiny streams down her face. Her hair was loose. It hung straight and gleaming, plastered to the sides of her head, clinging to her shoulders and chest, partly concealing the skin that showed through the front of the saturated shirt. 'Don't try and sit. Not yet,' she warned.

Ross lay on his back, opening his mouth, tasting the droplets of moisture. 'What happened?' His voice was croaky, parched.

'You drank the sunset rum,' she said. 'It sends some mad, others die if they drink enough of it.'

Ross sat up gingerly. Around them, branches had been torn down and a tree ripped from the wet earth, its stringy mass of tuberous roots naked in the rain.

'There was a windstorm. It happens at this time of year,' said Maria.

'How's Connor?' he asked through the rain. The house was some distance away, obscured by the bush.

'Asleep.'

Ross's hands were shaking uncontrollably. He wrapped them about his muddy body, noticing the rips to his shirt. He didn't know how long Maria had been by his side. Or how he'd managed to get from the bed to out here in the middle of the night.

'I couldn't move you,' she said. 'I tried.'

'You should go inside. You're soaked.'

'It's only water.' She tilted her head upwards, the rain running down her face and neck. 'You must drink lots of it,' she replied. 'Even if you sick it up, drink as much as you can. Here.'

Maria ladled water from a bucket at her side and Ross loss count of how many times he drank from the dipper. When he was finally sick, it was brutal and violent, as if his very insides were being torn free. He stayed on all fours as he brought up Sowden's vile concoction, pale slivers of his last meal massing on the ground to be washed away by the rain.

'You're not a drinker?' she asked when he could finally bring up no more.

'Whisky, occasionally.' Ross clutched at his aching stomach as he collapsed back against the trunk of the uprooted tree. 'Actually, I could count on both hands how many drinks I've had, and most of those have been this year.'

'It won't help, you know. The drink. It will only rob your chi, not help you to find it.'

Ross didn't understand what she spoke of. As the rain eased to a gentle spray she placed a hand on his chest. The action was so unexpected that he flinched. Unperturbed, Maria spread her palm across his wet shirt. 'Only a person who is lacking seeks release through drink. If not, why would you take such a vile thing?'

He looked at her hand on his chest and then into her eyes. He thought of the few girls he'd been attracted to in the past and the nerve it had taken to be the one who approached them. No woman had ever initiated contact or touched him the way Maria was. It unsettled him; the closeness of her, the words she used. As he wondered what he should do next, she drew away. The heat of her body dissipated, but he could still feel her.

Ross may have been thrust from Gleneagle, but it had been his choice to venture to Waybell Station. And now he was here he felt decidedly unbalanced. Nothing was as he imagined it would be. Everything was new and strange, from the dense heat to the thundering skies and the tangle of land that circled Sowden's hut. It was as if all progress stopped here. The worst of it was the creeping acknowledgement of how little he knew about this place and the people inhabiting it. Even this previously restrained girl, who knew things he'd never heard before and acted unconventionally. There was a knot of tension between her eyes. She looked tired. Ross guessed that he was to blame for that.

'Don't look at me that way. You're in a new place now. Remember when you saw me at the Tree of Knowledge outside the Terminus Hotel?' She sat back on her feet. 'The old Chinamen gather the youth there and teach them things. Well, they used to. Not so much anymore.'

'And they taught you?'

Maria appeared amused. 'No, but I listened.'

'So you're Chinese,' said Ross.

'I'm many things.'

'Well, if you're determined to sit out in the mud with me, you might as well tell me a little about yourself. Like why you chose to barely speak until we arrived here?'

Ross glimpsed again the shy creature of the past days. 'What would I talk about? The trees and animals?' she asked. 'The rain or the sun? I didn't know you. I waited.'

Ross drank more water. 'Waited to see what?' Maria spread the sodden material of her dress across a well-formed thigh.

'What kind of man you are,' she replied. 'Now I know.'

For some reason Ross recalled his grandfather riding off on a bicycle, armed with a net, a killing jar and some pins. The more exotic butterflies he kept fluttering behind glass, inspecting them with a magnifying glass before growing weary of the show and depriving them of oxygen. Once dead he stabbed them with a single pin through the body.

'Someone's coming,' said Maria. She got to her feet and ran off.

'Ross, are you out here?' Connor caught sight of Maria leaving. 'You're as white as a sheet.'

'I'd be a lot worse if it wasn't for Maria,' Ross replied.

'Aye, right.' Connor looked in the direction the girl had gone, his expression thoughtful. 'Wasn't that a brew and a half? I thought I had a bad night until I saw the state of your swag. Do you know that you ripped the netting clean off and dragged it halfway across the flat? I reckon you must have crawled out here, by the look of things.'

'I barely remember what happened. What about you?' Ross got to his feet. The rain had stopped, and with the parting clouds the morning sky grew bright.

'Me? Good as new, apart from a pounding headache.'

'Sowden poisoned us,' said Ross.

'I'd say it was more an introduction to life up north. He drank the same as we did. This morning, Annie made some beef tea and then I got the grand tour from Mick. There's a half-decent dray and a work shed. Well over one hundred horses. Most are hobbled and they roam about. The tack will keep us busy. Saddles, stirrups, bridles, halters, reins, bits, harnesses, martingales, everything has to be kept dry, the leather greased and checked for mould. But that's not all of it, I was up early enough to see Mick carrying Sowden from his bed to a chair.'

Ross gave a hoarse laugh. 'Good. I'm pleased he's suffering as well.'

'No,' said Connor sternly. 'You don't understand. Bill Sowden can't walk.'

⊰ Chapter 20 ⊱

'I didn't want to cause a bother.'

Ross was fairly stunned. 'It's true then. You really can't walk?'

They were seated around the table. The day shone through holes in the iron roof and walls, shafts of light spotlighting cracks, dirt and the mice running across the ground.

'It's only a trifling problem. Like I said, nothing worth bothering people about.' Sowden poured black tea from a battered tin pot, his movements verging on refined compared to the previous night. 'Sugar?'

Ross accepted the pannikin, adding a hefty dose of sugar, the sound of his spoon tinny in the room.

'Some might think it's a disability, but being paralysed in both legs –'

'Some? This is a cattle station,' replied Ross.

'Dinnae you think you should tell us about your, um, little difficulty?' asked Connor.

'Right. Yes. I'll not fancy it up for you. The gist of the story involves a poorly broken-in horse and a mad bull. We were up in the north when it happened. I came out of it the worst. Lay on the ground for a day, I did, before eventually being found.'

'And you haven't walked since?' said Ross.

The manager slurped his tea.

'When did this happen?' Ross demanded.

Sowden looked blank, as if he couldn't remember.

'When did it happen?' Ross enunciated each word slowly.

'Oh, about . . .' Sowden counted off time on his fingers. When he reached his second hand, Ross turned to Connor in disbelief.

'About nine years,' concluded Sowden.

Ross was stunned into silence by the manager's extraordinary revelation. 'Who's been running the property?' he finally asked.

The manager called for Annie and the woman appeared, padding across the dirt to her partner's side. She poured more tea for everyone, her features arranged in an expression of compliance. Then she slipped from the room.

'You haven't answered my question.' Ross tried to temper his anger. Sitting the pannikin down, he moved around the cramped space, past the newspaper pictures nailed to the wall, trying to comprehend the scale of the lie that had left his family property in the hands of the Aboriginal workers. For that was who must be managing it. There was no one else.

'The men have never done wrong by me,' said Sowden, as if reading his mind.

'How would you know?' replied Ross, leaning over so that his face was inches from Sowden's. 'Really, how would you know?'

'Because I damn well do!' Sowden slammed his fist on the table.

'Ross, steady.' Connor was standing, as if ready to stop a fight. 'Let's sit and talk through this.'

Ross regarded the tin trunk under the desk. 'Are the station papers in here?'

'Yes,' answered the manager, his voice straining with rage.

Ross carried it to the table, where he sorted through the contents. Once he had retrieved everything he needed, he dropped the trunk back to the ground.

'The station books are all there. Everything's up to date.' Sowden slumped back in the chair as if exhausted.

Some of the ledgers were mouldy, with pages ruined by rodents and weather. But the manager's hand was neat enough and the explanations regarding weather, pasture conditions and the general yearly movements across the property of men and stock were specific and descriptive.

Ross scowled. 'This is far more detailed than the reports you send to my father.'

He left the two men for a few minutes while he fetched the paperwork carried from Adelaide. On return he began comparing the two sets of figures.

Sowden wasn't expecting that. 'What have you got there, then?'

Ross peered at him over the top of the papers. 'The reports you've been sending my father.'

'I couldn't see the point of worrying him,' the manager hedged.

The figures didn't match. There had been a decrease in stock numbers in the first few years that Sowden was able-bodied, and although the losses fluctuated after that time, the final tally in the Waybell ledger showed a massive reduction in the cattle running on the property. Ross and Connor had been concerned by the figures in the Adelaide ledger, which had detailed several losses that ranged close to the two hundred mark, but that was nothing compared to this.

Ross pointed out the discrepancies to Connor and then directed his attention back to Sowden, who was beginning to resemble an animal in search of a hole to crawl into.

'We've gone from over eight thousand head fifteen years ago to a little over fifty-five hundred today?' Ross searched through the documents. 'And here.' He tapped the sheet of paper. 'You told my father that the number of cattle on hand this year is seventy-eight hundred. Where is the rest of the herd? What happened to them?' Ross slammed the ledger closed. It was little wonder that Sowden didn't welcome their visit. 'You're fired,' Ross told him bluntly.

Sowden's drooping cheeks wobbled in anger. 'You can't fire me, boy. The men won't work for you if that's what you're thinking. Not a young fella wet behind the years who's been hiding out on a sheep farm at the back of Burra for most of his life. That's why you came up here after all these years, wasn't it? To kick me out and take over the place yourself. Well, you can forget about it. Mick won't work for you, nor will any of the others without me, and you need them.'

'Based on these figures, I don't think Mick will be staying, either.' Ross gathered the Adelaide correspondence, squaring the edges of the pages. 'Particularly as I assume he's the one who's been giving you these numbers. Can he even count?'

Sowden gave a weak smile. 'Do you think we're a bunch of idiots?'

'No, you're certainly clever enough,' countered Ross. He had expected Sowden to relent, to admit to the disaster he'd helped create. Instead, the manager struggled furiously to hoist himself further upright in his chair.

'You have no idea what it's like here,' puffed Sowden. 'If your father ever bothered to set foot in the place, I would have told him plain. Waybell is naturally watered. That's what we depend on, year in, year out, on a big wet season that will fill everything up and give us hope. There's been no money to develop water in the south of Waybell, where we need it most. Do you understand, boy? Half the place is dry, too dry for cattle, and the north is so waterlogged it's not fit for running cattle. As for fences, well, you would have seen for yourself, there aren't any. The cattle walk for miles. Some of them could be on the other side of the Daly River for all I know. If there's cleanskins the neighbours nick them. What do you think you'd do if you came across an unmarked stray out here? Stand in the middle of nowhere and holler out what you've found and hope someone hears and comes a-running? Why, the first season I was on Waybell some wild blacks came across from the east. Those myalls ran off a few hundred head. So you tell me, how's a man to manage a place like this when he's told not to spend a brass razoo? When any money that's made goes down south to swell the coffers of a speculator?'

'Obviously we'll have to wait out the wet season before you leave,' said Ross. It was taking all of his willpower not to throttle the man.

Sowden thumped the table again. 'You're not listening. You're damn well not listening to a word I'm saying. It's not my fault. Where am I going to go? What am I going to do?'

'Ross, I think we'd better discuss this,' interrupted Connor.

For a moment Ross thought he'd misheard. However Connor was already at the door waiting for him. Ross followed him outside and across to the billabong. On its far side a fire threw a thin line of smoke into the air as children ran back and forth at the water's edge. Ross turned to his friend. 'Don't ever talk to me that way in front of staff again.'

Connor jabbed his hands into his trouser pockets. 'So why'd you bring me then? To be your lapdog, another Grant lackey?'

'It's you who's been doffing your cap to my family these many years.' Above them, the stony cliff shadowed them as the sun rose.

Drawing his hands free, Connor's usually mobile face grew still with fury. 'Dinnae talk to me like that.'

Ross hesitated. 'Sowden's got to go. The property is a mess. It's clearly been mismanaged.'

Connor took his time in replying. 'Aye, things aren't right way up but your father's not a stupid man, Ross. You know he's here for one reason only – the land increasing in value. I dinnae disagree that Sowden's done wrong, but your father can be pretty adamant. If the property has been managed badly then unfortunately he has to take his fair share of the blame. You cannae sit in your study thousands of miles away and expect everything to go perfectly.'

'So you're not as loyal in your allegiance to the Grants as everyone assumed,' accused Ross.

'I'm just saying how it is. You best decide, Ross, if I'm a friend or your employee because I cannae be both. Not out here.'

The question of Connor's role wasn't something Ross had ever considered, however employee *and* friend was exactly what was required of him. The Scot's grounding was in devotion to duty and

Ross couldn't understand why that needed to change. 'Sowden lied, Connor, and we're not talking about some bad decisions being made. There's theft involved.'

'We have no proof of that,' argued Connor. 'And we're unlikely to find any. So what are you going to do? Send him packing and then what? Hope the men will be happy to work for you? We've no idea what number might leave if you do fire Sowden. I'd hazard most of them,' he thumbed at the camp by the billabong, 'will be on his side. Clearly they've all been looking after him, otherwise Sowden couldn't have survived out here for so long. Their loyalty will be with him, not us.'

Across the water the children squealed as one of them was pushed into the mud. A woman sitting in a group pounding stones called to them and the boys reluctantly stopped their play.

'That camp depends on the station for meat, tea and sugar,' said Ross. 'They won't all leave.'

'Let's wait things out,' suggested Connor. 'Tell Sowden he can stay. That will keep everyone happy. When we're able, we'll send word to your father and he can advertise for another manager. Someone who knows this country and the people.'

Ross wasn't prepared to be bossed about again but nor could he afford to have Connor offside. 'I'll think about it. In the meantime, Sowden can stew.'

'If that's what you think is best,' said Connor, departing.

In the centre of the billabong a duck squawked and fluttered before disappearing under the water's surface. Up popped a boy holding the flapping bird by the legs. He swam to the bank, casually wringing the duck's neck as he walked to a cooking fire.

Ross decided to write to his father. He wouldn't mention Sowden's accident or the mismanagement. Highlighting the money that could be made from Waybell would ensure his father's attention, and attention was what Ross needed if a request for a line of credit was to be granted.

At the side of the house, Maria was cutting tall grass with a scythe, her brown arms damp with perspiration. Ross took shade beneath the wired-in veranda and the girl glanced at him, the blade hovering aloft before she resumed the task. The curve of each stroke made a gentle swishing noise as the blade sliced through air and plant. He remembered what had passed between them earlier that day, the warmth of her hand on his chest. The unexpectedness of the thought was not lost on him. He'd done his best to avoid women since the giving of the white feather in Burra, not that he'd been very successful with the opposite sex before that time, and yet here he was, watching Maria and admiring what he saw.

⊰ Chapter 21 ⊱

1920

January was behind them, lost in days of horizontal rain and heavy cloud-cast hours. Connor and Ross had celebrated the festive season quietly. Connor reflected on his first Christmas in many years spent away from the Grant family home, while Ross was pleased to finally be on the property, despite the tense circumstances. Two days after Ross's arrival, Sowden and Annie moved out of the house to the camp on the edge of the billabong, and with their departure he rearranged the household to suit its remaining occupants. Connor slept in the storeroom, surrounded by the tin trunks that held their supplies. Ross gave Sowden's space to Maria, which was only proper for a young woman, and he stayed in the sleep-out, grateful for the privacy but wary of the infinite area that stretched out beyond the chicken wire.

The poisoning he'd received from Sowden's sunset rum left a residue of tremors, dizzy spells and stomach cramps that at times made him bend with pain. Ross did his best to keep this illness from the others. He refused to confront Sowden about the concoction's effect on him and Connor's hardy demeanour was stiff competition. And, were Maria aware of his suffering, Ross suspected he'd feel twice the weakling. Three weeks passed before he felt fully whole again, although a lingering sensation of unease remained.

When the rain grew too heavy and the wind forced torrents of water across his bedding Ross strung a tarp over the chicken-wire, which stopped the worst of the storms, although nothing they did could caulk the nail holes in the roof or lessen the myriad gushing waterfalls that invaded every room. Unlike the countryside around Burra, there was no lulling silence when evening came. The rain sounded like buckets of stones being thrown continuously on the tin roof, and the chorus of frogs and other unknown things crowded the air the rest of the time. It was difficult to sleep most nights. The dark air was so thick with moisture that at times Ross believed he was being suffocated by the gathering dreams of his past. The darkness chased him as if he were a child, and he had to stop himself from dwelling on his dead twin and the part he'd been accused of playing in William's demise.

Soon after Sowden's departure, Ross began to be awakened during the night. He sensed from the beginning that the creaking noise of the bunk next to his was Maria returning to sleep by his side. At first, he imagined the girl scared of the night, of the thrash of thunder and the lightning that jagged like a catching thorn. And yet despite this reasoning he welcomed the distraction. In the brief periods of calm that the elements allowed, he lay waiting for her. Ross grew used to the pad of her feet as she passed through the dining room, the metallic flexing of the chicken wire as she groped her way along the sleep-out. The unmistakable hollowing whine the cot made as she sat. He'd assumed Maria only came out of fear but on clear nights she also appeared, and he began to consider that maybe she came for him alone. It more than pleased him, the way she sought him out, knowing that the choice to be with him was made by her, and that it was possible that the messy complications of the Great War might well be unimportant to someone younger like Maria.

As the weeks dragged on, their shared space made the monotony of the wet season more tolerable. To Ross there was an intimacy to this silent arrangement. In their steady breaths. Their unspoken decision to leave the bunks only feet apart when the sleep-out stretched ten feet on either side. But this closeness was difficult to replicate in daylight, and with each new day Maria was gone before Ross rose. And, with all of them restricted to the house during the ongoing wet, Connor was never far away, making the possibility of spending time alone with Maria difficult. He was tempted to reach for her during the night but worried doing anything that might alter what was developing between them. Ross felt condemned to making do with Maria's comings and goings.

When it wasn't raining Ross and Connor trudged through mud and water, like submariners cutting a path through the sea. The trees stooped under the mass of foliage they now carried and the grasses grew taller by the day. Birds, snakes and fish floated past on blue-green currents, a wash of fluid stretching into a heavy sky. The billabong was gorged by flooding; the escarpment had become a waterfall. They stood on the only square of unflooded land left and shot kangaroos and wallabies for dinner, while on either side the water crept among the timber.

Ross enjoyed their passage through this other world of swooping flycatchers and kingfishers, of schools of fish swirling by. But they were never quite alone. The Aboriginal camp remained by the billabong. Sowden sat propped up in a chair at the entrance to one of the wurlies, Annie sheltering him with a red umbrella as the manager followed their daily progress. Two children often waited for the men to appear. They marked time by trailing Ross and Connor, swinging their arms and pointing wildly as they mimicked their actions. Ross heard scraps of English in their talk and became mindful of what he said in their presence.

Ross chose not to mention Sowden after his departure from the house. If the manager did come up in conversation he promptly changed the subject. Connor was quick to share an idea, particularly reiterating his belief that a truce with Sowden would be more valuable during the wet than the current stand-off between the two camps. Ross held his ground, believing that a lesson needed to be taught about who was in charge, but with that decision it was becoming too easy to exchange heated words with Connor, particularly now as the days dragged. The Scot, as Mick christened Connor on account of his accent and the way he stumbled in and out of his native tongue, was not one for backing down, both about Sowden and on the point of Darcey.

'But you'll write to her at least,' said Connor, after a morning spent listing her many positive attributes. A one-way conversation that spoilt a good walk.

'I'll think on it. I don't want to give her hope, because there isn't any. Not for the two of us.'

'Aye, right. You married her, Ross.'

'I didn't want her,' said Ross firmly.

'Aye, but you married her. Truly, Ross. A piece of dirt in exchange for a woman's life.'

'A woman's life? I think you've been too long without female company, Connor.'

'You'd trade your grandmother if it meant you didnae have to do another's bidding.'

The gap between them closed until bare inches separated their noses.

'I might,' said Ross. 'I just might.'

They'd drawn the interest of Sowden and the rest of the camp. The manager gave a friendly wave, and Ross knew with the day so quiet their voices may well have carried clear across the billabong. 'I don't want Darcey mentioned again. In front of anyone.'

'You mean in front of the girl,' said Connor.

'I mean in front of anyone.'

Mick began visiting at the end of January. Appearing out of the rain to talk briefly about some happening he believed that the occupants of the big house should be made aware of: an old-man crocodile seen on the banks of the billabong, an outbreak of fever that had struck the elderly and weak but was now contained. Ross saw the sharing of these snippets as a pretext to check on what was happening in the whitefella's house. Invariably Ross was sitting at the table when Mick arrived, finessing the plans he'd drawn up for improvements to the homestead. Ross knew this information would be taken straight back to Sowden and was not backward in describing the alterations he had in mind. Two new rooms and pine floorboards, as well as proper windows with louvres, were met with interest. Mick remained angled towards the doorway during these meetings as if readying for escape, but he stared at the rough sketches and measurements ringed with the marks of plates and pannikins, the steady drip of rainwater smudging diagrams as Ross spoke.

'He's the better man,' said Connor one day, after Mick visited to tell them that flying foxes had taken up residence in a section of the stables. The warning was not to eat the bats, for they created such an odour in the body that they were usually only consumed if the mosquitoes were really bad and there was no other option. Even then, a person might rather have the mosquitoes.

'Why, because he assumes we can't fend for ourselves? He doesn't wade through the mud out of goodness, Connor. He gets things from us as well,' said Ross.

Connor was sitting at the other end of the cluttered table, greasing bridles in between examining his toes for mould. 'Aye, right. He's never even accepted a drink of tea.'

'You don't think Sowden's interested in the plans for the house?' said Ross. 'You don't think he's wondering if we're staying or someone new is coming to replace him?'

'No I dinnae. I reckon the only thing he's wondering about is whether we'd be stupid enough to kick him off Waybell,' answered Connor.

'They're thinking a lot more than that.' Ross ignored the sharpness in Connor's tone and concentrated on the map he'd found in the tin trunk. The plan showed the location of the homestead and yards, and Ross now knew that to the northeast lay country crisscrossed with stone, the beginning of a sandstone plateau from which water must spill outwards to fan over the lowlands, into rivers and billabongs, swamps and floodplains. All these were marked on the manager's map along with trails showing dry and wet tracks. He followed one dotted line with the stub of a pencil across waterways and through woodlands to the edge of the page, wondering what lay beyond.

≪ Chapter 22 ≫

'Another letter to your father?' Connor joined Ross at the table. He'd been gone most of the afternoon, promising fish for dinner. 'To my grandmother. How did you fare?'

'Well I'm not sure Herself would be partial to the swamp we're living in but if a person likes fish, this is the place.' Connor removed his wet boots and began stuffing them with part of an old shirt to stop them from shrinking. The consequences of the dispute with Sowden included a lack of red meat. They'd nearly eaten out the safety-seeking kangaroos and wallabies that camped on the slight ridge around the house trying to escape the rising moat surrounding them. While there was flour, potatoes and rice, rows of pickled vegetables, beans and a few wormy cabbages and carrots, the salted beef was all gone and the chicken eggs were a treat only if they could be gathered before a snake or bird took them first.

'Where's the girl? I thought she could make herself useful. Fillet them and fry them in a bit of flour. Aye, they'd be tasty then.'

'You mean *Maria*,' corrected Ross. 'We're lucky to have her, you know. She always manages to make something edible out of whatever we give her.'

'Well, dinnae get used to her, she doesn't belong here. Eventually she'll have to go to Holder. And I'll tell you another thing, if that girl is supposed to be a domestic she'll be ruined by the time she leaves here.'

'What are you talking about?' asked Ross.

'Dressing for dinner every night in that frock of hers. Sitting down at the table with us.'

'Are you saying she shouldn't eat with us?' asked Ross.

'I'm saying that she'll be in for a shock when she takes up her new position. Dinnae get me wrong, the girl does her share, but she's had things easy on Waybell. I'm reckoning that she'll be eating with the rest of the domestics once she gets to Holder's Run.'

Simply knowing Maria was nearby gave Ross some relief from the monotony of waiting for the rain to end. There was a wholeness about her. In the quiet way that she spent each day, cooking, scrubbing, airing bedding, keeping the grass cut low close to the house. There was no perfect ensemble of clothing or neatly styled hair. No challenge of opinion or raised voice. The girl was as distinct in her difference to Darcey as a person could possibly be. How was it that Ross could see what Connor could not? It was Maria who made Waybell civilised. She held their friendship together and kept the night at bay. Ross didn't want Maria going anywhere. He would have to send word to Marcus Holder when dry weather came and tell him that he'd have to find another maid.

'Listen, Ross, we should go and see Sowden. They're roasting something at the camp and it sure doesn't smell like fish or bird.' Connor placed the boots on the sideboard.

'I'm not going over there to beg for food. We can look after ourselves.'

'He probably took more than his share of supplies when he left,' said Connor. 'Dinnae you think we should try and get on with them? Food, for one. If this rain keeps coming they'll starve us out.'

'Leave them be,' replied Ross. He turned his attention back to the letter and addressed the envelope to his grandmother. 'We're not desperate.'

Connor returned to the table and sat, drumming his fingers. 'I dinnae know if I'd last another wet season out here. This weather drives a man to distraction.'

'Have you read all my books yet?' asked Ross.

'Just parts. The descriptions mostly. Some of the pictures are good,' replied Connor.

The illustrations were far easier to digest than the rambling discourses that lay between the pages of Herodotus, although the truncated version of Homer's *Iliad* rather appealed to Ross. A battle within a battle. That was the guts of the Trojan War. Agamemnon versus Achilles. The King of Kings set against a warrior. The patriarch opposing the unwieldy son. The book was well-thumbed, clearly a favourite of his brother's as well. Ross liked that.

Connor tapped the table for attention. 'It seems to me the Greeks bicker more than my parents did and that's impressive. I wonder at your brother wanting to be one of them as a boy. They're no better than us.'

'Perhaps that's the whole point,' argued Ross. 'They mightn't be any better than us, but they have moments of greatness.'

'Aye, right. What a load of tripe. If a man's going to fight he should do it for something worthwhile,' said Connor.

'Like what?' Ross wanted to know. 'What would make you fight?'

Connor concentrated on the funnels of water shooting off the roof, his voice louder as he strived to be heard above the din of the rain on the corrugated iron. 'Religion. Home. A woman.'

Ross sat back in the leather-hide chair. 'Connor Andrews the romantic.'

'Aye. Had I not been, I would never have left my village in Scotland. And what of your brother? Did Alastair believe the war was being fought for the right reasons?'

'You spent time with him before he sailed,' said Ross. 'What do you think?'

'He was a slippery one, Alastair,' said Connor. 'He knew when to say the right thing, the expected thing, but as to what was really going on in that head of his, well, I wouldn't like to fathom what made your brother tick.'

'He was a dreamer,' said Ross.

'Alastair? A dreamer? If what we heard is true, then I say a dreamer doesn't wake up one morning and pull a boot on the end of a shattered leg and escape from a hospital in France.' Connor followed the edge of the table with a thumb, stroking the timber. 'If they'd cut his leg off, Alastair might have come home. Aye, crippled but he'd have been home. Instead he disappeared. Why? For fear of amputation? Or of mending and having to return to battle? It's as I said, he was a slippery one, your brother.'

'Are you saying he's still alive?' asked Ross.

'No. I'm telling you that he might have been a dreamer once, but in the end he wasn't afraid to do what was necessary to survive on his terms. I dinnae think any of us realised that about him.'

'I did,' said Ross. 'I can't count the scrapes of his devising that we two got into, nor the times I took the blame for them. There was always an excuse, a reason as to why it was best I take responsibility. I look back now and think how the four years between us made a mighty difference. That if I'd been older, I may not have been so quick to follow him.'

'Aye, but a brother's love made you stick fast to his side and Alastair took advantage of that.'

'Yes,' admitted Ross. 'I suppose he did.' He tapped the letter thoughtfully on the table.

≼ Chapter 23 ≽

Out in the shack that passed for a kitchen Maria was kneading dough dotted with currants. Ross sat on an upturned bucket in the corner, a pool of water edging its way beneath the tin wall. He scraped at the dirt with the heel of his boot, enticing the moisture to run along the wall. Maria looked up at him, her expression changing from concentration to one of pleasure, then she returned to her bread-making.

A cream blouse hung dripping from a line strung across the room, and beside it a flimsy item of clothing blew back and forth in the draughty wind fed by the storm. Anywhere else, this blatant display of a woman's undergarments would have sent Ross immediately from the room but here the conventions of society seemed of no great concern. What was significant was his desire to reach out and touch the material.

Ross quickly turned his attention away from the washing. 'When the rain finally stops and we can order some supplies I'll get some dress fabric for you. You could do with some more clothes.'

Maria pushed at the hair falling across her sweaty face, a streak of flour smearing white against brown. 'You don't have to buy me anything.'

'I know I don't, but I want to. With the way the weather is, everything rots out here eventually.'

She moulded the batter into a tin, opened the door to the pot-belly stove and placed the mixture inside. 'I won't sleep with you.'

'I wasn't suggesting . . . I would never . . .' Ross stumbled over his words. 'Is that what you think of me?'

'I see you watching me.' She squatted near the stove, wrapping the folds of her skirt up into a bunch so that the hem didn't drag in the dirt, the action accentuating the roundness of her bottom. Ross didn't look away.

'And you don't like it?' he replied.

'That's not what I said.'

'It's you who comes to sleep next to me, Maria.'

She stood abruptly, wiping her hands on a rag tucked into her waistband. 'No one's ever offered to do anything for me unless they wanted something in return.'

'I'm not like everyone else.' Ross walked to the door. The rain was coming in sheets, gouging the mud as it fell. In the past he might have walked away at such an implication. He wondered if he'd misread her, if what he thought was mutual attraction was instead mere friendship. 'I came to ask if you'd like to stay on and work for me. As cook. I'd pay you and build you your own room. I intend to renovate the homestead as well as improve the property.'

'You're staying?' asked Maria, her voice inquisitive.

'Yes.' Although he'd been ruminating on the future these past weeks, the promise he'd made himself to never return to Adelaide held. It was here at the top of Australia where Ross believed he'd found something he could call his own. A place he could build on and improve. That could give him a sense of purpose, the beginnings of a new life.

Ross waited for Maria to answer. In the short time since meeting the girl, only once had she touched him, the morning after Ross consumed the sunset rum. Ever since then he'd felt restless and unsatisfied. Ross had blamed Sowden's horrible concoction and the endless rain. Now he was not so convinced. Connor's reminder that Maria would eventually leave had not sat well with him and the reasons had very little to do with cooking and cleaning. He wanted her.

This was a different need to the kissing and fumbling of youth. To the girl at Burra he'd cared for and may well have married if she hadn't told him how embarrassed she was to be outing with a man who wasn't going to war. Ross would never forget 1915. Alastair sailing away. His return to Burra. The questions and queries from older sheepmen of why he wasn't joining up as well. That single white feather.

'I want you to stay, Maria,' he said, despite being aware of the risk of repeating the question. The hard reality of being told no. The chance remained that she wasn't interested, that she didn't feel the same way. But what if she did? What if this girl, who was so different, also recognised the separateness in him and understood how alike they were?

She came to stand with him in the narrow doorway, a hand on the frame. He kept his gaze on the rain as she stared up at him, still giving no reply. Ross didn't want to ask her again. Not a third time.

'This blasted rain. I need to get mail out and supplies in,' he said. Above them sections of the bluff protruded from vertical rivers. 'And a bottle of whisky wouldn't go astray either.'

'You don't need it, Ross. It wouldn't help,' she said.

Ross could count the number of times she'd spoken his name.

'What about your family?' she asked. 'You and Connor talk about them. About your businesses in South Australia and your brother Alastair. The one that's missing.'

'He never came back from the war, Maria,' said Ross. 'I'm an only child.'

'One day it will all be yours. Everything here and there? You have to go back if you own so much.' Maria fingered his sleeve where it was rolled and bunched at the elbow. He was distracted by the intimacy of such an unexpected action, and it took him a second to reply.

'There is nothing for me there. Nothing except bad memories and an unforgiving family. They took what they wanted. Now it's my turn.'

'People are like that,' replied Maria.

The girl's hand was a light pressure on his arm as her fingers plied the material, crescent-shaped moons sitting at the base of each curved nail. He wanted to touch her, to feel the softness of her skin. Her dark hair was parted and plaited into a single thick rope that hung down the centre of her back. He ran his fingers down her long neck to the bony depression at the base of her throat, feeling the angle of collarbone and shoulder, his exploration stopping where the curve of her breast began to swell. Her heart thudded beneath his hand.

'Are you still going to tell me that you only sleep on the cot next to mine because of the storms?' he asked gently. He leant towards her.

Maria's eyebrows drew together as if she was sorting through the pieces of a puzzle. He kissed her, lingering over a sensation he'd long forgotten, feeling the fullness of her lips against his.

Then she was pulling away, and he worried that he'd rushed her. She scooped up a handful of mud, placing the sludge in his palm.

'Forget what your family took,' she told him.

The mass ran through Ross's fingers. He found it difficult to draw himself from the place he'd just been back to the reality of what Maria spoke of.

'Remember what was given. People don't live forever.'

She was right. One day his family would be gone, claimed by time. He simply needed to outlive them all.

Maria reached out into the rain and began rubbing her palms together to rid her skin of the mud. Ross stepped behind her and took her hands between his and washed them clean, continuing to hold her long after the water ran clear. The length of her back pressed against his torso, the scent of her hair in his nostrils.

'Are you ever going to tell me about yourself?' he asked.

'Maybe, yes.' She looked directly at him and then, as if suddenly coy, turned away. 'No.'

Ross didn't want that. He didn't want her to be like everyone else, manipulative and evasive. 'Why do you sleep next to me?' He needed the words to be said aloud.

She gave a thin laugh. 'I really don't like thunder.'

'Maria?'

'You know why.'

'Say it,' said Ross.

'I can't. It wouldn't be right. I can't be the person you want me to be, Ross,' she replied. 'I'm different to you. My life is different and it shouldn't be altered for anything.' She looked at him. 'Or anyone.'

'You're not different. We're the same. Can't you see that? Anyway, I'm only offering you a job. Or do you want to go to this Marcus Holder? Would you rather be there?'

'Things have been decided for me. It's better to leave things as they are. Safer.'

'I'd never do anything to hurt you, Maria,' said Ross, touching her face.

She brought his palm to her lips. 'Yes you will,' she answered. 'Eventually we will both hurt each other.'

149

⪻ Chapter 24 ⪼

Four weeks later the clouds dispersed. Ross woke to swifts chasing insects and sunlight glinting onto dewy webs. He rode through tall grasses and clusters of darting gold-brown dragonflies, across sodden country where the scents of flowering bushes and rank undergrowth drifted in the growing heat. Violent southeasterly storms had flattened the vast stands of spear grass, and he listened to the whoosh of falling foliage as trees dropped their heavy wet season growth. At night he, Connor and Maria feasted, laughing with the freedom that came with the end of the wet. Their conversations were filled with details of the extraordinary abundance of animal and birdlife and what they might achieve, now that the dry had edged in.

Tracing the wet track marked on Sowden's map, Ross and Connor rode through the tangled bush across grasslands and towards a clump of blue-green foliage, searching for timber for the planned homestead improvements. The horses wound through the cool woodlands as the men peered at the crowns of arching cypress branches, calculating that the pine was seventy feet high or more. Wordlessly they turned back to the edge of the stand of trees, where fire and past foragers had left hacked stumps and burnt wood. It was no small task that lay before them and Connor was quick to suggest recruiting some of the Aboriginal people from the camp to help. Ross dismissed this, telling his friend they would manage, somehow.

They returned to the same place a few weeks later when the track was dry, and cut and loaded lengths of timber into the creaking dray, which had not seen service since before their arrival nearly five months earlier. After a week camping out, the men left the cypress stand at daybreak. They halted their homeward journey when the sun was at midpoint and explored late into the afternoon, as the light slanted from the west.

The two men untethered their horses from the rear of the cart and, leaving the wagon in the shade, rode out to where the woodlands merged into flat marshy plains of grass. Large flocks of squawking magpie geese flapped upwards on their approach, forming a bridge of white between the lush green of the earth and the azure of the sky.

'Beautiful, isn't it?' remarked Ross.

'Aye. It's a fine stretch of land,' Connor agreed.

'Space, Connor. Space and grass and fresh air and not a soul to bother a person. A man can breathe out here. All I see is endless potential and nothing I think about seems impossible anymore.' He clapped Connor on the back, and thought of Maria.

'Aye, well, while I dinnae quite share your enthusiasm for living in the middle of a lake for part of the year, I admit the place does worm its way into a man.'

It did indeed. In the weeks since their initial embrace in the kitchen shed, Ross had been making quiet inroads with Maria when opportunity allowed, and her acceptance of his attentions was beginning to erode the bitterness of his previous relationships. He was not brazen enough to rush her, satisfying his growing ardour with the closeness of a brief embrace, or the touch of her skin.

He drew hard on the reins, and held up a hand to stop Connor from further movement. 'See them?' he asked.

His friend, who had been busy watching long-legged grey plumed birds, took a moment to focus.

There were eight buffalo a half-mile away, moving slowly towards them.

'Aye,' replied Connor. 'I see them all right. Where did they come from?'

A light breeze carried across from the direction of the animals. 'They haven't smelt us,' Ross observed. He touched his horse's flanks, and walked her forwards.

'Temperamental, they are.' Connor scratched at his beard. 'Charge a man without thought.'

The buffalo splashed on through the swamp. With the drying of the land, the floodplain was returning to mud as the water drained. The ground grew softer, the dense pasture concealing the unstable earth beneath.

'I think we've followed them far enough,' said Connor, when sludge replaced dry soil and the horses began to struggle.

'That bull must be close to ten feet long and nearly seven feet high.' The horses lifted their hooves nervously. Ross drew his rifle. 'Those horns are five feet wide if they're an inch. I wouldn't mind them hanging above the dining-room table in the homestead.' Sensing the intrusion, a mud-plastered bull came closer. 'He's seen us.' The animal dropped its head.

'Aye, and he doesn't look happy about it,' replied Connor.

Reluctantly, Ross turned away from the beasts. Were the earth drier he would have pursued them. There was money in buffalo, based on the number of hunters they'd seen in Darwin, and they roamed his land ripe for the taking.

'I see that look, Ross Grant. Dinnae go telling me you've a fancy to become a hunter of hides and bone.' Connor glanced over his shoulder as they retreated.

'Why not?'

'Why not? You've yet to progress from sheep to cattle. I'd rather thought the answer was pretty obvious.'

'Well, unlike sheep and cattle we don't have to yard them,' said Ross, feeling the prickle of Connor's insinuation. 'We only have to shoot them and skin them.'

'It's your use of the word *only* that's got me concerned.'

As Ross and Connor arrived back at the homestead with the loaded dray, members of Sowden's camp began gathering at the edge of the billabong. Finally the group was joined by the cane chair and its occupant, the familiar sight of the umbrella aloft above his head.

'That'd be right. Come to gloat at our efforts they have,' said Connor. 'Now, if we'd been friendlier, they might have given us a hand.'

The pine was long and cumbersome, and the pair struggled to pull the logs from the rear of the dray.

'Have you noticed,' replied Ross as he wiped sweat from his eyes, 'there's more of them? A good forty or so.'

With the onset of the fine weather the camp was beginning to swell with young men. They'd been arriving in small groups over the past few weeks and today they lingered at the edge of the billabong observing Ross and Connor's work with interest, until the crowd grew tired of their efforts and the audience dwindled to a handful of children who shyly approached the two men. Ross lowered the log onto the ground as Connor dropped his end, adding to the growing stack.

'You building big house?' one of the children asked. The boy wore trousers cut off at the knees and carried a stick, which he poked continuously in the ground, flicking dirt in the air. Behind him the other children laughed and pointed. Compared to the rest of the young ones, this boy was not quite as dark-skinned.

'Hoping to,' replied Ross.

'You bigfella Boss.' The child grinned. 'I'm Little Bill.'

'Sowden's been busy,' Connor said to Ross with a smirk. 'And who are all the other men that have arrived, Little Bill?'

'They come for the cattle round-up.'

'Do you think some of them might give us a hand?' asked Connor.

'Maybe,' the boy replied, walking back towards the camp.

'We can manage without their help,' reprimanded Ross.

Connor glanced briefly towards the encampment before resuming the unloading of the timber.

'Think of it this way, Connor,' said Ross with a smile. 'It could be worse. We're only cutting enough for a dining-room floor, not tackling the whole building. We'll leave that to the experts.'

'If we can find one out here.' Connor paused in his efforts of dragging a length of timber across to the growing pile. 'Let me ask you this, Ross. Have you ever done any building?'

'Fence posts,' he admitted. 'And you?'

'A pigsty.' Connor shrugged. 'I helped my father when I was a wee lad.'

'Well then, we're reasonably qualified,' said Ross.

'You sheep men have a funny sense of humour.'

Toby and JJ arrived with four other stockmen. Without being asked, they carried the rest of the timber to the stack of wood, and then Toby offered them further help, which wasn't refused. The bushmen spent half the day digging out a narrow sawpit and then took it in turns to cut the wood. Ross learnt from them that soon the wet season waterholes would begin to dry and when the cattle moved to the permanent watering spots, that's when the gathering-up of the cattle would begin.

Armed with the knowledge of action fast approaching, Ross and Connor spent the next few days concentrating on the construction of the dining-room floor. They made a framework for the new surface before resting the lengths of sawn wood across the scaffolding, chocking the ends with smaller pieces of timber, trying to ensure the surface was reasonably level. With the help of the men from Sowden's camp, there were now enough cut lengths to attempt to line the walls as well. Ross spent hours in the house on his knees with hammer and nails, only rising for food or for Maria.

'Ross?' she asked, appearing in front of him one afternoon with a bucket full of water.

He placed the hammer on the table and accepted the ladle of water, his hands brushing the handle where her own fingers grasped the dipper. He drank thirstily, watching her over the rim of the spoon, aware of Connor at the other end of the room, his back turned towards them. Although she'd not said yes to his offer of staying on as their cook, neither had she turned it down. If she wondered why he wanted her to have an official capacity on the property, she never questioned his reasoning. For the moment, Ross needed Maria's presence on Waybell to continue without query, although there was only one person on the station Ross worried would speak his mind when it came to their burgeoning relationship, and that was Connor. Ross released the dipper, and moved to the sleep-out, gesturing for Maria to follow.

Once alone, he pressed her against the wall, feeling her body fitting to his. He kissed her frantically, aware of their breathlessness, of the wanton sighs that surged between them. The drinking water she carried spilt to the floor. Ross placed a hand on her breast, vaguely aware of having abandoned all propriety, of finally having given into his desire. 'I want you, Maria. It's impossible being so close to you and –'

She placed a finger to his mouth. They could hear Connor in the adjoining room, continuing to saw the timber.

Ross shook his head. 'Don't worry about him.'

'And what about Mr Holder? Once it dries up he'll come for me and I'll have to go.'

'You don't have to do anything you don't want to,' replied Ross.

'You don't understand.'

'Then explain it to me, Maria.'

'Ross?' called Connor from the dining room. 'I dinnae know what we're going to do about this hole in the wall. We'll need extra boards for it.'

'Coming!' he yelled.

In the seconds it took for him to answer Connor, Maria was gone. He leant against the boards, balling his hand into a fist.

Each day was the same. It was difficult to find time to be with Maria. They were always busy working and, if not, someone invariably interrupted them. She was kept occupied preparing the game they shot for food, cooking endless dampers and tending the vegetable garden. The children from Sowden's camp visited the homestead daily now and Maria quickly gained a shadow in

155

Little Bill, who followed her everywhere, helping with any chores he could.

In the dining room Ross surveyed the area where the replacement boards were needed. The floor was nearly completed, and with its finishing the evenings of sitting with their chairs resting precariously on the unfinished surface would soon be at an end.

'Two more boards, Connor, and then we'll be done.'

'Aye,' said Connor, reaching for the planks Ross passed to him.

Finally, the last nail was driven into the boards and the table dragged back to the room's centre, where the two men gathered to admire their handiwork. The floor and walls, made of streaky gold-and-brown heartwood, with its knotty malformed whirls, were greatly improved, and the men spent an hour sipping tea and alternating between staring at the boards and complimenting each other on their achievement.

'It's a good job done.' Ross took another gulp of the tea and examined the lost branches and diseases that formed the grainy markings in the timber. 'We could build the extensions, you and I.'

'Aye, right. I'll not be coerced into that,' answered Connor. 'You mightn't recall the swearing and the arguments while we measured and fitted these boards but I do. Besides, if I was to drop a ball on this here floor it'd be at the other end in a skip and a jump.'

'Well I can't see us doing any more building for a while. I want to get the Darwin abattoir constructed so we can begin using it this season,' said Ross. 'There's a lot to work out after that.'

'We'll be here for a couple of years then?' asked Connor.

'At least,' confirmed Ross. 'I did warn you that I might not return home.'

'Och, aye. You said that, it's true. But a man with responsibilities can't live as free as a bird forever. Once the roads are open you'll be receiving mail from Adelaide, I'm sure. Best to keep a mind on duty, Ross, and not get too enamoured with the scenery here at Waybell Station.'

'What are you referring to?' he asked, his tone clipped.

'Nothing. Nothing at all.'

Ross knew Connor was thinking of Maria, and the rightness of his behaviour where Darcey was concerned. All the more reason to keep his thoughts private. The Scotsman only needed the tiniest of scratches to start peeling away at the layers of the situation, and Ross refused to be driven into an argument. He knew what it meant to ignore his marriage. And, in quieter moments, he did stop and consider the ramifications that lay ahead for Darcey. But that was all he could do. Briefly pause before moving on.

That night Ross waited for Maria. For the small sounds of her progress, the warp of boards, the familiar creak of the cot. He thought of the warmth of her fingers beneath his on the ladle. The way her gaze held his. How it had felt when he'd kissed her, as if the world had suddenly become a far better place and that in the future he might well be able to learn to forget those who sought to rule him.

She arrived later than usual. A waxing moon cast her in silvery light.

'Where have you been?' asked Ross.

She looked at him steadily. The shy, modest girl she'd been when they first met long gone. 'Asleep.'

She yawned. Ross extended an arm, spanning a gap of age and space and position. She took his hand.

'Will you let me lie beside you?' He waited for a reply, trying not to push her but no longer capable of existing on what they currently shared. 'Maria?'

Her eyes were closed, leaving Ross with only her breath and the rise and fall of slumber to remind him that she was not some untouchable marble effigy. And he was now too far gone to be saved.

≪ Chapter 25 ≫

Late one afternoon, two men arrived at the house. They hollered out, announcing themselves, and Ross came over to meet the strangers where they waited. They were accompanied by a wagon stacked high with crates and other supplies. The horses pulling it were big doughty mares.

'God's galoshes!' one of them called. He dropped the mailbag. 'Who are you?'

'Ross Grant, the owner.'

'The owner? We thought you'd be older.' He removed his hat, then slapped his friend's stomach, jolting him into doing the same. 'I'm Eustace and this here is Parker. We're stockmen. Well, after Mick, of course. He's the head stockman and we come under him. Not that he's better than us. No way. Parker and me, we've been gallivanting around these parts for years. We know what's up and what's sideways. So anything you need, Boss, just ask.'

Both men had impressive beards but where Eustace was red-haired, skinny and angular, Parker was stocky, with sandy-coloured hair.

'It's good to have you back. It's been wet,' said Ross sociably.

'Sure has,' replied Eustace. 'Everything's been in flood. It'll be a top year.'

'We would have got here sooner but we ran into trouble,' said Parker.

'A few days on the turps and we found ourselves part of a drover's camp out the back of Katherine. Well, we took off quick-smart, Boss, but how's a man to know where he is,' explained Eustace.

'Lost, we were,' added Parker.

'For three days. Spent the dark hours reading an old Bible we found lying on the ground, getting sun-blistered and heat-stroked until the toss of a shilling had us riding in the right direction. I hope Mick isn't riled up. You'll be about to go mustering,' said Eustace.

'So you two don't mind working for Mick?' asked Ross.

'Good fella,' declared Parker.

'Real good bloke,' confirmed Eustace. 'And he knows the country like nobody's business, and most people in it. 'Course he should, it's his country. Mick's been here forever and he and Bill are real tight, especially with Annie being Mick's sister.'

'Sister, you say,' said Ross.

'You do know that Mick's father was a king?' continued Eustace. 'A proper one. You might pay good money for Waybell but it's Mick and his people who own the land. You couldn't run it without them. Not that you'd want to.'

'I see. Can I ask you two, are you men aware of any funny business going on with the stock tally? Some of the figures don't add up,' said Ross.

'Don't expect nothing to add up here, Boss,' Eustace replied. 'Keeping track of the cattle is impossible.'

Perhaps Eustace and Parker were unaware of the severity of the discrepancies, but Ross wondered if they'd be that naïve.

Parker pulled on an ear. 'So are you paying us a friendly visit or staying for a while?'

'Haven't decided,' Ross informed them.

They seemed to accept that, and got on with unloading the wagon. Eustace pulled back the canvas tarp and clambered up into the rear of the wagon, which was crammed with crates and bags, and began passing the goods down to Parker, who sat them on the ground. He stopped suddenly at the appearance of Maria, who stared back at the new arrivals.

'Too right.' Eustace's skin grew a mottled red from the neck up. 'A woman. You brung a woman here? Well, now then, that's one for the books.' Whipping off his hat he gave a low bow. 'G'day, missus.'

'That's Holder's girl,' said Parker to Eustace. 'Remember?'

'Off you go, Maria,' said Ross. She looked at the men and then quickly walked away. 'Maria works here now,' Ross told them. 'I doubt she'll be leaving.'

'Righto, Boss,' said Eustace.

'Is Bill about?' asked Parker.

Ross explained the manager's move to the camp, including the fact that he'd left voluntarily early one morning a few days after Ross's arrival. There was a brief silence as the men realised the extent of the changes in their absence. They gazed around, as if looking for further evidence of the altered environment they'd returned to.

'Right. Well this is the standing order,' Eustace responded. 'We know exactly what's needed. It's the same every year. Except there usually aren't three more people. But we got Chin-Lee at the store to throw in some extra.'

'Yep.' Parker tugged at an ear. One lobe was longer than the other.

'There's your mail. You'll be pleased to get a letter from home,' said Eustace. 'There's also a couple of bottles of rum from Davis the publican, by way of a welcome.'

After the supplies were stacked in the storeroom and Parker and Eustace departed to the men's quarters, Ross settled down to go through the mail. There was no fizz of excitement in finally receiving word from the outside. Isolation agreed with him. Unenthusiastically, he upended the sack on the dining table. There were accounts for food supplies and other sundries used on the property but nothing to suggest that Sowden had behaved dishonestly when it came to purchases. The remaining post included a large box of

Connor's prized tobacco, mail for Sowden, months-old copies of the *Northern Territory Times and Gazette* and correspondence for both Connor and himself. Ross was surprised to find that one of Connor's letters was clearly written in his father's hand. He held the envelope up to the light and then sat it on the table, where it stared back like an unblinking eye.

There was a parcel from his grandmother. A letter from his father reminding him to send detailed reports, and another note in an unknown hand. Ross examined the handwriting on the off-white parchment, trying to place it. On the back were the details of the sender and for a moment he didn't comprehend the name.

Darcey Grant. His name and hers together. Intertwined. Darcey Grant.

Ross was as unprepared to receive a letter as he'd been to meet her last year. He resented her writing to him, reminding him of her existence, of their vows. This was not some pretty, amenable woman set upon by his parents to do as they wished. There was calculation involved. She'd been happy to exploit the Grant family's desires. Darcey's decision was made before they'd even met. If only she'd refused the arrangement brokered by his parents. If only she had opted to return to her home country. If only she'd been considerate enough to think of him. If, if, if. Even in the face of downright hostility, Darcey had been willing to become his wife.

Ross knew he must read what she had written, and that a response was required. He thought of the words that should be said and then of their wedding day. The unpleasantness of readying for the occasion, the choking atmosphere of the garden, the twig that caught on the slight train of her gown, the way Darcey flicked the material, expecting his assistance, and the photographer who jostled them to the portico where the family waited, assembled like jurors. Then afterwards of how Darcey came to his side, promising him friendship, reciting some fool's poem of maturing love until he stepped away from the discomfort of it all. Ross thought of Alastair and his careless love.

With deliberation Ross placed the letter down, opening instead the package sent by his grandmother. It contained two novels. At least Connor would be pleased.

My dear Ross,

It is a comfort to know that you arrived safely in Darwin. I have been told by your father not to expect any correspondence for some time as I believe the monsoon period is very great, leaving the land quite unsuitable for travel. Having read in the paper startling accounts of people being carried down flooded rivers never to be seen again and crocodiles entering homes, I do hope you are well.

Notwithstanding my consternation at your decision to leave Adelaide, my wish is that your new venture is everything that you hoped it would be. The family has every confidence in your success and your father is particularly looking forward to receiving your accounts of life in the North. We are all as well as can be expected with the march of the years, although I fear your mother has declined somewhat recently.

I will close with the pleasure I felt when your gift to Darcey arrived. The camphor box is quite a talking point for visitors to the house and your dear wife is a student these days, filling the hours learning about your new circumstances. I know the two of you were rather thrown together but small steps of kindness lead to firmer things.

You carry the banner for us now, lad. Hold it with pride. We await your news,

Your loving grandmother

Ross reread the letter. How was it possible that the gift purchased for his grandmother was delivered to Darcey? He distinctly recalled writing a note to his grandmother and Connor offering to post the Chinese woodwork. With a furtive glance to ensure he was alone, Ross prised open his father's letter that was addressed to Connor.

Connor,

Per our agreement, make sure you send me regular updates. I am depending on you for a true account of matters as they stand, as well as the conduct of my boy. Guide him as best you can, Ross will thank you for it in the future.

Morgan Grant

Ross stormed into the storeroom and kicked aside the Scot's bedding, which had been pushed to one side to make way for the newly arrived supplies.

'Interfering, meddling, ungrateful! Damn you, Connor.'

What was he supposed to do now? What could he do? He'd been tricked by the one person he thought he could trust to bring north, and what's more, Darcey had been misled into thinking he cared! Rummaging in the crates for the rum, Ross stared at the label briefly before pulling the cork and drinking straight from the bottle. His personal affairs were no one's business, least of all that of a paid employee. Ross could have throttled Connor for sending Darcey the gift meant for his grandmother, as he could his meddlesome father. He took another long glug of rum, silently thanking the unknown publican. The drink helped steady his thoughts, gain a more measured response. It was only one gift, reasoned Ross. The business of giving a simple wooden box could hardly be misconstrued for anything else other than a peace offering, for he'd not promised Darcey one thing, not that it mattered if Darcey thought otherwise.

Collecting Darcey's letter, Ross escaped the house. Outside, a blue sky pressed down on the too-green land. He kept on moving, past the vegetable garden and outhouse, to the place of fallen trees, where he'd been so ill months before. He carefully tore up Darcey's unread letter, scattering the pieces, and then flung the half-drunk bottle into the scrub. His mind re-ran every conversation with Connor, back to the day permission was granted by his father for the Scotsman to accompany Ross northwards. How easily that approval was given. Too easily. Ross should have known. Connor Andrews was a Grant man, through and through.

The remains of Darcey's letter circled to the grass, bits of paper catching in the pasture. The thought of never really possessing Connor's loyalty ate at him, and he decided that the Scotsman should learn that deceitfulness had its repercussions. Ross could do without people like Connor and their plotting. He now understood that in this new place, Maria was the only one he could trust.

≪ Chapter 26 ≫

Narrow-eyed, Ross stepped clear of the women, who were surprised by his arrival in the camp, and headed directly to Sowden's wurley. With the country drying out more every day, he'd expected to be informed of when the annual mustering of the cattle would commence. That hadn't occurred. Mick, having watched his approach, moved with the swagger of a man who knew his position. He called to Toby and JJ and by the time Ross was standing in front of the lean-to, Sowden was deposited out the front, Annie slightly behind her partner, a possessive hand on his shoulder.

Ross acknowledged them all with a stern nod, waiting for Mick to walk through the gathering tribe where he took up the place next to his sister. The camp heaved with young men who waited expectantly. Ross's workforce. Mick's people. Since the truth of Mick's heritage had been known, Ross realised that there would be no possibility of firing him. The Territory wasn't the southern states. The stockman and his people were here to stay. And if Ross wanted to keep Mick happy, Annie needed to be appeased as well, which meant Sowden was also saved. Ross faced a triumvirate of power. Everyone knew it. Now he did as well.

'How long before we start the muster?' asked Ross. 'With supplies having arrived, it must be dry enough.'

'We can be ready in a few days,' announced Mick. He pointed in a southwesterly direction. 'Knock-em-down storms nearly finished now. Ragul the red-eyed pigeon is laying her eggs, so it will be dry enough to the south. The first camp is near to where the Mary River and the South Alligator draw close. We catch them there.'

'You make it sound as if all we need is a butterfly net,' responded Ross. 'But it hasn't been that easy here over the years.'

Sowden gave a snort. Pieces of timber were nailed to the tatty sides of the manager's chair to provide extra reinforcement, although Sowden appeared leaner since they'd last seen each other close up.

'I'm hoping to establish the Waybell abattoir in Darwin this year. In the beginning we'll only be slaughtering our own stock that are fat enough for market,' explained Ross.

Sowden nodded. 'That's keeping a handle on the supply chain. It's a good idea.'

'You'll be staying put, Sowden, while the round-up's on?' asked Ross.

'Yes, me and Annie and a few others.' He stopped picking at the raffia on the arms of the chair, aware a grudging reprieve had been granted.

'There's mail for you.' Ross passed the manager his letters. 'While I'm gone you'll be in charge. We need some extra supplies other than what came today and I want to make a start fencing the southwest boundary. I'll also be needing a carpenter.'

'Yes, of course.' Sowden gave what passed for a smile. 'You're staying then?'

'Whether I stay or not, the house needs work. You'll do as I ask,' stated Ross. It wasn't a request.

'I'll do as you say,' said Sowden. 'I ain't going anywhere.'

'No,' replied Ross. 'I didn't think you were.'

Ross chanced on Connor on his return to the house. The Scot was carrying a rifle, and a brace of bloody ducks hung from a shoulder.

'I would have come with you,' said Connor, his attention switching back and forth from Ross to Sowden's camp, where men were milling about starting to pile gear and line up the horses. 'What's the matter?'

Ross squinted into the sun. 'That camphor box was meant for my grandmother.'

'Aye. You heard from Darcey? I'm sorry. I shouldn't have done that, Ross. The second I addressed it to your wife I knew I shouldn't have done it, but –'

'It's bad enough that you're up here as my father's spy but to interfere in my personal business, well, that's something else entirely.'

Connor rested the stock of the rifle in the dirt. 'I'm not anyone's spy.'

'Who are you loyal to then, me or my father?'

'That's unfair,' Connor protested.

'Is it?' asked Ross.

'Aye, it is. This property belongs to your father. He pays our expenses, yours and mine.' He swung around, taking in the house and the camp. 'Everything. He should know exactly what's going on.'

'And it's *my* right to tell him, not yours,' said Ross. 'As long as we have that straight.'

'Then tell him we need a new manager, but you cannae fire Sowden and Mick. We need them, regardless of what's happened in the past.'

'Anything else?' asked Ross, electing not to share the knowledge he'd gleaned from Eustace for the time being. Connor no longer needed to know everything.

'Aye. You cannae live up here for the rest of your life when you have a wife in Adelaide. Unless your intention is to bring the poor woman here?' said Connor.

'Connor, I think you'd better stop talking before you and I have a serious misunderstanding.'

'Och, aye, it will be a serious misunderstanding, all right, if you dinnae come to your senses.'

'It will be more than that if you don't watch yourself, mate,' said Ross firmly. 'Because you'll be out of a job.'

The ultimatum took the wind out of Connor. He rested the rifle at the midpoint of his shoulder, letting the stillness open up between them. 'Anything else?'

'Yes,' said Ross. 'Tomorrow you'll leave for Darwin. I want you to investigate somewhere suitable for the abattoir and start arranging the construction of it, as well as buyers for Waybell's beef. I have a letter to be mailed to my grandmother and two telegrams to be sent. One is for my father requesting funds for the improvements. The other is to Marcus Holder. I trust you to handle these affairs for me, Connor. *Can* I rely on you?'

'Aye.' Connor shifted the rifle a little. 'Aye, I'll do as you ask. But I worry about what you might be getting yourself entangled in. You've knots in you, Ross, and for the life of me I dinnae know how to slice them out without ruining the board. I hope you know what you're doing.'

⋘ Chapter 27 ⋙

Ross stepped out the dimensions of the planned extra room, using the activity as a distraction to whittle away at his anger with Connor. 'Big enough, do you think?' he asked.

Maria silently observed his careful measurements from where she sat cross-legged, resting against the rear wall of the house. She was a plucking a magpie goose for their evening meal.

'It's for you,' he persevered. 'Your own room.'

Maria turned the bird in her lap, its long neck hanging slackly, and resumed removing the feathers.

'It won't be ready for a while. We need a carpenter first but while we're away doing the round-up, with luck Sowden will have found someone for the job.'

With her head bowed, Maria's fingers moved nimbly across the bird's body.

'Is everything all right?' he asked.

She finally spoke. 'It's different now.'

'Different?' Ross asked. 'Nothing's different.'

'The wet is over.' She brushed her palms together to clean them. 'The men are back. I see them look at me, as you look at me, but there is a difference, for they know I shouldn't be here.'

169

Ross squatted beside her. He'd been patient, trying to reassure Maria of the rightness of their relationship by not pressing her for more than she was willing to give. He'd not tried to share her bed since the night she'd fallen asleep, for he had other plans afoot and the mustering camps featured in them prominently. He intended on having Maria accompany him on the muster, for it was not unheard of for women to do so, and once they were away from the homestead, and with Connor in Darwin, there would be ample opportunity to strengthen what lay between them. 'You belong here. We decided on that.'

'*You* decided on it,' she corrected, folding the goose in a piece of wet cloth. 'I have to start cooking.'

Ross gripped her arm as she rose to leave. 'Don't you want to be here?'

'What do you think?' she asked. She touched his hand, tracing a vein that ran twisting and rounded, her fingers sticky. He looked at her and kept on looking. With that simple touch, he felt like tossing his hat into the air or lifting her skywards.

She stepped away. 'I saw you drink the rum after the mail came,' she confessed. 'I know you have troubles with your family. I understand.'

'That has nothing to do with us,' said Ross. 'This is ridiculous. In two days we leave for the muster and I want you to come with me.'

'I can't, I'm bound to Holder,' said Maria. 'I shouldn't have let things get so far between us, Ross. It was wrong of me and I'm sorry, but I need you to listen – I am bound to Mr Holder and nothing and no one can change that.'

'The girl's right.' Connor had appeared and was leaning against the chicken wire, his weight bulging the mesh to one side. 'You better ask Holder what he thinks of your arrangements before you get too carried away, Ross.'

'Holder? He can find himself another maid,' said Ross.

Connor looked at Maria. 'You should have told him the truth, lass.'

Maria adjusted the goose in her arms and didn't say anything.

'She's promised to him. Has been for over a year, according to Eustace.' Connor's voice took on a solemn tone. 'And I figure that a man who pays good money for a wife won't take lightly to having another man stealing his bride.'

A gust of wind scattered the goose feathers. They rolled across the ground. Ross felt numb.

'It must be true, Ross. What advantage is there for Eustace to lie about it?' continued Connor. 'He also said that Holder's not an understanding man and that he was surprised he'd not already come for her.'

Ross waited for Maria to refute Connor's claims. She shrugged, lifting her eyebrows in a slightly dismissive way, as if none of this was her fault, and he knew then that Connor was right. But he still couldn't accept it.

'Even if it is true, it's up to Maria to decide if she wants to stay here.'

'Are you even listening to the words coming out of your mouth, Ross? She belongs to him. He *paid* for her.'

'What are you talking about? You make it sound as if she was sold.'

'She was.'

Ross flinched. 'How is that possible?' He again waited for Maria to reply, but her expression was unchanged. 'Slavery's been abolished.' The term soured his tongue. 'If Holder's paid for her then he'll be out of pocket. I'd hardly let Maria go to such a cretin and I'm surprised you'd even consider it, Connor, you being such a man of honour. You'll be ready to leave with me, Maria, when we head out. No arguments.'

'Let her go, Ross.' Taking him by the arm, Connor steered Ross away from where Maria could hear. 'For heaven's sake you've been following the girl around like some lovesick boy for weeks. God knows the boredom of the last months would strike a man silly and I can't disagree she's a beauty. But it must end now. You're making a fool of yourself and it's not fair on her.'

'It would be best if you stayed out of this, Connor,' said Ross tersely.

'By the saints, look at her,' Connor persisted. 'Take a good look. Apart from the fact that she must be only seventeen or eighteen years of age, she's a half-caste with enough mixed blood to put her on the far side of white. The very far side.'

At that, Ross punched Connor in the face, the force of the blow driving the Scotsman backwards. He fell heavily, tearing the chicken wire from its nails and slipping down the sagging mesh to land on the ground.

'What's the matter with you?' Connor scrambled to his feet, rubbing his jaw, and the two men faced each other. 'Have you become so obsessed that you won't even listen to reason?'

'Reason?!' yelled Ross. 'This from the man who claimed to be my friend and then went behind my back?' Maria was still watching them. Ross would have liked to hit Connor again but instead forced himself to calm down, afraid of scaring her.

'Ross, dinnae do this.'

'This is none of your business,' said Ross.

'Have you forgotten? You're already married. Did you hear that, lass? *He's married.*'

He couldn't help himself. Ross swung at Connor again, striking the Scotsman twice.

Connor straightened up. Blood poured from his nose. There was a cut above his eye. He struck back, and Ross fell to the ground.

'What is the matter with you? You have everything. A grand family. A pretty Sassenach willing to stand by your side. A name to be proud of. I dinnae understand. Why must you fight everything and everyone, including your own destiny? You're a Grant. The descendant of a line that reaches back to the old country and beyond. You might not like me or your own blood-kin, and we mightn't always like you, but we're all on the same side, boy.'

'No, we're not,' said Ross. He glanced back over to Maria in time to see her running away, disappearing into the trees.

'There is no honour in this,' spat Connor. 'In any of it.'

172

❧ Chapter 28 ❧

Ross wondered where Maria could have gone. It was no time to be hiding out in the timber with the sun soon to set. He called to her again, imagining her crouching behind a tree screened by dense leaves, or doubling back to sneak unnoticed into the kitchen. There weren't many places to disappear around here, unless a person chose to step beyond the ring of trees into the woody heartland, and even then, they would need to be aware of where they were going and to keep their wits about them in order to stay alive.

He moved around the property carefully, slowly. Stopping to listen for any sounds, judging the minutes it would take to walk from one building to the next. Leaving Maria alone, giving her time to compose herself, was an option Ross only briefly considered. He refused to jeopardise their relationship by allowing her to wallow in the revelation that he was not a free man. And what was freedom anyway, except the ability to do as one wanted? Here on Waybell Station, where land was limitless and the only boundaries were the ones constructed by nature or men, independence reigned so totally that the restrictions of his old life appeared antiquated in comparison. Societal ranking, the allocation of tasks and the seasonal changes by which every-thing was measured formed the days and months, but there was no authority holding a person to account. Except for Connor. It was as Ross always imagined. The Northern Territory was a new world and Waybell Station his domain.

He finally came across her sitting behind the stables. She was staring sullenly up at the stone escarpment, the smell of manure, horse hair and grease settling around her. The girl seemed wrapped in a placenta of anger.

Ross sat down next to Maria, relieved at having finally found her but also annoyed that she'd hidden from him. 'I'm sorry. I should have told you about my wife.'

'Yes, you should have.'

'And you should have told me about this arrangement with Marcus Holder,' said Ross. 'A person can't buy another person. If that's the hold the man has over you then you should know that it's wrong. Illegal and wrong.'

'And your wife?' replied Maria. 'This woman you never mentioned? I suppose that's different?'

'Yes. Totally. It was wrong I ever married her,' said Ross. 'Let me explain to you how it happened. I didn't want it. I didn't want her.'

'And yet you're married.'

'Maria, please.'

'It doesn't matter how it happened. You still belong to your woman as I belong to Mr Holder. It can't be changed. None of it can.'

'Anything can be changed, Maria. It'll just take time to work things out,' he insisted. 'I've told Connor to send a telegram to Holder telling him that whatever tied the two of you together no longer stands.'

'It won't make any difference. The wet season is over. Mr Holder will come for me and, even if he didn't, you'd still be married.'

'But she's not here,' said Ross. 'Darcey isn't here.'

Maria looked up at the cliff as if an answer could be found within its fractured surface. 'She doesn't have to be. She's your wife on paper.'

Ross felt the girl's anger gradually become his own. It transformed the air around them until it became fraught and tight with the electricity of a coming storm. How could she be so righteous when her own secret remained unshared? Why would she care so much about Darcey when she lived hundreds of miles away and he never intended to see her again?

'You want me to be with you, even though you're married, and I'm bound to another? Would your wife agree to such a thing if she were me?' Maria continued. 'Or is it because I'm not a white woman that you believe a girl like me wouldn't care about your circumstances? That I should be grateful?'

'No, of course not.' His denial of what she insinuated was swift, however Ross couldn't be sure that some truth didn't lie at the heart of what she was implying. 'I'm sorry, Maria, I would never hurt you.'

'You just did.'

He took her hand in his, holding her until the outline of the cliff darkened and merged with the night. 'You *will* come on the muster?'

'Yes, I'll come.' There was sadness in her reply.

≈ Chapter 29 ≈

The gelding was black, a scrag of a horse brokered by Mick in exchange for tobacco from a pan-shackled miner. The Rum Jungle mine site to the northeast was so hollowed out by digging that Mick reckoned the hills in the area could topple at any time and the horse was the only treasure left there. Ross wasn't so sure. The animal trotted when it should have been cantering and galloped when it should have been walking. The consensus was the gelding had contracted walkabout disease at some stage and with death or madness the predictable outcome, the horse's survival deserved respect. Getting acquainted with each other took some doing, and they were only just coming to an understanding. It was six weeks since their leaving, for the muster had coincided with the gifting of the horse.

They were in the mid-north of the property, working in a set of yards that had required a week's worth of repairs before cattle could be mustered in, the younger animals branded and the older ones drafted off for sale.

Ross sat on the rangy gelding thirty feet from the yarded mob, gripping a stiff green-hide rope. He plied the cord between his fingers as he waited to rope another calf, thinking of the wasted nights in the camps. It should have been possible to enjoy the simple pleasure of Maria's company at mealtimes or when they rode through the bush together, but it wasn't, not when she was so clearly still upset with him. She refused to talk to him about his marriage, or about Holder and the question of slavery that the exchange of money signified, keeping instead to the mundane occurrences of camp life.

The cattle pushed back towards the rear of the yards, stamping the dirt, their heads quivering. The horse quickened to a trot and, lifting out of the saddle, Ross leant forward in the stirrups, the rope twirling above his head. Flinging out his right arm the hemp unfurled, the lasso landing around the neck of a large bull calf. Ross jerked on the hide as the gelding began to draw the animal out of the herd. Instantly, the bull kicked and snorted, pulling against the rope, moving from side to side. The horse staggered under the weight before regaining momentum. Ross concentrated on his mount's deliberate progress, and on the bull that strained against the tight leather around its neck. He yanked the animal closer to the upright post and railings of the branding ramp and the waiting men. Angling off to one side, Ross tugged on the greenhide rope until it rubbed against the post, taking up the tension.

Toby and JJ rushed forward. They pushed at the animal's rump and as it took a step forward they managed to get leg ropes around it, then Eustace and another ringer threw themselves at the beast, bringing it to the ground until it lay on its side.

'Be quick about it!' Eustace yelled, struggling to hold the young bull's head on the ground.

Ross backed his horse up and the rope tightened. The bull snorted and puffed.

JJ positioned the brand on the animal's rump. There was a brief smell of burning hair as he left the iron on just long enough for the Waybell $\mathcal{W}$ to leave a distinctive mark of ownership. Suddenly Ross's horse jerked and the young bull struggled. The hot iron slipped down onto Parker's hand as he was finishing castrating the animal and he called out in pain.

Ross rode forward to lessen the tension, and the lasso and leg ropes were removed simultaneously. As the men stepped clear, the neutered bull gave chase. Ross cantered across the yard, positioning the gelding between the calf and Parker. The animal veered away and the horse abruptly changed direction and then stopped. Ross felt something solid hit his leg and he was flung sideways, hitting the upright post of the branding ramp. The newly made steer ran back to the herd.

'You all right?' asked Eustace.

Ross clutched at his side as he dismounted. 'Just winded me.'

'At least you can stick a saddle,' replied Eustace, with a grin.

'A man can be killed if he's not on the ball,' said Parker to JJ, his voice strained. He poured water onto the burn on his hand. 'You never brand and castrate at the same time. Never.' He spat on the ground.

'Not my fault,' answered JJ. 'Boss give too much slack too quick.'

Parker's left hand was red and blistered.

'Blame Mick and this nag he gifted me,' said Ross gruffly, discounting his part in the incident.

Parker gave a single tug to his ear. 'He's not your typical Bronco type. Reckon Mick knows his horse-flesh though.'

They were losing the light. The sun was already low in the west, obscured by the timber fringing the grassland. JJ put out the branding fire, and rested the iron on the top of a fence post to cool. With difficulty, Ross placed a foot in the stirrup and managed to get up in the saddle. While his leg ached from the accident there was something not quite right with his breathing. He clutched at his side, doubting the tobacco Mick received for the trade merited the horse he now owned.

Above the trees a thin line of smoke indicated where their camp lay, situated a mile away near a muddy waterhole. For the past two weeks they'd spent the nights listening to the mobs of cattle thrashing through the scrub towards the water for a drink before they were finally mustered in. Ross rode across to where Parker waited for some of the other men. 'How's the hand?'

'Not too bad, Boss. I'll put some rendered beef fat on it. Won't slow me down.'

'Good. Is there any fresher water around here?' Although they sieved the sludge from the waterhole before boiling it and skimming the surface, it tasted very ordinary even with extra tea added.

'Not that I know of,' replied Parker. 'You can check with Mick but he's not likely to say anything. I came across a nice little hole a few years back but could never find it again. The blackfellas like to have a bit up their sleeve. They don't want us whiteys or our cattle fouling up every spot.'

To the northeast, lines of smoke drifted across the horizon. Woodlands, grasses, drying swamps. All were touched with the firestick. Each day showed fresh burnings as the heavy grasses of the wet were razed for new growth. Ross looked for the people who tended the land, the communities that struck out into areas where hundreds of square miles might be home to a single white man, rarely sighting anyone.

'Tomorrow we finish branding at this place, Boss.' Mick appeared by their side. 'Eustace and Toby and a couple of the other boys can start walking the sale bullocks back to the homestead paddock.'

'Righto.' Ross clutched his side again, his breath still troubling him.

'You all right, Boss?' asked Mick.

'I'm fine. You sure this horse is worth persisting with?'

'You'll take to each other, eventually,' Mick assured him.

'If he doesn't kill me first.'

'Might help if you name him,' Mick suggested.

There wasn't much point complaining about the horse. It had taken some handling to muster the cattle in over the last few days and more than a few had managed to escape, dashing into the scrub to disappear in the thick growth. After many weeks spent on the move Ross now knew how impossible it was to get a true count of the livestock running on Waybell. Were the holding properly fenced, then the practice of waiting until the herd walked to the closest waterhole for a drink would have made the process easier, but up here the stock could roam freely in any direction. The wildness of the livestock was not something Ross had anticipated. He was used to the domesticity of sheep and the comparative ease of walking the mobs on Gleneagle to the yards, where drafting races and a network of timber fencing allowed for easy handling. Here there were few yards and many miles between them.

'Harder than I thought to get a clean muster,' Ross said. He'd bided his time in admitting this and was prepared for a cutting reply.

Mick nodded. 'Tell Bill when you get back.'

He'd only uttered a few words, but they were sufficient in their brevity for Ross to understand that Mick and Sowden undoubtedly considered him ignorant.

'Where to next?' asked Ross as they followed one of the many tracks of trampled grass created by cattle and horses.

'We sit down for a couple of days,' Mick told him. 'And then go northeast. Eventually we'll cross the South Alligator River.'

'Shouldn't we get moving as soon as possible?'

'You're not in whitefella country now, Boss. Men want sit-down time. Have a feed. Rest the horses.'

'I want to get the steers to Darwin before the wet season starts,' said Ross.

'Plenty time, Boss.' He glanced skyward. 'Nice hot dry weather couple months yet. Besides, further north the country's still drying out. You still out here when the white apple starts to flower then you're in trouble.'

'Why's that?'

'That's when *gunumeleng* comes and the storms begin.'

'What month is that?' asked Ross.

'Your time, October or November. But white man's calendar no good out here. Some seasons last weeks, others a few months,' Mick told him.

'We have four seasons. When is winter up here?'

180

Mick chuckled through a sheen of perspiration. 'Now. Couldn't you tell?'

The splayed imprint of a buffalo was visible on the ground. The pawing of soft earth trailed off to the north, where occasionally, the dark forms of the beasts wandered on the very edge of the grassland.

'The buffalo like this part of Waybell, Mick?' asked Ross.

'Swampy ground good for them,' he replied. 'Not so good for cattle. Walkabout disease, pleuropneumonia, ticks. Better for buffalo than cows, Boss. Lose plenty through sickness.'

They reached the camp. Two tents, a handful of wurlies, pack-bags, mosquito netting and swags were scattered among the trees a few hundred feet from the muddy water. Ross slid from his horse on arrival, the movement setting up a series of pains that stretched ruthlessly down the length of his body.

'You better get the girl to tend you, Boss,' said Mick.

One of the younger Aboriginal boys took the reins to Ross's horse. He held up a dead brown snake, its back smashed to a pulp. The boy gave a justified look of satisfaction. Ross kept moving towards the tent, and once within, he fell heavily onto the bedroll, tossing aside one of Alastair's books.

Maria knelt between the canvas flaps. 'Mick said you were hurt. What happened?'

'Nothing. Leave me alone.'

'But maybe I can help,' she offered.

'You can't,' Ross replied sharply. Tree-thrown shadows wavered across the tent's fabric walls. He thought of Maria's unhappiness over the previous weeks. It had been impossible to reach her.

'You're angry with me.'

Ross rested an arm across his face. 'Tomorrow you're to start off with Eustace. They're driving the bullocks home.'

Maria shuffled a little further inside the tent. 'You want me to leave. Why?'

'It's for the best,' replied Ross. Whatever once connected them had now come undone, the shared attraction splintered by Connor's outspokenness and worn sharp by twin declarations of guilt. He'd thought of apologising again for what had transpired between them, but couldn't bring himself to relinquish any more ground.

Maria knelt at his side and began to undo the buttons on his shirt. Ross brushed away her probing hands but she persisted in her examination, noting the discolouration beginning to show on his skin.

'It hurts when you breathe?' she asked.

He winced. 'Yes. It feels like I've broken a rib.'

Wetting a cloth from a waterbag, Maria cleaned away the day's grime, working her way down his neck to the base of his throat and then across his chest. Ross observed her movements, closing his eyes at her touch. He'd missed her. Outside, men talked as they rode past the tents to where the horses would be unsaddled and left to roam for the night. They could hear squeaks of leather, the jangle of bits being removed and whinnying as hobble straps were connected.

Ross wondered what Maria was thinking. A tiny blood vessel was visible on her eyelid, pulsating gently. It meandered towards a brow that curved downwards like a waning moon. She wet the rag again, wrung the excess water out of it, and ran it across the curve of Ross's stomach, following the edge of his trousers. Ross's hand closed over her wrist.

'You've been avoiding me for days and now this?' he asked.

Maria sat back on her knees, her head tilting to one side. 'You told me to come with you and I did. If you want me to go, I'll do that too.'

Ross tightened his grip on her, pulling her towards him. Maria was forced to move nearer, the neckline of her blouse allowing a glimpse of flesh. Ross released her, but she didn't move away. They held each other with their eyes.

'Ahem, Boss, you in there?' asked Mick from outside.

Maria was at the tent-flap immediately. 'He needs a bandage.'

'Ribs?' queried Mick.

'Maybe broken or cracked,' asserted Maria. 'I can't be sure.'

'Well as long as he's not coughing up blood,' said Parker, joining Mick outside the tent. 'A few broken bones don't hurt anyone but a damaged lung, well, we don't have the learning for that.'

Toby was sent to fetch supplies from the medicine kit, and he made a fuss of searching for the right type of bandage when there were only two to choose from. Eventually it was decided that something stronger was needed, so they cut a piece of canvas into strips and left Maria to wind the sturdy fabric around Ross's ribcage.

Her hair brushed his shoulder. 'I don't know what to do,' she whispered. 'I'm caught. You do understand, don't you?'

He cupped her cheek with his hand. 'I only know that I can't let you go.'

Maria tied the ends of the cloth. 'But you have a wife and Holder purchased me as his. These things are unchanged.' She sat back on her haunches, and then squirrelled about until her chin rested on her knees, her arms drawn tightly about her legs.

'Frankly, I'm having difficulty even imagining that possible,' said Ross.

'What, that a man was willing to pay for me? He has land. It's an opportunity. And what about your wife?'

Ross smelt pine on the breeze as the fires were stoked to repel the gathering mosquitoes. He didn't have a clue where to start or what to say. He wished he was like Alastair with his witty remarks and surety of position, however he was just a younger son with a dead twin brother and an older brother presumed deceased.

It was easy to think about what he wanted, to have a plan, to pitch the word *annulment* around in his brain, as if by repetition it would take root and grow into certainty. Except the consequences weren't guaranteed. If he deserted Darcey, Ross knew he would surely be estranged from his family. It was at this very moment he understood how hopelessly dependent he was on his people, for hadn't the years already proved that he'd not been enough, for his family or his friends? Nor would Darcey have ever set after him if not for the Grant wealth and name. This tore at Ross, for if he'd ever wanted to be considered as more than merely adequate, it was right now. He wanted Maria, but to have her properly, honourably, he needed to leave Darcey.

Maria shifted uncomfortably, her teeth biting into her lower lip.

'I care about you, Maria. You know that. But if I didn't own Waybell, if I came to you with empty hands, would I be enough? Enough for you to choose me instead of Holder?'

'So you don't love her?' replied Maria.

'Darcey was my brother's fiancée. I told you that Alastair disappeared in France during the war and is presumed dead. I would have fought but it was decided that I should stay at home.' He waited to see her response.

'You may not have returned either if you'd joined up,' she said.

There was no recrimination from her. Ross's relief was overwhelming. 'Better to have gone, I think. That's the thing about war. Everyone hates it. The death, the injuries, the sadness, but they hate a person more for not being involved, for not sharing the pain that so many others endured.' There was no way of altering the fact that his exclusion from battle made him an outlier. Even if time helped people forget, Ross never would.

'And your wife?' asked Maria.

'My family threatened to cut me off if I didn't marry Darcey. It was never consummated. The marriage,' Ross added.

At this Maria's nostrils flared ever so slightly. She studied his face as if seeing him for the first time. 'You did it for the money?'

'I did it for many reasons,' he answered truthfully. 'But yes, I didn't want to be cut off.'

'People do different things for money, perhaps yours is the least cruel.' Maria played with the rag, trailing it in the dirt until the sand was patterned with circles. 'I didn't choose Mr Holder. He was chosen for me by my uncle.' A slight line creased the space between her eyes. 'I haven't lain with any man. Ever. That's where my value lies for men such as my uncle and for Mr Holder. Men pay for the privilege, Ross. Mr Holder paid.'

'Your uncle should be gaoled and as for Holder . . .'

'Don't, please, Ross. You don't understand where I've come from.'

Beyond the tent came the sounds of the camp gathering around the evening fires. Soon their conversation would end with the bringing of food, the daylight noises replaced with the rustling and scratching of creatures and the intermittent bellowing of old bulls wandering in the scrub searching for the herd.

'Maria? Tell me about yourself.'

She concentrated on the tent's fabric, the cloth moving ever so slightly in the breeze. 'My grandfather came from the islands to hunt the trepang. It's said that he took a woman without her wanting and whispered to her beneath the mangroves, leaving her with child. A girl who would one day become my mother. He came back to hunt for many seasons and when my mother was old enough, although it was forbidden, she would watch for their boats with the large triangular sails. She helped him as a young child when the men came ashore. They would gather the wood to boil the sea cucumbers then lay them out to be smoked over a fire.'

'And your father?' asked Ross.

'I don't know. A Chinese woman, Lu Zhi, who was once a concubine, took my mother in and taught her many things. My mother belonged to no one, but in not belonging she also became no one, neither white, black nor Islander. The old concubine knew that and so did men. They gave Lu Zhi pearl shell and tobacco to lie with my mother. And then I was born.'

'Where's your mother now?' asked Ross.

'She died when I was young. Lu Zhi raised me. She told me that her mother sold her in exchange for a piece of pork and a bag of rice in China so that Lu Zhi could have a better life here. When Lu Zhi eventually died, a man arrived to claim me. He said he was my uncle and that he could buy me a better life.'

'And you believed him?'

'I doubted he was family, but it didn't matter. All I understood was that Lu Zhi was a concubine. A wife but of lesser standing. She joked that she was a gold widow, but when her husband did eventually die in a mine she was cast out and forced to make her own way. Holder offered marriage. Better to be married, I think, than a concubine to be thrown away.'

'But, Maria, it's wrong.'

Maria briefly held her forehead. 'I don't expect you to understand. You're white. You have everything.' There was a dull edge to her voice. 'When you ask me if I would take you as you are with nothing, first you must ask yourself that question. You've never been without money. I wouldn't give up such things for anyone and neither should you. In the end you would hate me for it.'

'Never. Anyway we'd never be poor, Maria. I promise you that,' said Ross.

'Perhaps not. But I'd still be your concubine. Not your wife.'

'I'll work something out. It won't be like this forever.'

'You should eat,' said Maria. 'I'll get us some food.'

'And you'll stay with me tonight?'

'No. It would cause trouble.' Maria got to her feet.

'It doesn't matter who knows about us or who doesn't. Who would care out here, anyway? I mean, look at Sowden.'

'Apart from your wife and Holder?' Maria crawled out the tent's entrance before turning back to face him. 'We haven't done anything to be ashamed of, but if we did, eventually you would care, Ross. You would care the most.'

⋘ Chapter 30 ⋙

Wallabies bounded from their path as the stockmen flanked the rushing cattle. Five wild bulls were leading the stampede. They'd broken down the wooden yards during the night, and Ross and his men were still trying to gather up the remaining escapees. Now only this mob remained and, at the head, five of the canniest beasts he'd ever seen. To his left, Ross caught sight of Mick weaving between the trees, closing in on the lead. Shafts of daylight highlighted tawny hides as the cattle bashed through the timber, the dust kicking up in their wake.

Ross ducked beneath branches with curled and yellowing leaves, trying not to feel the pain from his injured rib. The gelding cleared a fallen log and landed heavily but was quick to take up the chase. Ross swiped at a sticky spider web in his path as the sun sent spiralling shafts of light through the densely wooded area. He caught another glimpse of Mick as the barrel of the stockman's rifle glinted. Two echoing shots rang out. The lead bull changed direction, the herd following in a swift arc.

Ross drew level with Parker and Mick, and the three of them raced on, zigzagging madly through the trees. The mob ahead of them suddenly broke apart and one of the bulls turned back, spearing through the cows that were bringing up the rear. Mick aimed and fired, and this time the bullet found its mark. Sheer momentum kept the animal moving for a few more feet before it dropped to the ground. Mick drew to a standstill and let out a loud coo-ee.

'What's the matter?' Ross slowed and patted the gelding, who'd managed to obey most of his commands.

'No good following them anymore, Boss,' replied Mick.

Ross had been keen to at least shoot the renegade bulls so they wouldn't have the same trouble next year, but deferred to Mick and reluctantly agreed. Around them red, bell-shaped flowers grew from stubby, bare branches. They were on the northeasterly edge of the station, and with their progression to this last mustering camp it was as if the weather was turning against them. The days were intensely hot with little breeze and only the scarcest scattering of cloud. A few weeks earlier Ross had been in no rush to return to the homestead but now even he admitted that *gurrung*, the hot, dry weather season, was a testing time.

'This lot sure had a scatter on, Mick,' Ross remarked, as the other stockmen caught up with them and they headed back towards the yards.

'Cattle don't like being bothered,' Mick explained. 'One of the other tribe's been here.'

'So the mob was disturbed before we even arrived.' Ross thought of the bullocks that could well be wandering outside the borders of the property. He'd counted roughly eighteen prime ones over the last few days that hadn't made it into the yards. 'I guess they'll be doing a bit of hunting as well, eh?' He didn't expect a reply.

Smoke haze filled the eastern sky as Ross counted out the last of the cattle from the yards. He recorded the tally in a notebook with a stub-nosed pencil and then added each page together. Since the commencement of mustering, an extra eight hundred head had been rounded up and branded, but Connor was right. Proving theft was impossible.

He dragged the gate closed across cracking soil. The top railing broke off at one end, falling to the ground, and Ross kicked at the piece of timber. The gathering-in was finished for the season.

'We save working on these yards for next time we're here.' Mick stood with hands on his hips. 'Better we head back home now and get the rest of the sale bullocks organised.'

Ross made a note of the yard needing repair and sketched their position. Later, he would transcribe the descriptions into his journal and, with Mick's help, pinpoint their location on the map he carried. As he was marking the rocky plateau overlooking the yards he noticed a thin column of irregular puffs of smoke rising into the air. 'What are they talking about today?' he asked Mick.

'Long time since whitefella Boss been around,' Mick replied. 'They're telling their people to keep away from waterholes while we're here.'

'A bit late for that as we're about to leave,' said Ross. Behind them, an answering column appeared from somewhere in the dry woodlands.

'They're also saying another white stockman has come. The red-haired one.'

'Eustace? They're saying that now?' clarified Ross.

'No. A couple of days ago they said Eustace was coming back from driving those sale bullocks home,' Mick told him.

'Why didn't you tell me?' asked Ross.

Mick swung up onto the back of his horse. 'You didn't ask.'

'It'd be helpful if you'd just tell me these things as soon as you know about them.'

'Sometimes it's better to work a few things out for yourself.'

They came upon the rest of the stockmen slaughtering the shot bull. The beast's throat was cut and its testes had been removed, a large pool of dark blood staining the earth. Flies lifted and settled across men, animal and blood. Parker watched from nearby, a twig in his mouth, which moved from left to right as Toby separated the hide from flesh. Keeping the cutting edge of the knife turned towards the pelt at a slight angle he pulled at the skin while slicing, revealing a layer of white fat.

'Be a bit tough, won't it, after all that charging about?' commented Ross.

Down south, the animal would have been strung up in a tree so the blood could drain and the meat could stretch, but in this heat it wouldn't take long for the beef to rot.

Toby sliced into the bull's rump and removed two large chunks of dark red meat. 'It'll be good, Boss.' He then addressed the carcass, wiping the blade on his trousers. 'Thanks, mate. We'll leave you in peace now.'

Parker and the other stockmen mounted up and rode away. 'Any fresh waterholes around here, Mick?' asked Ross.

'Plenty water nearby.'

After Parker's revelation, Ross had made a point of talking to everyone about the possibility of permanent watering places at each new area they came to. None of the Aboriginal stockmen were forthcoming with information, simply saying that there was not much water around at that time of year. And Parker and Eustace, having depended on Mick's knowledge from the very beginning of their employment on the property, were of little help. This time, however, Mick was happy to oblige and they headed in a different direction to the rest of the men. They crossed a creek torn into deep channels. Debris from previous floods was piled high in the trees and the timber on the ground was dry-rotted and plastered with mud.

'How far back to the homestead?' asked Ross.

'Thirty mile as the crow flies,' Mick told him. 'Shouldn't be any problems travelling. All the country will be bone dry.'

They rode on through patches of timber where branches were devoid of leaves. The abundance of the wet season had been replaced with a land made barren by scorching heat. There were few birdcalls during the day now and the scuttling, slithering creatures of previous months, which at times made the country and sky merge with movement, were also gone.

Mick circumnavigated a paperbark swamp and led Ross to a stand of trees with odd-looking bulges protruding from their lower trunks.

'Bring your waterbag,' Mick instructed, collecting his own as he dismounted. 'And pannikin.'

Unhitching the tin mug and the canvas bag from his saddle, Ross joined Mick at one of the trees.

Mick tore away the outer bark and stabbed and prised at the swelling with his pocketknife. Water squirted out and he turned to Ross with a quick, pleased smile. They collected it into their pannikins, drinking quickly, and then took it in turns to fill their bags at another tree. Ross patted the trunk as the slightly discoloured fluid wept down the bark. They'd cut into the heart of the plant and drunk from its centre.

'Good for us,' said Mick. 'But for the tree it could be a year or more before it can give water again. There is always a time when blackfella and whitefella are more desperate. You ever get lost, Boss, you know one way to get a drink.'

Heat shimmered off the dried mud that stretched inwards to the remaining swamp water. Scratch marks were visible in the mud where wallabies had come to claw for morsels in the still-moist soil or graze on the fine grasses at the edge. A handful of ducks floated through the swamp's remnants. Ross would never have imagined that he'd find himself wanting to see those dense clouds that foretold weeks of lethargy and idleness. The wet season stretched a man's limits, or so he'd thought, until the dry season arrived.

'You said it's too wet up here in the north for cattle. Maybe we should let the buffalo have the run of things and hunt them instead. One day we might even be able to sell their meat,' considered Ross.

'Sure,' said Mick.

'Eustace said your father was a king,' Ross commented after a pause.

'No. My father was chief.'

'I didn't mean to offend.'

'You can't insult if you don't know better,' replied Mick.

'And you aren't a chief.'

'No, Boss. I'm not like you.'

Ross wondered if he and Mick weren't more similar than each other realised, but then cast the idea aside. Mick appeared to have a very strong sense of his place in the world.

Clear of the timber, Ross took a last look to the east where a rocky outcrop rose like a giant wall above the treetops. It was rugged landscape, with jagged upturned ridges rising from the plains to shadow the earth below. There were few pastoral leases that Ross knew of on the other side, except for a couple in the north bordered by rivers. Ross indicated towards the stone country. 'Have you been there, Mick?'

'Long time ago. You go through the hole in the rock, then across the plain to the East Alligator River to where the men speak something different.'

'What's it like?'

'The place is full of water, crocodiles, blackfellas and buffalo. Not whitefella land, that's for sure,' said Mick.

'You do know that telling a whitefella that only makes him want to see it more.'

Mick chuckled. 'You've got things to do first, Boss, like giving that horse of yours a name.'

Ross tweaked the gelding's ear. The horse remained a sorry excuse for an animal with its moth-bitten tail that refused to grow and a frame that belonged to an emaciated pony. 'I'll call him Nugget,' he said finally, 'and hope he turns into a chunk of gold.'

❧ Chapter 31 ❧

On their return to the camp, Ross and Mick went their separate ways. Maria met Ross at his tent. In her hands she held Alastair's books. Some of the covers were torn and a few pages were lying in the dirt.

'Your stories,' she said.

Ross accepted the novels. 'What happened?'

'You left them outside. Two of the boys found them and they got into a fight.'

Not far away, children were running back and forth, snorting and bellowing, then falling over as if shot.

'Do you want to speak to them?' asked Maria.

Ross shook his head, remembering his own boyhood. 'No.'

'It's good we're going tomorrow.'

The camp was dusty and hot, the air filled with the acrid stench of dying fish in a nearby muddy billabong, that had formed in a tributary of the South Alligator River.

'You'll be pleased to get back to the house, won't you?'

It was a long time to expect a woman to camp out rough, not that Maria had complained.

'I'm used to it now,' she answered.

Toby appeared at Ross's side with their horses. 'Boss, we shoot the buffalo that's stuck?'

They mounted up and Ross followed him to the edge of the water-course, where a mud-covered beast had struggled into the sludge, desperate for water, and become bogged. The old cow thrashed and bellowed at their approach. Ross dismounted and, rifle in hand, walked out across the cracked surface, testing the dried shell of the bed as he moved forwards. He loaded the rifle, pointed and fired. The beast slumped.

'Good feed for a crocodile,' commented Toby. 'There be one old fella here. Buried somewhere in the mud waiting.'

'G'day, Boss.' They turned to see Eustace riding towards them.

'Eustace, what took you so long?' Ross called. 'It's weeks since you left with the bullocks.'

The lack of a friendly welcome did nothing to dispel the red-head's grin. 'The Scotsman was there,' he replied. 'And the carpenter. It's a whirl of cattle and flying woodchips. The place has never seen so many comings and goings. It's like a regular circus. You'll be impressed, real impressed, Boss. They've even made a start on the western boundary. Connor got some Chinese in to help.'

'And the bullocks are on their way to Darwin?' asked Ross.

'Sure thing. We lost a few head along the way. Some of those real fat ones went for a gallop and the heat got to them.'

'They were plenty fat,' Toby agreed.

'Connor sold some to Vesty's meatworks.' Eustace sat a little straighter in the saddle. 'The rest are going to be slaughtered at the Waybell Station abattoirs.'

The pride in Eustace's voice matched Ross's own sense of accomplishment. 'That is news,' he commented. 'Very good news.'

On the way back to camp Eustace told them more about the carpenter, an Irishman named Brian Walsh who, by the red-headed stockman's description, was adept at entertaining everyone with his ribald yarns and spluttering laughter.

Ross looked forward to meeting the builder. As for Connor, he remained undecided. They'd parted on bad terms and though he may have proved himself capable of handling the business assigned to him, Ross wasn't ready to forgive him for the trouble he'd caused with Maria.

'This is for you, Boss.' Eustace handed him an envelope, which he immediately opened. The note was from Connor. Marcus Holder had been struck down with an illness last year and, although alive, was poorly. Ross crumpled the paper. Connor might yet redeem himself.

That evening they ate the fresh beef with damper. The camp was in high spirits with the thought of heading home and Ross sat cross-legged, drinking tea and enjoying hearing the men relive the stories from the muster.

'Here's to the boss,' said Parker, lifting a mug. 'We've done more this season than we have since I arrived on the station. Although I don't mind telling you all that I've seen enough of an axe for a while.'

'And I missed half of it,' complained Eustace. 'Which is okay by me, 'cause if ever one of us has to go to gaol, Parker, it'll have to be you as you've had so much practice with woodworking now.' He gave an amused laugh and, in return, Parker shoved him in the side so that he fell backwards onto the ground.

'It's getting late,' Ross reminded them. 'And we've an early start.'

The men discussed the packing up of the camp and once this was done, the conversation began to dwindle. Gradually the stockmen finished their tea and walked to their respective tents, leaving Ross alone with Maria. It was one of the few nights during the past months that they'd been by themselves at the end of the day, as Maria usually retired to her tent early. She'd rarely ventured beyond the established ranks of boss and domestic. Ross was certain it made no difference to what the men undoubtedly already assumed. Darkness hid many things, including the truth about who was sleeping with whom, even if it was only taking place in the imagination.

In the night sky, stars appeared in an arc following the earth's curve. Ross chose to hold off on sharing the news of Holder's illness. Their conversations regarding the man never ended well and tonight he wanted to simply enjoy Maria's company.

'You're sad about your ruined books, aren't you?' asked Maria.

'There's only a few that were spoiled. It's a pity, though. I like reading,' replied Ross. 'Especially in the wet season.' He threw buffalo dung on the fire to keep the mosquitoes at bay.

'Yes, but I saw the inscriptions,' she persisted. 'They belonged to your brother.'

'They were his favourite,' confessed Ross. 'He read them when he was young. Alastair used to pretend he was Hercules.' When Maria didn't respond he explained a little more. 'He was a Roman god known for his strength and adventures.'

'Men are just men,' said Maria flatly. 'They're not heroes.'

'He was a boy at the time.' Ross felt annoyed at having to justify his brother's juvenile fantasy. 'A child, really.' He poured the cold tea from the pannikin onto the dirt. Alastair's childhood games had altered their lives. *The Twelve Labours of Hercules*, an ancient tale of epic proportions, had been converted by the power of invention into a simple listing. An itemising of tasks, which ultimately carried them beyond innocent scheming into utter disaster.

'So why do you keep them, after everything he's done to you?' asked Maria. 'He went to war, when you could not. He shamed you all and then you were forced to take his woman.' Maria made a clicking sound of disapproval. 'You told me this, Ross.'

'I don't need to be reminded.'

Impulse had driven him to Alastair's room the morning he'd left Adelaide for Waybell. Ross wanted those books. He needed some small piece from the past. A shred of what had existed before everything unravelled. Contained within those pages were his dreams of a perfect older sibling. 'He's still my brother, Maria.'

'And when he went to war did he become a hero?'

'Briefly, yes.' And Ross would never forgive Alastair for that. For being better than him, for going to war and becoming the champion he once dreamt of.

'And he's dead?' asked Maria.

'Yes. I think he is. There's no other explanation.'

'The Chinese believe that after death the body is devoured by the earth and becomes part of the soil. That's why many Chinese want to be returned to the village of their birth so they can be reunited with the soil they came from. It would be the same for your brother. Maybe that is his punishment for what he did. No one knows where he is and so he can never be returned home. He will never be happy again. You should throw away his books. He's not worthy.'

Ross shook his head. 'I couldn't do that.'

'Why? Is it because it's like he's still alive when you read them?' asked Maria.

'Yes, I suppose.'

'See, that bright star?' Maria pointed. 'It's called Altair, *Qiān Niú Xīng*. It means *cowherd star*. The cowherd was in love with a weaver girl and they had two children. But they were separated from each other by what your people call the Milky Way. The father and children were on one side, the woman on the other. They are only permitted to meet once a year, when magpies form a bridge to allow them to cross the Milky Way.'

'Did the concubine teach you that?' Ross was pleased to be distracted from the subject of his brother.

'I wouldn't have any learning if it weren't for her. I like the stars. They tell their own stories and you don't need to carry the words in a book. They are there waiting. You only have to look up.'

A long howl carried towards them in the dark. It was answered by a much closer short bark.

'Dingos,' explained Ross. 'They've come to eat that dead bull.'

With the camp bedded for the night, Ross moved closer, tentatively placing an arm around Maria's shoulders. 'We could have been doing this every night, Maria.' He turned towards her, feeling the quickening of her breath. He pulled her hard against his body as they kissed. 'We *will* be together,' he murmured. 'We're meant to be together.'

'But nothing's changed.'

'Yes, it has. Connor wrote to me,' said Ross. 'Holder's been very ill. He may not recover.' He waited for a response from her. For he'd thought she'd be pleased at the chance of being released from Holder without intervention. 'Maria, what are you thinking about?'

In the blackness her finger stroked his cheek. 'You speak so angrily about Mr Holder and the money he paid in exchange for a wife and yet to me it isn't so bad, not when I think about Lu Zhi and what it meant to be *qie*.'

'And what is *qie*?' The spot where Maria had touched his skin went cold.

'A concubine. A female slave. And that's what I would become were I to be your lover, your mistress. I would have no rights. I'd be no better than Lu Zhi or my mother. I'd be nothing.'

'But we'd have each other, Maria.' He held her in his arms beneath the stars. 'I love you.'

'I know.'

'I'll work something out. I promise.'

≈ Chapter 32 ≈

The musterers' return to the homestead was met with enthusi-asm. The camp children, led by Little Bill, raced to greet the men, and the women who'd accompanied them during the months away, while Connor, standing next to Sowden and Annie, waited patiently.

'You're back then and all's well?' asked Sowden, as Ross helped Maria from her horse.

'You go in, Maria. I'll be there shortly.'

She squeezed his fingers. Ross watched her walk towards the house before replying. 'Yes. We found an extra eight hundred head of cattle. Mick can fill you in on the details.'

'Are you sure you can trust him to tell me the truth?' asked Sowden sarcastically.

Ross decided against starting an argument with him. 'I would hope so,' he replied.

Sowden had appeared ready to retaliate, but instead settled on levelling his gaze at Ross as if trying to understand the calmness of his response. Perhaps sensing that it would be wise to end the interaction, Annie called over to where the camp's occupants were crowded around the returning stockmen with their strings of horses. Two men came forward and carried Sowden away.

'I hear the abattoirs is a going concern,' Ross said to Connor.

'Aye. There'll be no shortage of Waybell steaks in Darwin.'

'Good.'

Connor took the reins of Ross and Maria's horses. 'It's good to see you, Ross,' he called out as he walked towards the stables. 'I see you've kept the fine piece of horse-flesh Mick selected.'

'Nugget. The gelding's name is Nugget.'

'Clearly a great deal of thought went into that.'

'Connor?'

The Scotsman turned, his expression wary. 'Aye?'

'I wanted to thank you for getting the slaughterhouse operational so quickly.'

'You dinnae need to thank me for doing my job. But I'm pleased you did,' he added with a smile.

'You better see to those horses,' said Ross, trying to sound authoritative but failing at the sight of Connor's cheeky grin.

He found Maria in the newly constructed room he'd promised her prior to their leaving. Brian the carpenter had done an excellent job. Ross closed the door, lifted her in his arms and sat her on the bed, and together they lay down on the narrow cot face-to-face.

'Do you like it?'

'Oh, yes. No one's slept in here before?'

'No,' said Ross. 'You're the very first.'

'Imagine that.'

'Sowden's old bedroom is now my office and through it is my room.'

'A bedroom each,' said Maria.

'Not for long.'

Maria's face grew crimson. She sat up abruptly. 'Ross, I –'

'I know what you said, Maria.' He ran his hands along her shoulders and down her forearms. The sweat of his palms stuck to the material of her blouse as he pulled the shirt free of the waistband of the trousers she wore. He expected her to stop him, but she

200

watched mesmerised as if she couldn't quite believe what he was doing, what she was letting him do. Beneath her chemise her skin was damp. Ross lifted the material and lowered his head to her breast. He grew muddled-headed by the scent of her, and when he finally looked at her again he was laying on top of her and her eyes were glazed. He reached down to where the tops of her thighs met, his fingers searching for buttons to undo.

'Boss, we out here. Mick sent us,' a woman called.

'Damn it.' Ross pushed hair back from his face, waiting until Maria had leapt to stand behind the door so that when it opened no one would see her.

'Yes? What do you want?' he asked, leaving the bedroom and closing the door behind him. Five women were standing in the dining room.

'Sorry, Boss. Mick sent us. I'm Becky. We cook and clean for you from now on. You have any trouble then you come to Becky first. I fix things.'

'Great,' Ross said, with annoyance. 'Thank you.'

The women giggled. 'We'll cook up a plenty big supper for you and the missus, eh?'

'The missus?' repeated Ross, finally concentrating on what the woman was saying. 'No. Maria is my cook.'

'Then we help,' said Becky. The women giggled again and then left.

He opened the bedroom door, but the space was empty, and the window was wide open.

Ross stood in the sleep-out as the sun struggled through the clouds. The beds were stacked in a corner, and the wire netting was gone, partially replaced by a wall of lattice work. Eventually there would be a proper doorway to match the new fixtures inside the homestead, as well as gauze to keep out the insects and glass for the windows in the two new bedrooms at either end of the house. Connor now slept in the men's quarters in a room of his own. The line of credit extended by his father was generous and Brian, the carpenter, who'd already departed, was keen to come back in the new year to keep working on the homestead once the dry season arrived.

In the few days since their return he'd sorted through the mail that had been delivered in his absence and, after having dutifully responded to his grandmother's many letters, Ross could feel a loosening of the ties binding him to the South. Apart from his mother, everyone else enjoyed good health and, other than ensuring his father's financial support was guaranteed, that was as much as Ross needed to know. Darcey's letters he left unread. Ross hoped that his lack of communication might make her reconsider her position, and he was beginning to formulate a plan. Surely another marriage would suit her better and Ross would be happy to assist.

Maria came into view. Little Bill was at her side, drawing a branch along the ground. He ran off towards the chicken roost and, kicking off her shoes and lifting her skirt, Maria followed the boy, dirt flicking up onto her bare legs. She'd kept away from Ross the last few days since their brief time together in the bedroom and he considered he may well have frightened her with the strength of his passion. But had she not been willing?

'Boss, we clean here.' Becky was waiting with a broom in hand, and Ross retreated to the veranda. He'd organised to go out riding with Connor to exercise their horses, and set about getting ready to leave.

The women had arrived, arguing among themselves who would be the one to give out orders, and had then set to rights what Ross considered a perfectly tidy home. Confronted with this feminine onslaught, he left the housekeeping routine to Maria to sort through. He figured the arrangement to be a simple one and Maria proved quick to delegate and then disappear into the bush, or retreat into her newly built bedroom. Little Bill remained one of the few people from the camp that Maria bothered speaking with beyond giving instructions.

The women continued sweeping out rooms and washing floors, arguing and laughing as they went about their tasks. The young women giggled if they caught sight of Ross seeking peace in the stables with Nugget, while Eustace only laughed when Ross complained about the intrusion. And Mick, such a frequent visitor during the first wet season, now only appeared after dark. Connor spoke of the benefit of everyone getting along, and the tentative peace between them that they'd forged on meeting again meant much to Ross. He hoped the Scotsman had learnt from his meddling.

'Ross?'

Maria returned from the chicken shed, drawing nearer to him as he sat on the top step of the veranda pulling on his boots.

'I have to go, Maria, Connor's waiting for me. And it's best I leave now before Becky comes out here and complains about me dirtying her clean floor.'

'Ross.' She looked demurely at the ground.

'What?' asked Ross, clamping a hat on his head.

'You're angry with me.'

Ross checked his belt, making sure the pocketknife was attached in its leather case. 'You've been avoiding me.'

'I . . . yes, I have,' she admitted.

'You'll have to make up your mind about what you want, because I won't put up with your childish games.' He took the stockwhip down from the nail on the wall.

Maria reached out and squeezed his hand. 'I'm scared.'

There it was. That little sign of interest. How was it that Maria knew exactly when to reach out to him?

'And I'm late,' said Ross, ignoring the quickening of his pulse. He stood and walked away.

Maria caught up with him at the edge of the yard, where a small pile of cut cypress timber lay waiting for the carpenter's return. She caught his hand and then stood on the stacked wood so that for once they were of similar height.

'What?' said Ross. 'You know I'm busy.'

'Do you think this is easy for me? It's different for men. They take what they want and then leave. For some, everything is a right.' Maria stood on her tiptoes, holding onto Ross's shoulder for balance. 'I know who you are, Ross, and I wish I didn't, for a part of me also hates you for making me want you, for being prepared to be the person I swore I'd never become. So you must promise me that you'll keep me from Mr Holder and that you'll find a way to be rid of your wife so that what we have can be made legal one day.'

'What are you saying?'

Her mouth was soft as she kissed him on the lips. 'That I'll be yours. That I'll wait for you to come to me tonight.' She jumped from the stack of timber and walked away.

Ross looked about to see if anyone had seen them. Washing fluttered on a line strung from the corner of the house to a tree. One of Sowden's dogs lay asleep in the dirt. A chicken gave an egg-laying cackle. Ross was struck by the sameness of things.

He walked across to the stables where Connor waited with their horses. The Scotsman gave him a knowing look.

'Now what's happened? I suppose it's the girl?'

Ross didn't respond. Not one hostile word had passed between them since his return from the muster and Ross was determined to maintain peace. He tightened the girth strap, placed a boot in the stirrup and swung his leg over the saddle. His hands gripped Nugget's reins.

'It must be hard to have such a pretty thing dangled in front of you every day. I suggest a trip to Darwin, mate,' said Connor. 'A man can't live on bread alone.'

'And did you find something to go with your bread?' asked Ross lightly.

'I did,' replied Connor, the corner of his eyes crinkling as he smiled.

Ross knew Connor would think him strange were he ever to discover that he'd never lain with a woman. But it seemed that part of his life was about to change. He clucked the gelding into a trot and began to whistle a tune.

'You're in a grand mood this morning,' Connor observed.

'And why not? It's as fine a day as I can remember.'

'Is it now?' Connor looked at him with interest.

Changing the subject, Ross remarked on the reduced size of the billabong. The country waited for rain.

'So are you sending me away to Darwin again next year?' asked Connor. 'I'd rather like to go on the muster.'

'It won't be like this season was,' Ross told him. 'I don't intend to stay away for months on end. We'll plan it and do one or two mustering camps at a time and come back to the homestead in between. It's only when we head to the far north of the station that distance obliges us to stay out there and get the job done. Besides, I want to keep an eye on the carpenter and those Chinese fencing contractors. And I was thinking that we should sink a couple of new bores in the far south.'

'And the Darwin abattoir?' asked Connor.

'We'll have to pay it a visit, yes,' answered Ross. 'There'll be time. The only reason we were away for so long this year was because of the yards that needed to be built.'

'You kept a good eye on everyone as well,' commented Connor.

'And after the year's results I'll keep my counsel and see what else we can catch with our nets, come mustering time,' Ross explained.

'I was surprised to return and find Sowden still here,' said Connor. 'Knowing how convinced you were of their shenanigans.'

'Annie is Mick's sister,' said Ross.

'Really? I didnae expect that. What a tight little ruling party we have. I can understand why you decided against Sowden leaving.'

Ross's palm brushed the tops of tall grass. 'It's tough country to manage. But with that escarpment in the east and the Mary River to the west forming natural boundaries, the losses can't simply be put down to a lack of proper infrastructure.' He was no longer the novice pretending to understand this new environment, but nor did he doubt that there was far more to learn in the years ahead.

'It's not all Sowden's fault then?'

'No, it's not. The country's too wet in the north for cattle. We'll have to try and keep that enterprise in the south and look at hunting buffalo in the north.'

'Really?' said Connor.

'Yes. Really.'

Behind them the snap of twigs alerted them to Toby's arrival. 'Hey, Boss. You come now, eh? Visitors at the big house.'

'A bit early for a caller, isn't it?' answered Connor.

The three men turned their horses in the direction of the homestead.

'Who is it?' asked Ross. Although he had a terrible suspicion.

'It's Mr Holder, Boss,' answered Toby warily. 'He said he's come for his bride.'

⋘ Chapter 33 ⋙

Ross would have preferred to have told Marcus Holder to be on his way. Instead, he was obliged to be civil to his neighbour, inviting the man inside his home, where tea was offered along with damper spread with honey from the native sugarbags.

'Good to meet you, Grant,' said Holder. 'I've heard grand things about what you've being doing here at Waybell. There's nothing like an owner's footsteps for putting a mark on a place. And you've been doing it in spades, I hear.'

'It's been a busy first year,' replied Ross. Holder dunked a wedge of damper into the pot of honey and then crammed it into his mouth, the golden threads glistening on his greying beard. The man was grizzled in appearance, cracked and sunbaked like dried fruit. Ross spread his own bread carefully with a knife and then passed some of the freshly baked dough to Connor. The Scotsman concentrated on stirring his black tea. He'd done as Ross asked, forewarning Maria to stay clear of the house and getting one of the Aboriginal women to serve up the food.

Holder cast a hollow-eyed gaze around the room and stomped on the floor testing the boards. 'My place isn't quite as fancy.

I've got floorboards in the bedroom.' He gave a wink. 'But the rest is antbed. Nothing quite like it for a good sturdy surface.'

'You received my telegram?' Ross pushed the half-eaten food to one side.

'Eventually. I picked up the fever early in the year and I can tell you at one stage I reckoned someone was lowering the sliprail and readying to push me through the Pearly Gates. He spared me, though.' Holder looked upwards. 'God bless him.'

Connor gave a sceptical glance heavenwards. 'You're a religious man?'

'I'm Irish,' said Holder. 'I say what I mean.'

Connor looked at Ross and began plugging his pipe with tobacco.

'Here's hoping for a good wet season,' continued Holder. 'Mind you, it was a beauty last year or so I heard. Can't remember most of it. I spent five months laying on my back in Darwin hospital. Still, while I was there I saw the plans for the soldiers' memorial that's to be erected at Liberty Square opposite Government House. A fine monument it'll be too. Lost my eldest in France. Harry was a good lad.'

'But you *did* receive my telegram?' Ross asked again, wondering if the reference to the war memorial was a pointed reminder at his own lack of service.

Holder laced his fingers across a concave stomach and gave a belch. 'I did, although I wondered at it. You met Hugh Carment. You agreed to deliver the girl to me.'

Connor took a sip of tea. 'Mr Carment didn't give us much choice.'

'He's like that, Hugh is. Does his best to help a mate out,' replied Holder. 'That's how things are up here, Ross. I don't mind telling you that Hugh's not the type of man who likes to be taken advantage of or to leave unfinished business. I'm the same.'

'The telegram,' answered Ross testily. He now knew extricating Maria from this man's grasp would be difficult. 'You know what I want.'

'I do. Indeed, were I not a man understanding of certain needs I would be quite in my rights to take you outside and give you a flogging.'

'You're right, and I would deserve it, Mr Holder,' agreed Ross amiably, deciding to change his approach. 'Particularly as you paid for a virgin and she no longer is one.'

Connor's mouth dropped open, the pipe hanging precariously on his lower lip.

The Irishman burst out laughing, his sun-aged skin turning bright red.

'I'm sorry,' he muttered between gasps. 'Strike me round if I didn't expect that to come out of your mouth. You coming from a gentlemanly family and all. Is that what she told you?'

Ross felt his insides constrict.

'Well, I thought she'd be a canny one.' Holder wiped away tears of mirth. 'I'll give her marks, I will, for trying to save herself for me. To do the right thing.'

'What are you insinuating?' Ross felt the familiar stretch of skin as his knuckles tightened.

'You'd like to know, wouldn't you? Is she a lass willing to sleep with a man for money?' Holder banged a fist on the table, spilling the tea and sending cutlery clattering. 'How long did it take before you forced yourself on her, eh? Or did you pay her?'

Across the table Connor's pipe was moving up and down as he chewed on the stem.

Ross toyed with the crumbs on his plate, pushing them into a neat pile. Holder could try to rile him all he liked, but Ross knew Maria. 'How much money do you want, Holder? Whatever you paid, I'll gladly double it.'

'Where is she?' asked Holder. 'I'd be in my rights to shoot you here and now.'

Connor reached down, retrieving a revolver from his side and sat it on the table. 'There'll be no shooting, Mr Holder.'

'Give me a price,' demanded Ross, more calmly than he felt. 'You're old enough to be her grandfather.'

'It's not about the damn money, or age for that matter,' replied Holder. 'Do you know how many white women there are in these parts? Do you? You can count them on your hands, boy. The ones who do follow their husbands out here either take off like Sowden's Harriet did, or they die trying to birth lifeless children like my Vanessa. The ones who stay and stick it out are like gold. And they're worth more to a man than any alluvial reef or tin mine. So don't sit there with that *it's my right to make an offer* on your tongue. The deal's already been struck. The money paid. The Chinaman was good to his word and I was good to mine.'

'Slavery was abolished some years ago,' noted Connor drily.

'It's not slavery, you fool,' argued Holder.

Connor's features tightened. 'Careful who you call names, old man.'

Holder lifted his hands in a gesture of apology. 'The Chinese do things differently than us. Some of their girls are sold to work as domestics and then returned to their family at marriageable age. In Maria's case, there was no kin left and the Chinese in Darwin didn't want her. They don't take to a polluting of their kind. Anyway, Maria needed a good home and I can do the providing. Slavery's got nothing to do with it.'

'And if she doesn't want you?' reasoned Ross.

'We were married by proxy,' revealed Holder. 'Now I'm sorry, but the time for talking is done. I'm taking the girl with me.' He placed his hat on his head and tipped it briefly in a show of thanks for the hospitality extended. 'I'll wait outside. Ten minutes only, and then I'll be coming in.' And with that, he left.

'You'll have to let her go, Ross.' Connor came to where Ross stood observing their unwanted guest through the shutters. The Irishman walked down the narrow dirt path to where his lone companion, an Aboriginal man, waited with their horses. 'The business has been done,' Connor continued.

'A marriage by proxy isn't legal,' Ross insisted. 'None of this is right.'

'It has a fair stink about it,' agreed Connor. 'But what can you do? None of this sits straight with me. We've just accused the man of slavery and you're offering to buy the girl from him.'

'I'm buying her freedom. It's not the same, Connor, and you know it. Maria should be allowed to make up her own mind.'

Connor pulled on a tuft of beard. 'Aye, but the thing's been done. An understanding was made between three people and you weren't part of the negotiations. You must leave it at that, Ross. We're in the middle of nowhere, where a man's word means more than the law.'

Ross tried to determine what he should do next. Maria leaving was the last thing he wanted.

'This isn't any of our business. Best to let things alone.' Connor glanced out the window. Holder was now cradling a rifle. 'He's armed.'

'Maria!' they heard Holder yell. 'Maria, you've got ten minutes to fetch your things and get out here!'

Ross took his own rifle from where it leant in the corner of the room, sitting a box of shells on the table.

'Cripes.' Connor spun the barrel of his revolver, each bullet he loaded sliding home with a soft click. 'I'm not dying over a girl of mixed blood, Ross, I tell you this now. I'll defend you and me if it comes to it, but that's it. There's too much to lose if things go sour. *You* have too much to lose,' he said pointedly.

Maria appeared dressed in trousers and a long-sleeved shirt, a tawny bag in one hand. 'I don't want to cause any trouble,' she said, sitting the holdall on the table.

Ross looked from his friend to the girl and back again. 'Connor, can you leave us alone please?' He waited until Connor was standing guard at the front of the house and then Maria ran to his arms, burrowing into his chest as she clung to him, sobbing. Ross briefly closed his eyes.

'You were right. I have to let you go with him,' said Ross before she could speak. 'I can't risk a fight here on the property or the possibility of the authorities getting involved. That wouldn't help either of us. Oh God, Maria. I'm sorry.' He kissed her forehead and then gently freed her arms from about his waist. Although he detested the idea of her leaving with Holder, Ross wanted no trouble on Waybell.

'If you let him take me, you'll never get me back.'

He took her roughly by the arms. 'I will come for you.'

She shook her head. 'If we'd been together as a man and a woman should, if I'd let you . . . forgive me, Ross. I didn't know what I should do.'

Wordlessly, Ross allowed her to draw him through Sowden's old space, which was now a study, and into his bedroom. Once inside she closed the door.

'Don't forget me, Ross.'

She stepped away from him and slowly began to remove her clothes. Ross couldn't draw his eyes away. He understood that a great journey had been unfolding, one that, over the past months, had taken him away from a respectable existence to this new situation of blurred lines and impossible boundaries. He'd travelled from a point of knowing right from wrong to this very moment, a place so filled with necessity that all he could do was stare at recesses and curves only previously imagined.

She pressed her body against his. Chest, stomach and thighs resting and hollowing out.

Ross ran his fingers down the length of her spine, feeling the taut bone of the woman he loved. Maria undid his shirt. Splayed fingers on his body. He fumbled with his pants, pressing her backwards until her body hit the wall. He lifted one of her legs and then the other, bracing a palm on the wooden boards. Ross felt her tongue, the slickness of her mouth. It was as if all the oxygen was being sucked from the room.

He didn't want to go to the edge where Maria drew him. Not yet. There was a darkness waiting there. A chasm of wonder that once breached would stay with him forever. It would be like water and he would have to keep drinking it to survive. Ross held on for just a little longer, until the clifftop came into view, then he allowed himself to fall.

They stayed tangled. Arms wrapping waists. Stomachs resting together in one breath. Their bodies glassy with sweat. A small scar showed on her breast and he bent lower to suck damp skin. Her back arched.

'Enough,' he whispered. Lifting Maria free of his body, Ross had the distinct feeling of having travelled too far to get to this shared moment. He cupped her face with his hands. 'I will get you back from him, Maria.'

He waited naked on the edge of the bed as she dressed. The room smelt of briny days spent at the seashore when he was a child. Ross imagined the sweaty salt of their wanderings etched into the timber wall.

Maria stepped into trousers. Fastened buttons. Tidied moist hair.

'I miss you already,' she finally said, patting her face with a shirt-tail, which she then tucked into the waistband. Ross went to her side and kissed her, their palms sliding briefly together.

'I'll wait for you to come for me,' said Maria. Then she was gone.

Only when she'd left to join Holder did Ross gather up his clothes, trying to remember the person he'd been before today. Before he'd made love to Maria and truly become a man. Through the window he saw Holder hoist Maria up onto the back of his horse. Then the riders left, the dust lifting beneath the horse's hoofs. The road emptying into the fringe of trees.

The void of the bedroom was absolute. Ross no longer cared about anything. He only thought of what it meant to finally have Maria, and he wanted her back. No matter the cost.

He found Connor and they made their way to the storeroom, where Ross found the rum delivered for the start of the wet season. Connor held out a mug and Ross poured for them both.

'It's for the best, mate,' said Connor. 'I know you were keen on her, but it could never have worked. Not the way things are. You know that.'

But Ross wasn't listening. He was forming a new plan.

Six miles or so, that was the limit of travelling available until the sun set. Holder would want to make camp before dark. Four miles then, Ross calculated, before they stopped moving. A distance easily reached in the dark. People talked about the Northern Territory being a law unto itself. Holder was still on Ross's property and Ross had his own laws too. He skolled the rum.

'More?' asked Connor.

'No,' answered Ross.

They sat on the steps of the homestead, listening to the children playing on the edge of the billabong, clouds shading the horizon.

He couldn't let Maria go.

⫷ Chapter 34 ⫸

It wasn't difficult to track them. For once the moon was high and bright, unobscured by cloud, and the camp was well illuminated. They'd travelled further than Ross had expected, Holder choosing to ride to the other side of the creek and another five miles onwards. It was a good spot to rest. The area was ringed by timber and the ground was soft, the type of soil that welcomed a swag.

Ross crept behind a tree and waited. The Irishman was snoring, a thin arm flung across Maria. A few smoking coals remained of the fire. A hunk of half-eaten meat was impaled on a branch that rested between forked sticks above the dying heat. Only Holder's travel companion was missing. Ross flattened against a gnarly tree trunk. There was no other swag near the fire and he concluded that the other man was camped with the horses, which were tethered close by. Holder would have demanded privacy. Ross swallowed bile at the thought.

He didn't want any trouble. He'd not come for a fight. But if pressed, Ross was prepared to do what was necessary to get Maria back. Whatever happened next was up to Holder. The law, the real law that came from books and that was regulated by learned men, didn't stand for slavery. If Holder needed to be tied up and personally escorted back to Darwin on the train to be handed over to the police, Ross would do it. But first he'd enforce his own rules. That of an owner, for, at the very least, Holder was trespassing on his land.

Eventually, when enough time had passed to suggest Holder's male companion was also asleep a little way off, Ross crept the short space to where the white man lay snoring. In the glow from the fire Ross could see that Maria had opened her eyes, and he pressed a finger to his lips as she held his gaze. He hated the sight of Holder's possessive arm slung over her body, the slackness of the man's fingers resting on the ground so close to Maria's face. Holder's weapon lay discarded in the dirt and Ross carried it to the safety of the trees. He concealed it, before sliding the bolt across on his rifle and walking quietly back to where Holder slept and Maria waited.

'No good sneaking about here, mate,' a voice behind him said softly. 'Blackfella's always better at such things.' The man snatched Ross's weapon, jabbing him in the back with a rifle. 'You make more noise than an old man.'

'You'd know,' sneered Ross. 'You work for one.'

'Hey, Boss,' called the man.

Holder sprung upright in his swag. Pushing Maria out of the way, he reached for the rifle, which wasn't there. 'What the hell are *you* doing here?'

'I've come for Maria. You're welcome to follow us back to the homestead. Then in the morning we'll sit down and discuss things properly,' said Ross in as friendly a tone as he could.

Holder squinted. 'Haven't I just sat down with you, Grant, and come to an understanding? At least, that's what I thought.'

'I made a mistake in letting you leave. Waybell is my property and as you're on my land I'm expecting you to adhere to my law. White man's law, which prohibits slavery. Not the oriental version, that suits a man desperate for a wife.'

Holder pushed Maria down when she attempted to stand so that she was crouching at his feet. 'Let's not talk about who's desperate, eh?'

'This predicament can be easily solved if we discuss it like gentlemen and ask Maria what she wants. You said your arrangement wasn't slavery. Well, here's your chance to prove it.'

'I don't need to prove nothing to you,' spat Holder.

'The law says you do. A magistrate in Darwin will soon sort this out,' said Ross.

'We're not in some fancy club in Adelaide now, boy. And there's no rich father to lend assistance. I'd spit on you if the illness hadn't robbed me of my curd. There aren't enough white feathers in the Top End for a coward like you. My boy lies dead and you waltz up here trying to make amends for your shoddy past and talk to me about gentlemen. Hogtie him onto his horse, Jimmy, and send him back to the little Scotsman. I ain't got time for this.'

'C'mon now, Mister,' said Jimmy. 'We don't want no trouble.'

'That's right,' confirmed Holder. He patted Maria on the head. 'I'm trying to catch up with my wife.'

'Leave her alone!' Ross yelled. Maria had the look of a scared animal, a rabbit readying to burrow.

'No,' replied Holder. He reached down and lifted Maria up, wrapping an arm about her shoulders. 'I have a husband's right and by God I'll not have the likes of you telling me otherwise.'

Without further thought Ross swung around, punching the Aboriginal man in the face with full force. Snatching up the rifle from the stunned Jimmy, he threw it into the shadows before rushing at Holder. They fell to the ground, scrabbling in the dirt. Ross yelled out as the Irishman bit him on the ear. They rolled over and Ross broke free, retaliating with a punch to Holder's head. The older man proved faster than Ross had anticipated. He drew a knife and smiled.

'Is that it, boy? A bit of a scuff and a yelp and you're done? Come on,' Holder provoked him. 'I never had a problem drawing a bit of blood, and if I have to stick you to make you realise the way things work out here I will.'

A whack struck Ross in the ribs he'd injured during the muster. He gasped for breath as he landed hard on his back.

'What did you do that for, Jimmy?' asked Holder.

'No good, Boss. No more fighting,' said Jimmy.

'Be damned,' Holder replied. 'Do you really think this will be the last we hear from him if I don't give him a sorting out? He's had a whiff of the girl, if what he told me is true, and I'll not leave here without him knowing that he's on the losing side.'

Ross rolled out of the way as Holder readied to kick him in his damaged side. But it was Maria who attacked, striking Holder in the back of the knee so that he crumpled to the ground, dropping the knife. She picked it up and stuck him in the thigh and then backed away, blood glistening.

'Maria!' called Ross.

But before he could stand, Jimmy lifted a rifle butt and hit him in the head.

When Ross woke he was upside down, his body hanging uselessly. In the darkness he heard the squeak of leather, smelt horse hair and saddle grease. Blood pounded in his head and through the thumping he realised he'd been flung across a horse, his wrists and ankles trussed together and connected by a rope strung under the animal's belly. With every step the ache in his ribs pressed on his lungs. His head flapped pathetically back and forth. There was pain there as well. The type of soreness that suggested serious harm. But there was little point in calling out. It was better to wait and see where he ended up, to pretend he was unconscious so that he could attempt an escape when he was finally set upright on the ground.

The horse moved steadily onwards and Ross came to realise that he couldn't hear any voices. Theirs was a silent procession of injured men and a heart-wounded woman travelling along a night track where the crunch of leaves and the flurry of evening creatures became a chorus of sorts to the methodical gait of the horses,

They finally slowed down, and Ross recognised Jimmy's voice calling for help. Ross readied for freedom, hoping for any opportunity to escape. If he got away, he could return later for Maria.

'What on earth?'

Ross recognised Connor's voice.

'They got into a fight,' explained Jimmy.

Ross felt a hand on his back and heard the cutting of rope, each twine unravelling as the blade sliced through it. Connor dragged him from the horse's back and sat him on the ground as his feet and wrists were freed. Ross fell back into the dirt, his head swirling unsteadily. There were people gathering. He recognised Parker and Eustace as they gave orders. Jimmy was asking for help for his Boss.

Connor raised Ross from the ground and half-dragged him into the house. Once inside, he helped Ross into bed, then lit a candle and a lantern.

'Of all the daft-brained things, Ross. You went after Holder?' asked Connor.

'Maria,' he replied. 'I went after her. Maria stabbed Holder.'

Ross noticed Mick standing in the doorway.

'He'll be all right,' said Mick. 'Only a flesh wound. We'll bandage Holder up and get Jimmy to take him home at first light.'

'And Maria?'

'She's not injured, if that's what you mean,' said Connor.

'Keep her safe,' muttered Ross.

'Aye, that I'll do,' answered Connor. 'But if she's the one doing the stabbing I think she can look after herself.'

⚔ Chapter 35 ⚔

Ross was sitting up in bed, examining the bandage around his chest and probing the dressing on his head. Annie slapped his hands away and forced another mouthful of stringy soup into his mouth.

'I can feed myself,' he complained.

'All night you lie here like baby and now you wake and cry like one.'

'Annie, can you leave me alone please?'

'You big Boss man. Know everything. But sickness you don't know.' She pushed the spoon into his mouth once more, the metal hitting his teeth. 'You lucky you're not deep in the ground with the worms chewing at you. Only because of this.' She pinched his bicep. 'Not this.' She tapped his forehead. 'That and Annie. Annie keep you good and strong. I tell you stories and you wake up. You listen to the frogs at night and they call as well. Time to wake up, Mr Ross. No time to be worrying about that girl. She's no place for a whitefella like you.'

'Annie,' said Ross.

She snatched the bowl from him and left the room. Ross leant back, the boards hard on his skull. A dry cough, which irritated

Ross's throat and tore anew at his injuries, struck as Connor entered the room. When the paroxysm finally ended, he clutched at his ribs. The house was quiet. He knew Annie had patched up Holder, and that he and Jimmy had left days ago. As for Maria, he could only vaguely recall her sitting at his bedside, clasping his hand.

'How are you feeling?' asked Connor, drawing Annie's chair closer to the bed.

'Like I've been dragged behind a horse at the gallop,' replied Ross. 'What day is it?'

'Saturday. Nearly ten days since your little escapade. I'd not be surprised if that thick skull of yours wasn't cracked through. It was a fair belting.'

'Where's Maria?' asked Ross.

Connor crossed one leg over the other. 'Annie gave you some type of plant concoction that kept you confused but mostly oblivious to the pain as well. I figured it was best you slept a while. So let me ask the question again, Ross. What on earth possessed you to go after Holder?'

Ross reached for a cup of beef tea resting on the table by his bed. 'I thought I could negotiate with him.' He took a careful sip. 'But I didn't count on his friend bashing me senseless.'

'It's Jimmy you can thank that you're still with us. Holder has notified the authorities at Pine Creek. You have to give the man some credit. A nasty knife wound to the thigh but that didn't stop him from going straight to the coppers. He told me before he left that he was going to make sure that you and Maria were charged for the attack. But he won't have any luck.'

'Why's that? We did attack him. But we had good reason.'

'There's no excusing what you did, Ross.' Connor clasped and unclasped his fingers, forming a pyramid with his hands on the point of his knee. 'It's your word versus Holder's. And apart from Maria, Jimmy was the only witness.'

'And they won't take what he says as evidence because he's Aboriginal?' asked Ross.

Connor shook his head. 'There's no evidence to be found because Jimmy won't give it. He's related to Mick. Eustace said they had a big discussion over at Sowden's camp about what happened and they decided that it was just a disagreement between neighbours. So that's the end of it, at least the attack part.'

'Where's Maria now?' Ross asked again.

'I packed her up and sent her back to Darwin on the train. She's staying with Howard Reece, the manager of the abattoir. I thought it would be safer,' said Connor.

Ross felt palpitations rise in his chest. 'You sent her away? Why on earth would you do that?'

'Why do you think? As it is, we cannae be sure Holder won't waltz in here to finish the fight you started.' Connor reached for a newspaper, passing it to Ross.

Ross looked down the page. He read slowly, his focus blurred. The article gave a colourful account of the confrontation in the bush before going on to state the theory that the owner of Waybell Station and a young mixed-blood woman were having an affair. 'Damn it.'

'I particularly like the part where the editor points out that you're a married man and Maria had been sold to Holder and you were trying to buy her back.'

Ross folded the paper. All he could think of was Maria running forwards to stab Holder as the man lifted a boot to strike him in the same ribs Jimmy had just broken. If Holder had succeeded, he may well have punctured a lung. Maria had saved his life.

'A bloke calling himself a civil libertarian is stirring the pot as well. And there's been a lot of noise about the Allies signing that League of Nations agreement last year. The stopping of slavery features fairly highly in it apparently. None of this paints you or Holder in a particularly good light,' said Connor.

'I was trying to *save* Maria,' said Ross in frustration. 'How far has the news travelled, do you know?'

'It's gone national.' Connor ran a stubby finger the length of his moustache. 'That's the wonderful thing about the telegraph line, it takes no time at all for news to get out. I read the paper in the pub at Pine Creek after I dropped Maria off. It was there that your father's wire found me. I forwarded a telegram immediately, explaining how Maria had ended up here at Waybell and that you were trying to protect her. It'll be managed, knowing your father. You'll come out of this debacle eventually.' The Scotsman rummaged in his trousers for tobacco, patting each of his pockets in turn.

Ross moved to the edge of the bed, carefully dropping each leg until his feet touched the timber boards beneath. He winced. The pain was still there. 'What a mess,' he said.

Having located his pipe, Connor filled it with tobacco but didn't light it, electing instead to chew the stem.

'Aye, it's a pig's poke, that's for sure. I have to tell you, Ross, I'm starting to wish I'd never agreed to come to the Territory. You're a Grant. You've got a pedigree that a man would sell his mother for, and everything's been handed to you on a platter.' Connor took the pipe from his mouth. 'Me, well, I don't have much of a reputation but what I do have I'd like to keep.'

'I never wanted to put you in a difficult position, Connor.' Ross moved unsteadily towards the window, where a blue haze filled the square of land and horizon. 'We're beholden to them now. To Sowden and Mick, Annie and Jimmy. The whole damn lot. Not to mention Parker and Eustace.'

'Aye. They know how you feel about the girl. Not that they didnae before this. All the papers have is innuendo and gossip but one word to the contrary and it would take some explaining to clear your name,' said Connor.

Ross walked to the opposite wall, running his fingers across the tongue and groove timber, where even in daylight the outline of Maria's body hung clear in his mind. 'I need Maria, Connor.'

The chair scraped noisily. Connor lingered in the doorway. 'You dinnae need her. You want her. There's a difference. So un-want her, Ross. You're headline news. And your wife is on her way.'

❊ Chapter 36 ❊

The thin line of smoke hung briefly in the air before a current snatched at it, muddling the white-grey stream against the sky. It had been there all morning. An intermittent signal that followed the approach of the riders. Now with the sun crossing the midpoint of the day, the outlying fire announced an arrival. Ross knew this by the tribe that had gathered a short distance from the house. They'd been waiting for the last half-hour, women and children lining the rutted track, giggling and talking, their faces turning repeatedly from the homestead to the timber from which the travellers were expected to appear. Last to join the group was Sowden, carried by two of his men and trailed by Annie. The manager was seated at the end of the line of his dark-skinned people, Annie's protective umbrella held aloft above his head.

Backing away from the stable door, Ross returned to his horse and resumed running the currycomb across the animal's flanks. Though most of the men had left for the expected start of the wet season, Darcey's anticipated visit had prevented any other departures. Ross drew the brush along Nugget's hindquarters. He'd never been one for strife. Now he was surrounded by it.

He thought of Darcey. How she'd been on their wedding day, dwarfed by a creamy whiteness and borne along the carpeted thoroughfare of the hall to the parlour for the brief reception. Ross couldn't even remember what she looked like. Only recalled the silver ring purchased by Connor, which was too large for her finger.

Why was she coming? It wasn't just because of Maria. He'd since discovered that Darcey had been close to arriving in Darwin the week Holder had appeared unwanted on the property. Ross flicked Nugget's ratty mane and left the stables, taking up a position inside the house fence. In the tin trunk, wrapped in an old shirt, were Alastair's books. Safely hidden away.

Connor was the first to appear through the trees, then Mick. Darcey followed, not in the loaded wagon with Toby but on a dark mare. At the beginning of the row of people she halted. Mick was quick to dismount, standing to the side of Darcey's horse like a royal attendant as she neatly slipped from the saddle, her feet finding solid ground. If she was tired she didn't show it. She moved slowly along the waiting line, greeting each person and shaking their hands, children and adults alike smiling as they called out the word 'Missus' in welcome. She was taller than Ross recalled, small-waisted and attired in close-fitting trousers, boots and a wide-brimmed hat. For some reason he'd expected her to be dressed in an extravagant coloured silk creation, as she was the first time they'd met. Across the heat-glazed dirt Sowden caught Ross's attention, offering a slow bemused smile.

Ross knew the manager had been waiting for this moment. Sowden fixed on Ross, and then gave a slow shrug. You're just like me, the gesture implied, no better than me with your lover and wife. Ross opened the house gate, making his way back to the homestead veranda as children began milling about the new arrival.

When the introductions were finally completed and Darcey had spent more than enough time talking with Annie and Sowden and meeting the remaining stockmen, including Eustace, Parker and JJ, who were all grinning like fools, she finally turned towards the house. She glanced neither left nor right. Her eyes were planted on where he stood. Ross tapped the floor impatiently with his boot as the crowd waited. There was a low hum of anticipation. He held out a hand as she approached him, clasped her cool skin in his and showed Darcey through the front door, shutting it firmly behind them.

In the dining room she removed a pearl-decorated hat pin, drew the sunhat from her head and, placing it on the table, turned to him.

'You have been busy, husband,' she said, peeling off her gloves.

Ross felt her scrutiny, saw the even set of her mouth, the cool detachment. His rehearsed greeting, curt as it had been planned, seemed pointless.

'I didn't know you could ride,' was all he said in answer to her rebuke. Her skin was flushed. The porcelain paleness he recalled from their last meeting burnished by the sun. Her red-blonde hair now suited her better.

Darcey helped herself to a glass of water from the water jug on the table. 'You have quite the station here, Ross. Everyone seems very friendly.'

'You're a novelty,' he told her.

'To everyone, it seems,' answered Darcey. 'Mr Sowden wasn't even aware I existed until recently.'

'My personal affairs are no one's business.' They sat down at the table.

'I thought when you sent that gift of the camphor box that there was some hope for us, but then you never answered any of my letters.'

'I can't be sorry if you had expectations,' said Ross. 'Anyway, that gift was not meant –'

Darcey gave a choked laugh. 'Only the expectations a new bride should rightly have of a husband, but then we're married only by document. The legality of which is obviously meaningless to you. Still, I'm surprised at this relationship suggested by the papers. There is truth to the rumour, I suppose? There usually is with these things.'

Ross refused to reply.

'They say that you became infatuated with this girl of mixed blood.' She took another sip of water. 'It's quite a story to be

226

presented with when you've just arrived. You can imagine my surprise, reading about the account in a Darwin newspaper.'

He was taken aback by her boldness. 'Why are you here, Darcey? If it's to ridicule me then you needn't have bothered coming.'

She played with the gloves on the table, moistening her lips. Ross knew he had caused her distress and had done so from the very beginning. He couldn't help it. He'd never wanted her in his life.

'Did my father assume I wanted you here? No doubt he thinks that the family reputation needs some bolstering. But your presence looks rather suspicious, considering the circumstances?'

'This trip has been planned for some time.' Darcey pushed the gloves aside. 'But I gather either you didn't receive my letters or chose not to read them. If you had, you would have known of my plans. Not that it matters now. Recent events make my coming here of even more importance. You only have yourself to thank for that. And if you think I have arrived here in the wilds unprepared, you should know that I've not been sitting in the parlour sewing since your leaving, if that's what you imagined.' She paused. 'If you imagined anything at all of me.'

She remained silent, and Ross knew that she was hoping for the even the scantest of kind words.

'I was an adequate rider, but not skilled,' she ventured, looking disappointed. 'I knew little of Australia on arrival in this country and nothing of the Territory, nor life on a property. All of these things have been rectified during your absence.'

Ross scratched his sideburn, which he'd taken to growing to hide the injury Jimmy had inflicted on him. 'With what purpose? To make yourself a useful wife?' He offered a crooked smile, trying to ignore the implication of her words. 'You would have been better off staying in Adelaide, enjoying the many benefits my family can offer.'

'I would gladly have remained there, especially once you became headline news, husband, except for one small thing.'

'Which is?' He held up his hands in mock amazement. 'Don't tell me there is something else more crucial than societal standing. That's all it ever usually is with my family.'

Darcey looked about the room, her expression not altering at the sparse surroundings. 'It's true that containing the scandal is of major importance. No family wants their name associated with such sordid goings-on. But there is another reason for my coming here.'

'Which is?'

'Your family wants an heir and I want a child.' She poured more water, the liquid tinkling into the glass. 'You have a duty to fulfil, which goes beyond your dislike of me, and frankly it is the one thing you can do, Ross, to make amends for the way you've treated me.'

'Children? You came here for children?' exclaimed Ross.

Darcey flinched at his loud words. 'I can't take a lover. Even if I was inclined it would ruin me, not to mention the hurt it would cause your family. But neither do I intend to spend the rest of my life treading water.'

'I can offer a divorce. An annulment. Whatever can be done to release us both from this situation. You would be well provided for.'

At this, she pushed her chair back from the table, and he watched as she moved about the room. She reminded Ross of his father, always standing or walking when deliberation was required.

Reaching the desk in the corner, Darcey turned to face him. 'A divorce?'

'Yes.'

'You expect a lot, Ross. Very well. I would consider what you offer, if you agree to what I ask. I'm older than you and regardless of the Grant desire for continuity I would like babies of my own. You would have to be the father. You owe me that at least.'

He was at a loss as to how to answer her. How was it possible for a woman to have the gumption to ask for such a thing? Ross had forgotten what it was like to be in the company of a forthright woman. There was a spirit to Darcey but also a learned confidence.

'How is my grandmother?' he asked, delaying having to reply.

'Well enough for her age, although I've heard she's become quite agitated with what's happened recently,' she explained.

'She shouldn't have been told,' argued Ross.

'What a small place you've allowed yourself to inhabit, Ross,' replied Darcey. 'Why are you continually fighting to be anything other than what you were born to be? I know the truth of our union. That you only married me to ensure your inheritance.' She moved towards him. 'That's what's ailing your grandmother. In trying to bind you to the family she only succeeded in pushing you farther away. People only want to help you, Ross. Your family –'

'You know nothing about my family!' he yelled.

Outside, dogs barked in response, a series of rapid yaps that soon died away in the afternoon heat.

'This is a pretty mess for two people to find themselves in, isn't it?' She walked about the room again, running a finger across the pages of the ledger sitting on the table. 'Do you love the girl?'

'Yes.' Ross was surprised at how readily his response came.

Her shoulders stiffened. 'Would you be prepared to give me a child?'

'No.' He wanted no further complications between them.

Darcey turned at his reply. 'You truly are all take and no give, as only the privileged can be.'

'And coming from far more modest circumstances, you would know that for a fact, I presume?' he retorted.

A brief expression of sorrow crossed her features. 'You've done a lot with this house based on Connor's accounts of the place when you first arrived here. It's a credit to you.' She sat back in the chair. 'I don't want to fight with you, Ross. Let's just agree to provide each other with what we both need. I want a child. You want to be free of me. When I have that child in my arms I will agree to whatever terms you wish.'

'You're prepared to raise a child alone?' he asked.

'I wouldn't be alone. The child would be brought up in the Grant home.'

Ross exhaled noisily. 'You've discussed this with my grand-mother, of course?'

'Regarding the child, yes. I didn't realise you'd be so keen to be rid of me. But I expect once a child is born your family would be happy for me, as the mother of the Grant heir, to stay on in the family home regardless of whether we were still married or not.'

She was right. Darcey was assured of a secure future if there was a child. 'So you'd be comfortable as a divorced woman?' he asked.

'Comfortable? No. Resigned to compromise? Yes.'

'And if you remarried afterwards?'

'Remarried? I'd not considered such a situation, but the child would retain the Grant surname,' said Darcey. 'If I were to move out of the Grant household in the future, any child you and I have will always be yours as well, Ross.'

Darcey may have journeyed here on his father's command but she'd arrived with her own agenda. A child in exchange for freedom. And if the arrangement ended in birth, what then? Becoming a father was something he'd never considered. He was caught. But he was also desperate. 'Fine. I will do as you ask. Then you'll do the same for me.'

Darcey dipped her chin in acknowledgement.

Ross never would have believed that he would be bargaining to go to bed with a woman. 'I'll come to you tonight.' If he were given more time to think he might well renege.

'Tomorrow, Ross.' Darcey gave a shy smile. 'I've been travelling for weeks. I'm tired.'

≪ Chapter 37 ≫

As he hesitated outside the bedroom, Ross thought of Alastair and his brother's passing love for the woman within. The three small shots of amber fluid he'd drunk did little to remove the anxieties circling in his mind. The idea of Alastair and Darcey's love having been consummated years ago made Ross uneasy. As it always had. Darcey would forever belong to Alastair, as did everything else that his brother had cast aside the day he rejected his family. Ross was simply the custodian of the remains of someone else's life.

Being with Darcey might have been easier if he knew for certain that she was untouched. There was a purity to the idea of it, but more than that he was bothered by a lack of total possession on his part. Everything in his life had been owned by another before him. Even Maria, although Ross knew in his soul that, despite Holder's insinuations, he'd been her first lover, just as she had been his. There was a sacredness to their relationship, and when the business with Darcey was complete Ross intended to go to Darwin and reclaim her.

He gave a brief knock and entered the room. The stub of a candle burnt on the bedside dresser and insects massed around the brightness. Darcey was stirring something in a glass. She didn't acknowledge him immediately, instead drinking the contents before enveloping herself inside the netting suspended from the ceiling. A glow of light highlighted her face, hair and bare shoulders, her eyes betraying the calm image she was trying to portray.

Ross undressed, a strange mixture of anticipation and guilt making his movements clumsy. The netting untucked easily and he lifted the sheet, settling in the bed next to her. Ross didn't want to be the one to begin this charade. He'd spent the day out riding, spurring his poor horse to the gallop until sweat lathered them both. Keeping clear of Darcey was his only objective.

'Connor said you were very sick after the attack,' said Darcey, breaking the silence.

'I survived. I don't believe in slavery, Darcey. I was trying to protect —' He stopped before saying Maria's name aloud. The girl need never know of the pact made with his wife but still Ross saw the act that was to come as something of a betrayal.

'Connor also told me that your intentions were right,' she said gently.

The insects droned noisily.

'Perhaps you should blow out the candle,' suggested Ross.

Darcey ignored the request. 'Thank you for agreeing to this.'

He turned towards her, readying to drag her body beneath his.

The kiss she offered was unexpected. He pulled away, not wanting such intimacy.

'Don't,' she said softly, drawing him back to her. The candle spluttered and died.

Ross had imagined they would be like two rutting sheep, the business over with only the barest of interactions. That's what he'd visualised. One of Gleneagle's stud rams and a docile ewe. It made the thought of the venture achievable without the encumbrance of emotion. But the woman beneath him didn't allow for such rudimentary coupling. Darcey was persistent, patient, halting his rushed progression with a firm hand planted on his chest. In the end Ross returned her kisses, his need fed by her gentle persuasion that left his earlier thoughts wrecked by base desire.

He departed immediately after, clothes clutched to his chest, feeling like a thief as the bedroom door clicked shut. In the study Ross lit the kerosene lantern and dressed quickly, swilling a mouthful of rum straight from the bottle. He was wide awake. Every muscle in his body pulsed. Sleep would be impossible so how was it that a vagueness was centring itself in his body, making him feel uncertain?

It was so different with Darcey compared to Maria. Ross knew that, despite his wishes to keep Darcey a stranger, as a husband there were certain rights requiring no justification. The dilemma, however, remained. The act itself. The moment of abandon, the agonisingly slow march to an ending made possible by Darcey's uncompromising restraint. Perhaps that's what bothered him. Her self-control and his lack of it. It struck Ross that Darcey's self-possession was more than the singular issue of self-control. He'd been led to that place of satisfaction by experience. His wife had not come to their marriage bed a virgin. It had been just as he thought, and yet he had enjoyed the experience.

≪ Chapter 38 ≫

1920—21

Ross avoided Darcey. Craftily, rudely, desperately. There were the hurried excuses of a buffalo sighting, a crocodile, a dispute in Sowden's camp. Ross was late for meals and then went straight to sleep in the room built for Maria, having abdicated his own bedroom for his wife. He lay on Maria's bed, staring at the few items of clothing he'd purchased for her, which were still hanging from a wall peg. A red skirt, a lace-edged blouse, a length of ribbon. His own clothes, hastily moved from his bedroom before Darcey's arrival, were piled on a chair near a washstand. Alastair's novels had been moved from the tin trunk in the common area to an iron bucket in Ross's current room, where they remained safe from termites, protected from Darcey and the sentimentality she would attach to Ross for his possession of his brother's boyish things. Ross hated the room for its emptiness. For its monastic space, which pushed in on him as he tried to reconcile what he wanted and what he had.

He grew used to absconding at daybreak and going bush for three or four days at a time. It was easy to disappear. The wet season was late arriving, and the days were predominantly clear.

Brian the carpenter returned early and unannounced, having fought with his wife at Pine Creek, and so the house became noisy with his saw and hammer. The women continually complained about the mess his building made as they went about with their housework. Christmas came and then New Year. By mid-January Ross had ridden southwards several times to camp out alone away from Darcey, each fall of rain limiting the distance he was able to cover as water spread across the land.

Ross ruminated on that first night with Darcey and the subsequent nights they spent together, trying to find some reasoning for the predicament he was in. He talked it out with Nugget, welcoming the lack of response. He rode until exhaustion bit hard and then slept feet away from the mangy horse that had become his ally. Try as he did, Ross could unearth no logic as to why Darcey was now at Waybell and Maria was not.

And he couldn't go to Maria. Not yet. He would keep her safe from Holder, who still threatened them with legal action. The last he'd heard, the knife wound had become infected and an ulcerous sore was keeping Holder in constant pain. Ross knew he had no choice but to wait. It was too soon since the scandal. That was an awakening of sorts. Learning that he wasn't totally undone by his time in the Territory, that shreds of Grant respectability still held firm. There was no accounting for any of it except for what Homer drew on so often: fate.

After another week camping rough Ross returned to Waybell, handing Nugget over to JJ for tending. The gelding was exhausted and hungry, his black coat gritty with sweat and dust.

'You trying to kill this horse of yours, Boss?' asked JJ.

Ross patted Nugget and the horse whinnied. 'Just tend him.'

He drank from a waterbag hanging in the stable and with his belongings over a shoulder circumnavigated the homestead, doing his best to keep clear of people, especially Darcey. Ross chose the place of the fallen trees at the back of the house, not expecting to be disturbed, planning on waiting until late evening before going indoors.

'There you are,' said Darcey. 'I saw you arrive home.' She was dressed in pants and a shirt and was wearing boots.

'You've been riding,' said Ross, trying not to show his annoyance at being interrupted or the exhaustion he felt, concentrating instead on Darcey's use of the term 'home' as if theirs was a normal relationship.

'Yes. Connor saddled up one of the mares for me. I didn't get very far. The country's waterlogged, although from what I've heard it's not as wet as last year. Apparently Brian will be able to get through to Pine Creek if he takes a detour to the south.' She looked at him expectantly, clearly hoping for a reply. 'He's nearly finished the windows and will be leaving in a few days. And you've been exploring?'

'I'm tired, Darcey.'

'Ross, I know you're avoiding me. This is –'

'Awkward? Yes. I'm not sure I can go on with it,' said Ross. 'It feels wrong.'

'Is it so very bad?' asked Darcey.

He sighed, unsure of how to reply.

Darcey sat down on a stump opposite him. Grease from the saddle ran in a line down the inside of her beige trousers. 'Don't you want a child?'

'I hadn't thought of it,' replied Ross.

'Until I asked for one?'

'Yes,' said Ross.

'We are husband and wife, Ross.'

'You slept with Alastair in London. Didn't you?'

She plucked at something in the grass. 'Yes. I'm sorry if that bothers you.'

'I'm surprised and disappointed,' he admitted.

'In me or your brother?'

'Both, I suppose,' said Ross. 'For what he did to you and for what you –'

Darcey's smile crinkled her nose. 'My husband the puritan. Alastair would laugh at you if he were here.'

'I'm sure he's laughing anyway,' Ross snapped.

'I didn't mean to upset you, Ross, it's just that love is only love. It can't always be contained neatly according to everyone's expectations or with a view to what might possibly happen in the future. Look at us, we're married and yet you've fallen in love with someone else.'

'We were talking about my brother,' Ross reminded her.

'Yes, we were. During the war no one knew what was going to occur. It seemed such a small thing to be with the man I loved. Do you hate me for that? The fact that I loved him?'

'As it turns out, I guess you're glad you slept with him,' said Ross.

Darcey rubbed something in her palm and smelt it. 'Actually, I'm not,' she answered, flicking the herbage away. 'Now I know he wasn't worthy of what I gave him.'

How Darcey felt about Alastair's behaviour wasn't something Ross had ever contemplated. It seemed to him she was a willing enough participant at the time.

'And you,' asked Darcey. 'Have you loved many women?'

Ross didn't answer and they sat for a while, neither of them speaking. He thought of Maria alone in Darwin and her parting words that she would wait for him. This business with Darcey needed to be resolved and there was only one way to be free of her.

'I don't know what I need to say to make things better between us. Perhaps one night we could start by eating a meal together,' she said. 'I brought some wine with me. You might like to try some. Would you like to try some? Now?'

Ross knew that if he didn't accept an argument might follow and then they would be back at the starting gates of this badly thought-out race. He followed Darcey to the house. A little table was arranged on the rear veranda with two glasses, a bottle and a small plate of cheese. Ross poured the wine, noting the alcohol had already been sampled.

Darcey tapped a file of powder into the glass and stirred it. Ross wondered what it was. He'd first noticed her consuming it when he'd come to her bed. But he didn't ask, he didn't care to know.

If they were to live together a little longer it was far better they remain strangers in all but the flesh.

'Thank you,' said Darcey.

'For what?' he queried.

'For giving me time.'

'This arrangement can't last forever, you know.'

Darcey moved a square of cheese on the platter. It was already drying in the warm air.

'Then you'll have to stop avoiding me,' she replied.

≪ Chapter 39 ≫

Darcey held the child's wrist, wrapping a length of calico bandage around the cut. Next to her, Annie tutted loudly, complaining that the medicine couldn't possibly work when it came out of a white man's tin. Patiently, Darcey explained that it was only salve, a simple ointment that would aid healing. If it didn't, she promised they would try Annie's way, the old way, however she was to give it a week first and the young girl was to return every day so that Darcey could check the wound.

'You're a regular Florence Nightingale,' said Connor, walking past Darcey where she sat on the homestead steps. He nodded to Sowden, who was waiting for her attention.

Ross greeted his friend at the door to the house as a young woman hobbled up the dirt path to join the waiting queue.

'Your wife's clinics are getting more popular by the week,' observed Connor. 'Settled in very well, hasn't she? Sowden's been seeing Darcey quite a bit, you know. It seems the poor blighter has sores on the backs of his legs the size of dinner plates, and since Darcey told him to lay on his stomach for part of each day there's been an improvement. If ever a missionary was hoping to convert a flock, it seems your wife is winning on the medicinal front.'

'She had some training in London,' replied Ross. 'Nurse's aide or something like that. Anyway, sprains and cuts are the worst of things here.'

'She's been here for nearly four months and you're still not taken with her, are you?' Connor drew up a chair and the two men sat at the dining table, a large map spread out between them.

'She only came here for one reason, Connor.'

'Aye, maybe she did, but I'd not be complaining for you mightn't have a bairn yet but it must be rather pleasant trying. A bit of lust in the dust, eh?'

'I'm glad you see the funny side of it,' said Ross.

Connor frowned and shook his head. 'A child, Ross. Think on it. It's something a man like me can only dream of.'

'I never gave much thought to children,' admitted Ross.

'That's because you're still young.'

'Her coming here. Wanting a baby. It's not what I expected. None of this is.'

'Few people get what they want in life, and if they do manage to it's never quite what they anticipated. Anyway, this situation isn't all bad.' Connor nudged Ross in the arm. 'Darcey might just manage to lift a wee corner on that prickly hide of yours. Now that would be an achievement. So, we'll be ready to leave for the muster in a week. Is Darcey coming with us?'

'I haven't invited her. She isn't used to this life.'

'Maybe not, but she's taken to it,' stated Connor.

'Still, I'd feel better if she stayed here with Annie and Sowden. Besides, I have other things to attend to.'

'Such as?' queried Connor.

'I've not seen the Darwin abattoir yet.'

'And there's a reason for that,' said Connor. 'We're waiting for the fuss to die down.'

'I'm sick of waiting. It's been over five months. People have short memories.'

'Not if you stroll into Darwin and knock on a certain young woman's door, they won't. Dinnae look at me like that. You've been itching to get back there. It's bad enough you've been writing to her, Ross, but one of these days someone's going to discover that you're still in contact with each other. Have you ever thought that she might not have your patience? She's smart enough. She will have heard that Darcey's around.'

'Darcey and I have an understanding.'

'I'm sure,' he answered cynically. 'But the rest of the Territory mightn't be so free-thinking.' Connor glanced at the pannikin sitting on the table displaying an arrangement of wildflowers and shrubbery. 'Your wife likes it here, Ross, and I haven't heard you mention receiving any letters back from Maria.'

Ross passed Connor the ledger with last year's livestock tallies and Connor began transferring the figures into a pocket notebook to take on the muster when they left. 'You haven't thought about it then?'

'What?' said Ross.

'About how you'll feel when you're a father?'

'I've thought about it. It hasn't happened though, has it?' said Ross sharply.

They heard Darcey call goodbye to Becky and some of the other women. She'd set parameters around their housekeeping with late morning the cut-off time for everyone to depart the homestead. Only Little Bill and a few other children stayed on for a limited time each day. Darcey taught them basic letters so that they could spell out their names in the dirt.

'Can I get you some tea?' Darcey placed the medicine chest on the table where the men sat.

'No, nothing thanks, Darcey,' answered Connor.

Darcey left the room as noiselessly as she'd arrived.

'So what do you think about Holder's land?' Connor pushed a squat thumb on a portion of the map to the south of Waybell. 'He's still in Pine Creek. Eustace heard from the publican that he's not expected to last much longer.'

241

Their neighbour's failing health was reported in the newspaper on a regular basis, making Ross wonder at the length of time it was taking for the man to die. It now seemed it wasn't the knifing that ailed him but a battle with cancer that had been going on for years.

'We'll make an offer on Holder's Run when the time comes.' Ross took another look at the Territory map that highlighted Holder's portion. Once he was dead and buried, there was one less obstacle in his path to Maria. The land would be a bonus.

'There'll be talk,' replied Connor. 'About you being the one to buy his land, if you're successful.'

Ross rolled up the chart. 'I'll be successful, Connor. You'll make sure of that.'

≪ Chapter 40 ≫

After dinner, Darcey asked Ross if he would walk with her by the billabong. It wasn't the first time she'd made such a request and, as Ross was leaving before dawn to travel to the first mustering camp with the rest of the stockmen, he found himself arm-in-arm with his wife. They dodged the muddy edges of the waterhole, disturbing scurrying water rats and lizards. The awkwardness of the situation was not lost on Ross. They were like young horses, sometimes nervy and flighty in each other's company, at others strangely comfortable and capable of coming together in the most intimate of ways. But walking together at dusk was different ground. It required manoeuvring Ross was ill-equipped for.

The half-light that came just after sunset darkened the water, accentuating the long-necked birds stalking for prey.

'Egrets,' said Darcey. 'Once I would have asked you to shoot one for me. They're in great demand for women's hats.'

'And you no longer fancy them?' asked Ross, as the birds lifted into the evening air.

'Most of what I know about birds and animals came from books, Ross. The fripperies I once enjoyed aren't so important anymore.'

Ross caught her profile, contentment showed. They knew every inch of each other's skin, but little else. He'd not allowed it. Since Darcey's arrival, it was plain to Ross that more than the hope of a child kept his wife at Waybell. He was sorry for her dreams.

Only once during her months on the station had Darcey complained, and that small comment was made during the height of the monsoon when a number of dry days had created relentless heat and the humidity made the brightest of souls irritable and depressed. Connor coined the phrase 'suicide season', the antidote to which he believed was keeping well clear of people. When the cloudbursts eventually arrived Darcey countered the stifling weeks by enticing him to play cards, then she cut up some of her clothes and sewed them into curtains. Ross observed the way she laid out the useless gowns, tracing the patterns, collars and cuffs before unpicking the fabric and winding the pulled thread onto an empty reel. There were scissors and measuring tapes and much holding of fabric against walls to check the suitability of her choice and careful, neat stitching as the rain poured down. At the end of each day Darcey poured a large rum for him and a small glass of wine for herself, adding the tincture that she explained was for nervous tension. Why she required the mixture, Ross could only speculate. Darcey Grant was the most singularly composed woman he knew. Silk now framed the gauze on her bedroom window, heavy brocade in the dining room. It was a small thing. A simple decorative touch like the native flowers on the table and the sharing of drinks at dusk, and yet it felt like a gradual encroachment. As if, inch by inch, Darcey was staking a greater claim.

'My father called this time of night the gloaming.' She picked up a stick and threw it into the water where a lily pad cushioned its entry. 'Often he would sit in the garden until dark, enjoying the changing sky.'

'A man of simple pleasures,' responded Ross. 'You must miss him.'

'I do. He died a few months after we were married.'

'I'm sorry,' said Ross.

244

'Don't be. You didn't know him, however he knew of you. I wrote to him the day after our wedding. He knew that I was cared for. That's all he ever wanted.'

'We should go in.' Ross directed them towards the homestead, wondering about the letter Darcey had penned to her father. He imagined it full of a woman's wrath and regretted her writing it, firstly for her father, who undoubtedly hoped for better things for his only surviving child, and secondly because of the negative portrayal it would have cast on him. Not that he was undeserving.

Across the water, the fires of the camp sent spiralling embers into the sky as fresh logs were thrown onto the flames.

'Will you be away for long?' she asked. 'Mr Sowden told me that there is the opportunity to stop at the homestead, instead of staying away for so many months.'

'The men will certainly be back here in a month or so, but I'm considering buying another property, so I'll head south at some stage with Connor and leave Mick and Eustace in charge.' He didn't mention that he also intended on going to Darwin.

'They seem like good, reliable men.'

'They're as trustworthy as their conscience stretches, Darcey, but yes they do a good enough job.'

'You sound like your father. It suits you.'

Ross stiffened. 'I'd rather hoped I was my own man, not a carbon copy of another.'

'Of course. I didn't mean to offend you. And this property you're thinking of buying. Is it very large?'

'Large enough.' A hand on her elbow, Ross guided her up the stairs into the house. The rooms were dark. The floorboards creaked as they walked across them.

'Our house in England had a nightingale floor,' Darcey told him. 'My father said it was built by smugglers who worried about the authorities coming for them in the night. It squeaked and groaned when you walked on it, and I never could sneak downstairs for a glass of milk in the middle of the night without my parents knowing. It's the same with this floor. I know when you're coming.'

Ross lit a candle, replacing the flue. 'Darcey, it's been months. This situation can't go on forever, you know.'

'Will you come to me tonight?' she asked.

'I have to leave early in the morning,' Ross told her.

'Please. If you don't, more time will pass and I know you don't want that. I'm afraid my age might take away any chance I have of ever having a child.'

'That's ridiculous, you're still young.'

'Older than you,' she reminded him. 'And yet to have success.'

'All right,' he relented. Ross had given thought to the possibility of Darcey being incapable of bearing a child and where that would leave their agreement. 'We'll have to talk about the future, Darcey, if nothing happens soon.'

It was a difficulty neither of them broached, for want of hearing the other's expectations. Ross now struggled with the possibility of never having a son, an outcome that mattered more than he'd once thought it would. What had taken root was the inevitability of time and the plain truth that Ross didn't want his name forgotten. Even if all that remained of him was a yellowing photograph atop a piano. It was mortality that kept Ross returning to Darcey's bed. The thought of a son.

For once there was no prearranged time to their meeting. When Ross entered the bedroom unannounced, his wife was not already waiting in bed, a sheet preserving her modesty. And Ross realised that he'd forgotten to partake in the bolstering shots of rum that had usually been his custom.

Darcey lit the bedside candle and began taking the pins from her long hair. Ross tugged off his shirt and splashed water on his face from the washstand, smelling the lavender soap that he'd come to associate with Darcey. She struggled with a button on her skirt and Ross went to her, standing behind, their hands catching as he helped. The material billowed at her feet and Darcey stepped from it, her hair falling over a shoulder. Ross bunched the lengths in his palm, and turned her around. She lifted her face to his.

❧ Chapter 41 ❧

Ross left the next morning before dawn, when the sky was inky blue. He rode westwards all day, the sun warming his back. The woodlands unspooled in a disturbance of orange, yellow and mauve flowers. Miles behind him, in the centre of the dining room table, anchored by a mug of wilted flora, lay the letter he'd left for Darcey. Its composition proved harder than Ross expected, so in the end he'd given up trying to find the right words. There were none. It was a brief note, direct. They were playing at marriage and Ross wasn't prepared to wait forever, and neither should she. Surely the woman wanted a better life. And so he'd told Darcey to leave.

It wasn't the expected parting. If Ross had thought of their goodbye at all it was in vague terms, a handshake at her bedroom door, a hug. Neither seemed proper. Both were awkward, as was the whole unusual messy time that they'd lived together. Yet they'd never once argued after that first day and as their time together had worn on, simple respect had led to understanding. It was as if Darcey had lit a fistful of twigs under their relationship, fanning it continually until it became a small fire. She was clever. She had seeped into his pores. This morning he'd woken up by her side, and he'd wanted to be there.

'Where are you going then?' Connor rode out from among the timber to where Ross had made camp for the night.

Ross lifted the rifle at his side and then returned it to the ground. 'Did I ask you to follow me?' he questioned. He resumed turning the wild ducks on the spit, the juices dripping onto the embers with a hiss. A light easterly wind stirred the air, carrying with it scattered fluffy clouds. Ross glanced at the wispy sky and back to Connor, who was now tying his horse to a low branch.

The Scotsman squatted in the dirt, hands dangling between his legs. 'The rest of the men should be at the first mustering camp by now. I had it in my head that we were going with them. What happened?'

'Nothing,' said Ross bluntly. He poked at the fire, jiggling the billycan in the coals. 'I told Darcey to leave.'

Connor took out his pipe, tapping the stem in his palm. 'Ah. That must have been tough. On both of you. How did she take it?'

Ross slid the threaded ducks from stick to plate, then he dug a damper from the coals, dusting the ash and dirt from its hard crust. 'You hungry?'

'That well, eh?' Connor stabbed at one of the ducks with a knife and began pulling at the steaming flesh with his fingers. 'Man shall not live by bread alone. So what's your plan? Darwin, I presume?'

'You deduct that from the fact I'm heading in the direction of the train lines?' replied Ross.

'Lucky guess.' Connor grinned. 'While you're inspecting the abattoir I can find out if Holder has finally passed on and who's handling the sale of his property.'

'Keeping an eye on me wouldn't be on your agenda too, I suppose?'

Connor tore a chunk of bread from the loaf. 'Never crossed my mind.' He bit into the hot damper. 'Not bad. We'll make a cook out of you yet.'

Ross added a handful of tea leaves to the billy, which was nestled in the coals. 'Tea?'

Connor retrieved his pannikin from where it was tied to his saddle and returned to the fire. 'Don't mind if I do,' he replied, holding out the mug for Ross to fill. 'This will be a good test for Mick and the rest of them. Leaving them in control again.'

'We'll see,' said Ross, taking a sip of the scalding brew.

'Are you sure it's what you want, Darcey leaving?' Connor asked between mouthfuls.

Ross picked at the damper, throwing pieces of it in the path of a trail of ants. 'I didn't ask her to come.' He ate a portion of the duck and then, sitting his plate aside, pulled one of Alastair's books from his belongings. There was barely enough light and Ross read the same paragraph twice before giving up.

'The gloaming,' he said quietly, recalling the previous evening's walk around the edge of the billabong. The fire brightened against the coming dark.

'You not eating then?' queried Connor.

Ross took a few more mouthfuls and then passed the plate to Connor, who quickly shovelled the remaining food into his mouth, and made a show of licking his fingers. 'It's a fine thing to finish the day with a good feed in your belly. That and a sip of tea and a pipe. Now, if we had a bottle of something hard and you played the harmonica, Ross, we could make a night of it.' Connor rolled out his swag.

Ross lay looking up at the stars as a layer of smoke settled over them, a remnant from the burning off of wet-season growth by the Aboriginal people further to the east.

Connor filled his pipe and then lit it, sighing contentedly. He began to hum.

Turning on his side, Ross moved back and forth until he managed to carve a slight depression in the earth with his hip. There was something to be said for being alone but the occasion was rare when that happened. At least Connor's music, a melody of Scottish

249

notes with the odd word thrown in, didn't ask anything of him. Ross listened with some pleasure, wincing when the Scotsman tested the higher octaves.

Finally, he stopped. 'Darcey got under your skin, didnae she?'

'She cornered me. That's what she did, Connor. Coming all this way.'

'But she didnae, not really, Ross,' Connor told him. 'You took what she offered and now you've had enough, you're sending her away.'

'It's not like that.'

'Then tell me,' said Connor. 'Spell it out, man, for I'm a daft highlander and I can't make sense of this. You've been living together as man and wife. Sharing a bed. And now suddenly you tell her to leave? I dinnae understand. You were getting along just fine. Better than fine. And what about her? Didnae you ever wonder how she feels? How hard this must be?'

'I didn't ask her to come, Connor.'

'What happened? What happened last night that's made you run? I'll tell you what I think's happened. I think you've realised that maybe you dinnae want Maria quite so much, or maybe, *maybe* you want them both. Aye. That's it, isn't it?'

'I don't want to talk about it, Connor. I know you think I've done Darcey wrong,' replied Ross.

'Aye, mate,' Connor said. 'And you do too.'

≪ Chapter 42 ≫

Darwin

A week later, Ross arrived in Darwin. Leaving Connor to meet with Marcus Holder's solicitor, he went straight to the Reece residence. A woman was in the garden pruning an overgrown shrub, the branches of which were twisted around a picket fence. She rose unsteadily at Ross's approach, clutching the railing with a gloved hand so that her plump figure made the timber squeak under the strain. Ross introduced himself and Mrs Reece's bland expression immediately changed to one of interest.

'Mr Grant.' She peered from under the brim of a tatty felt hat. 'This is a surprise. My husband wasn't expecting you until this afternoon. It's such a pleasure to finally meet you.' She gave a small puff of exertion. 'He's at the slaughterhouse. Giving it a thorough going-over. He's expecting a big season. Connor wrote to say that the cattle numbers will be up on last year.'

'Hopefully, Mrs Reece, all going well,' replied Ross.

'And we've been hearing great things of your improvements. What with your new homestead additions and the work on the western boundary.' Mrs Reece removed her gardening gloves. 'You will come inside for tea. I've just made a cake. It only needs a dash of cinnamon and sugar to finish it off. Oh, and did you bring your wife? I didn't meet her when she came through last year but those that did sang her praises. Pretty and refined, that's what people said of her. We never took much notice of that newspaper gossip. You coming from such a fine family and all. And once Mrs Grant arrived, we knew everything was codswallop.'

'Thank you, Mrs Reece, but I've only just arrived in town. You'll tell your husband that I was here and that I'll call on him later.'

'Of course. You'll join us for dinner, won't you? And Connor, if he's travelling with you. Charming man he is, with a cheeky sense of humour. Of course, once the Administrator knows you're in Darwin you may well find yourself siting on the veranda at Government House with that lovely sea breeze. Such a well-situated building. Only the best for our public servants.'

'I was wondering about the young woman who was put into your care. Maria,' interrupted Ross.

'Maria isn't with us anymore.' Her tone sounded slightly prickly now. 'I did write and tell Connor but the way the mail is sometimes during the wet . . .' She lifted her hands, palms up. 'I don't mind telling you it was a kerfuffle last year, Mr Grant. Not that we minded the responsibility. My husband said it was only proper we help, us being the face of the Grant family business here in Darwin.' She leant a bit closer. 'We had all sorts of people hanging about the house. The clergy, the do-gooders, newspaper journalists, all sorts. It was a hard time for Mr Reece and myself. Maria told us very little, however I did as Connor asked and intercepted any letters addressed to her and those she tried to mail. All of them were for you, Mr Grant.'

Ross thought he had heard her wrong. 'What?'

'I figured she was trying to obtain further help but we all know you'd already done quite enough. It was a difficult time. Why, people trailed us in the street, trying to find out the truth of things. We never did hear, not really,' she hinted.

The woman continued to speak, but her words blurred together. Ross may well have walked away, stunned by Connor's manipulations, were he not so struck by the extent of his plotting.

'And poor Maria. Well, I was pleased when things turned for her. Not that I minded having her in the house. She was a worker and I've never been one to turn my nose at a good domestic, Aboriginal or otherwise, but you never can tell. If you know what I mean. Still, when you look the way Maria does, trouble follows a woman no matter the blood. Especially here, where girls of a marriageable age are hard to find.'

'What do you mean Maria's not with you? She's meant to be in your care,' said Ross, when the woman finally paused to dab at perspiration.

Mrs Reece straightened. 'She was, Mr Grant, but Maria left here over a month ago with her young man.'

'What young man?' queried Ross, his voice raised.

'Why, her fiancé, Edward. Hugh Carment's son. And Maria was very fortunate to catch his eye. Very fortunate, indeed. Why it weren't two months before they were outing. I was doubtful the young man would pursue her, for it takes more than pretty looks and we all know the rubbing needed when the silver's tarnished. But Edward isn't your average young man. He's principled like you, Mr Grant. Anyway, they're married now, so you don't need to worry about the likes of Marcus Holder taking advantage again. May he rest in peace. Died ten days ago, he did. The minister said there was no record of a proxy wedding having ever taken place, not that such a thing is legal. But bless you for trying to save a girl like her. You will come for dinner, Mr Grant, we eat at –'

Ross wasn't capable of listening to her anymore. He looked at the Reeces' neat weatherboard house. The angled slats on the windows made the home appear heavy-lidded, the low-slung tin roof like a lined brow. He made his excuses to leave, and shut the garden gate forcefully. He only just remembered to tip his hat in farewell.

He turned left and left again. The deserted street unfurled to a narrow point where a speck of blue swam on the tilt of the horizon. A dray went past, the pop of a whip hastening its progress. Ross pursued the driver until the wagon turned at the end of the block. Still he kept walking, his direction fixed on the sea.

The long avenue gradually filling with movement. Ross shouldered his way past men in grimy collars and tunic-clad Chinese people, quite unable to believe what he'd just heard. The laundries with their crippling heat propelled him onwards until the strange aromas of oriental cooking were left behind and neatly dressed sun-hatted women strolled along Smith Street. As if by instinct, he'd found his way to the Victoria Hotel. He stormed through the door into the public bar, jostling the early drinkers to one side.

Miners, graziers, labourers and hunters turned at his entrance. Ross didn't hear the words of greeting or the offers to buy him a beer. His focus was on one man.

Connor sat at a table near the window reading the newspaper. He looked up as Ross approached. Raising his hand in acknowledgement, the Scotsman called to the woman behind the bar and ordered Ross a drink.

'Well then, I have news.' He tapped a folder that sat on the table. 'Holder's solicitor is meeting us here. The place is to be sold. Holder's died.'

'Why did you do it?' hissed Ross.

There was no mistaking the uneasy look on Connor's face. In another world, Ross may have said his piece and left but this was different. Since the beginning of their time in the Territory, he'd been troubled by Connor's meddling, however he was the closest thing to a friend Ross had. Not since Alastair, or before the war when his childhood friends still spoke to him, had there been one person whom he'd trusted as much, who he believed understood the pressure placed on him by his family, and Connor knew he loved Maria. It made the man's deceit so much worse.

Slowly, Connor stood. 'You've seen Mrs Reece?'

'You knew I would find out about Maria,' countered Ross.

'Aye. Although I wasn't aware until recently that they'd planned to marry so quickly,' said Connor.

Ross could barely believe what he was hearing. 'And I suppose my father knew of Edward Carment's interest.'

Connor thrust his hands in his pockets. 'I didnae tell your father. After what happened last year I doubted either of us would still be in the Territory. And now as far as he's concerned you're with Darcey.'

A billowy middle-aged woman placed two beers on the table. 'If you boys are going to argue take it outside, otherwise I expect the both of you to sit down and drink up.'

'I'm leaving in a minute,' replied Ross bluntly.

'Good.' The publican left them alone.

'You knew how I felt about Maria,' Ross continued once she'd gone.

'That's why it had to be done. You'd ruin yourself for her, Ross.' Connor held up a hand, index finger and thumb barely an inch apart. 'You came this close to that happening. I thanked the day Darcey turned up at Waybell, and then when I saw how well you two were getting on –'

'I don't want to see you again, Connor. Pack your bags and go back to Adelaide.'

'Listen to me –'

'Listen to you?' Ross let out a mirthless laugh.

'People can hear what we're saying, lower your voice,' cautioned Connor.

'Listen to you?!' Ross repeated, louder. 'I'll never listen to you again! Who would know what's fact or fiction? I knew from the beginning that you were my father's man. If you weren't keeping watch on me, you were making sure your own position was never blackened. Bugger what *I* wanted in life.'

'Hell, Ross, I'm your friend first and foremost.'

'No you are not!' yelled Ross. 'You've never been my friend. You're just like the rest of them. Trying to trap me into doing your bidding. Ensuring I adhere to what the family wants and never giving a thought to what I care about. Well, no more. Do you hear that, Connor Andrews? I'm *not* going to be controlled *anymore*. This is *my* life and I refuse to have people interfering in it.'

Connor's face was stormy. 'I'm not falling out with you over a whore.'

Ross rushed at him but the Scotsman was quick. He sidestepped to the left and punched Ross in the middle of the chest. Ross staggered backwards but held his ground and answered with a hard blow to Connor's jaw. The Scotsman flinched and responded in kind. Ross dipped and weaved, avoiding the next strike but Connor didn't miss on the following attempt. The watching crowd let out a collective groan. Ross hit him again and received a quick response. They stood, matching strike for strike. An intolerable anger fanned Ross's need to cause pain, and he lost sight of the individual standing opposite him swaying gently under the force of each blow. There was only fury within him and a rush of resentment that found the briefest relief when his knuckles grew smeary with blood and snot. The strength of his blows forced Connor against the wall and still they persisted at each other. He was prepared to go on until he dropped from exhaustion if need be, until a stranger landed such a clout to the side of his head that Ross fell to the floor.

Two men dragged Ross upright, constraining him, as a tight circle of drinkers looked on. A dark-suited man stepped forward from the crowd.

'You're Ross Grant?'

Ross rubbed at his jaw. 'Yes.'

'I'm Charles Pike, Mr Holder's solicitor. I can't in good conscience proceed with the sale of my client's property to you, Mr Grant. Everyone is aware of Mr Holder's unsuccessful attempts to have you stand trial for the attack on his person, and considering what I've just heard I think he had good cause. Mr Holder might be dead but I very much doubt he'd want to sell you anything.'

Then the men holding Ross dragged him upstairs and dumped him in one of the rooms. He sat up, one hand on the floor to steady his balance as a brusque woman's voice explained that the punches he'd received didn't warrant the laying about he was currently enjoying.

'Mr Andrews, on the other hand, is deserving of a bed,' she continued. 'He can stay here rent-free until he mends but you, Mr Grant, you can pay double. Get up,' she demanded. 'Connor Andrews is well thought of in Darwin, however you always were an unknown quantity and you've proved yourself such.'

Piano music filtered into the room. A coverlet hung from a bed and Ross pulled himself upright, sitting on the groaning springs. The woman sat near a washstand, a ribbon of blue-yellow flame from a kerosene lantern throwing her bulky shadow on the wall. A thick arm held a pipe that she sucked on savagely, puffing smoke through her nostrils. He vaguely recalled her from the public bar. The door opened and one of the men who'd hauled him from the bar dropped his belongings on the floor. The room was small and cheaply furnished. It was not the accommodation he'd paid for.

'There's a bottle of rum on the table,' she said. 'I imagine you're a drinker. If you weren't when you arrived in the Territory, you will be by now.'

Ross poured a nip of rum and swallowed. The liquid was harsh. Diagonally across from where he was slumped, stars showed through an open window. 'Who hit me?'

'My first husband was a boxing champion.' She rubbed at her right hand. 'He taught me a thing or two, which comes in handy when there are problem drinkers or men who aren't right in the mind.' She tapped her forehead for emphasis. 'You have to use your noggin, love, before you revert to fisticuffs. The little Scotsman isn't to blame for your poor choice in women.'

Ross tipped more rum into a glass.

'Not interested in how he fared, are you? Well, Connor's damaged, but he'll mend. You, on the other hand, are going to need more than rum and a good dose of castor oil to put you back together. No one can help you, lad, except you yourself. If you're willing. Having a bit of fluff on the side is one thing, expecting something to come of it is just plain stupid. I should know, I'm on my third husband.' She opened the door to the room. 'By tomorrow the whole of Darwin will be dredging up last year's story about the attack on poor Marcus Holder, and you'll have made us front-page news again with the stink of adultery and slavery added to whet the Southerners' appetites. Thanks for that. We have enough troubles with our image without no-hopers like you making things worse. You know trial by jury's been abolished in Darwin except in cases of murder. The authorities said it was impossible to obtain a conviction against any Darwin citizen by a jury of his peers, but you know, I think they'd make an exception in your case. I'll send up one of the lads with some food but I want you gone by morning.'

Ross took a long swig from the bottle as the door clicked shut. The drink slid down his throat until the flask was nearly empty and a numbness replaced the throb of his skull. The ceiling hung low and close, pulsating back and forth, matching each wave of air that passed through his lungs.

Maria was married. He repeated the phrase again and again, reliving the months she'd spent at Waybell. There were so many images he could draw on but none so provocative as the last time they'd been together. He thought of their bodies that day. Entwined. Recalled the taste of her on his tongue. Were he back at Waybell now, he would press his mouth to the walls of his bedroom and she would be there, infused into the wood.

He was woken the next day by a figure in the doorway. Ross shielded his face from the sun's glare. Lifting his head from the lumpy pillow he wiped at crusty dribble, stepping square into a plate of untouched meat and vegetables as he righted himself. The rum bottle fell to the floor and rolled towards the door. Connor stooped to pick it up, setting it on the washstand. His face was bruised and swollen, a busted lip and broken nose the most obvious injuries. He coughed, a spine-hacking noise that caused him to take a breath, bringing him to stillness.

'What time is it?' Ross ran his fingers through mussed hair.

'Afternoon. I see you dinnae look much better than me.' Connor placed a folder on the edge of the washstand, clearly not wanting to step further inside the room than necessary. His two front teeth were missing.

'That's the surveyor's map of Holder's station.' He gestured to the paperwork. 'The lawyer asked me to return it to you. He thought you might like it for a souvenir.' Connor's words were tight and inflexible. The lilting accent – usually all ferny glens, hills and burns – was gone, replaced by desolate moorlands.

'Nothing like having a sense of humour.' Ross lifted his fist, swollen to twice its size. Dried blood caked his skin. The fingers wouldn't straighten. He raised the sash window a few more inches and stared out over the town. The view faced south, away from the water, taking in the neat framework of the city and the mass of trees that marked the division between progress and where he'd come from.

By tomorrow, much of Darwin who'd previously only guessed at the truth of his relationship with Maria would know of his love for her. By the end of the week, Pine Creek and Katherine would be crawling with the news. The telegraphers would be busy. Not that it mattered. He'd taken care of himself for long enough to know how it was done and he wasn't so useless as to be unemployable.

'You should go back to the station. One of us has to be there,' said Ross.

'Aye and you?' asked Connor.

'Considering everything that's happened, I'm sure you'll understand that what I do is none of your damn business.'

Outside, a wizened black man was standing on the corner. A passing horserider and two people walking in opposite directions were the extent of the traffic, until the noisy chug of the Sandfly locomotive, and the blast of her whistle, stung the air.

'Where is she?' asked Ross, still fixed on the street scene.

'Dinnae do this. You have to let her go. She's married, which is good for a girl like her. People said she was a prostitute in Chinatown. That she was bought up by an old concubine who taught her –'

Ross faced Connor. 'You knew how I felt about her.' That was the cut of it. Connor's treachery was absolute. 'Where is she?'

'At Hugh Carment's station. I can't do this anymore, Ross. You have a wife who cares for you, and whether you want to admit it or not, you care for Darcey as well. I'll leave and head back to Adelaide if that's what you prefer, but dinnae throw it all away.'

'You can go back to Waybell, Connor,' said Ross.

'And what about you?'

'Thank you.' Ross held open the door. 'You can go.'

Connor left quietly, his boots muffled by the red carpeted runner that threaded its way to the end of the hallway and the largest room. The Scotsman moved slowly. He remained a wiry man unchanged by heat or damp, infuriatingly consistent in his approach to life. Ross waited until he entered the end room that had once been his on their arrival in 1919. He remembered that there was a view of the sea from that balcony and a writing desk positioned at the window with a cushioned cane chair. There was no way to explain Connor's actions and no chance now to right what was wrong. Ross would never forgive him.

He tore a strip from the bedsheet, poured water into the wash-stand and gradually eased out his damaged fingers in the cool liquid. He pressed down hard on the ceramic base, feeling the stretch of ligaments, and then wound the strip of linen around his hand. He tipped the remaining water over his head.

Downstairs, the publican wiped the bar with a frayed cloth. She looked up as he approached, her brow creasing. 'We have towels, you know.'

Taking a wad of notes from his wallet, Ross sat them on the counter.

She licked her thumb and flicked through the money. 'That's too much.'

'I'm surprised you'd say that.' Ross poured water from a pitcher on the bar and drank. His stomach was complaining. 'It seems everyone wants their pound of flesh.'

'And you?' she asked. 'What do you want, Ross Grant?'

Ross hoisted the swag on a shoulder. 'To be left alone,' he said.

⊰ Part Three ⊱

1929

❧ Chapter 43 ❧

Central Australia

Not much pushed Ross onwards other than rage. He and Nugget travelled west and south. Paddled up rivers, walked rangy hills and skirted the Tanami Desert. Eight years had passed, and in that time he'd sunk bores on the Barkly, trapped wild horses and constructed so many fences in the south that he hazarded Australia was now cut in half. Miles and miles of boundary lines constructed for big-hatted men with lofty ideals such as those he'd once dreamed. With each post that split the earth, with each swing of the mallet, Ross killed off a little more of his life, hammering the past into the ground. When he stopped and thought of the broken world left behind, he'd step over the pile of cut poles waiting to be bedded and move on.

He considered returning to Waybell, to the place of lost women, but hard labour became so ingrained in the hours that stretched out between dawn and the evening star that Ross now doubted he'd ever feel whole without the thrust of exhaustion and the uncertainty of what lay ahead. He sensed defeat in the prospect of going back and he speculated that life was better alone, that it would get better and, if not, he could exist with what he had.

At last he was an explorer. Of lands already settled and tamed, of his own ability to survive. He rode with Afghan cameleers, led pack mules loaded with mail to red-crusted stations that treated him like a dignitary and went far enough south for white dots to reveal the sheep of his younger years.

Ross had arrived at the Mount Wells Tin Mine nearly a year ago. He'd taken a dogleg west to avoid Pine Creek, and the mine was simply in his path when he came back from the south. The Chinese miners weren't partial to his arrival. They may have been working for a company, however, with their kind having laid claim to the site some forty years earlier they'd dug, died and gone mad chasing the vein that dipped deep under the valley, and they weren't inclined towards any outsiders entering their domain.

There were few white men labouring there. Conditions were rough and the fever claimed many. Ross remained because the desire to move had been beaten out of him for a while. And when he considered leaving, there was really no fixed place he could think of to go.

Unused to the business of keeping his thoughts hidden and his fists by his side, the first few months were painful and difficult. What struck him the most were the people. There were too many of them, living in tents and small timber structures. It was like entering a city, where some streets were safe and others not, but it was *their* city, where they wielded pickaxes by day and chatted at night, carried lumps of rock from the bowels of the earth and scooped up rice with their fingers. There was little choice for Ross: either he got along with these men or got out. So, he got along with them and by the time of his leaving, just prior to the wet, and ten pounds lighter in weight, Ross had a higher regard for them than on arrival.

Don Hart was a teamster, whose job was to haul supplies to and from the site. The boy, sixteen years of age, and thin and scraggly like a yard of pump water, nearly ran Ross over with a dray the first time they met. The second time, the boy bashed one of the workers over the head when he came across Ross and the man rolling around in the dirt.

'What was that about?' Hart asked, as the attacker ran away.

'A book,' Ross panted, wiping the blood from his chin. He held up the last of Alastair's novels. 'It's called *The Twelve Labours of Hercules*,' he explained.

'Don't look like there's much reading left in it,' the boy commented. 'And you don't look like you'd be much of a reader.'

The book was dog-eared and missing a whole wedge of pages. 'It's the only thing I've got left.' Ross stuffed the book inside his shirt.

'Well then, you'd better hang on to it,' the boy replied.

Ross thought on those kindly words. Hart spoke as if he understood what it was to lose something dear.

The boy was a curiosity. He had the eyes of an old man and was friendly to all, although he was no skilled driver. If there was a wheel to be broken, Hart's navigation managed to find every rock and stump. Ross suggested the boy leave before Ping, the Chinese overseer, killed him and fed him to the pigs for the damage he'd caused. There were a few graves but not the number to match the deaths he'd heard about and fresh pork fetched a good price. Ross guessed it was natural that he and the teenager would leave together. Hart was like an old boot with a busted sole that you kept on mending. It would have been easier to buy another pair but somehow Ross couldn't afford to throw the old shoes away.

They headed east, sharing food and fires and stories of what they'd done. Hart listened quietly and rarely asked questions. Ross tended to exaggerate the little good he'd been party to and omitted details from his yarns when they became sticky with wrongdoing, so the versions the boy ended up hearing became narratives that belonged to a better man.

Nearly twenty years separated them. Hart had limited knowledge of the war or of what it meant to be a coward, except in terms of being ready for a fistfight. He wasn't partial to women due to a girl he'd liked who'd died of smallpox. And he hardly cared for where a person had come from or who their family was. Rather, Hart talked about where a man might go and what he could do, given the opportunity. Ross admired his hopefulness and decided against setting the boy straight.

Sand dunes and scrubby plains, anthills and sentinel termite mounds, rocky outcrops and salt lakes. Ross had seen the best and the worst of man and country while his skin cracked like aged cowhide and his legs became bowed from gripping the flanks of his horse. He'd driven himself until hours meant nothing and day and night became one. There were times when he'd sunk so low that carcass-putrid water nearly ended the odyssey for him, when men grew sick of his gnarly tongue and bashed him to a stupor, where he was an outsider among outsiders and he began to find solidarity among sinkholes, death adders and predatory birds. The things that scared others offered him a sort of belonging. So it was strange that being in Hart's company somehow made the days better.

Then, one morning, the horse Hart rode had shied at a snake. The boy had come unsaddled, and landed in the dust near the agitated serpent. It was as ordinary as that. Ross was quick to place a ligature above the bite on the boy's leg to stop the poison's progress, but the last few hours spent slackening the leather strap on the boy's skinny leg hadn't lessened the severity of the symptoms. Gently loosening the strap above Hart's knee and retying it, Ross made shallow knife incisions across the snake bite. The cuts overlapped the previous welts he'd cut into the boy's skin, the area burnt by the Condy's crystals he'd applied. Ross doubted the potassium-based concoction would help.

Hart was propped up beneath a rocky overhang painted with tawny outlines of animals and people. He drank from the waterbag as Ross worked. 'You know what you're doing, mate. I could've died.' His speech was slow.

Ross didn't answer. A small abscess was forming over the wound which, combined with Hart's continuing tiredness, suggested that it would be up to the kid if he were to pull through. Ross lifted a trouser leg, revealing a scarred calf.

'Are they both bites?' asked Hart.

'Nope. That's from a lancewood tree. Come dry season, when it sheds, the branches are hard and pointed. I've seen a man impaled on them.' Ross stretched the skin on his leg, showing another injury where a lump was missing from his flesh. 'This one is. He got me near Wild Man River but I was fortunate to be with someone who knew what to do. Not sure I needed a chunk cut out of me but I survived so I'm not complaining. You will too. Wish it.'

'My mother used to say that. Make a wish and maybe, one day.' The boy's poison-addled eyes were fixed on the drawing of a fish on the rock above. 'Funny, isn't it? How they draw the insides as well. Like they can see the bones.'

'Gives them something to do, I suppose,' answered Ross.

'How come we never see them?'

'They're out there.' During the dry seasons in the snarled back country, where a slurp of water was worth a life, Ross became aware of the Aboriginal warriors trailing him. 'Friendly' remained a loose term when they dragged unseen spears between their toes. Staying away from their women, he kept his rifle handy and always gave out tobacco before moving on, regardless of whether it was deserved. He'd come out of the worst of it with a waddy in the small of his back and a limp that would be with him for life.

'I should be right to ride soon,' said Hart, his skin shiny with perspiration. 'Thanks RG.' His eyelids fluttered as he rested.

That was the name Ross used. Two letters that meant everything and nothing. Next to him, Hart gave a nod of gratitude to match his words. Ross wasn't used to appreciation, in any form. He watched the boy carefully. Hart depended on him. Asked him things. As if Ross knew how to live life properly. Sometimes at night when the boy snored and Ross lay awake, he gave thought to what it would be like to have a son. He figured Hart was the closest he'd ever get to that and he was grateful.

'We'll have to get going today,' Ross told him. Another twelve hours wouldn't make much difference, and at least if they were moving Hart would have something else to fix his mind on. Before the snake bite Hart had been enthusiastic for a kid, but maybe Ross been like that at that age too.

'Do you like horseracing?' asked Ross. The boy slept.

One day, in the past, northwards of Lake Eyre a speck changed shape in the distance. Ross lifted his head, flopping the brim of his hat, which had torn from the crown, and peered through the gap of rabbit pelt. The next day, more figures could be seen in front and behind. Like trailing fly-spots spoiling a surface. He wasn't expecting to see many people on the road. They in comparison were keen to gather in like woolly lambs traversing a great expanse to a single watering point. Ross reluctantly merged with riders, overland travellers and fly-blown camels crossing the border near Charlotte Waters, from the south into the Territory.

'You going to the Alice, then?' said a squashed-nosed man who'd taken up the space next to Ross when there were hundreds of miles available. 'I am. Trying my luck at the races. The stakes are five hundred quid. Five hundred. I'll give it a go. You from Oodnadatta?'

'Nope,' said Ross.

'Adelaide then? You look like you've come a-ways.'

'You riding that horse in a race?' asked Ross, taking in the youth of the gelding. He'd probably been cut too early, leaving no time to grow out. 'Fine-boned and flighty. You won't do any good with him.'

'Hey. How the hell would you know? Look at that piece of scruffy horse-flesh you're sitting on. Why the only thing it's good for is couch-stuffing.'

Ross smacked the man in the face and the stranger fell from the saddle. 'Come on, Nugget. Don't you take any notice.'

He squared closer to the telegraph line, keeping his attention on the single wire suspended from the top of the pole. Eventually the choice needed to be made of whether to go left or right. Ahead lay Darwin. A ranging eight hundred miles or so.

Ross veered westwards, guided by a dry riverbed, which furrowed up behind them like a canoe's wake. The sand made for heavy going and he wrestled Nugget clear of the powder, the pastel pinks and golden tinges of the McDonnell Ranges beckoning in the distance. It was there that the carcasses of the caterpillars lay. The ancestors of the old people of this land. The spaces in the hills showed where they had fought the enemy and had their heads bitten off during the battle. Ross reckoned he knew what that was like.

He kept moving on until lack of light forced him to stop. He made a fire and tipped water into his hat for Nugget to drink, wishing he'd made for the Alice. He was skint. And while being broke wasn't so bad out bush, a bit of flour and salt wouldn't have gone amiss. Mostly he existed on one meal and a glug of rum a day and, if need be, could go for seven before the weakness set in. So a ride down the straight at the Alice could have been an opportunity.

A few years ago he'd met up with a man called Joe Davies at Katherine. They'd won a pile at the races, Ross riding Nugget and Joe laying bets. They blew the winnings in a week but not before he'd procured a new saddle and blanket for Nugget and a set of clothes for himself and kept enough for the odd bottle of rum. Horseracing. It was a cattle-king pastime in the dead centre of Australia, a way to make a quid if you owned a stripling like Nugget and didn't mind people. Which Ross now did.

Except for Joe. Joe said what he meant. He was a ringer from Queensland who'd taken to buffalo hunting and Ross had already done one season with him, shooting the beasts for their horn and hide. He was to join Joe again very soon in the northeast. God willing. He'd not mentioned this potential job to Hart before, partly because he'd not expected the boy to stay with him for so long, nor could he be sure that Joe would welcome a young stranger.

Hart was awake again. 'Have you ever been buffalo hunting?' asked Ross.

'No. But I could learn.'

Ross walked to the edge of the rock shelter, flicking his blade back and forth on his shirtsleeve to clean it. The lowlands stretched below. A vibrant green mat of rain-pooled land trimmed with the resinous smell of drying grasses and fringed by pandanus palms. Sheer sandstone ridges several hundred feet in height extended southwards, while in the east they dropped away to the valley below. The crude map in Ross's pocket outlined the Magela Plain and Cannon Hill. They lay before him. New way-markers on a trail with an unknown end. Ross planned to reunite with Joe Davies's outfit downstream from the river, crossing near the Oenpelli Mission, and do a season of hunting. They'd formed a tight partnership three years ago when they'd met by chance at the top end of the Mary River but Ross refused to stay on for another year. The past was a jagged reminder of what it meant to trust someone.

'Is it far?' asked Hart.

Ross recalled Mick's description. 'Remember that hole in the rock we rode through? Well, that's step one. Out there is part of the plain we ride across to get to the East Alligator River, and eventually we'll reach the place where the blacks speak something different.'

'So you haven't been there?'

'Not there, no.' Hart was one of the few people he'd known who didn't feel the need to empty his mouth by the minute. Ross appreciated that in a person. Words were useful but they wore out quickly. 'We'll have to make a move soon.' He cupped water from a rocky pool edged by ferns and drank. Stains on the rock's surface showed where run-off drains had already dried. There would be more water at the base of the hill.

'I think we're near Waybell Station,' commented Hart. 'It's the last place before stone country. You heard about the owner who up and disappeared? Real mystery.'

'I'm not from around here,' answered Ross. 'I told you that.'

'Sure. I just thought you might have heard. Happened a while back. I was a kid myself then, but there was a real stink about it. My father said he had money. Pots of it.'

Ross left a small amount of tobacco on the ground. Then he shouldered Hart, and the boy hobbled towards the horses.

'Who's that for?' asked the boy.

'That outcrop was someone's home. Best to thank them, eh?'

Behind them an Aboriginal man appeared from the direction of the rock overhang. Naked except for a small string bag tied about his neck and bands of scarlet ochre dotted with white, he stood quite still leaning on a long spear. Finally, he walked over and picked up the tobacco and then disappeared.

≪ Chapter 44 ≫

They passed red paintings on a rock face. Long-limbed stick-figures that could have been running or swimming, Ross couldn't decide.

'They give me the creeps,' said the boy.

'They're *mimi*,' Ross told him. 'Spirits.'

'You mean like ghosts?'

'I don't know rightly,' replied Ross. 'Down south I saw bright lights once or twice. They came out of nowhere and disappeared just as quickly. The bloke I worked for called them *mimi* lights. Reckoned an old blackfella called them spirit people. That some were good and some were bad. I guess it's better if you can't tell.'

Hart nodded. 'I suppose.'

It was hard going crossing the plains. They rode through dense palm trees and shoulder-high grass, trying to avoid the green carpet of weed, which floated above the waterholes hiding boggy pits and crocodiles. Some of the land was already burnt, the savage decaying growth of the wet season razed by the local Aboriginal population so that fresh young shoots would appear. The fires were eventually put out by the rivers, creeks and the numerous water-holes that crisscrossed the grasslands.

They made camp at the base of a hill, in a cave filled with animal bones. Their fire threw spluttering light onto painted walls drawn vivid with stencilled palms and tall-hatted men with rifles. Ross swigged from a bottle of rum, treasuring each gulp. He knew it should be saved. That to drink it all in one go would condemn him within a day to violent sweats and uncontrollable shaking. That was the worst of being unable to live without alcohol. Ross undid the ligature on Hart's leg and then retied it.

'It looks better,' said Ross, lifting his gaze from the festering bite to where Hart tongued at a capful of water. 'Couple of days, you'll be good as new.'

The boy nodded and lay back, exhausted.

Outside, Ross scratched around for kindling. Nugget snorted, edging closer to the shelter. Ross set the wood near the resting boy and scraped his knife on stone until a spark finally took.

'You hungry, Hart?' But the boy was asleep.

Ross stood at the mouth of the cave and held up the rum bottle. Brittle light from a waning moon revealed it to be half-empty. He'd not planned on going near the Oenpelli Mission. Venturing back into real society was not something he was at all keen to do. Ross was better out in the bush where there were no expectations constraining him, but Hart wasn't getting better. The boy needed to stay put and either recover or at least be able to spend his final days with better care than Ross could offer. But he knew the company of white men would lead to questions he couldn't answer. The choice played in his mind.

Wedging his swag until it fitted in the hollow of his back, Ross emptied the saddlebag, lining up the contents in the dirt. Quart-pot, tea, the last of his tobacco, rifle shells, fishing line, and the book he now had difficulty reading, *The Twelve Labours of Hercules*, both due to the missing pages and failing vision. His eyesight had begun deteriorating earlier that year. 'Here's to us, Nugget.' He swigged the rum and swigged again until it was empty, feeling bereft by the finishing of it.

Ross held the bottle by the neck, envisaging another flagon years ago, one filled with sunset rum, and the man who'd poured that first pannikin. Sowden.

'Makes some men mad and kills others,' Ross muttered to himself, recalling Maria's warning, his voice tumbling into the dark. He thought of her hand on his chest as she sat by his side in the rain that long-ago morning. Then he lay down in the sand as the alcohol took effect, reflecting on the places he'd been and what he'd done after Waybell. After Maria. Brawls had been often and vicious. Not much was needed to rile a man in places where it took more spine to survive than stand upwards, and Ross had grown adept at irritation. A bitterness had leeched its way inside of him. He wasn't good with people anymore and he wasn't any better alone. But he was trying with Hart.

Women had tended some of his injuries and slept with Ross when they'd felt inclined. Mostly he didn't remember them. Except in terms of relief, when he couldn't get his stomach filled with grog. Between times he chopped wood, saddled drover's horses and searched for water. Always moving on, taking one road and then another as had the explorers of old, except this expedition had no end.

There were turning points in a person's life, and his were dotted unceremoniously across a spate of years that made him feel shrivelled by time. It made the original romance of Waybell, the dream shared by two brothers, pathetically ignorant. All of it was. Women, love, new land. Settlers' dreams rarely touched the truth of life up North. Ross knew that now.

The night was spent with the fierce crack of thunder breaking the noise of Hart's breathing. If the boy were a dog Ross would have cut his ear and bled him at the first sign of the bite, hopeful that the pump of his heart would purge the venom from his body. Feet away, Nugget snorted at the storm. Every time Ross hooked at the reins and tried to coax the horse inside for protection, the gelding tossed its head in defiance, rain glossing the animal's coat until it shone like wet coal.

Ross woke with a start, his stomach paining and body shaking. The sun cracked through an overcast sky. Nugget gave him a hurt expression. He packed their belongings and roused a listless Hart, looping a rope around the boy's waist, securing him to the saddle. He threw the empty bottle in the dirt, thinking of the crows he'd dreamt of during the night. This wasn't the place to stay. He looked about at the mouth of the cave and the broken rocks and shiny plants and stared at Hart, slumped over the saddle, then he swung himself up onto Nugget's back. After an age of trying to keep his mind still on windy days, Ross blinked and turned east. Living proved difficult, but not as difficult as trying to kill himself through drink. That took some doing.

❧ Chapter 45 ❧

The horses waded through mangroves and across the muddy yellow river towards a rickety landing platform as the incoming tide swept to meet them. Waiting for them on the other side were four Aboriginal people. There was little Ross could do but make for the platform. It was the shortest, and appeared to be the shallowest, crossing and the surging tidal currents weren't going to slow while he debated a better route. Ross's index finger was poised curled and tight on the trigger of the rifle that lay across his thighs. Having almost crossed the river and reached the lands where men spoke something different, he didn't fancy being the recipient of a barbed point in the flesh, or becoming crocodile prey.

The horses struck sandy soil just as the deceptive bough shape of a crocodile sunk beneath the water. Nugget's haunches flexed as the gelding found purchase on dry land and then drew up hard where the men stood. Each held a spear and smoked a pipe. One of the men, who had a frizzled grey beard, stepped forward and Ross picked up a mix of pidgin English and an indecipherable language, which might have been Japanese for all he understood of it.

'You follow us to the mission, eh?' said a younger man.

He'd not expected to feel relief at passing the boy into someone else's care. The welcome suggested they'd known of Ross's coming, courtesy of the smouldering fires that stoked the sky. Ross tapped Hart on the shoulder but the only response was laboured breathing. The men gave the sagging boy a cursory glance and then waved eastwards and began to walk.

'Young fella crook?' asked one of them.

'Snake bite,' Ross told him.

'Looks pretty buggered.'

Ross tugged on the lead and Hart's mare drew level with Nugget. The cave had been a far better resting place. They shouldn't have left it. When confronting mortality, a person didn't need movement. A man required peace to ready himself.

Eight miles of rough ground later they reached the mission. It consisted of a collection of neat stringybark buildings, hemmed in by water, hills and plains. Mobs of pelicans were paddling about on a lagoon while, to the north and south, rocky ranges spread angular and sharp against the sky. A slight man of fair complexion emerged from a small house and introduced himself as the missionary, Mr Dyer. He listened intently to Ross's explanation as he cut the rope that tethered Hart to the horse.

'Bring the boy,' the man directed.

Ross followed Mr Dyer to the broad veranda at the rear of the house, and placed Hart in one of the hammocks. The boy was listless. A thin arm fell to the floor, fingers brushing the timber boards. Ross placed it carefully back by the boy's side and then removed his own hat, toying with the brim. Mr Dyer touched Hart's brow then lifted the trouser leg to inspect the wound. A thin red line spread up the boy's leg from the fast-growing abscess.

'He's too far gone,' said Mr Dyer apologetically. 'I'll leave you to say your goodbyes.'

Ross looked at the departing missionary to Hart and dragged a stool to the boy's side. There were no words he could think of that seemed right or proper, so he simply sat and waited for the young face to turn away from life. Small foamy bubbles gathered at the corners of Hart's mouth. Ross swished at the flies. The boy stared out at the neat garden, which stretched to the lagoon. Ross searched for a story to share, a few words that might ease Hart's journey but instead he felt his own lips tremble and berated his uselessness. He took the boy's hand.

It took some time for Hart to die but when his last breath was finally taken, Ross closed the boy's eyes and thought about what it had meant to him to have a friend.

'Thank you,' he said quietly to Hart's still form.

In the afternoon Mr Dyer returned and read from a Bible. When he'd completed the passage he patted Ross's shoulder. 'I'm sorry for your loss. Was the boy family?'

'No. I met him at a mine and we sort of stuck.'

'Hard life. Hard death,' pronounced Mr Dyer. 'You never said what your name was?'

'RG.' He lifted Hart in his arms for the final time. 'Where do you do your burying?'

'This way.'

Later, Ross sat on the stool near the empty hammock, his thumb rubbing the worn cover of Alastair's book. The missionary's wife was busy in the schoolhouse and Ross was yet to meet her, having respectfully specified that only he and Mr Dyer were needed at Hart's graveside.

Mr Dyer stayed close, returning to the veranda frequently as if he eventually expected Ross to need him. Ross suspected the missionary saw him clearly: an anonymous drifter stripped bare of excess fat, the colour of burnt beef, a shady man of indeterminate beliefs who may well have gone to war for the scars he carried.

'I best be going.' Ross knew Joe Davies was waiting, camped somewhere along the river.

'Geese, ducks, ibis and crane.' The missionary handed Ross a pannikin of tea, noticing the tremors in his hands. 'Beautiful, aren't they? I could sit here all day watching them out there. Are you a bird lover, RG?'

'More a bird eater,' he responded, gulping the liquid.

'Well, we all see beauty in different things for different reasons.'

'I was to meet Joe Davies,' explained Ross.

'I figured as much. Joe said you were coming.' Mr Dyer took a sip of tea. 'He's camped about five miles away. Why don't you wash up? I can find you a clean shirt from among our stores.'

Ross scratched at his beard, which stretched down to his chest. 'I'm not a taker for your ministrations, Mr Dyer. It's not that I don't appreciate it. I've just been out in the scrub for too long.'

'You're a reader?' asked the missionary.

Ross held up the book. A portion of the title was missing. 'It's done some travelling. Like me, I guess.'

'And is it really as hard as the Greek myths would have us believe? All those labours?'

Ross squinted at the volume, wondering what the man was getting at. 'It's just a book.' He placed the tome on his swag and waited for the man to finish staring at him.

'There was an Aboriginal reserve here before the Church took it over,' said the missionary. 'Many of the children here are of mixed blood and we expect the numbers to only increase. I suppose I'm telling you this because family comes in all forms. Young Hart was family to you.'

'I barely knew him.'

'Out here it's not unusual for men to ride miles to save a sick friend. There's few of us about and we're scattered by distance, which means that the word "reliance" takes on powerful significance. It's knowing why we go out of our way to help someone who's important.' The missionary stomped on the boards, frightening away a foot-long lizard ambling along the veranda. 'We'll do up a headstone for young Hart. Is there anything that you'd like for an epitaph?'

Ross wondered at the point of a few words scratched on a piece of wood that would be worn blank by weather and eventually rot. But had he sunk so deep that even a remembrance to the dead meant nothing anymore? Across from him the missionary waited.

'He was a good boy,' said Ross, wondering at the moisture in his eyes. All he knew was that he wanted Hart back by his side.

'How about "saved by a friend"?'

'But I didn't save him,' argued Ross. 'It would have been better if I'd stayed put and let him die in peace.'

'And how do you know that he didn't?' Mr Dyer asked him.

'I have to go. I'm obliged to you,' said Ross, finishing the tea.

The missionary walked with him to where Nugget waited in the shade. 'My wife wanted you to have this.'

The package contained a half-dozen johnnycakes still warm from the fire. Ross didn't know what to say. It had been many years since anyone cooked for him, let alone a woman. He pocketed the food. Out to the west he'd once stolen a leg of meat from a drover's fire when the man would have undoubtedly been happy to share a meal and a yarn.

'We came across from the Roper River Mission,' Mr Dyer said as Ross tightened the girth-strap. 'You hear many a strange thing in these outlying places. Stories that are fabricated in the scrub, worn smooth around the campfire. There's one about a man who left his family, wandered into the bush and disappeared. Many think he's dead and he may have been forgotten, except that he always did the right thing by the local people, giving out tobacco and sharing food.'

'Maybe he was being smart,' said Ross.

'Perhaps, or he could be more human than some of us and not realise it.'

'Don't know him.' Ross placed his boot in a broken stirrup and swung up into the saddle.

The missionary held tight to the horse's reins. 'He carries a book with him. A story of Greek heroes. Some say he goes by the name of "RG" and I suspect that stood for his real name, Ross Grant.'

'I think you've got me confused with someone else, Mr Dyer.' Ross looked about the mission, with its cleared land and sundry outbuildings. It was a neat enough holding, carved as it was out of the guts of the Territory. Children of mixed degrees of colour played chase in the dirt. Ross jerked on the reins, freeing the leather from the man's grip. 'I appreciate what you did for Hart.'

The missionary gave a flat smile. 'See that hill? It's about a half-mile away. If you climb to the top, you'll get your bearings.'

'I'll do that.'

The mound was easy to climb. Ross guessed it to be about six-hundred feet high with a fine view of the surrounding plains, the mission with its lagoon, and Joe's camp, which lay four miles further on. A scatter of horses and tents. There was a wooden cross at the top of the mound and Ross imagined the missionary praying for guidance, caught midway between the vastness of the universe and the responsibility that lay on the ground. Solitude and perspective. Maybe he and Dyer were not so different.

He kicked Nugget's flanks and they cantered off.

⋘ Chapter 46 ⋙

At the edge of the camp, three Aboriginal men were methodically going through a string of thirty packhorses, checking and paring down the shoeless hooves, which grew quickly in the soft country and regularly split. Ross led the two horses towards them – Hart's was now a handy spare. From their furtive glances, he could see the men were suspicious at his arrival. A lanky individual ran a hand along fetlocks and hindquarters, sneaking closer to the other two, who were stern-eyed. A file tapped the palm of a hand. The curl of a whip readied for action. Accounting for the odds, Ross immediately sought an advantage. He could slash a couple with his knife but if it came to it he'd have to fight or shoot, or both.

'Who are you?' one of them called.

'I'm looking for Joe Davies.' Ross's gaze skimmed over the group to the clutch of wurlies where women and children were gathered, and then to the tents a few hundred yards away, where a man was shaving, a piece of mirror tacked to a tree. 'I'm RG, he's expecting me.'

The men looked doubtful. 'You're RG?' the lanky one asked. Then he turned towards the tents. 'Hey, Joe!'

The man abandoned his shaving and wandered over, patting at his chin with a rag.

'Who are you?' He came close enough for Ross to recognise the fine scar above Joe's cloudy eye. 'RG? What the devil happened? I didn't recognise you.' They shook hands. 'You look crook and –'

'You're unchanged,' interrupted Ross.

'Except for a few more aches,' answered Joe. 'I wondered if you'd come.'

'Within ten days of the end of May, beginning of June. That's what we agreed,' said Ross.

'It was a while ago.' Joe studied him thoughtfully. 'Over three years. Either one of us could have changed our minds. Taken on something else. Still, you're here now.'

'Your team aren't very welcoming,' commented Ross.

'You look like a tramp, mate, that's why.' Joe turned to the horsemen. 'Best shot at the gallop you'll ever see. You can still shoot?'

'Better than you,' answered Ross.

He noticed a man weaving towards them through stacks of supplies – tea, sugar and Worcestershire sauce for the humans, salt and arsenic for the hides and enough cartridges to start another war. A string of fish hung limply from the man's hand.

Joe squinted a whitish eye. 'You're not looking your finest, mate. You sure you're up to this?'

'Do you want me or not?' countered Ross.

'Better have a wash, eh?' said Joe, although he sounded unconvinced about Ross's capabilities. 'You smell like you could have something living in that chin growth of yours.'

Ross grabbed a rusty saw, the teeth cracked and stained like those of an old man. Propping his rifle on one knee, he grasped the barrel as he cut through the stock, sawing it clean off. He lifted the weapon, checking it for balance.

'This is all I need.' Ross stroked the attachment where a sword bayonet had once been fixed.

'I would have thought the missionary would have gotten you bathed and churched at first sight. You did see Dyer?' asked Joe.

'Yes, I saw him.'

'Maybe he needs something, or someone, to get cleaned up for,' said the fisherman, with a hiss of air through two mismatched gold teeth. His Scottish accent was painfully familiar.

Ross waited a moment for his mind to settle as the catch was deposited in a bucket. The fishtails stuck out the top, all crescent-shaped scales and grey-silver tones. The bearded man who'd been carrying them was now standing next to Joe. Ross found himself remembering the hours they'd spent together cutting pine for the Waybell homestead, the air in the grove tangy and almost too full of oxygen for his lungs. The splinters of memory washed through him like light through fog.

The fisherman held out his hand. 'It's been a while, Ross,' said Connor, his voice was cautious but also tinged with emotion.

Both of their grips were strong and tight. 'Yes. It certainly has,' replied Ross.

⊰ Chapter 47 ⊱

The cooking fish was spitting and hissing on the skillet. Ross wanted to know how Connor had managed to track him down but he worried that by asking the question a cavern would open beneath his feet and he would fall straight back into a place long left behind. The Scotsman served up the fish, slapping the meat onto an enamel plate, and pointing to a selection of cutlery. Ross studied a fork with its neat, shiny prongs, his fingers shaking, before reverting to what he was used to. He stripped the fish quickly with teeth and hands, demolishing it in an instant, and belched loudly.

Connor looked from Ross's plate to his own. He'd taken only one mouthful so far. 'I've been chasing you for a while. Thought I'd caught up with you at the Marriots' place on the Barkly but you'd gone by the time I got there.' He pricked the fish with the fork, a line of puncture marks running the length of the catch. 'I even paid a black tracker but when you went northwest he refused to go further. Reckoned you knew the country better than him. Either that, or it was sheer luck if you survived.' The sentence ended with the hint of a question. 'People said you weren't worth finding.

Others said that you were a ghost, or maybe I was chasing the wrong man. There's a lot of lost souls wandering around out here.'

'Are you one of them?' Ross asked. 'I figure you must be, to come after me.'

'So what does that make you?' Connor replied.

He was as feisty as always and not short of a comment. Grey hairs and latticed skin may have altered the man's appearance but his cockiness was undiminished. Ross skimmed the dinner plate with his tongue, thinking of Hart alone in a box, untroubled.

'I met Joe Davies in the pub in Darwin a few years ago,' Connor continued. 'We got talking about rough riders and stockmen and he told me a yarn about this bloke who stuck a horse like nobody's business. Won the maiden at Katherine on a niggly gelding a few years back and then picked a fight with anyone interested. Betting on himself. Davies ended up spending a season with him around Wild Man River. Nearly died from a snake bite. Well, you know the rest.' Connor chewed on his catch. 'I never cottoned on to the RG name. It seemed too obvious, and there was a drover by the name of Reg Garnet who covered a fair bit of the Territory down south. He used the same initials, so it never struck me that it was you until Davies mentioned the book that RG always carried. That gave you away. Alastair's childhood obsession.' Connor stabbed at the fish and took another mouthful. 'I never would have figured you to turn out like this. Look at you. Your hair's past your shoulders. Your clothes are barely holding together. How old are you? A few years off forty? You look closer to sixty.'

Ross had no idea how to respond to this question. He was unused to the restrictive ideas of time and place, of pinpointing someone by the years they'd been alive as if it were the only way that a man could be defined. He'd come to know life as a daily path where age meant nothing other than the ability to witness another sunrise.

'Why are you here?' he asked finally.

'A lot's happened since you left.' Connor was chewing so vigorously on the fish that slivers drifted to his lips. He sucked them back into his mouth. 'Haven't you given any thought at all to what took place after you cleared out? Like what happened to Darcey? Your family? Or who's running Waybell? It's been years.'

Ross stretched out his legs, wondering at the options left. Joining Joe's outfit was something he'd planned on and worked towards. Having it ruined by an outsider never came to him as a possibility. 'If you open your mouth again, Connor, it will be a sorry ending.'

'So you really dinnae care at all? About any of it?'

'I left for my own reasons and they haven't changed,' said Ross flatly.

Connor ran a finger around the plate and sucked the juices off it. It itched at Ross, the fact the Scotsman had chased him. Trailing him like a villain through desert and scrub with the same unforgiving stars shining down on both of them.

'You're heading out with Davies, I hear,' said Connor. 'Mind if I come along?'

'Why?' asked Ross.

'Because short of staying at the mission and waiting for the next supply-lugger to take me back to Darwin, I haven't got many options. Besides, I haven't been buffalo hunting before.'

Ross considered what it would mean to have Connor by his side again. He couldn't tell if it was the risk of gladness or the sureness of heartache that made him so undecided. The latter he'd grown accustomed to, while happiness he didn't know anymore except in terms of space and shifting light. It wasn't much, this life he'd chosen, but it proved useful when it came to erasing the past.

They were both older now, different on the outside and in. Like a pair of birds stuffed and mounted on opposite walls. Glassy-eyed and glaring at each other. 'And then what?'

'Then I'll go home,' the Scotsman promised.

'To Waybell?' The word lodged in Ross's throat.

'No. Adelaide. Even if it ends today at your bidding, I'll have done what I set out to do. Find you and tell what's left of your family that you're still alive.'

'I'll think about it,' replied Ross.

Connor retrieved pipe and tobacco from his pocket. His sun-riddled hand stuffed the bowl with dark shreds.

'I wouldn't mind a smoke.' Ross could feel his tongue itching for the taste of something pungent and strong. It had been too long since his last drink in the cave. The bottle was all that remained from when he and Hart had stopped the north–south train, claiming they'd been robbed, and managed to elicit enough compassion for rum and tobacco.

Connor tossed some tobacco and a pipe to him. Ross didn't say anything, simply concentrated on packing the wooden pipe, willing his fingers to stop shaking. Finally, he drew back a lungful of smoke, closing his eyes to savour the pleasure. It was going too far to be asking Connor for a nip of rum as well, although he knew Joe always ran with a couple of crates for emergencies. Dead man's last rites, Joe called the stash. Alcohol for medicinal purposes.

Instead, Ross delved into his shirt where Mrs Dyer's squashed johnnycakes were lodged next to his skin, half-expecting a hint of something womanly to waft up from the wrappings. The paper rustled under his uncontrollable trembling and it was only when Ross became aware of Connor examining him that he sat the parcel on the ground and pushed the round bits of damper across with a boot. The Scotsman took one and ate it. An offering of sorts, given and received.

'I haven't forgiven you,' Ross told him.

'I know,' replied Connor.

❧ Chapter 48 ❧

With horse spittle speckling his face, Ross lurched forward, calves gripping hot flesh, his backside barely in the saddle, beard and hair flying. A resounding noise obliterated everything. It came from the pounding of the horse tilted at full gallop beneath him, the buffalo that was hurtling across the plains that he pursued, and his own breath, quick and gasping.

Holding the sawn-off rifle in one hand like a pistol, Ross readied for the bloody strike, closing the gap until the thudding of the fleeing buffalo's inner workings matched the rapid beats within his own chest. Ross aimed. A single shot escaped from the gun, striking down into the buffalo's loin alongside its spine. In an instant, Nugget was swerving away light and fast across flattened grass from the toppling beast and the sweep of its horns. The buffalo dropped as if struck by lightning, paralysed but still alive, awaiting the knives of those that followed.

Twenty-three for the day. Seventeen shot by him, six by Joe. It was a good tally and as much as he and the skinners could handle. Ross drew up on the edge of the swamp. Oozing, churned-up mud showed the trail taken by the remaining herd across to the safety of the palms, which stood thicket-close and impenetrable a mile away. He laid a hand briefly on the gelding's neck, offering encouragement for a good day's work, and nudged the horse away from the swamp. In the distance the other stockmen killed the wounded beast with a final shot before setting down to the business of skinning it warm, so that rigor mortis didn't make the paring of skin from meat impossible.

Ross didn't enjoy thinking about the animal's last moments. The buffalo lying in wait, frightened of the unknown, unable to move, forced to endure the final insult of hopelessness. Still, the skinners were a good team. In twenty minutes the hide would be off and loaded onto a packhorse ready for the trip back to camp.

He rode over to meet Joe and Connor, and Joe gave a pleased nod. They both knew that, if not for Ross, Joe's takings wouldn't be anywhere near as profitable. He had easily shot at least eight buffalo a day since they began almost three weeks ago, which made today's takings particularly impressive.

'You might want to change horses tomorrow, Ross. Give that nag of yours a rest. He mightn't last the distance with you riding him so hard,' suggested Joe.

Ross shook his head. 'Nugget's a stayer.'

'He always was a sorry-looking excuse for an animal but Mick would be pleased to know how good the trade turned out.' Connor explained to Joe: 'The head stockman on Waybell traded tobacco in exchange for the gelding.'

Ross tugged at the reins, riding clear of the men. Nearly every day the Scotsman dredged up the past. Connor flushed memories out of him like the men drove the buffalo clear of the brush.

'Didnae manage to kill yourself today, then?' asked Connor, giving him a wry smile.

'Not yet,' said Ross. He had a pact with Joe. If he killed at least seven head every day for a week, Joe would give him a bottle of rum. They laughed about it as being a bonus of sorts. Reward for effort. It would be funny, Ross agreed, if he weren't so desperate. It had been five days since the last swig of blessed cane-sugar, a span of hours that led to sleepless nights and a desperation for the speed of a horse and the chance of death to forget the pitiful needs of his body. There'd been moments when he'd been close to stealing Joe's supplies. It wasn't pride that stopped him, but respect for his friend. Joe had never once asked him to explain his past and he'd given Ross a blunt apology for Connor's continued presence.

The day they rode out from under the shadow of Dyer's hill Joe admitted that if he'd known who Ross really was three years ago, he would have asked him to become a full partner in the buffalo-skinning business, to help with the costs. But as Ross's value lay in his abilities and Joe's one good eye was showing strain, he was content having him as part of the team. Joe's description of their professional relationship reminded Ross of how he'd valued Sowden's men. Capital and labour tied together, as if Ross were a principled man of America's Deep South. And now here he was, riding for another man's benefit, all for the promise of a bit of grog.

At the camp Ross handed Nugget over to one of the men and collapsed near a fire, drinking the black tea a woman poured for him. Then she resumed cutting up hunks of buffalo meat. The amount of food at the camp overwhelmed Ross. A meal a day was as much as he could stomach and even then he felt as if he was one of the old ewes on Gleneagle blocked up by a gutful of indigestible grass. A bit of kangaroo or fish would have been enough. A side of roots. Anything other than lumps of bloody meat.

Around him, women had spread the buffalo skins on the ground and were salting them. There were four women to each stinking skin, talking and laughing as they rubbed coarse salt into the hides. The coats had been washed in the waterhole, and the fat and remaining meat cleaned away. Under the cover of a lean-to, hides were turned and restacked, drying out in the air. Another pile was being reordered so that the top hides now sat at the bottom. Ross stared at the stacks. In time, some of the skins would become leather belts driving steam engines, running even in death.

One of the younger women in the camp sauntered past the fire. The older woman preparing the meat shooed her away but not before she'd smiled. He didn't mind the look of her, and she appeared interested in him. He'd never slept with a black woman. Ross liked to believe it was out of respect but, deep down, he knew that taking one of their women could cause trouble, and that's what had stopped him previously.

The last of the packhorses arrived with the fresh hides. Joe was at the lean-to where the skins were stored, speaking to a Chinese worker named Manny, whose job was to ensure that the hides were sufficiently dried and cured properly for transportation to London. On days when the kill exceeded the sunlit hours the camp worked through the cold night, cleaning and rubbing, using salt harvested by the Greeks at Ludmilla Creek near Darwin. It would be no different this evening. Ross knew he would lie shivering in his swag as others prepared what he had brought them.

Ross swirled the tea with a dirty finger, his free hand feeling the solid form of the novel tucked within his shirt next to his skin. The book was all that remained of his brother's stories, a sorry collection of stuck pages and missing sentences that no longer formed a reliable storyline. But it didn't matter, as he hadn't been able to read the book properly for months. Now he only stroked the pages like a blind man reading braille, for he could no longer see the written word close up. It was as if his eyes had been blunted by wind and rain and fibrous light, and with the deterioration it seemed that a part of the civilised, educated world he'd been born into was now lost to him. He was grateful that other, everyday objects remained clear and that the disability was yet to affect anything other than his capacity to read.

'Good day, verily good day, Mr Ross,' called Manny. He did a little dance around the creamy-yellow piles of buffalo horns that were kept near the lean-to of hides.

Ross studied the pyramid of bone. Having been told by Joe that the calcified material would eventually be ground into a powder for the Chinese to use as an elixir, somehow, he knew that those horns would be the closest he ever got to the exotic. He imagined Alastair curled between the front paws of the Sphinx or walking in the footsteps of Kubla Khan while he collected medicine for an ancient culture on the other side of the world.

'You verily good, Mr Ross, verily good.'

This was industry. The Top End kind. Where horses could get filleted by horns and men could be impaled through dumb luck. Chance exchanged for horns and hides. Hunters and the hunted. He only had to kill and stay alive. Ross hated it and loved it.

'Dinnae think I don't know what Davies is up to.'

Of course Connor had taken the space beside him when they were surrounded by a mile of vacant bush. Ross hunched over the chipped mug. He longed for Hart and the boy's quiet ways. The amenable conversation.

'He urges you on to keep the kill high with promises of grog, waiting until those delirium tremens of yours are too bad to aim straight before giving you a bottle. Some friend,' said Connor.

'And you'd know about that.' Ross twisted the cup back and forth deeper into the soil. 'Being a friend.'

'You're a damn alcoholic. You'd drag yourself through the dirt for a drink. I dinnae know why I bothered looking for you,' Connor snarled.

'Why did you then? If I'd wanted finding,' Ross said quietly, 'I wouldn't have tried so damn hard to disappear.'

Connor's shoulders slackened. 'There's many a reason but I'll start with the worst.'

Ross stopped fidgeting. He'd known that this was coming. How Connor managed to keep counsel for so long undoubtedly amazed them both.

'Herself is dead. Your grandmother. Remember her? Died in her bed. And your father. Heart attack. Died within two years of each other. Your father first and then Herself. Two boys missing. Both gone walkabout. What did you expect?'

Ross thought of his grandmother, loving, crafty and hard. Bound to protect the family name, no matter the cost. She'd blackmailed him with his inheritance to ensure that he'd marry Darcey, but he'd never blamed her, not really. She'd been mother and father to him. He would always love her.

'Did you hear me, Ross?'

As for his father, Ross never really knew him or had understood him and he certainly wouldn't miss Morgan Grant.

'Dinnae you have anything to say? They're your blood kin, Ross.'

The gap was so large between this day and his departure from Adelaide. So filled with the clutter of action and inaction that where there might have been at the very least the sense of an ending there was now only dullness.

'You saw your life as a war from the very beginning, Ross. But it's them that lost.' Connor stood, his chest heaving as if he had run a mile. 'You were the one they pitted themselves against, trying to make you understand. But they may have well been tossing pebbles against a rock wall for all you cared.'

'G'day,' interrupted Joe. 'Thought we'd celebrate as it's nearly the end of the week.' He held a bottle ready to pour a nip for each man.

Ross wanted to toss the remaining tea over his shoulder and shove the rim of the pannikin under the flagon's neck but Connor watched, eyes needle-sharp. Ross hated him, hated that he actually cared what Connor thought of him.

'None for me. Give it to Ross,' said Connor. 'He's having his own private wake. For himself.'

'You all right?' asked Joe when Connor left.

Ross took the rum, drank it down and held the cup out again.

'Let's save it for the morning. Steady your nerves for the shoot, eh?' said Joe. 'You know, I never got on with my father, either.'

Ross moved away from Joe and wandered through the camp. They'd been talking about him, no doubt discussing the reasons behind his desertion, trying to find purpose in the choices he'd made. The idea of being judged by these two men made Ross prickle with anger. Connor's presence had ruined the season and damaged the bond he'd once shared with Joe.

A half-mile away at the river, women were digging up mussels that had grown fat deep in the soil. Ross moved aimlessly, the taste of rum still strong in his mouth. At a tree hollow a fly emerged.

Ross stuck his hand inside to plunder the native honey, scooping the dark substance into his mouth. He licked his fingers. Wild honey. The Greek asphodel of the dead. Said to grow in the Elysian Fields. He laughed at this useless knowledge.

Somehow, the young woman from the campfire had known to follow him, and she met him where pandanus palms edged towards thickening bush. He waited, concealed by a tree's shaggy grass skirt of leaves, stepping out from the cover of the plants to grab the girl as she passed. She made a startled noise but didn't try to leave, and allowed him to lift the material of her dress. He nodded encouragingly. Leaves rustled. It didn't take long for the business to reach a satisfying conclusion and he rested against her, feeling suddenly remorseful for his treatment of her, even though she'd been willing. He found himself thinking of Sowden. How the manager once stated that one day a person might be grateful for a little black velvet. Sowden, the man he'd scorned.

He let go of the young woman and stepped away.

'Are you all right?' she asked.

He told her to leave and she ran off. He sank to the base of the palm tree, his hands cradling his face. It had meant so much to him. To have been loved by Maria.

⋘ Chapter 49 ⋙

Ross guided Nugget along a track that led to several rubbing trees, where tufts of buffalo hair were caught on bark and freshly twisted saplings showed a well-defined trail. He ran a callused palm over the rough surface and looked at the hoof-broken ground that would lead to a watering point and a wallow. It had been five days since the last big hunt. Eight since the last drink.

Ross counted the buffalo signs with grim determination. This herd had been hard to find. The dry season was at its peak and the buffalo had taken to camping in the timbered country on the edge of the plain. But their preference for a home range was their undoing. The land dried up a little more each day and ten miles away over one hundred buffalo lay rotting in the earth that bogged them. Ross wanted to tell the brainless beasts that familiarity and security could bring a slow death but his job was to slaughter.

Waiting for the first kill always unsettled him. He distracted himself by thinking of the girl, and the brief couplings that had occurred when the sun dropped low and fast. The camp was too occupied with the task of living to notice the absence of the outfit's crack shot and the young woman he'd taken up with.

Ross wanted the girl to go with him when the hunt finished, except now he agonised over the rightness of the plan. If Hart had been there, the boy would have spoken plainly and told Ross to do what was best. Best for Ross and for the girl. Ross saw benefit in their shared company but he couldn't be certain of the girl's safety. He'd just as likely go on a bender and leave her behind, or worse.

Aboriginal men and women walked through the long grass, beating lengths of timber, tin plates and cups. Anything capable of making a noise. The clamour stirred the buffalo and they moved from the timber, gradually being shepherded towards the edge of the plain. Ross waited for the mass of dark bodies to edge out a little further from the wedge of trees, his mount lifting each leg from the ground like a runner warming up. The herd stopped and sniffed the air. Far to the right sat Joe and Connor like stockmen on a wing of cattle, readying to drive the herd across the plains.

Connor's shooting had been fair to poor. It wasn't that he was incapable, he simply lacked courage. Ross knew this by the way he hung back, giving chase but never quite committing to the final strike of spur to hair. Doggedly tailing a man, that Connor could do. But ride and shoot because he must, for a feed at the end of the day, to feel the suck of speed and the mind-altering swoop of the pursuit, that was something Connor couldn't do. Or maybe didn't care to.

They'd talked little since their argument a month ago, and Ross sensed that Connor had given up on him. He expected that the Scotsman would see out the season and then depart in the company of hides and bones on a lugger from Dyer's river landing. Ross would be relieved when he left. Connor looked at him sideways now, as if he couldn't quite face the person Ross had become. That, at least, Ross understood. He had seen his reflection in Joe's shaving mirror and had to step away before he set the razor blade to his skin and the de-bearding revealed more than Ross wanted to know.

Finding themselves in open country, the buffalo began to run out across the flats. Ross eased Nugget into a trot. The ground was like cement made rough by twelve-inch-wide hoof impressions that formed in rain-soaked country and dried during the water-less months. The horse extended to a canter. Ross felt the draw of the kill as a wide-horned cow took the lead. He bided his time, knowing distance and speed would eventually wear her down. Hoping the rush of the chase would still his shaking hand.

At full gallop Ross was close enough to see the bristles on the beast's hide. He lifted the sawn-off rifle and fired. Simultaneously, Nugget stumbled on the rough terrain. Ross was pitched into the air and the wounded cow, briefly grounded, impaled the founder-ing gelding through the belly and then tossed the horse skywards. The sun was briefly obliterated. Ross heard a whoosh of air and whinnying and then the horse hit the earth. A rip of pain jolted through him. A cracking of fibre, tendon and bone. The gelding had landed on his outstretched legs. He struggled into a sitting position. Now he was like the beasts that he had slain. Paralysed but still aware.

The wounded buffalo was panting and blowing, setting dark eyes on him from over the top of Nugget's body. Ross grunted with effort as he reached for the spare pistol holstered near the saddle. The trigger was steel-cold as the cow lowered its head, readying to charge.

Ross lowered the gun to his side and waited.

❈ Part Four ❈

1929–1939

≪ Chapter 50 ≫

Darwin

Ross tugged at the straps tying him to the railings of the cot. He thrashed and yelled, trying to free himself, and then gave in to the pain and frustration. He lay sweating and aching, his breath slowing until the pounding in his head eased and he could hear beyond the internal struggles of his body. Mechanical music was playing somewhere. It was so long since he'd heard a tune. He was briefly mesmerised.

'Morning, Mr Grant,' said the doctor, who came to stand by his bed.

'Untie me,' Ross demanded. He strained on the bindings, noting the people in the beds lining the room. There were so many of them. Myriad strangers weighing his uselessness, waiting for the opportunity to attack, like meat ants stalking a freshly staked-out cowhide. 'I need to get out of here.'

'Just relax,' the doctor told him.

He pulled on the fastenings until the bed began to rattle.

'Fine.' The doctor cut the restraints with a pair of scissors and stepped back. 'You won't be able to get very far.'

Ross tried to sit up and was blinded by pain. 'What are they looking at?' he yelled at the patients in the ward. A nurse appeared and stretched out a panelled screen around his bed.

'Mr Grant.'

'Stop calling me that.'

'Mr Grant,' the doctor repeated. 'How are you feeling?'

'I need to get out of here,' answered Ross.

'You can't. You can keep on ranting as much as you like but the fact is you're too unwell to be released. So stop asking.'

Ross breathed heavily. His legs felt useless. 'Give me something for the pain.'

'We've had this discussion. You'll have to bear the pain from now on. You've needed more morphine at night than the average man, which corresponds with your addictive illness, but as of today you will have to draw on your own strength.' The doctor pulled up a chair. 'I assume at some stage in the past you were capable of controlling your impulses. You haven't always been addicted to alcohol, have you?'

Ross thought of taking a punch at the man but the doctor was canny. He'd sat just out of reach.

'Do you know why you're here?' The man wore a white coat. His curly red hair and freckled skin suggested Irish origins. Ross hated the Irish. They reminded him of Marcus Holder.

'I was hunting buffalo.' Ross recalled the piles of hides and horns at the camp.

'Yes. Your horse was gored and crushed your legs.'

Images played in Ross's mind as he tried to remember what had happened. All he could recall was a litter being dragged across the ground and the lugger that floated along the river to the sea.

'Once the morphine wears off your memory will improve. Now I need to place this stethoscope on your chest. As you hit the last doctor who attempted to do that, I'm hoping I won't need to tie you up again.'

Ross grunted assent and the cold stethoscope was moved about his chest accompanied by a hollow-sounding two-fingered tap. His skin felt inflamed as if it had been scrubbed with a currycomb. 'Why was I tied down?'

'Apart from the punching incident? Delusions. Pain. Anger,' the physician replied. 'You will control yourself?' Ross picked at the material wrapped around his wrists until it came loose and rubbed at the red marks. 'Let me remind you that you have two broken legs, a fractured pelvis and cirrhosis of the liver, along with some sundry complaints that include jaundice and weight loss. The malarial infection has gone. All in all, you're lucky to be here. You should be aware, however, that the damage to your liver may well shorten your life. No more alcohol, Mr Grant, if you want to live for another twenty years. And I can't promise you that time, either. I have no idea how much damage you've done to your other organs.'

Having long ago given up considering more than one day at a time, Ross was disappointed at being told an end point. Twenty years. It was something to work towards, he supposed.

'When you're more yourself I will bring the nurses who attended on your arrival so you can thank them. You were a mess, Mr Grant. There is no excuse for such filth.'

'And my things?' asked Ross.

'What things? You only had the clothes you were wearing, and as they were full of lice everything was burnt.'

'No book?'

'Nothing. You'll have to improve your attitude, Mr Grant, now you're back in civilised society. You've been in the papers on and off for many years. Some of it good, like, for instance, that young man you took to the mission, but most of it bad. Don't expect people to take to you right off. They haven't yet decided if you're man or madman. Me included.'

The doctor left and Ross was moved into a wheelchair by two orderlies. The pain lashed out, strong and throbbing.

'So, mate, we're taking you outside,' said one of the orderlies.

'Moving me out of here?' asked Ross.

'No, mate,' the man answered. 'The doc thought you'd like a bit of sun. Normally we wouldn't move someone as banged up as you, but the doc said you'd live with the discomfort and you don't strike any of us as the indoors type.'

With his bandaged legs extended in front of him, Ross was wheeled feet-first out of the ward like a man in a wooden box. They travelled along a corridor and down a sloping surface until Ross was finally out in the sun. A hard sky met the cobalt-blue of the ocean. It was too bright. Too fine a day for the way Ross felt, but he was so relieved to be away from the hospital ward. He wondered if he could escape and then looked down at his legs. Unlikely.

The orderlies deposited him beneath a shady tree next to a rattan table where a bowl sat on a tray, shielded from flies by a doily. A nurse arrived and, holding the dish up, waited for Ross's agreement. The woman was middle-aged, and she smelt of menthol and starch. Ross stared at her as he had the other nurses, marvelling at their different faces, at their familiarity with a place he no longer understood. She held up a spoon and leant towards him. Ross snatched the bowl from her grasp and slurped from the rim, his stomach gurgling and groaning as if being slowly strangled. She looked at him as if he'd lost more than the use of his legs. Then she got up and left.

She was replaced by Connor. Ross was used to the man turning up when least expected, but his arrival jolted him awake far more than the trip across the bumpy hospital grounds. Connor took up the seat left warm by the nurse and together they stared out at the sea. Ross imagined that each was waiting for the other to speak. For his part, he had both too much to say and not enough. Ross recalled so many things: paintings on cave walls, the bloody welts made by a knife in a boy's leg, a cross in the middle of nowhere and the fisherman waiting at the bottom of a hill.

'How are you feeling?' asked Connor eventually.

There was no comfort in seeing his old friend. It was because of him he had just been dumped like wreckage at the tree's base instead of laying stiff and cold, oblivious. It was the Scotsman who'd appeared with a blood-curdling yell to take aim at the wounded buffalo, dropping the beast in its tracks.

'I lost Alastair's book,' was all Ross could say. It was a long time since he could remember what his brother clearly looked like but with the loss of the novel it was as if the last shred of Alastair's existence had finally disappeared.

'Aye,' replied Connor. 'It's probably still lying next to the carcasses of that horse and cow. Joe sent his regards. He's gone south. How are the legs?'

'Not working,' said Ross.

'He was a good horse, Nugget. They say you won't ride again and walking will be difficult. Have they told you that?' Connor fumbled with his empty pipe.

'No.'

'Well, now you're prepared for when they do.' With an embarrassed smile, Connor tucked the pipe back into his pocket. 'It took so long to get you back here. I wasn't sure we'd make it in time, and then when the malaria set in . . . There's a lawyer who's keen to have a word with you, Ross. There are things that need settling.'

Ross couldn't think beyond a few minutes at a time. 'You handle it.'

'I cannae. I have no authority. I don't work for the Grants anymore and I haven't for some time.'

If he probed, Ross knew that the reason behind Connor's leaving would point back to him. It was best to say nothing. In the end, Connor's motives were his own, although Ross appreciated that the man's separation from the Grants would have come at a personal cost. Connor still remembered a Scotland of clans and chieftains, whereas Ross identified with none of it.

'There's someone here to see you.'

'I don't want to see anyone, Connor. I'm not fit.'

'Fit or not, you have a visitor.' Connor briefly gripped his arm. 'I don't know when you crossed the line from running away to punishing yourself but it's time to stop. I'll be back in a few days.'

A woman was walking across the lawn. Ross knew the face and yet didn't know it. He looked to the ocean and then back again, just to make sure it wasn't a drug haze that was altering what he saw. He fidgeted with the wheel of his chair. An onshore breeze stirred the branches overhead. Leaves caught in the wind and fluttered downwards to rest on his useless legs.

Darcey waited to be invited to sit and then finally claimed the chair next to him, positioning it a little out of the harsh sun so that they almost faced each other. The returning memories were unwanted. The farewell letter on the dining room table. The smell of her on his skin. It took months to forget Darcey and it came as a shock when those last few hours returned, vibrant and real. Ross thought of her hair fanning across his chest, the nestling of a leg over his thigh, her warm arm outstretched.

'Hello, Ross.'

There was a fragility to Darcey that showed in the fiddling with a silver ring about her finger. Her hair was short, styled so that it framed her cheeks, lessening the slight sagging that made her jawline uneven. Still, she was pretty. Ross scratched at his face and then reached for his hair. The beard was gone, the hair cropped close. The doctor most likely believed that he had cut off the wild parts. The pieces that fought men, killed horses and drifted onwards without purpose.

'I never left the Territory,' Darcey told him.

It was because of her that Ross abandoned Waybell. Because of her and Maria. And other things, a tangle of other things. Ross was taken aback by the knowledge of Darcey waiting. By her coming to see him after what he'd done to her.

Darcey he could have. Maria he couldn't. Had it been as simple as that? A fool's game of rebellion.

'I stayed at Waybell for a time and then I moved here to Darwin,' she went on. 'I have a nice house.'

Darcey couldn't hold his gaze for more than a few seconds at a time. Ross knew a woman like her shouldn't be in his company.

'You should go,' he told her. Darcey moved uncomfortably, her back straightening. There was an explanation for her staying in Darwin. A bargain made. A pact. Ross clasped the arm of the wheelchair. 'Why did you stay?'

'You have to ask?'

Ross didn't know how to respond. His stomach was rebelling against that sloppy meal. The child. A child for freedom.

'At first it was because of that last night.' Darcey played with the strap of the handbag in her lap, snapping the metal clip open and closed. 'Things seemed different between us. As if it wasn't an obligation.'

'So there's no child,' concluded Ross, swallowing the rising bile. Without warning he leant sideways, bringing up the food. He collapsed back in the chair, embarrassed by his feebleness. Darcey offered him a lace handkerchief but he used the back of his hand. He could smell lavender and something sharp and clean, like cut grass. Ross seized her wrist, seeing his own sun-dark knuckles, swollen and glutted by endless fights.

He told her to leave. And moments later she was gone.

'Making a fuss, are we?' A nurse appeared and wheeled him further into the shade.

'I need something for the pain.' Ross clenched his teeth.

'We can't have one demon being replaced by another, can we?' the nurse retorted.

'I don't want any more visitors,' said Ross.

The nurse shook out a thermometer and held it questioningly in front of him. Reluctantly Ross opened his mouth. 'Better,' she concluded on reading the temperature. 'No visitors it is, then. For how long?'

The sea was hard and flat. Between the hospital grounds and the ocean a car motored along the road. There were bicycles and people. Normality.

'Until I can walk,' he answered.

'That might be some time.'

'So be it,' he replied.

≪ Chapter 51 ≫

Ross sat across from his lawyer, Mr Maitland, at a desk over-flowing with papers and files. Outside, a woman swabbed the floor with a mop, the looped yarns dropping lengths of fibre onto the wet surface. Mr Maitland frowned as the doctor left, closing the door. They were using the physician's study and disturbances were frequent. The lawyer shuffled his papers and waited for Ross to resume speaking, his gaze drifting to the crutches leaning on the wall. They had started poorly. For his part, Ross had little interest in spending time satisfying the lawyer's inquisitiveness regarding his long absence. All the lawyer required was an autograph book to make Ross truly feel like a pariah.

'So my father's assets are intact?' confirmed Ross. That was unexpected. It had been over three years since Morgan Grant's passing. Ross assumed at least a portion to have been sold by now.

'The majority, yes. A trust was set up to administer the estate after your father's death. It was decided that the winery should be sold, and one of the sheep stations. Wool prices have been on the decline since the end of the war.'

'Which one?' asked Ross. 'Which property was sold?'

Mr Maitland read the document, removing his spectacles before speaking. 'It was located near Burra. Gleneagle. I believe you were there for a time. Are you sure you don't wish to discuss your personal situation, Mr Grant? I'm told you've allowed no one to see you these past weeks. Sometimes it helps to talk things through.'

Ross set his mind on the loss of Gleneagle. He was sorry that, of all his father's acquisitions, it was this piece of dirt that had been traded to the highest bidder. The thought of that unrelenting square of red country, the place where he grew, unfettered by family, belonging to another, brought home some of what he had thrown away. 'Whose decision was that?'

'The trustees,' answered Mr Maitland. 'Business associates of your late father's. As I said, they were placed in control of the estate. Had your whereabouts been known, things may have been different. I must say I find it quite extraordinary that with the size of the legacy involved and your older brother only recently declared dead –'

'I thought that had been done years ago,' said Ross.

The lawyer placed the paper he held on the table. 'I wasn't involved in those legalities, Mr Grant, but it's been more than a decade since the end of the war. Consider it closure for you and the family.' Mr Maitland toyed with the reading glasses, flipping them over and over. 'What's left of them.'

Ross thought of the novel that lay rotting northeast of Mr Dyer's fragile Christian cross. White-anted in disregard. He couldn't sit there much longer discussing the property of the dead. He felt like an intruder in someone else's life.

'Your mother retains the right to stay in the family home until her death.' The lawyer read each clause precisely, taking a heavy breath as the remaining contents of the document were announced. 'There are funds set aside for a paid companion and a live-in nurse.'

'And everything else,' asked Ross, breaking Mr Maitland's studied explanations. 'Waybell Station, the other properties? After my mother is finished with the mansion? What happens to all of it?'

'It was about to be transferred to a new beneficiary, however your turning up the way you did has rather changed things.' The lawyer waited as if expecting the words to have greater effect. 'Currently, in the event that you were found alive, you were to be the recipient of a modest yearly stipend. The remainder of the estate was to go to your wife.'

'Darcey?' said Ross.

'Yes.'

The word wife suggested warmth and caring and honesty. It was a grim reminder of the complications of a marriage he never considered real.

'I understand your concerns, Mr Grant. It is one thing to be on the brink of losing a fortune, quite another to discover it was to be placed in the hands of a woman, even if she is your spouse. And there were no stipulations as to how this bequest was to be managed. Mrs Grant was to receive it unencumbered. But now you can easily contest and lay claim to your late father's estate. After all, you are her husband and unlike your brother, you were never legally declared dead and even if you had been, the situation is far from irreversible.'

Ross thought of Darcey's father buried in England's cold, loamy soil. He had wanted his daughter cared for and she would be. 'Let her have it. All of it except Waybell, and that stipend, I'll take it too.'

Mr Maitland sat the spectacles on his nose and fussed with the settling of each curved end over an ear. He appeared baffled. 'You should think about this, Mr Grant. We can delay. The house in Adelaide would be a comfort to you in your condition.'

'I'd like to see Connor Andrews. Can you arrange that? You should be able to get word to him at the Hotel Victoria,' said Ross. 'I'm leaving here today.'

Mr Maitland promised to do so.

Ross pointed to the crutches and waited as the lawyer fetched them. He stood awkwardly, crushed bones trying to arrange themselves into once-strong lines. His emaciated legs bowed. They'd told him it might be weeks before he walked. Ross couldn't wait that long. Nor could he stand being cooped up surrounded by people and noise. He'd spent four months in hospital. With effort, he wedged each crutch into an armpit and staggered forward. One leg laboured harder than the other and Ross managed a shambling walk like a hobbled horse. The pain was excruciating, like a red-hot poker fresh from a fire, running in a line from ankle to hip.

The lawyer blocked the exit. 'I must advise you, Mr Grant, it is quite ludicrous to take that property over the Adelaide estate. The doctors say that you'll never regain the full use of your legs. That you won't ride a horse again. And these two impediments are on top of serious health concerns that may well shorten your life. I would be doing you an injustice if I didn't ask you to reconsider.'

'You'll be doing yourself more of an injustice if you don't let me pass,' said Ross, shuffling through the door.

❧ Chapter 52 ❧

Ross wanted a boarding house somewhere out of the way, near the sea, and the widow Mrs Guild, who'd lost two sons in the war, was eager for someone to care for. She set up a little table on the back veranda and Connor dragged a sagging cot next to the wall so that Ross had only a few steps to walk. He used a pot under the bed when nature beckoned, saving the continual struggle to the outhouse, and spent the long hours dragging his body the short distance to the end of the veranda and back. He rarely entered the house. It smelt of unwashed pillowcases and inside were sporting pennants and ribbons, photographs of serious young men in slouch hats, of troopship carriers, palm trees and one of a dead crocodile, the hunter leaning on his rifle. The living room contained the remnants of a long-gone family. It reminded Ross of what was lost to him and he wasn't prepared for that.

At dusk he ate, looking out across unkempt grass to the water, the brawny currents layering the surface in different shades. Mrs Guild, doing mending for a well-to-do family, sewed close by, making sure he consumed what she gave him and ensuring no food was wasted. Her skin was crosshatched with age and she was cranky most of the time, pecking away at life like an old boiler hen. Ross thought they made a fine pair, taking turns to grunt at each other, always quick to complain. Although come evening a truce was forged, as if they both understood the difficulties of having made it through another day, and it was then that Mrs Guild spoke and Ross could do nothing but listen.

'You might be better somewhere else,' she told him a month into his stay. 'My place is out of the way and I'm past talking to folk.'

'I'm fine,' answered Ross.

She sorted through the basket of clothes on the floor, selecting a shirt. 'How long will you be staying?'

'Until I can walk better.'

'Is that ever going to happen?' she asked.

'I hope so.'

'Well, if it doesn't you can remain here, I suppose.' She held the needle to candlelight and threaded a length of white cotton through it. 'That'd be all right but eventually you're going to have to move inside. This isn't a swagman's camp. If I leave you out here long enough, next thing I know you'll be bedding down in my garden and lighting yourself a fire. And I can't have that. What would folk think?'

'As if you'd care. Besides, the only neighbours you've got are bats and birds.'

'Not the point, is it,' she sniffed. 'You may have my eldest's room.'

'I won't move inside,' Ross told her firmly.

'Charles never came back. Like you, he was. Tight-lipped and fernickety, wouldn't take a helping hand from nobody. That's how he died, they told me. Kept on fighting after he'd been shot instead of going to one of those field hospitals. Bloody-minded like his father. Anyone would've thought he had the world on his shoulders. My Ben, he did come home. They shot him in the chest. Sent him back all stitched neat and tidy but then they had to open him up again. And every time they cut him, something else would come out of there. A bit of shirt, a piece of his tunic. Bits of shrapnel. We used to joke. I'd say, "Ben, you didn't need to bring your mother back any souvenirs." And he'd say, "Mother, you said you wanted something from France. That's all I've got left now." Those things his chest spat out. Ben got the doctor to put them in a glass jar.' She cut the thread with her teeth, folding the shirt she'd been working on. 'Connor said you've got family here. Why don't you want to see them?'

'I haven't got anything to say,' replied Ross.

'Well, if you're not careful you're going to end up like me, taking in strangers to make up for the family you lost. You might be paying me to be here but I'm taking your money so I've got someone to talk to. You understand what I'm saying.'

A little later she made tea, sitting the pot on the table near his elbow. Next came a plate of biscuits, the kind made with rolled oats. Mrs Guild classed them as one of her specialties and called them Anzac biscuits. Ross wasn't going to argue.

'That keep you going?' she asked. 'I hear you. Up half the night, stumbling around, knocking into things. Can't they give you anything for the pain?'

'No.' Ross bit into the tack-hard mixture.

'A bit of training to knock off those rough edges and you'd be quite a catch. Nothing a person likes to hear more than a please and a thank you. The name's Mrs Guild, by the way, if you've forgotten. I expect you to use it. It makes you feel appreciated. Manners and all.' She placed a kerosene lantern on the table and lit the wick. 'If you're not willing to forgive your family for something they've done, then that doesn't make you any better than them.'

'How do you know it's them who need the forgiveness?' asked Ross.

'Forgive yourself, then.' Mrs Guild plumped the pillow on the narrow cot and straightened the coverlet. 'I see you day after day staring at the ocean. I did the same, waiting for my boys to come home. Nothing out there but fish and crocs and the sea-slug chewers. If you need to, say twenty Hail Marys and half a dozen Our Fathers. Add a few more bruises to those damaged knees of yours.'

'I haven't been to church in a long time,' admitted Ross. There were few insects gathering around the lamp with the seabreeze but as Ross turned down the light, a mosquito hit the hot glass and flew away. 'Anyway, I'm Scottish.'

'A press-button, eh? Hmm. It's finding a beginning that's the challenge. Now, those relations you have up here. Are they close family?'

'Reasonably.' Eventually Mrs Guild would discover that Darcey lived on the other side of the city and then he imagined his ear would be tugged long and hard.

'Connor came this morning as he does every week. I said you were sleeping. He's complaining that I'm keeping you all to myself but we both know you're capable of doing that by yourself. You don't need me to keep people away, it's a talent for a person to be able to do that. I know cantankerous and you've got it in spades.'

His and Connor's past loomed like a wedge between them, and for Ross there was enough to think on without pretending friendship. 'Sometimes I don't think you like me at all, Mrs Guild.'

'These are for you.' She handed him a pair of spectacles. 'My husband couldn't read the newspaper without them, and I'm figuring by the way you peer at the pages you have the same difficulty.'

'Thank you.'

'That's better.' She picked up his plate, prodding at the morsels of roast beef that were left. 'I like having you here but I don't like the reason that brought you.'

Ross patted his thigh, feeling the wasted muscle. 'They'll mend in time.'

'Stupid boy. I'm not talking about your legs. You're sore on the world. And there's nothing sorrier than a person who feels sorry for himself.'

❈ Chapter 53 ❈

Ross leant on the crutch, catching his breath. The air was salt-filled and blustery. It blew from the incoming storm, shreds of lightning turning the sky mauve as waves gathered in lines of two and threes to rush at the shore. Fine drops of rain sprayed across the headland. Ross wondered if the squall would be strong enough to wash him clean.

'Dinnae you think you should wait a wee bit longer? Are you sure you want to do this?' Connor stood with the horse, an old mare the colour of roasted walnut with a greying muzzle and tolerant eyes.

'I still think of young Hart. Carrying him into the cave,' said Ross. 'It was right before we reached Oenpelli.'

Connor paid attention to each step Ross took. 'Who was Hart?'

Ross handed Connor a crutch, then placed one hand on the mare's mane and another on the saddle. He wished Nugget were there. It was the worst of his legs that needed to be lifted high enough to reach the stirrup iron and he wondered if his body was capable of the effort. 'A friend. Hart was a friend.' He kept forgetting, about who knew about which bits of his life. During the sleeplessness of night Ross recalled events and locations, mixing

316

up people and places so that reality was skewed by more than absentmindedness.

'I dinnae think this is a good idea, Ross.' Connor held tight to the horse's bridle. 'We can get hold of a motor car or a dray instead. The doctor said your hips and pelvis couldn't handle the strain. No need to bust yourself getting there.'

'Just give me a hand.'

Connor interlaced his fingers, forming a cup for Ross's boot. He said on the count of three he would lift, and Ross cringed with the ache of unused muscles as he threw his right leg over the saddle. He gritted his teeth, then grabbed at each leg beneath the knee, levering them up so that finally his feet rested in the stirrups.

'Are you all right, Ross? By the saints, you look like you'll pass out.'

Ross lifted a hand to show he'd heard.

'Can you stick her?' asked Connor. 'There's no shame in admitting you cannae, mate. A walk around the yard is one thing but riding to the other side of town is asking a bit of yourself.'

His legs refused to press firmly to the warmth of the animal and Ross found it difficult to stay square in the saddle. He thought of the humiliation if he fell, of needing the Scotsman's strength to get up from the ground.

'I could rope you on, just to be sure,' offered Connor. 'A neat little slipknot you can loosen when you get there. Aye, that would be the trick.'

'Maybe you should go back to the wharf,' replied Ross.

'You asked me here, remember?' Stuffing a knob-headed walking stick into a rifle holster, Connor detained him. 'I still think I should go with you. How are you going to get off, or get back on for that matter?'

'I mightn't do either. I might just turn around and ride home.'

'No you won't,' said Connor. 'You've been thinking on this for some time. If you dinnae do it now then you probably won't ever do it.'

'Is that so,' said Ross.

'Aye. As sure as I know that you'd drag yourself along the road before you let Darcey see how you really are.'

Ross wished that Hart was still alive. He wouldn't have minded the boy accompanying him part of the way. There was no use explaining to Connor his preference. That the boy's simple need for friendship made him a better companion than Connor ever was, or that Ross deserved. The boy wanted nothing more than company and direction, and expected little in return, relying on blind faith and Ross to get him through his troubles. But with Connor, Ross couldn't hide. He was too close to everything that had once filled Ross's life and that had always been the problem.

'The papers have to be signed,' replied Ross. 'I could ask Darcey to come here but I'd never hear the end of it from Mrs Guild.'

The widow stood on the rear veranda holding a glass jar up to the light. Ross knew she examined the fragments taken from her dead son, and that when she finally went inside the house she would pat at her eyes as she sat the container on the windowsill. He held his hand up in acknowledgement and she gave a reproachful nod that signified her disagreement with what he was about to attempt.

'She's an old cracker, but she's kept you alive, and you're looking better,' said Connor. Together they rode away from the house. 'Always is a better view from atop a good piece of horse-flesh.'

Ross didn't reply. He was too busy concentrating on breathing through the pain. At the end of the street they parted company, and Ross continued on alone.

≪ Chapter 54 ≫

Darcey's house was at the end of the street, so close to the bush that the timber was shuddering about it in the wind. There were palm trees and potted shrubs at the front and a paling fence so white Ross was sure he could smell the fresh paint. It was showering but the storm had headed east. Plumes of blue-grey cloud hugged the coast and he thought of the open country that lay outside the gridded streets of Darwin, so dangerously seductive. The mare had kept to a steady gait. Ross yearned to break into a gallop, to head south to the cover of the scrub but his body was rigid with discomfort and there was no returning to where he came from. That shadowy outer place that inhabited him as much as he inhabited it.

Ross wondered at the height of the house and then looked with dismay at the steps leading to the front door. The dwelling was perched on stilts ten feet above the ground, the garden gate closed. He thought of Connor laughing at him, wounding his pride. Ross leant down, judging how far he could reach before his body rebelled or gravity pulled him over. The latch lifted and he entered the garden. There was little point in trying to dismount properly, as he knew his legs wouldn't bear the weight, so he lifted each foot from their stirrup, flung a leg over the mare's back and fell to the ground.

The thud of the earth juddered through his bones and he lay still, panting like a dog from the shock of the fall. He breathed through the effort of rising, hoisting his body by relying on the horse and tree for support. Eventually he managed to tie the mare to a whip-thin branch and had the knob of the walking stick planted in his palm. At the foot of the steps he stopped. He'd already undergone a beating, but the final trouncing was yet to come for he doubted he could climb the stairs.

As he contemplated whether he was capable of attempting the steps, Darcey appeared from his left at the corner of the house.

'Ross?' she said. She wore a white sundress, the brownness of her limbs evidence of time spent outdoors. 'I wondered what time you'd arrive. Come this way.'

Instead of up the stairs, she led him between the posts supporting the house to where a table laden with tea things sat waiting. He followed her with difficulty, the walking cane catching on the uneven ground, his legs tackling movement as if they had anchors attached. An easel sat in a corner and a stack of painted canvases leant to one side. Ross noticed a hammock strung between trees in the garden and wished he could collapse into it.

'It's good to see you.' She poured cordial into tall glasses and added water as Ross eased himself carefully into a cushioned seat. 'I didn't know you could ride. I thought Connor would bring you.'

'No need for that.' He doubted Darcey usually entertained there beneath the house but he was grateful to be on ground level and glad to be stationary. She looked well. A hint of red coloured her cheeks and her hair had grown since they last spoke at the hospital. Ross tried to remember what it meant to be in the company of a lady. A woman similar in age to his. There was a folder full of papers in front of her bound by a twist of string, suggesting that his wife was straight to business.

'I'm glad you're better. Connor tells me that Mrs Guild is looking after you extremely well.'

'Yes, she's a good woman. Darcey –'

'Please,' she interrupted. 'Let me go first. I knew nothing of your father's intentions when he was alive. I just want you to know I've told Mr Maitland that I would prefer it if you were the main beneficiary and that I only require a small yearly income. He tells me that he can do nothing without your consent and that you were quite adamant when you met, but I don't want all your money, Ross. Truly, I don't.'

When she finally paused there was a brightness to her. Ross couldn't tell if it was false or whether Darcey was pleased at having been able to speak her mind. Now it was his turn, and in his current state there was no riding off in a hurry if what he'd dwelt on proved to be incorrect. The risks he'd taken over the previous years seemed nothing now that he was compelled to speak the truth.

'When we last spoke, Darcey, you said that you stayed all these years because of the last night we shared at Waybell.' She shifted a little, her fingers twisting in her lap. 'You said,' continued Ross, 'on that particular night, it didn't feel as if there was an obligation between us anymore.'

Darcey lowered her chin. 'That's true.'

Ross sipped at the cordial, feeling the rush of sugar course through his body. It was strange being sober. 'Could I have some more of that?'

'Yes, of course.' She rose and began to manoeuvre glasses and bottle, making a fuss of removing and replacing the cork and the doily covering the water jug.

He waited as Darcey mixed the beverage, noticing the slightness of her wrists. Ross still couldn't reconcile how they'd ended up in bed together. It was so businesslike. The discussion. The bartering of one need for another. Until that last night, when he'd overthrown Maria, the first woman whom he'd loved, for Darcey, the woman he'd been compelled to marry.

'You were right.' Ross took a long drink and exhaled. 'There wasn't an obligation. I wanted to be there as well.' He leant on both the cane and tabletop to stand, and moved to where sunlight slanted across the dirt floor. He thought it would be better to speak in movement, as discomfort and awkwardness sharpened his thoughts. It also gave them space, distance to hide how they felt now that he'd finally sorted truth from fantasy and been honest with her.

'I want you to have what was left to you, Darcey. That was my father's wish. However I would like Waybell and the stipend. I'm living on that at the moment.'

'Are you sure?' Her voice was tentative, wary.

'Yes.' Ross thought of how comfortable the hammock looked. It was nestled in a corner, free of the worst of the day's heat but angled so that there would be a fine view of the night sky through the branches. 'Were you upset about Alastair? My father declaring him dead?'

'I imagine you found it difficult to hear,' replied Darcey.

Ross was aware that she hadn't answered the question. 'And did *you* find it difficult?' he asked again.

'I was sad, of course. But his disappearance was so long ago. Alastair is dead to me in so many ways and he has been for years.' There was a catch in Darcey's voice, as if she was struggling with something unsaid. 'You've always been judgemental of me, Ross, as if I were the cause of many of your problems. And yet, in the beginning it was Alastair who betrayed us both and still you let his ghost hover about you. This man who changed our lives forever. Let him go.'

Once, when he was young, three older children had chased Ross home. Alastair and he had been calling out names to some troublemaking town boys who'd taken offence and given chase. The brothers had become separated as they ran away, and the boys caught up with Ross. They'd circled him and prodded him, until, growing braver, they began to shove him back and forth. Ross had been terrified. At that moment, Alastair had charged into the group, yelling and screaming. One of the boys had been knocked over in the attack and Alastair managed a punch that stunned another. He told Ross to run and he did, sprinting the rest of the way home. Alastair returned a little later, nose bloody and clothes torn. Ross was six years of age. Alastair ten. A boy rarely forgot something like that. A brother, never.

'Are you all right, Ross?'

'Yes.' There was another question that needed to be asked. One that had been with Ross since Darcey's visit to the hospital. If she answered the way Ross believed that she would, he wasn't at all sure what it would mean to him or for them.

'Did you stay here all these years because you loved me?' he asked.

'No.' She hadn't even paused.

What had he expected? He was a fool.

Darcey came to his side. 'You never let me. You might have come back, Ross, but I don't think you intended to.'

'No, I didn't,' he admitted.

'After you left, I decided not to go back to Adelaide. I couldn't, really, after everything that had happened, and there were opportunities here. I have a good life. I work at an orphanage during the week and in the maternity section of the hospital on the weekends.'

'Oh.' What had he expected? That she'd be unable to go on with her life in any meaningful way after he'd deserted her? He was embarrassed by his assumptions and it struck him that he'd not known her at all. How could he have, until this moment?

'I'm sorry if you thought otherwise,' she said.

'I'm pleased for you,' he replied, not knowing what else to say.

Darcey bent over to tuck a straggly branch of a potted plant within its clumpy interior. This wasn't a woman who waited and pined. Darcey Grant expected a partner to be equal in intelligence and ability and wasn't prepared to settle for second-best. This was a woman who set her mind to a problem like chisel to wood and worked at the challenge until the result was fashioned in her favour. He should have seen that. Why hadn't he seen that? Especially knowing what she was like when they first met.

Her rejection stung, and Ross wanted to leave but he was incapable of sitting on the horse for the return journey and he refused to ask for help. A message to Connor, and the Scotsman would have appeared with a dray to cart him away like the invalid he was, but the idea of needing assistance and Darcey witnessing his utter uselessness was not something he could bear. Not now. So he stayed on, hoping that with rest he might be able to leave of his own accord.

The clouds finally cleared, and they spent the remainder of the day sitting in the garden. Ross read the newspaper as Darcey painted. He fell asleep often and woke to see her framed by the vibrant mauve of a flowering turkey bush. She'd set up her easel in the shade and was trying to capture the waterlilies on the Waybell billabong, a piece she'd apparently been working on for some time. There was something about the light that she couldn't capture, Darcey told him, and the work had become something of a preoc-cupation in a life that revolved around homeless children and the birthing of babies. Ross dared not to tell her to leave the painting alone, that every time she added another hue she took a little majesty out of a scene that to him seemed already perfect.

She'd arrived in Darwin three months after Ross left her at Waybell. Connor helped select the house and found a young girl to help with chores, but the garden Darcey tended to herself, and her interest in plants was evident. There were myriad sketches of the kapok bush in the folio she showed Ross, the delicate flowers patched with vibrant yellow, and other specimens familiar to Ross that Darcey had labelled with great detail. She was happy to do the talking while she painted and Ross was thankful that not much conversation was expected of him. If she'd wanted to know of his travels Ross wasn't sure he would have been able to explain the years of absence. He guessed that Darcey, as a female, would be interested in a pretty description or witty tale. However there was nothing remotely appropriate he could think of sharing. His self-imposed exile was a plodding, unnavigable course almost leading to extinction.

As the afternoon lengthened, the trip back to Mrs Guild's was not mentioned. Ross knew the impossibility that riding presented. It would be daylight before his body could be forced into movement again. The hammock was the only bed he considered. Darcey left to buy some food, and his gaze fell upon Mr Maitland's nubby binder left on the table. Carrying the contents of the folder to the light, he slanted the pages and then reached for the spectacles stored safely in his buttoned shirt pocket. His eyes strained through the magnification as letters and then words began to take shape. The full extent of his father's life was summed up in neat rows and columns, a series of holdings represented by names and acreage and current values. Nowhere did the document mention the personal cost exerted on the man and his family from the accumulation of his fortune. Nor could the tally of assets ever reveal the father Ross knew. But Morgan Grant had accomplished far more than he. Ross had built nothing, created no empire from the dirt, governed no family home, or a family, for that matter. He'd not even managed an heir.

He'd been on few outings with his father as a child. Trips included a day's fishing and horserides when he and his brother still wore short pants, but there was no significant time spent together that Ross could recall. No experience that bonded them. That made them separate but whole. Possibly there wasn't meant to be that type of connection between a father and son, or if there was, perhaps the complex start to his early life ruined any chance of a relationship like that. Ross believed, though, that Alastair had enjoyed what had been unobtainable to him, and a niggling theory made him explore the chance that he and his father were rather alike and that was the reason they'd never got on.

Ross stretched out his fingers and then, manipulating each stiffened knuckle, formed a series of fists. The pen felt unfamiliar in his grasp, and the length of time since he'd last written anything was beyond remembering. The ink left a blot as Ross pressed the nib to the document and scratched out his initials. Leaving the greater part of the fortune to Darcey lessened the wrongdoing on his part. Then he closed the folder on a better man's life.

Darcey returned with bread and fresh oysters, which she insisted she was quite capable of shucking. She prised the lip of the mollusc open by inserting a pearl-handled knife at the hinge between the two valves, twisted the blade and then slid the knife upwards. The oyster revealed its fleshy insides. Ross tried to do the same, but nicked his palm in the process.

'Too hard,' chastised Darcey. 'You must be gentle and firm,' she explained. Moving the kerosene lamp closer, she demonstrated the process. The shell parted and she shook Worcestershire sauce onto the oyster and then, lifting her chin, tipped the soft shellfish into her mouth, licking her fingers free of the juice.

'What?' she asked, noticing his interest.

'It seems years since I've seen a woman eat,' he replied. 'A woman like you.'

Darcey selected another oyster, opened it and passed it across the table to him. 'I never thought you'd be without admirers, Ross.'

He swallowed the shellfish. 'And you, have there been others in your life, Darcey?'

'Of course. Don't look so shocked. Why is it that the things men consider to be their right are frowned on when a woman partakes?'

Unsure how to reply, Ross began pulling the bread apart.

'Let me.' Darcey reached across, cutting the loaf into slices. 'And there is a napkin. For when you finish eating.'

Ross glanced at the neatly folded triangle.

'You place it on your lap, Ross. Remember?' she asked.

He fingered the material. 'I should apologise to you.'

'Not if you don't mean it.' She poured herself some water, then tipped a dash of something from a small bottle into the glass.

'What is that?' asked Ross. 'I remember you took a powder when you first came to Waybell.'

'Laudanum, to calm my nerves. You don't really believe that a woman could do what I did without some assistance, do you? I'm not that brazen.'

'And you still take it?' questioned Ross.

'Why not?' she said. 'None of us is perfect.'

326

When the meal was over, Darcey gathered the dishes. Ross listened to her footsteps as she padded through the house overhead. In the garden he relieved himself in the bushes and then, placing his backside in the hammock, lifted one leg followed by the other until he could lay down.

'I wondered where you'd gone,' said Darcey, coming to him. 'Can I get you anything?'

'Nothing. Do you mind?' he asked.

'Of course not. I could bring a mattress down if you prefer,' she offered.

'This will be fine. I suppose Connor told you that my progress has been steady.'

'I knew when you arrived at the hospital that if you did survive it would be a long recovery.'

'You were there that day?' asked Ross.

'No. Connor told me he'd brought you back and that the doctor wasn't hopeful. I only visited that one time, in the garden. You sent me away, if you recall, and told the nursing staff you didn't want any visitors.'

'I wasn't ready,' conceded Ross.

'Neither was I. I came out of curiosity and for the simple fact that, after all these years, we are still married.'

'Yes, there's that,' said Ross.

'I also went for your family's sake. They were and continue to be, through their legacy, very kind to me. Your mother's nurse writes to me occasionally. If you visited her now, Ross, it would be doubtful she would recognise you. Her mind has slipped.'

'That happened a long time ago.'

'It's not your fault,' she told him.

'I know.'

Darcey touched his arm. 'No, really. It's not your fault. Any of that.'

There was no moon, and the deep blackness made the stars distinct. Once, on a strip of sand near a river he'd sat and talked to two old blackfellas. They told Ross that the celestial bodies he

327

knew as the Magellan Clouds were the campfires of the dead. He'd lifted a finger, pointing out the galaxies that appeared to have broken away from the band of light that was the Milky Way, and they in turn roused at Ross for his whitefella stupidity. Everyone knew that if you raised a finger in their direction, the dead would curse you and bring down all manner of troubles. Ross thought of his family, saw them sitting around one of those campfires, shifting through the ashes of his life. He would always wonder what they thought of their younger son. They'd been far kinder to Darcey than he ever had.

'What will happen now?' asked Darcey. 'What will you do?'

She deserved an ending and a new beginning, and the Grant money offered his wife many options. Ross hoped she understood that.

'I have no idea,' he said. 'But I'd like to come back here to visit you.'

'Why?'

'Because I want to. I didn't expect to say that,' he confessed.

'And I didn't expect to hear it.'

'Is that a yes?' he asked.

The darkness hid her hesitation but it was there in the growing silence. 'As you've just given me the larger part of your fortune, yes.'

⫷ Chapter 55 ⫸

Ross visited Darcey regularly. As his body grew sturdier and the return trip to the widow's house became less of a struggle, he stopped staying the night. It was not for the want of enjoying Darcey's company but rather concern at his own expectation of what might be possible in the future, when he could only live by the hour and the day. It was impossible to know if Darcey was pleased or disappointed by these impromptu visits, for she never varied in her welcome. There was always good food to share and she seemed to understand when he wanted to speak or was content to listen. She talked about art and plants or a book recently read and, as the topics unwound, the tightness linking them slowly unravelled and Ross gradually re-entered the world. It was this easing back into normal life that he most appreciated, and one of the reasons he kept returning. His general health was also improving, and he found himself thinking more and more about Waybell and the possibility of a life there.

Mrs Guild commented that he was like a push-me-pull-you, a reference to a character that was in a children's story book. 'It's like you have two heads, Ross. You have no idea in which direction you should go. Indecisive. That's what you are. You'll spend four days in a row with that poor woman and then you won't go back for a week. If I was your wife, I'd clout you in the ear.'

'Maybe it's because I've made some bad decisions,' he replied.

'Now that's a confession I wasn't expecting to hear. So when are you planning to leave?' the widow said one night after the plates were cleared and the tea and biscuits were set before him.

'Did I say I was going anywhere?' Ross poured and handed her the teacup with the blue and white pattern she so liked.

'You can walk. Not very well. And you can ride. How far I've no idea but I'm thinking you'd get further than the rest of us, even if your body complained.' She tipped the tea from the cup into the saucer and blew on the steaming liquid. 'And you've worn a track down to the headland with your continual walking. A young man's greatest enemy is boredom.'

Ross was perched on the veranda railing, trying to improve his balance. 'I was thinking of heading back to my property.'

'Ah, the famed Waybell Station.' She took a sip of the tea, nodding in appreciation.

In the final glow of sunset, Ross saw the woman she'd been. Handsome, with a narrow chin and once prominent cheekbones now curtained by lined skin. 'You knew all along who I was, didn't you?'

Mrs Guild's mouth lifted in one corner as she picked up some darning work she'd started earlier that day. 'Yes. Age doesn't make a person dim, Ross. I said nothing and I asked nothing. I figured you'd get yourself out of the black spot you'd found yourself in if you wanted to. Either way, my opinion wouldn't make one bit of difference in the end.'

Ross thought of his family. If ever there was a group of people willing to give their view, wanted or not, it was them. 'That must have been difficult, not telling me what you thought.'

Mrs Guild took another mouthful of tea. 'Considering the state you were in, yes, it was. But then, I've reared two boys and buried three men, so I've grown used to keeping my counsel. No one listens anyway.'

'I'll miss you, Mrs Guild.'

'But not my biscuits,' she said.

'No,' admitted Ross. 'Not those. You're not a very good baker.'

'And you, my boy, have a long way to go if you're ever thinking of setting foot in a fancy drawing room in Adelaide again.'

'I didn't go to war, Mrs Guild,' Ross told her.

'I know,' she replied. 'You were saved. I'm glad for it. Now, there's nothing else that needs to be said on the matter.' She returned to her darning. Ross had not expected her to be so forgiving. 'And what about that wife of yours? Is she following you out to the middle of nowhere as well?'

Resolving to return to Waybell had not come without great consideration. Ross knew the difficulties ahead. Every time he pictured the station and the part he might play in its future, he only saw the limitations of his own doing. Running the property with the injuries he'd sustained worried him, as did the reception that he knew would await him. A whole mass of people were meant to be under his care. They may well have managed without Ross prior to his arrival but he'd thrust himself into their lives, turfed Sowden out of the house, and in the early months of his stay done very little to befriend any of them. Then he'd disappeared, slinking off without a word. Not for a few weeks or months, but years. Far from going back as the proud owner, Ross would have to start again. Intentions would have to be laid out and explained. Friendships reforged. Belief somehow restored. Ross had no idea how he could show remorse without chipping away any more dignity. There was so little faith left in him that the miniscule shred of self-respect he still retained barely clung on.

And yet, another reason preventing his swift return to Waybell was that he knew he would miss Darcey. But how could he presume that she would be interested in accompanying him, particularly after revealing that she'd never loved him? So why would he even consider approaching her with such an offer, knowing of her feelings and the full life she enjoyed in Darwin? Darcey would decline any proposal he put to her. For his own part Ross couldn't promise a long life or a happy marriage, and he feared the lure of the bush would hit him afresh. It was seared into him, the need to keep moving.

Mrs Guild waited for a reply. 'She's made a good life here in Darwin,' he eventually said.

He listened to the familiar tut of her tongue. 'So you haven't spoken to her about going with you?'

'No,' Ross acknowledged.

Mrs Guild paired a darned sock and selected another. 'Maybe you should just ask her straight out. Then you'll know.'

'I don't have the right,' answered Ross. 'And there might be someone else.'

'Don't you think, after the weeks you've been visiting her, that she would have said if there was another man?'

'Darcey told me she didn't care about me,' said Ross.

'And you're surprised by that, are you? You disappear for years without a word. And now you're back, not looking your finest, I might add, you expect a woman to be enamoured with you? Ross. Ross.' She clucked her tongue. 'I know men can be soft in the head at times, but really. If she's not thrown you out the door yet then I'd say you have as good a chance as any other with her, and you have the right of a husband. Don't leave her to drift in the wind, lad. Show your interest.'

'And if she says no?'

'It's a no. You tried.' The widow put her half-darned sock aside and disappeared inside the cottage. She returned with paper and pencil. 'If you can't say it . . .' She placed the writing materials on the table and pulled out the chair.

'I can barely hold a pen.'

She retrieved his spectacles and sat them next to the paper. 'Scratch it out, boy. You've done harder things, I expect.'

Ross rolled his lips inwards, slowly clambered down from the veranda railing, and took the seat. The blank page taunted him with all the words that could be said, and those that needed to stay concealed. But the page also offered something he'd not imagined in a very long time. A new start.

> Dear Darcey
>
> I'm returning to Waybell. I'd like you to consider joining me. I don't expect it and I won't be blaming you if you choose to stay where you are. I can't promise you anything.
>
> If you can't see your way clear to this, I'll understand.
> I'll also be sorry.
> Ross

He gave the letter a final once-over, and passed it to Mrs Guild for inspection. She held it at arm's length, gradually drawing it closer.

'That took near to a half-hour?' She read the note again. 'Well, your writing's so poor I can barely make out one word from the next and you'd never be accused of being over-flowery, but you got your point across.'

Ross folded the note and scribbled the address on the front.

'I'll get the milk boy to take it to her,' said Mrs Guild, sliding it into the pocket of her apron.

Ross dunked an Anzac biscuit in the now-cold tea and decided it tasted better than anything out of a bottle. 'And you, Mrs Guild. Will you be able to make ends meet without me?'

She gestured to the pile of mending. Shirts, socks and pants were scattered about her stockinged feet. 'You might think you're indispensable, but the Carments have been very good to me over the years.'

'The Carments?'

'Yes.' Mrs Guild scooped up a sock and made two quick stitches. 'I knew a Hugh Carment years ago,' said Ross slowly.

'I know you did. That would be the father you're talking about. It's his family I take in the mending for,' she explained. 'They've a big house right on Myilly Point. Hop and a skip from the hospital. You never see Mrs Carment there,' continued Mrs Guild. 'Doesn't mix much around town, from what I've heard. A bit fernickety about the company she keeps, but it's more the other way around for some. I don't know the whole story, not that it matters, because I'm sure you remember,' she said pointedly. 'I was nursing my boy and had just buried a husband. A few years of my life are blighted by grief and anger, but what I do recall is hearing that the young Mrs Carment was caught in a delicate situation and the Carment boy, Edward, saw her and fell in love. If the gossips are right then the girl's always been trouble and her husband was caught line and sinker, unlike the lover who managed to escape her. That lover was you, Ross.'

Ross levered his body up from the table. His heart was suddenly pounding.

'Yes, I knew about her, Ross. It's up to you what you choose to do, but I thought you should know she's still here. And regardless, I'm sending that letter to your wife.' Mrs Guild said goodnight and went inside.

The day had long ended and a duskiness spread out towards the ocean. The air heavy and humid. It was as if he were out in the back country again. Knuckles scabbed over. Inhabiting some grubby space, existing, only to be drawn out. Punched in the guts. Swift and hard. He sat on the edge of the bed, the springs flagging, creaking with age. In one deliberate disclosure, every single step taken in retreat from the wasteland of his previous years had come undone.

≪ Chapter 56 ≫

The house was shuttered and pitched towards the ocean, and low-slung to withstand the buffeting of storms off Myilly Point. The garden was brittle pale from lack of rain, and clearly required attention. Shrubs were overgrown, the path needed sweeping. A wooden bench sat under a lone tree and a child's swing – two pieces of rope and a plank – hung from one of the branches. If not for the basket of mending sitting in Mrs Guild's cottage, the signs suggested that the occupants were not home and hadn't been for some time. Ross waited for an hour at the end of the street and then walked further along the point to where tussocky grasses clung to the white edges of the beach.

The sky was banded to the ocean by blue, the horizon impossible to define. Not far away, people enjoyed the airless morning. Two children dashed ankle-deep into the sea, racing each other, skipping over the smallest of the waves. Whitewashed foam crept across the shore as a woman gave chase, dragging them free of the water. The children circled their carer as she held out something she'd unearthed. A shell perhaps, or a piece of drift-wood. Further along the stretch of sand were muddy flats where mangroves waded. That was how Ross felt, caught between the sea and the land.

He was deliberating whether he should wait a little longer to see if anyone returned to the house when he noticed a figure approaching from the opposite end of the beach. He watched the woman walk towards him. With each step closer he began to identify characteristics that were familiar. The smallness of her, the way she slightly swayed as she moved, the darkness of her hair. It was her. Maria. With that recognition, every noise that had been a background to her arrival – the swish of the waves, the call of birds, the hum of distant motor vehicles – dropped away until there was nothing except her, growing nearer until she finally stood before him.

'Ross?' Her face was blanched white in surprise.

Ross removed his hat, fiddling with the brim before replacing it. 'Hello, Maria.'

He'd come here to find her and now she was before him, older and yet still so young. Her face firmer than he recalled. The long black hair pinned to fall over one shoulder. She was wearing a pink dress and straw hat edged with lilac ribboning. Still beautiful. Like a picture from another age. He'd formulated so many words during the night, replayed exactly what to say. How he'd feel. The rush of excitement. Holding her in his arms again after so many years. But he was no longer the brash boy he'd once been. The shock of learning that Maria still lived in Darwin had been replaced by unutterable joy and then, finally, as pre-dawn glowed, his emotions were tempered by fact. A reality he acknowledged as she stood before him, her features almost rigid with disbelief. They were still separated by circumstance and time and Ross no longer knew how he felt about her. He was like an old man who'd thrown a coin into a wishing well and, with a dream made real, he wasn't sure what to do with his prize, or if he even wanted it anymore.

'I almost didn't recognise you.' Maria took in his appearance from boots to hat. 'I saw a man limping and guessed you to be one of the patients from the hospital.'

'It's been a long time,' he replied. He tried not to stare, at the slight angle she wore her hat, the slope of her hips as she moved from one leg to another, at the gold wedding band.

'I knew you were back,' she stated flippantly, waving at the woman with the two children further along the beach. 'You made the front page of the newspaper when you arrived at the hospital, no doubt across Australia as well. You were always good at making headlines.'

She'd collected herself quickly. While he, in comparison, had not.

'I only found out yesterday that you were here,' replied Ross. He couldn't believe that, while he had rushed to find her, it seemed that she'd ignored his existence all these months.

'Really? I'm surprised Mrs Guild didn't hurry to tell you. This is still a small town. Everyone knows everybody's business. Maybe she was too simple to make the connection.'

'She's been very good to me,' Ross said sharply.

'The old woman's a good worker,' Maria agreed. She looked at her feet then to the wandering children. 'I heard most of your family died. You must be pleased.' There was an edge to her voice.

'Not so much,' said Ross, unprepared for the subject and her harshness. 'My father and grandmother had been dead some time when I got the news.'

'I see.' She gave a smile like a shared conspirator. 'Come on. You were so angry with them and rightly so. Still here you are, pulled from the wilderness by your faithful servant.' She bobbed a curtsey. 'The great man. Resurrected. Heir to a fortune.'

'Don't do this, Maria.'

Her false gaiety soured. 'Why not? You deserted me. It might be years ago but that's the truth of things. You made me a promise and then you ditched me like a piece of trash. But what does it matter now? We've both moved on.' She signalled again to the other woman, and in response the woman walked to where the children were tossing sand at each other. Maria appeared fascinated by their game. Ross searched for something more to say.

337

'I have my respectable life,' she said. 'And you have yours. Whatever that might be. So why are you here?'

'Stop it, Maria.' He felt awkward, being faced with such disdain. He'd had little idea what Maria's reaction would be, but he'd not expected this. She looked confused.

'I never deserted you,' said Ross. 'I made sure you were safe and –'

'It was Connor who made sure I was safe,' Maria interrupted brusquely. 'Made all the promises in the world, didn't you?'

'You hate me,' stated Ross. 'Well, you'll never be able to despise me as much as I hate myself for what happened. I didn't know about your marriage until it was too late. But don't think I ever forgot you. I came to find you. I wanted you but you'd already gone, already married. In the end it was you who didn't wait.'

Maria's palm hit him, sharp and stinging across the cheek. Ross grabbed her arm tightly. He knew he was hurting her. He observed how her lips pressed tightly together, the slight flare of her nostrils, her eyes never leaving his face.

'I swear I'll hit you until every single person in this town sees what's going on,' she hissed. 'Then it will all come swimming back into the public's glare. Your sordid past. The way I was bundled away to hide your shame.'

Ross let go of her wrist, battle-ready for what she'd promised. If she was angry then surely she was also suffering. It would be something, at least, to know he wasn't the only one to have been rubbed raw.

She flinched and took a step away as if expecting to be struck. 'When I needed you the most you didn't come.'

'What are you talking about?' Ross wasn't interested in games. He'd come for an explanation, some justification of her actions. Even though nothing Maria said would alter their current situation, Ross needed to try to grasp how they'd reached this point where they fronted each other like enemies.

Maria regarded him closely. 'The child, of course. It was then I understood that wanting me was one thing, being father to a bastard quite another.'

338

'A child,' repeated Ross. With those two words it was as if he'd been thrown into the sky and then spun straight back to earth. 'We have a child?'

Maria's mouth opened. 'Truly. You didn't know?'

'No.' Ross turned and began to walk away, the sand pooling around his boots. He needed air and space. A bird was diving into the sea, flapping its wings and trailing a spray of salty water. Maria chased after him and laid a tentative finger on his arm.

'You're not lying to me?' she asked.

'Why would I?' He spun around, seeing the hurt, feeling his own.

'I wrote a letter. Addressed it to you,' she said. 'I gave it to Mrs Reece to post.'

'I never got it. As you never received any of mine. Connor made sure of that. He had a strong assistant in Mrs Reece.'

Maria paled. 'I thought she was my friend.'

Ross placed an arm about her waist, afraid she might faint and then drew her to him. He felt resistance, the stiffening of a body that once melded to his. Years ago Ross believed that to hold Maria again would be a healing, a coming home, where everything else would be unimportant compared to the woman he loved. They stayed like that for some minutes, Ross holding her, she unmoving, arms by her side, until she gradually returned the embrace. He still cared for her, but whether it was love, he could no longer tell.

'A girl or boy?' he asked.

Maria broke away and started fussing with her dress. Ross collected her hat, which had fallen to the ground. She glanced cautiously to where the woman and children were now leaving the beach, walking away from them towards the scatter of houses.

'A boy,' she finally told him, pressing each eyelid free of tears. 'He'll be ten this year but, Ross, he can't know about you.'

'What do you mean he can't know about me?' said Ross. 'Don't be ridiculous.'

'Think of him. He already has a father,' countered Maria.

'Not the real one.'

She looked at him. 'You've changed.'

'Answer me this, do you love your husband?'

'As much as you love your wife,' she retaliated. 'Actually, that's wrong. You never cared for her.'

'I loved *you*. I wanted *you*,' answered Ross. 'When I realised . . .'

'What? You packed up and went walkabout! Please, Ross, don't blame me for deserting everyone. I have enough of my own problems. Real ones, not issues created by a poor little rich boy. Connor was right. You followed me around like a fool. Treated me like a plaything. You were no better than Holder, bartering for me, weighing my value like a mob of cattle. A white woman wouldn't have been treated that way.'

Ross shook his head. 'It wasn't like that,' he insisted.

'It was for me, Ross. I grew up with people assuming I was a whore because of my childhood, because I belonged to no one and had no family, because of the colour of my skin. And so I became one. Is that what you want to hear? That I slept with men for a bowl of rice, a trinket, a few shillings? Would you have fought Holder if you'd known that, or would you have been disgusted? What if I told you that I searched through the bones of those Chinese waiting to be sent back to the home of their ancestors? Gold dust and pearls. All concealed in skeletons to avoid tax. What do you think of me now?' she breathed defiantly. 'I have a family, Ross,' she said more quietly. 'So what do you mean by coming here? What do you want? A quick roll on the beach or something more lasting? You with your wife and me with my husband.'

This wasn't the person Ross remembered. This new Maria was all sharp edges and harsh notes, but she was the mother of his son. 'Is it Carment you want to be with, Maria? Can he give you every-thing you deserve?'

'He's not as pretty as you once were, nor so determined to carve a path,' Maria told him. 'And there is no great fortune. No grand home in Adelaide. But he's enough for me.'

Ross heard her words as the soft hiss of the outgoing tide dragged at the sand. 'Do you love him?'

'You and he are completely different,' she replied.

'And that's good, no doubt.' He felt renewed anger at another man taking what was his, and refreshed disappointment that he'd given up so quickly on finding her once he'd learnt of her marriage. If not for Holder's claim and Darcey's obstinacy, they might not have reached this point, might not have destroyed what was once so engulfing, at least for him.

Ross knew that the days of wandering since he'd last seen her had placed a heavy burden on them both. If there had been anything left of their love to save, the remnants of it were fast disintegrating as they fronted each other on this deserted beach.

There was nothing to be done. This wasn't one of Alastair's Greek myths. No fleet would set sail to capture his Helen a second time. He'd fought for Maria once before and suffered the consequences, and then he'd walked away. Beaten. Sick of everything and everyone. His years in the bush were self-inflicted penance for having lost her. For having been unable to deal with the machinations of those closest to him. For being addled by confusion and guilt. And for loving two women. It was a hard admission.

'Our son deserves to know who his real father is. I'm sorry about your husband but you will have to tell him about us.'

'No,' said Maria. 'Edward knows Hugh isn't his. He believes Marcus Holder is the father. Pretending I was pregnant to that man and not you provided me with some sympathy, and I'm grateful to Edward for marrying me against his father's wishes. I needed a father for my son and I wasn't going to say no. And, Ross, you were and still are married.'

'I wouldn't have cared less. You know how I felt about you.'

'Some of us can't afford to be so reckless. I know what it's like not to fit in, to be unacceptable. I didn't want that for my child.' Maria tugged once at his sleeve as if to ensure he was listening. 'Hugh thinks his father is dead and it's best that way.'

'And is Edward a good father to my son?'

'Of course.' The answer was curtly given.

Ross sensed there was more. 'Maria?'

341

'We have four other children, Ross. It's natural that Edward favours them over Hugh.'

'Meaning what exactly?'

'Nothing.'

'Maria?' he said again,

She looked out to the ocean, clearly hesitant. 'It would be easier for everyone if they got on a little better.'

'In other words, Edward wanted you but not another man's child?' He watched as the truth of what he said showed itself in Maria's eyes.

Yesterday, barely a shred of Ross's own making existed and now he'd discovered that there was one extraordinary thing he'd had a part in creating. And yet he was being asked to walk away, before he even had a chance to meet his son. It was hard to give up something so sweetly found. There was a mangling going on within him, a twisting of knowing and having and wishing and wanting and all the time Maria waited for an answer, scrappy sand blowing on and around them as if the wind didn't give a damn.

Ross imagined escaping Darwin with the boy. Cutting cross-country through clusters of termite mounds aligned according to the passage of the sun. Camping rough. Hiding. Moving in the shadow of the stony escarpments until the creeping ferns and paperbark swamps dried up, until the rocky outcrops dwindled in size and the land grew flat and smooth, dust-riddled and mazed by things that walked and hopped and slithered. Ross could be the father that the boy needed. He could teach his son how to survive on the land, knowledge that could not be found in any book, like finding water when there was none to be found, of the type of horse a man needed for roping cleanskins in a yard, and the ones that were fearless and agile, that glistened with sweat on the buffalo plains. These were all things he'd once thought of sharing with Hart, had he and the boy been given time.

'I could take him with me, Maria.'

'No!' she shouted, her cheeks red with rage. 'If you take my boy he'll be your shiralee. Maybe not to start with, but you'll think of him that way eventually. Once people start hunting you it won't be as easy to disappear. There is more to consider here than what you want, Ross.'

He stepped away from the incoming tide, from the bubbles popping up through the sand, and the anger of the woman in front of him. 'I won't leave without meeting him. That's final.'

Ross thought of the girl on the buffalo hunt. Even now, a child of his blood could be resting beside her as she salts hides at another's man's request. There'd been women. And maybe other children. This one he wasn't letting go of.

'I mean it. It would be wrong of you to deny your son. You know that, Maria. Particularly if Edward isn't the father to the boy that he should be. You've said as much.'

Maria glanced briefly down the street to her house. 'If I let you meet him,' she said, 'will you leave us be? Will you promise not to cause any trouble? Or do you intend to hurt me twice? You owe me, Ross.'

She knew how to strike, he'd give her that. 'I have no other children, Maria. In the end, what property I have should be left to my son. I'd *like* it to be left to my son. I won't say anything to him about it today, but at some stage in the future Hugh needs to know the truth. You need to tell him so that when I return he won't be surprised to see me.'

'Not while he's a child,' she warned.

Ross waited on the bench outside the house while Maria went indoors. The young woman from the beach emerged, with a red-haired child on a hip. She told him that Mrs Maria wouldn't be long. She seemed interested in him, and lingered on the veranda, sitting the little girl on the bannister. Eventually the child's kicks drew her back to the present, and then she too disappeared down the long hall. Ross pulled on the knotted swing supports before sitting on the bench. A row of shrubs planted sporadically along the fence leaned away from the onshore wind. There was a hole near the gate big enough for a dog to crawl through and above it, on the top railing, a magpie stared at the house.

Maria's voice could be heard and then there was a stomp of footsteps and a boy ran outside and down the three stairs from the veranda to the garden, stopping directly in front of Ross.

'Hello, Mr Grant.'

The boy extended an arm and Ross rose. Hugh was tall and skinny with black hair. His grip suggested he was used to mixing with men. 'I know all about you. How you saved my mum and then roamed the bush with the blacks.'

'This is Hugh,' Maria puffed, catching up. 'Named after his grandfather.'

Ross thought of the old bastard he'd met in the Hotel Victoria the first week he'd set foot in Darwin. The man who'd placed Maria into his care. 'I know Hugh Carment. How is your grandfather?'

'Still running the property. My dad says he'll be running it even when he's got one foot in the grave. But I don't think he'd be able to do that, do you?'

'Probably not. And where is your father now?' asked Ross.

'He's with him. I'd like to be there to help with the muster-up, but Mum says I have to go to school.' He screwed his feet into the ground, scuffing his shoes.

'There's plenty of time for cattle work,' said Ross. 'School's important too.'

'What was it like when you were out bush, Mr Grant? My dad says you went mad. Is that right?'

'Hugh!' Maria admonished. 'I'm sorry, Ross.'

'That's all right.' Ross met Maria's gaze. 'For a while there I almost certainly did.'

'And Mum said that you got hurt when you were hunting buffalo.'

'Did she tell you all that just this morning?'

'Oh no.' Hugh stuck his chin out. 'Mum told me some of that stuff ages ago.'

'Did she now?'

'That's what I want to do,' continued Hugh. 'Hunt buffalo. Grandfather says I'm already a crack shot and that I can stick a horse like nobody's business.'

'Is that right? Well, I wouldn't doubt it,' said Ross.

'Time to go, Hugh,' urged Maria.

'Bye, Mr Grant.' He ran up the steps. The front door squeaked on its hinges, and he was gone.

'So you have five children?' asked Ross.

'Three boys and two girls.'

So many, Ross thought. A household of little ones to carry on the Carment name. 'Does he need anything?'

'Nothing. Hugh's a good student.' Pride showed in the way she glanced back towards the house. 'He likes reading and sports and he gets into a fair bit of trouble. More than some other boys, but he's strong and healthy and headstrong. Like you.'

'Can I write to him?'

'And say what?'

'I don't know. I could tell him about buffalo hunting.'

'And nothing else?' queried Maria. 'Hugh's too young. Be content with the fact he considers you a hero.'

'Nothing else,' promised Ross.

'All right, then. Yes. But don't flood him with letters, it will make Edward suspicious.'

They walked in silence to where Ross's horse waited in the shade. Unsure whether Maria's company meant she didn't trust him to leave, Ross said nothing more about the boy. He didn't want to break the fragile bond he had established that morning, but he hoped Maria appreciated how much it tore at him to go.

The sun was already high, a blur of light that Ross needed to shield his eyes from when he glanced up, which he did often. He focused on anything that attracted attention. A piece of newspaper on the ground, mail wedged in a letterbox, the sound of a child's laugh. Little things that meant nothing but would become permanent fixtures when he recalled that day.

The whiskery mare nickered on their approach. Maria patted the animal as Ross lifted his leg, sliding the boot into the stirrup, then heaved himself onto the horse's back, his face almost touching the mare's neck with the effort. With difficulty, he straightened in the saddle.

'You shouldn't be riding, Ross.'

'So they tell me,' he replied.

'You're as stubborn as ever.'

The mare flicked its tail. 'Maria.'

'Don't say anything, Ross.' She folded her arms across her chest.

He thought of his hopes of reconciliation that morning and of the enormity of what had now replaced those vague expectations. Maria stepped further away and he in turn pushed the crown of his hat down hard. Ross measured the distance connecting them and the son, which now created a triangle. He'd wanted Maria once. But what he recalled and what was before him no longer corresponded. And yet if she'd come to him, willing and happy . . . but there was no point in speculating, not anymore.

⫷ Chapter 57 ⫸

Waybell Station

The old mare trudged next to Mick's young gelding, growing more reluctant as the miles increased. Ross figured the horse smarter than him, that the animal could sense that rushing to an uncertain welcome wasn't something to be advised. Tread carefully, the old horse cautioned as she stepped hesitantly through the undergrowth. Boss he might well be, however his entitlement was neither warranted nor proven.

'You need to stop?' asked Mick.

Ross pulled the mare up and caught his breath. Three hours in the saddle was testing his pain threshold. 'I'll stretch my legs,' he said. He gripped the saddle, swung a leg over and, on hitting the ground, buried his forehead in the horse's rump. When the discomfort lessened he began to lead the mare. 'I'll walk for a while.'

'Ross, are you all right? Perhaps you should ride in the dray,' called Darcey. Parker sat next to her. The wagon was loaded with supplies and her most favoured pieces of furniture, her easel sticking up on one side. Eustace tailed the small party.

Ross gave a dismissive wave in response, knowing how much worse the ache would be if he was to sit on that wooden seat with his legs crooked up at right angles. He thought of the walking stick in the rear of the wagon as he stepped over some fallen timber, and of the woman who observed him from the advantage of height and full health.

Darcey's presence had come about through pity.

Yes, she'd said a few days later, answering his correspondence in a neat, concise reply. Darcey had taken it into her mind that Ross wanted her on the property to care for him and organise the household, and accordingly she offered to live on the station for a period of one year until he became more settled. Refusing the offer was an impossibility, for then Darcey might have assumed he'd expected more from their relationship. Twelve months. Ross thought of the weeks allotted to him. The time was undeserved and he still berated himself for writing the letter and presuming that she cared. He wished that Darcey had refused him. He wasn't sure what he wanted from his wife, but whatever it was, it wasn't pity.

'Are you sure you should be walking, Ross?' she asked again.

'I'm fine,' he replied.

Mick slowed his horse. 'It's a long way yet, Boss.'

'I know, Mick, but I'll just walk for a little while.'

'Must have been a big buffalo to smash you up so bad.'

'It was Nugget that fell on me. He got flipped into the air,' said Ross.

'That weedy nag?'

'Yeah.'

'Shouldn't have swapped that tobacco for him. It *was* good tobacco,' said Mick.

'No, it was a great trade, Mick. Nugget was the best horse I've ever owned.' He didn't add that his recklessness killed the animal, and that he'd ridden too hard, too fast for far too long.

'Boss, we run buffalo in the north now and cattle in the south. Better for the cattle,' explained Mick.

'Sounds like a good idea to me.'

'Your idea. We talked about it. You be here for a while?' asked Mick.

'It depends. Staying mightn't be the right thing to do. For anyone. Waybell might be better off without me.'

'This country go on no matter who's here, Boss. Best that you ask if you'd be better off without Waybell,' answered Mick.

The land was spoilt from the heat, and the dry crackled about them. They journeyed for the rest of the day, Ross feeling more settled now he was back in territory he knew, despite the aches that tormented him. Timber-framed turrets of rock could be seen in the distance and it was towards these craggy projections they headed until the bluff that hung cold and straight above Waybell came into sight. A ridge, an incline, a well-gouged track and then the trees separated.

The station's inhabitants were lined up to greet Ross and Darcey. A string of people, distantly familiar. Old men sitting in the dirt. Children in hand-me-downs, stockmen leaning impatiently on rifles and women who, Ross supposed, figured he'd gone *womba* and waited with interest to see what might happen next. Mick led their small procession to the front of the homestead.

Lifting his boot free of the stirrup, Ross dismounted. He staggered a little from the weakness of his legs, and waited until his balance evened out before limping slowly to where Sowden sat in his cane-bottom chair. The manager was older and smaller. Long grey hairs sprouted from his eyebrows and spiky chin-grizzle gave him a dissolute air. Annie held the familiar raggedy umbrella aloft, the woman and the bent parasol both showing signs of age.

'Boss.' Sowden nodded.

'Sowden,' answered Ross.

They shook hands. Sized each other up. 'You look well,' commented Ross.

'And you not so much.' Sowden took in the slope of Ross's waist, which was kinked up on one side.

'Hello, Annie,' said Ross.

'How long you back for this time, Boss?' Her fingers moved along the handle of the canopy.

'Long enough.'

Further back the women and children gathered around Darcey, calling out 'Missus' and touching her. She greeted each person. Shaking a hand here and there, asking after children who had since grown and meeting new additions. When she reached where Ross waited with Sowden, he noticed she held a package wrapped in brown paper and twine.

'Hello, Bill.'

The manager smiled, taking Darcey's hand in both of his. He nodded and grew watery-eyed as Annie and Darcey exchanged hellos, and there was a brief discussion of camp news. Darcey enquired about medical ailments that might be troubling the tribe and offered her services if required. Annie said she might just send one or two who never listened and see if the Missus could do better.

'We kept the house just as you left it, Missus,' Sowden told her.

'Oh, Bill. I did tell you and Annie to move in. You know that.'

'That wouldn't have been proper.'

'This is for you.' Darcey gave Sowden the package as women and children crowded in.

Sowden, puzzled at first, carefully unwrapped the gift. Inside was a canary-yellow umbrella with navy stripes. 'Thank you, Missus,' he said.

Everyone moved back so that the sunshade could be opened. The old parasol was thrown away to be fought over by some of the children as Annie set the new one above the manager's head.

'It's the best thing someone's ever given me,' he snuffled, folding the brown paper into a series of smaller and smaller squares. 'The very best.'

'Mick tells me you've got the place in good order,' said Ross.

'Fair enough.' Sowden set the paper and twine in his lap, slapping away the eager children. 'Mick's been in charge since the little Scot left.'

'With your help.' He'd planned on taking Sowden aside and having a private conversation, but now he was back on the property he felt the familiar hierarchy come into play. The camp waited for one of them to speak. Ross hesitated. Sowden's lips curled into a slight smile. It was as if he understood Ross's predicament as he tried to find the right words, if not apology for the accusations of the past, at least indebtedness for what had been done in his absence.

'Thanks for looking after the property. I appreciate it,' said Ross finally.

Sowden bowed his head.

'You figure things out now?' Sowden asked, without a hint of cynicism.

How to answer the question when the whole camp was eavesdropping? 'Am I meant to?' replied Ross.

Sowden's mouth twisted to one side, the skin bunching. 'Don't know rightly. My father couldn't read or write very well. He used to mark time with a stick. Scratched on a bit of wood with a knife to count off the days. Six upright strokes and a slash through the lot of them for Sunday. That's how I learnt to tally numbers as a boy. Staring at the passage of time. Lost days, my mother called them. That's the only thing that's certain. Time. One day we'll all be gone. And everything we've done, the good and the bad, the mean and the kind, well, it's gotta count for something, otherwise why would we put ourselves through it? You stick a piece of wood in the ground with my name on it or burn me and place my bones in the hollow of a termite-rotted trunk, doesn't matter to me. Shouldn't matter to anyone. All the remembering and the doings got to be done now because no one will be doing it for you in the future. So it's not so much about working things out, but living. Making use of the time we've got.'

Almost the entire camp was on the ground, limbs crossed and attentive. Even Parker and Eustace had halted their unloading of the wagon. One of the horses whinnied and the disturbance roused Sowden. He tapped the chair, and two young men grasped the arms on either side.

351

'A place needs a boss,' Sowden said to Ross as the chair was lifted and everyone got to their feet. 'And get yourself a better horse,' he called as he was carried away. 'That old mare might be all right for a cripple.'

'He tells a fine story,' commented Darcey as they walked up the stairs and inside the homestead.

'They missed you,' Ross told her. 'You stayed after I left. That means a fair bit to them, I'd say. I don't think many women would have done that, Darcey. Live in such an isolated place without a man's protection.'

Darcey removed her hat and set it on the table. 'Oh, Ross. This place is full of men and women and children. And anyway, Connor was here at that stage. He only left when I did.'

'But still, you know what I mean,' he persevered.

Eustace and Parker called out to say they had Darcey's belongings and they entered the house, sitting the travelling trunk in the dining room.

'Only two more to go,' said Eustace cheerily. 'You must have gutted that house of yours, Missus.'

'Not quite.' Darcey smiled. 'I left the icebox.'

'Now that's one thing worth staying in Darwin for,' said Eustace, as he and Parker departed.

Ross opened the bedroom door and walked inside. He wasn't expecting the large wardrobe and matching dressing table, or the floral bedcover.

'They came from Pine Creek,' explained Darcey. 'Connor and I made a trip of it. We stayed at the hotel for a few nights after the furniture arrived. I hope you don't mind.'

It was just as Sowden had said. Life went on. Changes were made. People moved into spaces previously inhabited by others, erasing old memories and creating new ones. On the wall hung a patchwork, although it looked incomplete. It started square-cornered at the top, the cubes of material falling to a zigzag, like a flight of stairs.

Darcey examined the wall hanging. Insects had made a feast of it. There were various sized holes and dark spots blotted the material. 'Oh well, I'll have to make another. The room's so plain and that wall so bare. It always felt to me as if there was something missing.'

'You should take this room,' said Ross, unwilling to think of the time when he was young and whole and Maria had offered herself to him. 'You've made it yours.'

'Are you sure?'

'Yes.'

Leaving Darcey to unpack, Ross moved through the house. The rooms were slightly changed. There were new pieces of furniture and a few of the original items. At the threshold to Maria's room, he stopped. The space held a bed, wardrobe and washstand, the few items she'd left behind long since removed. Maria was gone. Exorcised from the homestead by the years, through their recent meeting and because another woman had managed to supplant her through patience and mercy. It would have been better if all contact with Maria could have been ended that day at Myilly Point, but there was a child now. His son.

≪ Chapter 58 ≫

A dreadful howling punched the air. Ross woke with a start, momentarily forgetting where he was, though six months had passed since his return. As he lay in the dark listening, a choir of wailing rose, increasing in volume. He rolled onto his side and sat upright. Darcey knocked on the bedroom door, pushing it open so that it hit the wall with a thud.

'What's happened?' asked Ross.

'I don't know.' The kerosene lamp shone on his naked body and Darcey half-turned in modesty before changing her mind and gathering the clothes strewn about the floor. She passed each item to him, staring at the scars on his body. Ross did up buttons on his shirt and the fly of his trousers, concealing the marks from the years of wandering. Snakebite, knifings, burns, lancewood welts and ruined hips and legs – a map of events linked by anger and alcohol, many of which he couldn't even recall.

Finding his boots, Darcey knelt at Ross's feet, her features composed and unquestioning.

'Thank you,' said Ross, leaning on her shoulder as he tugged each boot on.

'Do you want your walking stick? It's very dark outside. The moon hasn't risen yet.'

'No.' He'd been trying not to rely on it as much, which was testing him.

'The noise is coming from the camp,' said Darcey.

Ross heaved his body from the bed and got to his feet. 'Get a pistol and stay in your room.'

'But, Ross.'

'Do as you're told, Darcey. Please.'

'Be careful.' She stepped aside to let him pass.

Ross stumbled downstairs and into the night. He met Eustace and Parker along the way, bleary-eyed and worried, the click of cartridges and the sliding of bolts accompanying their steps as they slowed to keep pace with him.

Dogs skirted their heels as they passed the billabong, the light from a campfire guiding their direction. Most of the commotion was centred outside Sowden's wurley and it was here that Ross went, pushing through the gathered people to the empty rattan chair near the entrance to the hut.

A piercing wail sounded. A woman's voice.

'You go inside, Boss,' said Eustace, sounding nervous. 'See what's what.'

Once indoors, Ross could see that the wurley had been enlarged and that there was another room partitioned off with hessian from the main bit of the hut. The interior was lit by a single lamp and as the cry repeated itself, Ross realised what had occurred. He was far from prepared to face this particular death and he delayed going further into Sowden's space. A table held foodstuffs, books and a leather-bound diary, while clothes spilt from the top of a forty-four-gallon drum. Having until very recently given no consideration to Sowden's reduced circumstances after he'd left the homestead over a decade ago, being confronted with the manager's personal belongings made Ross feel deeply ashamed.

The adjoining section of the hut was supported by a tree, branches sloping from bark to earth. It was here Ross found Annie.

The woman was kneeling, bending back and forth from the waist, wailing. It was dreadful to see the way she bashed at her chest, grasping at Sowden, who lay on his back, eyes open, his spindly legs white and bare.

Sowden's skin still held heat. Ross closed the man's eyes and whispered his sympathies. Annie swished at him like a fly.

'I'm sorry, Annie.'

'Are you?' She rose from the ground. 'You never liked my man. He was good. Very good. Better than you. He looked after all of us.'

'I know he did,' replied Ross. Annie was contorted by grief. A different woman. Broken.

'He looked after this place,' continued Annie, the whites of her eyes red. 'Mick and the others, we all did, and what did you do? Treat us badly. Walk away. All those years. Bill never said anything when you left. Except that you'd gone walkabout and that we should respect that. And when we heard Connor found you, my Bill was glad. I said, why be glad? He doesn't care. And he said to me, because when a man's lost he should be found.' She ran an arm across a snotty nose and hiccupped, waiting for Ross to refute her claims. 'He always thought the best of a person. You never did,' she spat.

'You're probably right,' replied Ross.

'Then when we heard about you in the hospital, Bill was worried because he knew what it was like not to have legs.'

'I'm sorry. I'm very sorry,' said Ross. 'I have no excuses for the way I've lived my life.'

He went back to the adjoining room and stood there as Annie's grief welled up once more. The floor was covered with layers of cowhide, and pages ripped from newspapers lay in one corner. Curious, Ross gathered up the clippings and carried them to the lantern. They were all about his family. The Grants of Adelaide and the sole surviving son gone missing. The articles noted suspected sightings of Ross, his father's obituary and the beginnings of Connor's search, which was widely condemned as foolhardy and a waste of time. A lengthy interview with Mr Dyer of the Oenpelli Mission, who hailed Ross for trying to save young Don Hart's life, completed the collection. Ross held the papers, and glanced through the brief record. The bones of a family nearly all gone. With care, he replaced the clippings where he'd found them.

Outside near the fire, Eustace and Parker were talking to Mick. 'Sorry business,' Mick commented.

'Yes,' answered Ross. 'Very sorry. How do you want to bury him?'

'Old Bill was more blackfella than white.'

'Well, if you need anything,' answered Ross. He took Mick aside. 'You're in charge now.'

'Yes, Boss,' the stockman replied.

'There'll be no new manager coming to take Sowden's place. We both know you were running this property long before I arrived. Having the title of manager only makes it official.'

'Better you stay on too, Boss. Better for everyone.'

'We'll see,' said Ross.

Darcey sat at the dining room table, waiting for Ross's return. There was a pot of tea on the table and two mugs. A kerosene lamp provided the only light. Ross joined her and explained about Sowden's death. 'It could have been a heart attack. I don't know.'

'I'm sorry he's gone. He'll be missed. Here, have some tea.' She poured for them.

Ross stared at the black liquid. Darcey added sugar to his cup.

'Annie mentioned he'd not been well. I think he was waiting for you to come back, Ross.'

'What for? I'm of no use on the property. I can't even read the station ledgers without my glasses.'

'To see you one last time. Annie said there were things that needed to be said,' Darcey explained.

'More on my part than his. I accused him of mismanagement a long time ago and I was wrong. I never found any proof. I should have told him that. I should have apologised. As it is, we've barely talked since my return. So whatever he wanted to say he thought better of.' He took a sip of the tea. 'Anyway, Annie pretty much summed things up,' he said grimly.

'Don't be so hard on yourself.'

'Wouldn't you be?'

'Ross, not everyone holds their resentments as close to their heart as you do. Remember the day we arrived on the property? Bill talked about time and making the most of it.'

'Yes,' said Ross.

'Well then, he had plenty to say. Lost days. I remember that phrase distinctly. That speech was for you, Ross. No one else,' she said. 'Besides, if you needed to apologise to Bill for the past, then consider this: for a wrong to be righted properly he also had to forgive you. I'm not saying he had, but I do believe that after everything that's happened he came to understand you a little better, perhaps he even saw similarities. The both of you have led hard lives.'

The tea was dark and hot. Steam rose from its surface. Ross had seen Sowden laid out on the hut's floor, Annie crying beside him. How people presented themselves and who they really were didn't always match. Or maybe it was his perception that was lacking. He'd wronged the man who grew cold in the hut by the billabong, and making amends was now an impossibility. He could only hope that Darcey was right. That in the end he and Sowden had reached a silent understanding. He'd seen a glimmer of that the day of his return to Waybell.

Few mistakes of his doing could be repaired. He glanced across at Darcey. Not settling for her pity could. 'I appreciate everything you've done for me, Darcey, but this isn't much of a life for a woman.'

Darcey took a sip of tea. 'Caring for children, mending cuts and broken bones, helping to birth babies. Painting and walking in my spare time. The only thing that's changed in my life is location, Ross, and you. You've changed a lot.'

'So you don't miss Darwin?' he asked. They shared a quiet existence. She with her ministrations and he with his daily rides, only coming together at mealtimes to talk of Waybell and life there.

'Yes, I do,' she replied.

Ross slurped at the tea and Darcey patted his arm. He shrugged off her attentions but nonetheless placed the mug down and straightened his shoulders. She was still trying to re-educate him, to draw out the dormant characteristics of the culture he'd been born into as if she were a potter and he the clay. A part of Ross refused to be recast into that previous state, for too much ignorance came with his earlier existence.

'I know what your letter said, Ross. No promises. It was the same for me. I followed you here for the reasons I gave in my note. Duty lay at the heart of my decision and that obligation was centred on my love for Waybell and its people. Your difficulties were secondary.'

'I see,' said Ross.

'You're not offended, I hope?'

'If I was, I wouldn't have a right to be.'

'Exactly.' She smiled. 'I feel a greater sense of need here, or perhaps I feel more needed. But I don't know if living together is a possibility for us, at least in any ongoing capacity.'

'So the company you're keeping is making you reconsider your obligation to stay?' said Ross.

Her face was unreadable. 'It's been over six months since our return and now I find myself thinking about other things. What life would be like if I went back to Darwin. If we divorced.'

'You want a divorce?' repeated Ross. The scratchy letter composed at Mrs Guild's house had been remarkably stupid. Extricating Darcey from his life had once been his primary objective. They'd bartered divorce for a child. He'd lost Maria because of their marriage. And now, these many years later, Darcey was offering what had then been unattainable: the freedom to do what he wished with who he wanted.

'Well, it's worth considering,' she explained.

'You'd remarry?'

Darcey twisted the knob on the kerosene lantern, the light flickering up and down. 'I'm not sure. I rather like my independence. The idea of travelling.'

He was to lose Darcey as well, then. Ross thought of mounting an argument, of reminding his wife of her contractual obligations. He had the right of a husband, but the knowledge that Darcey retained some rights too stopped Ross from speaking immediately. She was a spurned woman, one who was wealthy and intelligent enough to reach the reasonable assumption that a man such as he, useless and ageing, was of no value to someone like her. Pity only extended so far. Ross refused to degrade himself further by asking her to stay. What was the point of explaining that it wasn't for reasons of loneliness or selfishness but the simple acknowledgement that he'd come to recognise her many fine qualities, and that those qualities were more attractive than beauty or youth. He should tell her. Ross knew that. Leaving so much unsaid would burn what was left of his body. And if Darcey did leave, what then?

'Ross? What's the matter?' asked Darcey.

There was one overwhelming reality. He wanted Darcey in the way that a man wanted a woman. As a husband desired his wife. It was years since he'd been with a white woman. The last white girl Ross remembered was the daughter of a station owner out west, and as she was keen and he desperate he'd made a feast of her at every opportunity. Taking her on the sand near a bore head, against the side of the house. Ross left the job when the girl became more than relief to him. He had nothing to offer her.

'Tell me what you want, Ross?' Darcey waited, patient, watchful.

He wanted nothing and everything. He wanted items he couldn't have, like Alastair and the full use of his legs, and to get a decade back that he'd wasted through stupidity. The ability to run and rope and gallop without pain. The time to sit with his son and to talk to Sowden and Hart. To write to his grandmother one last time. There were so many entries on this list that they were impossible to count.

'Ross?' Darcey spoke up.

'What?' he asked.

'Talk to me.'

'Do you want me to ask you to stay, Darcey? You need my permission? Fine. I want you to stay. I never would have sent that damn letter if I didn't,' he admitted. He scraped back the chair. It was time to leave.

'Why? Why do you want me to stay?' asked Darcey. 'Tell me.'

'Because I can't manage. Because I'm useless. Some mornings it takes all my willpower to move. To even feel like getting out of bed. My body aches continuously and if there was drink about I'd be onto it. I'd be gone. Maybe even already dead. I'm an alcoholic, Darcey, and although I haven't touched a drop for months I still think about drinking nearly every day. The taste of it. How it made me feel. Numb. It's the deadness of it I crave. What comes from that single swallow. God, I can't even talk about grog without breaking into a sweat.'

'Yes, but why do you want me to stay?' she asked again.

'I've just told you,' said Ross.

'No you haven't,' she argued. 'If you are that feeble, perhaps you should return to Darwin. I'm sure we could arrange for a paid companion or nurse.'

'No,' he said loudly.

'Then what do you want?'

'*You*, damn it. I care about you. But it's one thing to care and another to have the ability to do something about it. I doubt I'd even be able to take you to bed.'

Darcey's eyes widened.

He looked away from her to the tongue and groove boards, the enamelware on the sideboard and a vase of wild flowers.

'I always knew you weren't quite the bastard you made yourself out to be,' she said.

≪ Chapter 59 ≫

With the mustering season having already begun, the home-stead and camp was quiet. Only women, children, old men and the infirm remained, along with a bereft Annie, who every morning placed Sowden's chair in the sun, hoisting the umbrella like a flag before withdrawing inside her hut. Ross wandered outdoors, considering the recently arrived mail. The letters were few, and the ones that came from the South were from managers and accountants providing updates on the running of the Grant empire on behalf of his wife. Darcey grew wealthier by the month. Only one message remained unread, and on the edge of the drying billabong he reached for the telegram, reading the brief lines from the family solicitor. His mother was dead. Buried already by the date of the wire. Leaden eyes and reclusive habits, that was all he recalled of her. Not much else.

The Adelaide house was to be closed. The gardens tended to in Darcey's absence. One day the property would be sold but for now Ross hoped that his wife would retain the residence. He wasn't quite ready to relinquish what was left of his childhood. At the water's edge, children poked at a turtle, snatching it up before it disappeared into the muddy hole. They held the hard-shelled creature aloft for inspection and ran towards one of the cooking fires, where their mothers waited.

That afternoon, late clouds gathered on the horizon. The unexpected rain kept Ross indoors and he wrote to his son in the study next to his wife's room, noting that the painting of the billabong waterlilies had been hung opposite the desk. It seemed to him that the lives of two women were now commemorated on the walls of his home. Maria, infused into the timber through the heat of their lovemaking, and Darcey's far more substantial contribution made bright and tantalisingly real by her continued presence.

His son had not yet been told of his true parentage but when that day came, something extensive was needed to explain how the business of living had gone so awry for Ross. He'd begun collating pages from scattered memories until a sort of log took form. The chapters of his life divided and depicted by the variegated colours of the earth and its formations. Weathered patterning on a rock face. Grassy plateaus. Rugged hills. The lifelessness of pale sand. The red soil of the plains. It became a difficult obsession, committing to paper his existence, for there were things Ross had forgotten or never wanted to reveal, choices made that were so poor he didn't recognise the man who toiled across the page. It was an inadequate chronicle for a father to write for his son, made worse by the absence of time. Having been informed by the doctor in Darwin of his limited mortality, each dawn sky underscored what he'd squandered and the dearth of fine days and rainy ones that lay ahead. Sowden's lost days were now etched into Ross's mind.

Outside, Darcey walked past the window. He'd been avoiding her since the night of Sowden's passing. He'd tried to fill the hours with riding and stumbling about outdoors, his inadequate body a barrier to what he yearned for the most: the liberty to return to where he'd come from. The wild lands, where questions and answers were wiped clean by the simple struggle to survive. But there was no chance of dodging the embarrassment he'd felt at her making him admit his need for her.

Darcey entered the room. 'Ross?'

He closed the journal and stood up, as a gentleman should in a lady's presence. 'Yes?'

'Was there any news?' asked Darcey. 'In the mail?'

'Letters from the solicitor and . . . and my mother died.'

Darcey positioned herself on the edge of Sowden's battered tin trunk and Ross resumed his position.

'I'm sorry.' Darcey appeared troubled.

'Difficult, is it? Giving condolences to someone who barely recalls the deceased and doesn't really care,' replied Ross.

'Come now. She was your mother. Even if you feel nothing today, you will tomorrow.'

He questioned if that was possible. At young Hart's passing, he'd held his hand during his last breaths and hoped it had been of some comfort to the boy. It was for him. Ross wondered if anyone had done the same for his mother. 'Anyway, they're all gone now. Every one of them.'

'Except Connor. He mightn't be family but he cares,' said Darcey. 'Are you ever going to ask him to return?'

'We've had too many disagreements,' replied Ross.

'So he told me.'

'I'm sure his version made for interesting listening.'

'It did. I know about the child. Your son. I assume that's who you're writing to so regularly?'

Ross stared at her. After a while he got up and limped about the room, then he sat down again. Darcey hadn't moved.

'Have you known for a long time?' he finally asked.

'Within a few months of moving to Darwin after you disappeared. Mrs Reece informed Connor of Maria's pregnancy and when the child was born he thought I'd find out eventually, Darwin being such a small place.'

Learning that Connor had known of the baby's existence from the beginning stunned him into momentary silence. He was furious.

'You didn't know that, Ross?'

'No.'

'Connor was trying to protect you. That's all he's ever aimed to do.'

'But if I'd known –'

'What? You wouldn't have gone walkabout?'

'I don't know,' he answered truthfully.

'She was already married by the time you arrived in Darwin,' said Darcey, as if reminding him that there was nothing he could have done.

'My life is my own. It always was, Darcey, and it always will be. It's not for anyone to interfere in.'

'We all know that now, Ross.'

He assumed Darcey would be angry. Being a father was fresh and new to Ross but it was ancient news for his jilted wife. Still, he rather thought she'd take the opportunity to condemn or complain. Any woman deserved that retaliatory jab.

'I wished it had been me. My child. I blamed myself for not falling pregnant and then I blamed you,' confessed Darcey, twisting the ring on her wedding finger. 'That's silly, isn't it, because it wasn't for the want of trying.'

Neither of them spoke. The original wedding band had been too large. The one she now wore fitted snugly and she twirled it constantly like it was a string of worry beads.

'I've heard Maria has a number of children. She's been blessed,' said Darcey.

'Yes, she has.'

'Have you come to an arrangement with her regarding your son?'

'You're very calm about all this,' he remarked.

'I've had time to grow accustomed to the situation.'

'You're fortunate,' said Ross. 'Maria's preference is for me to remain invisible, but as he's the only Grant heir, that's impossible. I intend to tell Hugh about me next year.'

'You don't think that's a little young?' suggested Darcey.

'No, I don't,' said Ross.

'And the properties and money your father left me? It is yours by right and so it must go to Hugh eventually, but only after I've finished with it. Let's just agree to that without debate.' She paused and then asked, 'And what about Maria? She's happily married, I hear?'

'It's over, Darcey,' said Ross firmly.

Her expression revealed little. 'And to think I only disturbed you to enquire about the mail,' she said, still fiddling with the ring. 'I'm sorry about the other night, provoking you the way I did.'

'You wanted answers,' said Ross.

Darcey ran a thumb over a palm, the nail tracing the lines in her flesh. 'Yes, I did. I also needed –'

'To make me experience how I made you feel all those years ago, unwanted?' asked Ross.

She laughed quite loudly. 'Heavens, no. I was angry with you for a long time, Ross. You treated me poorly and humiliated me but I learned to accept my part in our relationship. I was naïve to believe that a forced union could ever work. No, I simply wanted the truth as to why I was here.'

'I see.'

'You've always been one of the most difficult people to speak with.'

'It's a talent,' said Ross flippantly. Darcey's tone suggested that a more serious conversation was taking form and he worried, lest she draw out some other fault or desire within him, for he knew there were many.

'You've been very quiet since that night.'

'I've been busy.'

'Oh Ross,' she said, smiling. 'There's no shame in being honest. Haven't we put each other through enough? Let's not complicate things any further.'

'I don't understand.'

'Let me put it plainly,' said Darcey. 'I don't love you.'

'You've made that quite clear.' There were any number of accusations he could withstand but not more of this.

'Wait.' Darcey gestured for him to sit still. She rubbed her hands together and then along the length of her skirt from thigh to knee. 'You've changed.'

'As have you,' replied Ross.

'I never renounced society and embarked on extinction. But I want you to know what I see in the person before me. Most of the less-than-attractive parts of you are gone. What's left is better, finer.'

'Apart from being a cripple and unfit for society.'

'You'll never make a gentleman but then when we first met you were hardly the drawing-room type. I like this Ross Grant a lot better than the old.'

'You do?'

'Yes.'

Ross set his attention on the woman before him. There'd never been much order to his life once the short pants of childhood had been tossed aside. His was a rootless existence comprised of harshness and obsession. Yet here was the wife he'd forsaken telling him he was a better man. He had wronged her and even then she offered what he'd been incapable of giving, to anyone, especially his own family: tolerance and understanding. He was stunned by the scale of her compassion. It was so different to what he believed Darcey thought of him that he dropped his head, concentrating on the warped timber at his feet. He was like a ghost in a shell. Unworthy.

'Ross?' said Darcey.

Was it possible for a man such as him, who'd fallen so low, to finally make peace with everything that had gone before? Was he capable of the same kind of mercy? And if he was – if he could forgive the family who had wronged him – would he too be able to move on?

She was kneeling before him, a hand on his knee. 'There are five great tragedies in life, Ross. Ignorance, foolishness, poverty, a life without purpose, a life without God. You have lived through all of that needlessly, appallingly, and you almost killed yourself in the process. Think about that. About how you came to such a sorry place when you had family who loved you. Perhaps not in the way you wanted or believed was right, but there was love for you.

People cared. They still do. Think about what you have. What you can do tomorrow and the day after. What lies ahead.'

'I made a mess of everything,' he replied quietly. 'Maria, my family, even Sowden. But especially you, Darcey.'

'We all live in the margins of other people's tragedies. You in Alastair's. Me in the middle of two extraordinary brothers.'

'I'm sorry. For everything. Sorry for leaving you all those years ago.'

'I know,' said Darcey. 'I know you are.'

'I don't want you to go,' he said, taking her hand.

'And I don't want to leave.'

'But you don't love me,' answered Ross.

She leant forward and kissed his cheek. 'No, but there is always the hope of love growing, Ross, and fool that I am, I do care.'

❧ Chapter 60 ❧

1937

Hugh held firm in the saddle as the horse bucked around the yards, an arm held high in the air as if he was one of the American cowboys he so admired. At seventeen, he was tall and lean, with features that leant more towards the Grant bloodline, although the almond shape to his eyes and black hair was unmistakable. Ross observed his son as the boy drew blood from the spurs he wore until the horse finally threw him. Hugh landed heavily, rolling across the dirt in a clearly practised manner and then jumped up in disgust, Mick coo-eeing at the failed attempt to tame the gelding.

'Well, you should have seen that coming. What did you expect, riding him with the spurs like that?' commented Ross as Hugh dusted earth from his clothes.

The boy slipped through the railings so that he was on the same side as his father. 'Didn't you kill a horse hunting buffalo?'

'It was an accident,' countered Ross.

'That's not how you wrote it in that story you gave me to read.'

'It wasn't a story. It all happened. And ease off on the spurs a bit. You'll only scare him. You should know better.'

Hugh brushed dirt from his shirt. 'My horse, my methods.'

'I gave you the damn horse and this is my place. I don't have to leave any of it to you,' said Ross.

'So you keep telling me.' The boy walked to the stables.

Ross slammed his palm on the railing. If he'd known how damn difficult being a father was, he may not have taken the role on. Hugh itched for an argument nearly every day, to the extent that Ross was beginning to question why the boy even bothered to visit the property. He speculated it was only for the inheritance. It certainly didn't appear to be for the love of being Ross Grant's son.

'Young fella's pretty angry,' observed Mick, resting the gelding's saddle on the top railing.

'Yes, he is.'

'He'll be all right.'

'I hope so, Mick.'

'Sure he will be. First he's got to get to know you better, and you him. That'll take some doing. Best though if you don't go at each other like black snakes, eh?' Mick lifted the saddle and headed for the tack room.

Ross limped back to the house. Sitting on the top step of the veranda, he pulled out his pocketknife and found the sharpening stone he kept on the landing. It was only proper that, after everything that had occurred, Hugh's loyalty would lie with Maria. It had been his mother who'd broken the news of his parentage and while Ross chose not to think the worst, occasionally he blamed Maria for the boy's hostile attitude towards him. Although he reasoned that tensions in the Myilly Point household might well add to Hugh's angst and confusion, Hugh's manner towards him certainly wasn't due to the love of his stepfather. Hugh's relationship with Edward Carment had not improved over the years, according to the brief letters he received from Maria providing updates about their son. A situation made worse with the revelation that Ross was his birth father and not the long-deceased Marcus Holder. Ross had no idea how the outing of their affair had affected Maria's marriage, but assumed the ramifications would be significant. Maria's union of convenience had been based on a lie. Years ago, these unpleasant facts would have found their way into the reading public's hands, however even the papers weren't interested in revisiting the sordid details of the past. For once, Ross was old news.

'There's going to be a war, you know.' Hugh was standing in front of him, a stockwhip curled around a shoulder. 'It's in the paper. Nanking has surrendered to Japan. They reckon the empire's killing thousands of Chinese.'

'That's not our war,' said Ross.

'No, it's mine,' countered Hugh.

It was the first time the boy had made reference to his mixed blood.

'It's between the Empire of Japan and China,' Ross told his son. The boy stared at him almost dismissively. 'So you want to fight? For the Chinese. As a mercenary?'

'Maybe.' Hugh fingered the plaited hide he was carrying. 'I've talked to a few of the old men who came back from France. They've told me not to go. You'll say the same, I suppose?'

'I might, except that I didn't fight in the Great War, so it's not for me to say. You have to make your own decision.'

'Really?' Hugh toed at the ground with a boot and then squatted in front of Ross. 'All those notes about your life that you gave me. I didn't believe most of it, apart from the bit about you deserting my mother and what you said about the war. About how not going made you feel like an outsider.'

'This is a different war, Hugh. There's only two countries involved and Australia isn't one of them.'

'And that makes it less important?' argued Hugh.

'Of course not. But your Uncle Alastair fought for Australia. You'd be fighting for a place you've never seen with people you don't know and a language you can't speak.'

'I don't think of you as my father, you know,' Hugh said suddenly.

'And I'm not speaking to you as if I am. I'm just saying how it is,' said Ross.

They eyed each other off, Hugh's anger showing in the way he pursed his lips. 'You feel more like a distant relative,' he said, his tone insolent.

'That's something, I suppose,' Ross answered calmly.

He expected Hugh to stomp away, instead he unfurled the whip, flicking it across the ground as if trying to prolong the conversation.

'I never got on with my father, either,' Ross told him. 'He was a complicated man.'

'Bossy?' asked Hugh.

'Yes. I guess you reckon I'm the same, which wouldn't be an unfair assumption. I've often wondered if the reason he and I didn't have a great father–son relationship was because we were too alike.'

The boy stopped playing with the whip. It was obvious that he was considering Ross's words. 'Why did you leave my mother?'

'You know why, Hugh. You've read what happened from my point of view and heard your mother's side as well.'

'It was wrong. Everything was wrong.'

'Everything *went* wrong. Yes. I agree with that. And I'm sorry for what happened. If I could change things I would.'

'But you can't,' challenged Hugh.

'No, I can't.'

'I'm leaving tomorrow.'

'Tomorrow? But you're meant to be here for at least another week.'

'I don't want to be stuck here over the wet season, and if I go now I can ride out with Eustace and Parker.'

He considered forcing the boy to stay on, however such an action wouldn't help their relationship. 'Go then, if you want to.' He couldn't hide the disappointment from his voice.

Hugh lingered for a few more moments before walking away.

Ross stretched out his legs, the familiar ache lessening as tendons and bones eased into the different position. He hated the lead-up to the wet season. The humidity woke every part of his skeleton, making portions that functioned reasonably well in the dry brittle and painful during the tedious months of rain. He was like a wristwatch that couldn't be repaired, gradually slowing until one day it eventually stopped.

Darcey, knowing how he suffered, suggested that he head to Adelaide for a few months and this year he was almost willing to see something of the South and the changes he'd read about, however the idea of sitting on a train or horse, even a ship, for long periods tormented him. Ross still couldn't manage more than three to four hours in the saddle and after years of preferring a swag, these days by dark he looked for a bed. It bit at him, the inability to ride across the land he owned, and the very notion of leaving only to return to the property worse than ever crippled him more than his shattered body. He wasn't yet fifty years of age, but his youth was long gone and returning to Adelaide seemed pointless at this stage.

'Ross, where's Hugh?' Darcey leant against the wooden pillar on the veranda, framed by a spray of bougainvillea that trailed around the bannister.

He looked up from the pocketknife he was sharpening, the blade worn thin from hours of rubbing. 'I have no idea. Now he's got the idea into his head that he wants to fight for the Chinese, in China. Ridiculous idea. Why Maria would condone it when she spent the time I knew her trying to disassociate herself from them.' Ross stopped talking. He did his best not to mention Maria in Darcey's company. 'The Empire of Japan's invaded Nanking,' he finished more evenly.

'I was just reading about that in the newspaper Hugh brought with him. Do you think it will affect us?' asked Darcey, sitting next to him on the step.

'No. I'm more worried about Hugh and this childish scheme of his,' answered Ross.

'He's only testing you, Ross.'

'Is he? If I'd had the chance to go at his age I would have. Anyway, Hugh's leaving tomorrow. Apparently he's had enough of Waybell. He's worried he'll be stuck here for the duration of the wet season. And he hates me.'

She stroked his arm. 'Give him time, Ross.'

'Time? The boy's been coming to Waybell for the last three years. I still barely know him. The moment Hugh arrives he takes off and camps out for days, and when he is here he barely talks. Today was the most conversation I've had with him since he arrived.'

'I seem to recall someone else who was like that,' said Darcey. She rested her head on his shoulder.

'You on the other hand must have been born patient.'

'Don't you mean long-suffering?' she replied.

He squeezed her leg just above the knee and she let out a small squeal of complaint accompanied by a titter of laughter.

Their delicate courtship had been a renewal of faith that stretched the better part of two years before the night came when they finally lay together. The first time, it had been a clumsy reunion. Having succeeded in claiming his wife in every way but physically, Ross feared stepping back into the world of passion. Not only because he remained unsure of his ability to do the expected but because of where love once took him to, beyond the boundaries of reason. There was no mad desire. Instead, a mutual appreciation strengthened the growing bond between them until he understood how gentle and kind love could be.

'Truly, Ross, Hugh will come around eventually. He hasn't had the easiest of beginnings.' She interlaced her fingers with his.

'I hope you're right.' He worried for Hugh. In putting his life down on paper and giving the document to him to read, he'd run out of conversation to share with his son. Talk was difficult at times. There weren't any incidents from his own childhood that Ross could draw on and portion out when advice appeared to be required. At least, not the kind that showed how a boy became a man. Detailing his life, thus giving Hugh ammunition to throw back at him, now seemed a poor decision.

'Well, with our child you'll have more opportunity for fathering,' said Darcey.

Ross folded the knife. 'What?'

'A baby, Ross. We're going to be parents.'

Ross looked from Darcey's face to her stomach. 'How is that possible?'

'Ross . . .' she teased.

'I mean. I thought –'

'What?' She wagged a finger at him. 'That I'm too old? I'm not yet fifty, Ross. It's rare but it's not impossible.'

'I don't know what to say.'

'Be pleased. I am.'

'Of course I'm pleased. I'm overwhelmed.' He took her in his arms and hugged her tightly and then released her carefully. 'How do you know?'

Darcey laid a hand on her stomach. 'There are signs, Ross. And I've put on weight. Didn't you notice?'

'It seems to me everyone swells with age.'

'Well, this swelling comes with a child.'

'Is it safe? I mean . . . why now? After everything that's happened. After all this time?' asked Ross.

'I have no idea.' She smiled.

Ross took her hand and squeezed. 'How long?' he asked.

'Maybe five or six months.'

'We should go to Darwin. It'd be better if you're near the hospital. We can stay in your old house until the monsoon's over.'

'No, I don't want to go to Darwin. I want the child to be born here at Waybell.' She tapped his cheek. 'I want you to carry our little one outside as soon as he's born and show him this marvellous property. Let him breathe the air and feel the space about him.' She lifted her face to the sky.

'Just as well the child will be born in the dry season,' said Ross solemnly. 'I wouldn't like him to spend his first few months staring out at the rain. Wait. You said "him" – a son?'

'Yes. I just feel as if I'm carrying a boy.'

'How do you know?'

'Women's intuition.'

Ross didn't query his wife. It was far beyond his capabilities to know the workings of a woman's mind.

'Once Hugh hears the news you may well find him a bit more amenable, Ross. Competition can do that to a person.'

'How's that?'

'Our child will be your legitimate heir, male or female.' Darcey gave Ross a cheerful wink. 'I'm going to tell Annie about the baby.'

Darcey touched his head on passing, an old dog keeping tight on her heels as she headed towards the camp. Ross observed the gentle sway of her movements, the mother of his unborn child. The children from the camp raced towards her, circling Darcey and running around her excitedly. Ross was grateful for her support of his relationship with Hugh, particularly as his wife had lived in Maria's shadow for years. If he could be granted anything at that very moment, Ross hoped that, with a child of her own, Darcey would finally enjoy the complete fulfilment he so wanted for her.

He speared the pocketknife into the ground, looking towards the heavens, trying to contain his smile. 'There you go, Father. Two heirs,' he announced loudly. 'Two male heirs,' he repeated slowly, contemplating what the birth of another child meant. Hugh wouldn't be happy about the news and Ross worried for the boy's sake. He didn't want his firstborn to experience any sense of inferiority, but how to ensure that would be difficult. Hugh carried an entitlement to inherit of which he was aware, however with this new child Hugh's share would decrease substantially. There was no other way.

❈ Chapter 61 ❈

1938

Hugh lifted the rifle and pointed the barrel at the wedge-tailed eagle gliding on the air current. A loud crack rang out. The bird hung in the sky for the slightest of seconds and began to fall. Ross closed his eyes in disbelief as the eagle plummeted to the ground, and then busied himself with remounting the old mare he'd taken to riding. They'd been out hunting for dingos and, having only shot three of the feral canines, Hugh had grown bored, resorting to shooting anything that moved. Wallabies, snakes and rats, geese and ducks all fell under his aim.

'We don't usually shoot the wedge-tails,' said Ross.

'Why not?' replied Hugh.

'They're beautiful birds, don't you think?'

'Not really. I've seen them pecking the innards out of kangaroos and other dead animals,' said Hugh. He holstered the rifle and swung up into the saddle.

'Well, that's how they live. It doesn't mean they deserve to die.' Reminding the boy that a person should only kill when necessary, and usually then only what they could eat, was futile. Hugh wasn't worried about droughts or floods or where a next meal might come from, nor was he particularly concerned about the wildlife. 'So how's that horse of yours going? Mick's been riding him while you were away,' said Ross.

Hugh flicked the gelding's mane. 'You can tell. He's too hard in the mouth. I've got to yank the reins to make him take any notice. I don't think he'll make much of a horse.'

The boy's opinion of the gelding reminded Ross of another young man, nearly eighteen years ago. A brash know-all who'd doubted the ability of a piece of horse-flesh bartered for tobacco.

'Maybe you should name him,' suggested Ross. '"Horse" isn't particularly original.'

'It'll do.' Hugh ran his knuckles lightly between the horse's ears. 'How's the roping coming along?' he asked.

'Fine,' said Hugh.

They rode through the woodlands towards the homestead. Hugh hadn't once mentioned Darcey since his arrival five days earlier. Having explained that his wife was in bed suffering from exhaustion, Ross waited for the right time to tell Hugh about the imminent birth of the child. He knew the news must be shared, and soon, but the occasion never seemed to arise and Ross began to grow angry at his procrastination. It was a task he dreaded. Hugh's last visit had been fleeting and awkward, so it was with a pleased wariness that he greeted his son's recent return.

This was Hugh's second visit to Waybell in six months following three years of being cajoled into undertaking an annual trip south to the property. Hugh's arrival, unrequested and unannounced, timed to coincide with the commencement of the mustering season, only served to make Ross more concerned about their relationship with the coming of another child. In the past, Ross contemplated if there was some greater power at work apportioning out difficulties that were weighed unfavourably against him. Now he was convinced of it. Hugh, having returned to help for the duration of the dry, was about to discover the existence of a soon-to-be legitimate heir.

'I won't be going on the muster,' Ross told him.

'I know. Mick said you can't do much anymore,' answered Hugh, supporting the rifle across his thighs.

Ross thought of the days he'd ridden across the plains. The wind glassing his eyes, foam from Nugget speckling his face. In another time he may have been offended by the comment. 'I still do a bit. It's my legs. I can ride for three hours or so but any more and I'm useless the next day.'

'You really buggered yourself, didn't you?' said Hugh.

'It was an accident.'

'Except that there was drink involved.'

'Yeah,' agreed Ross. 'There was a lot of that. So you decided against going to Nanking?'

'There'll be other wars,' replied Hugh casually. 'Besides, it didn't feel right leaving my mother. She's been abandoned too many times already.'

Ross wanted to tell Hugh that it was time to move on. That reliving the past only served to pull a man down until he was bogged in a drying waterhole like a failing beast. However he was not the one to give the boy a lecture on the subject.

The boy rammed the rifle in its holster, a stricken look on his face. 'You don't care, do you?'

Ross drew the mare to a halting stop. 'I wouldn't have made a point of making sure you knew about me if I didn't,' he answered carefully, at a loss as to where the outburst came from.

'But that was before this new baby,' countered Hugh.

Ross was furious. He vowed to have strong words with whoever had told the boy. He didn't reply immediately. Ross was used to conversations where Hugh would complain about something and he would give an ineffectual answer, but on this occasion he doubted any response would improve things.

'I'd intended to tell you, Hugh, but most of the time you're either too disinterested or angry. It doesn't make a person inclined towards conversation. Anyway, don't worry, you won't be cut out of my will.' Ross set off at a quicker pace.

'Don't you have anything else to say?' Hugh called out.

Ross pulled hard on the reins and rode back to face his son. 'You've been here for five days and not once have you asked after Darcey. Not once. If you'd cared just a little, I would have told you immediately about the baby. That the child was not planned and that Darcey has had a hard time of it lately. Instead I waited, hoping you might show some kindness towards her. That this visit might be easier with you making the decision to come here without my asking and offering to be involved.' Ross rode closer to Hugh. 'You know why I didn't say anything? Because we were getting on better and I hoped that things might be stronger between us. If not as father and son, at least as two men trying to make the best of things.'

'You're just making excuses,' accused Hugh.

'This isn't a damned boarding house. It's my home and my wife's. If you can't show respect to Darcey and the half-brother or -sister she's about to bring into the world, then you should return to your mother!' yelled Ross.

'I never really wanted to come back here, anyway!' Hugh yelled back.

'Then why the hell did you?'

'I needed a job.' His knuckles grew white as he clutched the reins.

'You can get work in Darwin or on someone else's property.'

'No. I don't want that,' said Hugh. The words caught in his throat as he looked intently at Ross.

'Why not? You don't like it here. You argue and whinge. Arrive for a week and then clear off again. What's the point of coming, Hugh, if you don't want to be here? You're wasting both our time.'

'Because you're my father! You're the person who wrote to me every month for years! Who taught me about life and how not to live it. I took to keeping a calendar so that I'd know roughly when a letter from you might arrive, and I'd run back from school to check the mail, sure of eventually hearing from you again. I'd reread them at night when everyone was asleep, and I still have them. Every one of them.'

Ross felt something inside him begin to break.

'I know more about you than the man who raised me. I know more about horses and buffalo and this whole damn territory because of you. I know where to find water in a dry time when there's none worth finding, how to rope a bull calf come branding season, and I dream of owning a coal-black horse that can race across the plains. I know how much a person can live through before they go bad from the inside out, and I understand that some families can hurt. You've done everything a person possibly can do and more, and all I've ever dreamt about is one day being like you.'

The boy's eyes were wet with tears. Ross swallowed. He slowly got down from his horse and shuffled to Hugh's side. He tried to speak but nothing came to him. He simply looked up at his son and then he rested his forehead on the boy's leg. He thought of what Hugh had said and what it meant to him, and eventually Hugh's hand settled on the back of his hair and they stayed that way. Hugh in the saddle and Ross leaning against him.

Overhead, the escarpment bore down hard and glittered in the noon light. The boy would grow to be a man unafraid to speak the truth of things. He would know right from wrong. And Ross had helped forge that, as the boy had made him realise that his own life was not without purpose. It was the strangest sensation, being a father who had been saved by his son.

❧ Chapter 62 ❧

Darcey lay on the bed, a number of pillows supporting her. The shutters were closed, the room darkened to combat the heat. Her eyes were ringed with tiredness. Annie had taken over her care, making her eat small meals of soup, and this appeared to restore her energy for a few weeks until her growing size and the increasing heat worsened her lethargy. Ross sat by her side, the springs making pinging noises under his weight, then he lifted his legs and lay down beside her, boots and all.

'Has something happened? You look concerned.'

He rested a hand on her exhausted body. 'How are you?'

'Tired and ready to have your baby. I look like a whale.'

'Never. I had a talk with Hugh.'

'Oh.'

'Actually, he was the one that spoke. I listened.'

'And it didn't go very well? I suppose he's angry about the baby.'

From somewhere in the house came the sound of whistling. It was Hugh, readying his gear for the muster.

'He admires me, Darcey. Me? We had a fight and I told him to go back to Darwin and it all came out. How he'd read my letters

382

and kept them. It was –' He broke off, conscious of the tremors rising from the very centre of his body.

'Oh, Ross. Of course he admires you. You're his father.'

Ross struggled to his feet and at the window he opened the shutters and lifted the sash. Hot, dry air pushed into the room, along with the slight scent of land burning in the east. 'I didn't expect him to say what he did, Darcey. After everything –'

'You don't believe you're deserving of his love?' she asked.

He turned to her. 'I don't think I deserve much at all. I still can't understand how I earnt you.'

'Come here, Ross.'

He walked to her side reluctantly. A well of emotion remained bottled within, as he feared making a fool of himself in front of the woman he loved.

'Don't you think you've punished yourself enough?'

'You don't understand.'

'What? That you've spent your life fighting the desires of others, until you ended up fighting yourself. Look at you, standing there in that unbreakable body, days away from being a father again, unable to see what I saw from the very beginning, that you're a strong man. The man who I grew to love, against the odds, but a man who still hasn't managed to absolve himself from the errors of the past. It's time to do that, Ross. It's time to forgive yourself. It's time to let go and move forward.' She patted the bed and he sat next to her once again.

'How does a person ever excuse himself for the bad choices he's made?'

She gripped his fingers. 'The first step is recognising the wrongness of those decisions.'

'And the second?' he asked.

'Is letting go of the past and learning how to love yourself again.'

He noticed how tired she seemed. 'I should leave you to rest.'

'Perhaps,' she agreed.

Darcey was asleep before he reached the bedroom door.

❧ Chapter 63 ❧

Shooed away by the female Elders, Ross toed the caked mud
of the billabong. It drew inwards to where newly hatched fish
hugged the shallow weed beds. It was the time of dragonflies and
hoarding mosquitoes. The dry season, when the slightly cooler
nights made for easier sleeping. He pictured Hugh and the other
stockmen, racing on the wing of a mob of cattle, dust and sweat
smearing their eyes, the tang of the bush sharp in their nostrils.
It wasn't for wanting to be away from his wife that he wished to
be among the thick of the gathering-in, but men were useless
when women's business was afoot. And he was no different.

He'd spent the past fortnight relegated to Hugh's room, the
one that once belonged to Maria, and had scratched out so many
children's names that he'd totally confused himself as to what
he liked or disliked. Eventually he reached a shortlist. If the
child was a girl he rather liked Bridget, in honour of his grandmother. If a boy, he was partial to Cameron, Angus or James. If
Connor had been present he'd have been quick to point out the
merits of each, and more than once Ross had considered making
contact with the little Scotsman, but of all the people he'd

managed to begin acquitting of blame, Connor was proving the hardest to forgive.

Darcey's suggestion to wait until the baby was born to see which name suited seemed too logical for such a miraculous occasion. However Ross stopped pestering her for an opinion and instead began giving consideration to the child's education. He was beginning to view the baby's birth as a new start for all of them and, accordingly, a Brisbane-based boarding school appealed, not only for its proximity to the Territory but also for the detachment it offered from the Grants of Adelaide. No child of his was ever going to suffer from his or his family's wrongdoings again. And so he stood at the billabong and mapped out the first ten years of the baby's life, deciding that regardless of gender it would certainly be intelligent and have its mother's saintly disposition.

The pondering and planning stopped him worrying about Darcey, who was nearing two days of labour. Discomfort had kept her awake for the last week, and although Annie had been attentive with meals it appeared to Ross that his wife had lost weight. Her swollen belly sat heavy on her slight frame. He'd spoken to Darcey earlier that morning where she'd confirmed what he knew, that the birthing business was long and tedious, fraught with false starts and chattering women, before Annie had shoved him out of the bedroom.

'Boss,' said Annie. She didn't stop, turning instead to walk back to the house and beckoning for him to follow.

'How is she? It's taking a long time for this child of mine to come, Annie.' Ross thought of the Magellan Clouds and his folk looking down from above. For once, they would be proud.

'You come now,' she called over a shoulder.

'Yes, all right. Slow down. I can't walk as quickly as you. How's Darcey? How's the baby?'

She halted for just a moment then, flicking at a fly, she resumed walking quickly towards the house. 'Baby must come.'

'Is it on the way?' he panted, moving as fast as he could in a shuffling manner.

'Missus very tired. She tell you she was tired, Boss. Too tired for baby.'

'That's ridiculous. She was tired, not sick. Why is it all taking so long?'

'Maybe baby not want to come. Maybe you not whisper hard enough or strong enough for baby to come in the first place,' Annie told him.

'Don't tell me that mumbo jumbo, Annie. Darcey's a white woman.'

'Different but same,' she muttered, running on ahead.

Once in the house Ross entered the study. The bedroom door was closed. He knocked on the door demanding to be informed about what was happening and was told to wait. Ross shuffled the length of the room anxiously. Five minutes passed. Then twenty. From inside the bedroom came the sound of women weeping. The door finally opened and the women filed out. He glanced at their faces and then into the room. Darcey was laying in the bed, a sheet drawn to her chin as other women tidied up around her. A bloody sheet was carried from the room and then another bundle, held close to an older woman's chest. He heard a soft sound, like a mewling kitten and took a step after the woman. Annie stopped him.

'You have boys, Boss,' said Annie.

'Boys?' asked Ross.

'Missus have two.'

'Twins?' he clarified. He found himself thinking of his own birth, so many years previously and he grew fearful.

Ross caught up with the woman, and took the swaddled infants into his arms. He unwrapped the cloth. Inside, two tiny bodies lay huddled together, pink and warm. He lay them on the desk and stared at the perfectly formed limbs, counting fingers and toes, the knot in his stomach loosening.

'There's nothing wrong with them,' he said in wonder. 'Nothing at all.'

He tried to fathom how they could be so perfect, when the horrors of his own birth had left such an indelible mark on his early life. But before him were two small people, exquisitely made. Crafted from pain and longing and regret. Ross stroked the lick of a curl on a forehead, his own skin dark as stirrup leather against the healthy colour of his sons. 'James and Cameron,' he said quietly.

'Boss, you see the Missus now,' said Annie. Gently, she pushed Ross aside and, rewrapping the infants, held them close.

Ross couldn't take his eyes off them. 'Boss . . .' Annie persisted.

'Yes.' He went to Darcey's side as the room slowly emptied, dragging a chair next to the bed. 'Darcey? Darcey, are you awake?' he said excitedly.

'The baby, Ross? The baby?' queried Darcey through sleepy eyes. She was very white, as if the colour had been leached from her skin.

'We have two, Darcey. We have twins.'

Her eyes flickered about the room, coming to rest on the empty cot. 'Where are they?'

'Annie's with them. She'll bring them in soon.' He kissed her on the cheek and took her hand. 'How are you feeling?'

Before she could reply, Annie arrived with a moistened cloth. She held the material against Darcey's lips, gently wringing the cotton so she could drink. 'You want me to send a message for Hugh, Boss?'

'No, not yet,' replied Ross.

Annie left and returned with the babies. She placed a child in the crook of each of his wife's arms and Darcey touched their downy skulls with her lips and then looked at Ross. A single tear slid down her cheek.

'You're tired, Darcey. You should rest.' Ross nodded to Annie and the woman took the children again and left the room. 'I'll be back in a minute,' Ross told her.

He found Annie in the adjoining study staring at the waterlily painting.

'We wash your boys, Boss.'

'Thank you. Annie, the Missus is very pale. Can you make some chicken soup? Or beef tea? Yes, beef tea might be better and fish for dinner.'

'Food not help, Boss. Missus lose too much blood.'

'Of course it helps,' said Ross.

'Not this time, Boss. I'm sorry, Boss,' replied Annie.

'What are you saying?'

'That Missus not stay with us.'

He dropped his hands and stared at her. 'What do you mean, she's not staying with us? That's ridiculous. She's just given birth to two healthy sons. She's tired, that's all.'

'Boss, haven't I always told you things straight?'

The room grew so quiet that Ross was sure he could hear the dragonflies hovering at the edge of the billabong.

'How long?' he whispered finally. 'How much time do I have? Time to fetch a doctor from Pine Creek?'

'Boss, even if you weren't all mangled up like you are, no riding would make any difference. Missus probably be gone by sundown.'

The blood in him seemed to stop running. Ross hit the wall with a fist and then leant on the timber, feeling nothing except the richness of what he'd once had slipping away. He looked to the bedroom door and back to Annie. He wasn't quite sure what was to be done. People needed to be informed. But there was no one. No real family. Maybe Connor. Definitely Hugh. Perhaps no one. Not yet. He'd be incapable of forming a sentence, of holding a pen. Did he tell Darcey or wait? Or did she already know? A hopelessness had taken hold. He looked to Annie for answers.

'Boss, better you be with the Missus,' she told him.

He nodded and in a daze he returned to Darcey's side, cupping her hand in his, observing the little tremors that shook her every few minutes.

'I was an idiot all those years ago,' Ross told her.

She smiled weakly. 'I wish I'd met you first, Ross, before Alastair. Before the war. For I would have chosen you over your brother. You have more honour than Alastair ever did, and you asked nothing of anyone except to be allowed to live your life on your own terms, right or wrong. And that's how a life should be lived, with persistence and passion and courage. I'll always love you for that and for giving me our precious children.'

'Darcey –'

'You've carved a fine life here, Ross, and you have our sons. Be good to them.'

'But how will I manage without you?'

'You know what to do. Guide them, love them, be an example.'

She had no idea of the enormity of the task that she asked of him, and for the first in his life he felt truly afraid. How would he go on without Darcey? And what chance did he have to raise their children alone, when his own childhood had been without real fathering? Ross kissed her and held her close as she drifted deeper into sleep, the sun's rays patterning the room as it slipped lower in the sky. He looked again and again at the bassinet, and thought of the children she'd given him, and each time he held Darcey a little tighter until he was sitting on the bed, holding her in his arms.

He felt her stir and he squeezed her fingers and kissed her on the lips one final time and told her that he was with her, forever. The smile she gave was magnificent and Ross reached out to touch the softness at the base of her throat as her breathing stilled. He stayed with Darcey until her skin grew cool and the room lost all light and the day came again.

Then he found a shovel and dug a hole a short distance from the house. Ross wrapped Darcey in a sheet and carried her outside, his legs straining under her weight, pain searing through him. She was white, shrouded in white, and Ross thought of their marriage and the unconsummated wedding night and how all the long years later he was carrying his wife across a far different threshold, one he was not quite ready to span, while the attendants of her later life walked behind, wailing.

He collapsed on the ground and lay Darcey in the narrow grave. There were words that needed to be said. A long, grateful, pitying prayer that spoke of suffering and love and begged for help but Ross was so far removed from church and religion that although he searched, nothing appropriate came to mind. Had he been at

Oenpelli he would have clawed his way up the missionary's hill and chopped down the wooden cross and its false ideals of hope. Instead, he drew on his fragmented memory, sorting through partial passages and quotes until one rose whole.

'You will never be lovelier than you are now. We will never be here again.'

In the end, it seemed that some good had come of reading Homer.

The old men, women and children who crowded in on her resting place left silently soon after. Annie was the last to go, a sleeping baby in each arm. Ross sat at the foot of Darcey's grave for the rest of that day and long into the night, his body cramping as the hours dragged. The nightbird's songs became her requiem and as the moon rose he touched the freshly turned earth. He'd never be able to express his gratitude for what she'd said, about his life and his brother. He thought that perhaps honour came in different forms, and how extraordinary it was that in the eyes of Darcey he'd finally found his.

≪ Chapter 64 ≫

Although in the end, messages were sent to Hugh and Connor telling them of Darcey's death, neither boy nor man returned to the homestead or relayed their sympathies. Ross gave up waiting in the silent house and left a fortnight later, riding northeast. He rode for two hours at a time, stopping each night, barely able to move. Each morning, the effort of realigning and urging his body onwards became more difficult. Ross ate up the pain and lived on it, existing on tea and bread and little else. He knew that if he kept on going, eventually he'd become exhausted and the return trip would undo him. Ross depended on that.

He rode to where schools of eel-tailed catfish swam lazily in pools sheltered by stone, and as light fell softly, he led the old mare around the edge of a waterhole carved out in the shade of burgundy cliffs. Ferns and other wet-rooted plants grew from recesses where dried moss clung and Ross looked about at the still water, at the paintings of spread-out hands on the cliff wall and another that resembled a crocodile.

Then he sat back on his haunches and cried for the first time since childhood. He thought of the wasted years and the love he'd always borne Alastair in spite of everything, and the fortunate life that remained, and decided that maybe it was time to forgive his family without exception and put aside regret. When he was ready, he rode back towards the homestead and his children, aware of the responsibility they presented and knowing that this time he couldn't run away.

He saw Hugh first. His boy was leading a horse towards the stables when he arrived home and for the first time since Darcey's passing Ross smiled at the sight of his elder son. The boy was a fine rider, a loner at times, but already Ross could see the man he would become. Strong and smart, willing to try anything, but stubborn enough to ensure that whatever he attempted would be accomplished his way. He'd not seen the similarities linking them as clearly as he did at that moment, and the recognition made Ross value the importance of being patient, of guiding and caring for the next generation. Something his own father had not managed. He refused to be like that. The distant patriarch. And Ross made up his mind to try and be the father figure he'd needed in his own life and had never experienced.

As if knowing he was being observed, Hugh turned towards his father and, dropping the reins, ran to him, slowing as he reached his side as if worried about the level of enthusiasm he should display at Ross's return.

'Where have you been?' Hugh chastised, waiting as Ross dismounted. Then, steadying his father's descent with a braced arm, he said with concern, 'I came as soon as we got your message.'

'I needed to get away for a while.' Ross leant on the horse for support before clasping his son's shoulder in greeting.

Hugh gave a tentative smile and untied Ross's swag, swinging it over a shoulder. 'We were miles away. I'm sorry about Darcey.'

'Thanks for coming home,' said Ross.

'I would have been here sooner had I known. You look pretty crook, Dad.'

It was the first time Hugh had ever addressed him that way. As his father. Ross took in the length and breadth of the young man before him, searching for a word that could express his happiness. 'I'll be right. A cup of tea will help.'

'And a feed, by the looks of you.' Hugh offered an arm and Ross leant on his son as they walked slowly towards the house. 'I've got a couple of new brothers.'

Ross halted. He was too exhausted to argue. 'I hope you're okay with that, Hugh.'

The boy didn't answer directly. 'I think it's good, Dad. They'll come in handy when I'm running the property. You can never have too many workers.' He grinned. 'While you were away Annie organised for Little Bill's wife, Jo, to care for the twins. It seems to me you're going to have your hands full, Dad, so I thought I'd stay on through the wet and maybe next year. If that's all right?' he asked.

Ross couldn't answer. His throat swelled up. 'That'll be just fine, but what about your mother?'

'I'm grown up now, Dad. I don't need to get permission.'

'No,' said Ross. 'I suppose you don't.'

✠ Chapter 65 ✠

1939

The pedal radio tapped out the letters on the Morse keyboard. Hugh leant over the contraption. 'You know, Dad, you can get a voice transceiver these days.' He read the message aloud. 'Prime Minister Menzies has announced the beginning of Australia's involvement in the Second World War.' His concentration reverted to the machine, as if willing more news to be relayed.

'War,' Ross repeated. He knew it would happen. That they'd be drawn once again into a bloody conflict. How was it possible that such stupidity existed in the world?

Across the room his son waited for the machine to reveal more details. Alfred Traeger's radio device had connected the vast stations of the outback, however with the technology came knowledge. Ross preferred the old days, when folk lived in isolation and other people's difficulties carried more chance of remaining their own. It'll save a life, Hugh had claimed, upon returning from Pine Creek with the invention. Ross doubted it. The radio wouldn't have helped Darcey or Sowden or Annie, who'd passed earlier that year in her sleep. The radio, Ross judged, was a bad investment.

Particularly now. He knew the boy would enlist. He stirred two spoons of sugar into tepid water and drank.

'He had to do it, Dad. Germany's invaded Poland,' said Hugh.

'And so it starts all over again,' replied Ross.

'We won last time.'

'Sure we did, Hugh. But we also lost much.'

Ross balanced the ledger on a knee, holding the magnifying glass so that the numbers doubled in size. He could just make out the figures. His vision had long since deteriorated. Mrs Guild's husband's spectacles and another three pairs besides were long discarded. Hugh had walked the sale bullocks back to the main yards yesterday and was stopping in for only two nights before heading north and rejoining the mustering team, who were now concentrating on hunting and domesticating buffalo in the top portion of the station. Theirs was a strong partnership. The type of working relationship Ross once envisaged he and Alastair would share. Only twenty years of age, Hugh had earnt the regard of the men on the property and was mature enough to consider other people's opinions, even if they were at odds with his own. For his part, Ross had learnt to give his son praise when it was due and to quietly reprimand when required, although it had taken some time for him to grasp the fundamentals underlining their relationship, mutual love and respect. As he became more accustomed to parenting he was hopeful that when the twins were older, the task wouldn't be quite so challenging.

'We won't make the money we have out of hides next season,' said Ross. 'Turkey's been the main buyer over the last couple of years, but if this war is anything like the last one that will change.'

'You know I have to sign up,' interrupted Hugh. 'Don't you agree with the Prime Minister that if Britain's defeated, then Australia could be as well? We have to help them because we might need their support one day.'

'Beef will rise in price. It's a pity we don't still own Gleneagle. Wool and meat, that's what armies march in and on.' Ross averted his son's gaze. The boy hadn't left since Darcey's passing and Ross didn't want anything to change.

'Dad?' Hugh screwed up a page from an old newspaper and tossed it at Ross to get his attention. 'The government will call for volunteers. The papers have been talking about what might happen for weeks.'

Ross shut the ledger. 'This is war, not some jaunt overseas. What happens if you don't come back?'

'I'll come back, Dad.' Hugh sat on the chair opposite his father.

If only it were that simple. That a young man could do his duty and return justifiably proud of the contribution made to a family eager to embrace him. 'It took a lot of winning, the last war. Visit the Anzac Memorial when you're next in Darwin.'

'I have,' replied the boy.

'Hugh, plenty can happen in a time of war. Let someone else go in your place. We'll wait and see what happens. If things get worse then consider enlisting, but don't rush in. You're my eldest son. If you don't come back, what happens then? To Waybell and everything else we own. It's taken generations to amass it all.'

'To not go would be wrong,' argued Hugh. 'It should be my decision.'

With the twins still so young, Hugh was all he had. A single person who he felt he could truly rely on, who was not just his son, but also a friend. A word he could never have used in association with his own father. Somehow, every wrong turn in his life had merged to form this young man and bring him to the place he now occupied by Ross's side. How was it then that, for a second time in his life, a dictator's decision on the far side of the world in an unknown country had the potential to wreck their lives? Ross felt Hugh slipping away, receding like a mirage until the day of departure came and they locked hands one last time.

'Dad?' questioned Hugh.

He marvelled at Morgan Grant's fateful determination to send Alastair to war, while keeping him at home. How could a father do that? Make a decision that could result in the loss of a son, while allowing the other to live with the consequences of not serving, as if his two boys were toy ships at sea and he was the errant wind that filled their fragile sails.

Ross wasn't like his father. He wasn't going to assume he knew better and make decisions on his grown son's behalf. However by not overruling Hugh, every wound he carried would be torn open. And if the boy didn't return, Ross understood he would truly be lost.

Hugh waited for an answer, his face a mixture of excitement and concern. And Ross saw that it was not the worry of having to obey a father that made the boy uneasy but that of a son determined to do what he wanted. Ross saw the difference, recognising the strength of character and the sharp aspect of defiance. He'd lived with the consequences of having the terms of his life dictated and he knew the ache of ostracism. He'd felt like an outcast most of his life. Men could be cruel. A father needn't be.

'When do you want to leave?' said Ross, the saliva in his mouth drying up.

'Soon,' answered Hugh with relief. 'I'll start off with the cattle and then go on from there.'

'You can go via Adelaide,' suggested Ross. 'Make yourself known to the solicitor and check on the old family home.'

'Sure,' answered Hugh. 'You know, I reckon Edward will volunteer as well. He's under forty years of age. The cut-off point for volunteers.' Hugh inclined his head to one side. In the light he resembled his mother. 'I thought you'd like to know.'

'What Edward Carment does is of no interest to me, Hugh,' said Ross.

'I know that. I know you hate him.'

'I don't like or dislike him. I don't know the man. If anything, I should probably thank him for raising you,' conceded Ross.

'We never did get on very well, especially after he found out about you. Not that it matters now.' His face brightened. 'I thought that if Edward did enlist I might tell Mum that if anything happened, you know while he and I were away, you'd help her. Can I tell her that?'

'Of course. You tell your mother to contact me if she needs anything.'

'Thanks. It's just in case.'

'Sure,' said Ross. He doubted Maria would make contact even if the need arose. They were strangers, connected only through their son. The slender memories of what might have been long bested by Darcey.

'I might go and see Eustace and Parker.' Hugh nodded in the direction of the camp, getting up to leave. 'They've got a concoction they've been brewing.'

'Have one for me,' said Ross. War. He hated wars. If he was abroad right now, he'd walk straight up to Hitler and shoot the man in the head. 'Hugh, can I ask one thing?'

'What, Dad?'

'Come back to me.'

Hugh lingered in the doorway, framed by dwindling light. For Ross, it was a moment he knew he would recall forever.

'I will. I'm not your brother, Dad.'

Ross nodded. There were things he wanted to say but the words wouldn't form. He closed the ledger, resting the magnifying glass on top. 'I'm proud of you, Hugh.'

His boy smiled. Then he was gone.

❦ Epilogue ❧

In the middle of the night, when he often woke, Ross thought of God and the Being's expectations and the missionary's cross on that shabby hill. And, spreading out from that lonely place, he imagined people praying as if by pressing palms and dirtying knees answers might be given. He wasn't one of those folk who scrabbled for reasons. He knew the truth. That it was up to men to help themselves. Ross reckoned that although he'd made a mess of things, maybe that was the way his life was supposed to be, for in the end he'd come out of it all right.

Wrestling his body out of the chair, he leant on the cane for support. The aches and pains rarely varied, but today a general feeling of unwellness struck him to the point of exhaustion where even breath became a difficulty. It was as if the mechanism of living was coming undone. Ross had never been afraid of death but he wished for a good day tomorrow so that he might write Hugh one more letter and tell him again that he was proud.

In the kitchen he levered open one of the storage tins with a screwdriver, rummaging around for the bottle of brandy the cook used for cakes on special occasions. He'd not drunk since his accident, and Ross wasn't sure why, after so much time and so many years of pitying desperation, he was finally close to succumbing, except that with Darcey's passing and Hugh's leaving, the prospect of the coming years seemed limited. And as a father he wanted to toast his son to battle. The 6th Division had been formed during October and November in 1939 and had embarked for the Middle East earlier this year to complete their training. Hugh was already abroad serving his country as his uncle once had, as Ross would have liked to. Had the boy waited a little longer to enlist he might not have been accepted, for in early 1940 each of the armed services had introduced regulations that banned the enlistment of people not 'substantially of European origin'. It was a sore point for Ross that, if not for Hugh's hastiness and determination, he'd still be home, and safe.

Ross held the bottle to the light and looked past the dark fluid to the distant cliff. It hung as always, starkly impenetrable, dwarfing the homestead and the happenings around it. He dropped his gaze to the grassy plain and caught sight of the twins playing under a tree with Jo. He chuckled at their antics and then, uncorking the flask, he sniffed at the alcohol. The scent of it was pure and sweet, tart and enticing. He raised the brandy a little higher in salute to his son and in respect of that other war long ago, when life was still vague in terms of destination and he'd laid on the lawn in Adelaide, smoking and drinking whisky with his brother, outwardly smiling and laughing, inwardly desperate to be going too. To have the chance to prove that he too was a man.

'Ross?'

Ross set the untouched bottle down and pivoted on the cane. The man before him was grey-haired and tall. Dark-eyed and tanned. And he was big. Not fat but solid. Well fed. The sleeves of his white shirt were rolled to his elbows and a waistcoat fitted neatly across a trim stomach. Ross squinted at the visitor, trying to place him, cursing at his fading eyesight.

'It's me. Alastair.'

Ross took a stumbling step forward.

'How are you?' The stranger's faced was lightly creased with worry.

Ross took another step.

'Don't you remember, Ross? It's me, your brother.'

He walked closer and Ross saw with a start that it *was* his brother. Older and fitter and still handsome. The cane wobbled under his grasp. The wonder of seeing Alastair struck him speechless. How was it, after all this time, he was alive and standing before him barely altered by the years? Ross wanted to hug him and shout. To reach out and touch this person from another age, part childhood fable, part ghost; a dream. When he blinked Alastair still stood in front of him in the kitchen doorway, smiling broadly as if everything was unchanged.

'How are you, Ross?' Alastair asked again.

Ross took a step closer and, lifting his fist, punched Alastair in the face.

'Fine. How are you?'

❖

'You've broken my nose,' complained Alastair, stemming the blood with a tea towel. He walked outside and Ross trailed him, noticing the slight limp. 'I travel all this way and this is the welcome I get?' A flock of geese flew overhead, honking loudly.

'Where the hell have you been? What happened?' Ross thrust the cane in Alastair's direction.

'Connor said you'd be riled but I didn't expect this.' Alastair reached for a pocket-flask, took a sip and then offered the flagon to Ross. He refused. 'Have some. It'll help settle your nerves. Anyone would think you were the one who went to war. Cripes. Connor said you were crook, but really, Ross, you look like you've been run over by a Cobb & Co. coach, not by one mangy gelding in the middle of nowhere.'

Ross reached out with the cane and whacked Alastair in the side of the knee.

'Steady on, Ross,' said Alastair.

'You've seen Connor?' he asked.

'Yes. When I reached Adelaide I contacted the family solicitors, who told me everything, and then I tracked down Connor on reaching Darwin. It was him that brought me here. I'm sorry, Ross. For all of it.'

'Are you? You know Darcey's dead?' said Ross.

'Yes.'

'The rest of the family are as well.'

'I know.'

'What the hell happened? We were told you were wounded and that you'd deserted.'

Alastair examined the tea towel before balling up the material and dropping it on the ground. 'I'd had enough. They wanted to cut my leg off, so I pulled my boot on and left.'

'What do you mean *you left*?' asked Ross.

'I'd been caught up in a bombardment. We went over the top one stinking night and Fritz gave us an absolute pounding. I ended up buried during the shelling. I figured I was dead, but a bloke saw an arm or leg sticking out and decided to pull on it to see if anything was left on the end of it. I don't remember much else. Just the noise of the attack and this solid weight taking the last of my breath. I woke up in a field hospital with this pommy doctor telling me that if the wound didn't heal properly I might well get an infection, and I looked across the ward and there was this soldier getting his leg sawn off.' Alastair lit a cigarette and inhaled. 'They had a bucket in a corner that they were dropping the amputated limbs into and it was then that I decided I wasn't going back to the front. So I waited until I was stronger and I got out of there. I stole a French ambulance-driver's uniform from a soldier who didn't need it anymore, and with the help of my schoolboy French pretended to have amnesia. Eventually I was taken to another field hospital. I moved hospitals a few times, until one day I was fit enough to leave. I left during the night and kept on walking away from the front. France was in a mess. People continually queried who I was but usually they were kind.

They'd feed me and put me up for a few nights. Eventually I met up with some Catalans in the south of the country and made it into Spain with their help.'

'And what about us?' asked Ross. 'Your family? Why didn't you come home?'

Alastair pinched the bridge of his nose. 'I think you broke it.'

'Why didn't you return or at least let us know that you were alive?'

'Return to Australia to be court-martialled? To have Father tell me how disappointed he was? How I'd let down the whole family? I couldn't do it. I didn't want to do it,' he stated bluntly.

'But Darcey?' argued Ross.

'Yes. Darcey. Out of all the people who were hurt, it was her I thought of the most.'

It was as if Ross had been physically struck. He found himself thinking of mighty Achilles dragging the slaughtered Hector by the neck, in one final insult. Ross stared at his brother, recalling the years that he'd mourned him. Over half his lifetime. It was all for nothing. Alastair had never really cared about him.

'You're a coward,' said Ross, his voice shaky. 'A snivelling coward.'

Alastair shrugged. 'You might see it that way,' he said. 'But I'm alive. Which is more than can be said for the thousands of young men who died in the mud of France. You didn't go, so you'll never understand what it was like over there. The days of monotony and then the sheer carnage. Men charging into machine-gunfire and barbed wire at the blow of a whistle. Hundreds of men dead in the time it takes to drink a beer. That's not war. It's murder.'

'You have no honour!' yelled Ross. It was impossible to bring together this man standing before him and the brother he remembered.

'There are many kinds of courage, Ross. Maybe I had more of some and less of others. What I didn't have is what it takes to be a slaughterer of men. Some of the boys enjoyed it, or appeared to. Your mate Drummond behaved as if he were at a duck shoot. I refused to. They're the same as us, those boys we fought, and yet someone in power states we're enemies and we blow each other up.

There's a different law that comes into being when you're given a rifle and told it's all right to kill another man, and it's wrong. Some take to it. I didn't choose to.'

'I never would have done what you did. Abandon your regiment. Disgrace the family,' replied Ross.

'We'll never know, will we?' countered Alastair.

His older brother looked so well, completely unbroken by events. 'Why did you come back after all this time?' asked Ross finally.

Alastair took a last puff of the cigarette, casually flicking it aside. 'This new war, of course. We knew Hitler was causing chaos, most likely long before you people learnt the extent of it, and I wasn't going to wait around to be seconded by the Allies to assist in some manner and be caught up in one of their bunfights. I figured after all this time I'd be forgiven for my misdeeds. At least by the family.'

'And you never gave thought to any of us?' asked Ross.

'Yes, but you were here, Ross, and you always were more interested in Father's rural properties than I was. Not that, as it turns out, you could be relied upon to pick up the pieces in my absence. From what the solicitor told me in Adelaide, you don't really have the right to comment on my life. You disappeared just like me and you also abandoned Darcey.'

'You and I are nothing alike, Alastair. Besides, Darcey and I had reconciled.'

'So I hear,' replied Alastair coolly. 'Remember when we talked about coming up here to Waybell? You were so keen. Well, here we are. I must say, it's not much, is it? Hardly the great adventure that you dreamt of, and yet you stayed.' Alastair glanced at the cliff. He gave only the slightest indication of unease but Ross could tell his brother was uncomfortable in this environment. 'I should have written, I suppose. At least to you. The longer I stayed away, the more difficult it became to make contact. Time gets away. You know how it is.'

'No, I don't.'

'It was a shame having to leave Cairo. I managed to wrangle a position as an assistant to a British archaeologist and we'd just returned from eight months in what was southern Mesopotamia. George was investigating the Babylonians, who developed a new approach to astronomy, which the Greeks continued with. The Tigris River, Ross, you should have seen it.'

Even if he'd had the strength, he was beyond the task of punishing Alastair for his selfishness. It was impossible to hurt the man he'd idolised from childhood, but the profound disappointment he felt as his brother talked on about his adventures had the same rank taste of blood and despair that came with being on the losing side of a severe clobbering. He realised that grieving for Alastair these many years in the hope of keeping his brother close had done them both an injustice. His brother wasn't worthy of his devotion.

'Where are you going, Ross?' asked Alastair.

'For a walk. Alone.'

Ross could see an older, slightly stooped man lingering at the front gate. He recognised who it was immediately, and shuffled down the stairs past Darcey's flowering bougainvillea to where the visitor waited.

'Connor,' he said. The Grants' former righthand man was grey-haired.

'Hello, Ross,' the Scotsman answered. 'Alastair showed up at the docks looking for you. Everything all right?'

'Not really,' admitted Ross. 'It's been a while since I've seen you. Too long.'

'Aye it has. I was sorry to hear about Darcey.'

Ross was shakily leaning on the cane and he rested on the fence, feeling worn out.

'I should have written, Ross, but too much seemed to have passed between us, and I guess I was angry that you never asked me to join you here on Waybell when you returned. Are you listening?'

'It's the shock of it, Connor. The shock of seeing him again.'

'Aye, it's a long time since any of us have seen your brother. Has Alastair explained himself beyond running away and digging in the sand?'

'Yes and no. Is he aware of everything that happened?' asked Ross.

Connor was not so adept as he had been in the past at concealing his thoughts. Ross saw that he struggled with how best to answer. 'Not all of it. It's your life he's querying, not mine. It might have taken me some time, but I've learnt that a person's business is their own. Best you share what you want. I only told him about the accident and that the years had been tough for you.'

'Tell him everything, Connor. I'll not blame him for my mistakes in his absence, but I can't forgive him either. Tell Alastair all of it and then escort him off Waybell. I can't speak to him anymore.'

'Aye. If that's what you want, Ross. I'll do it. He'll be looking for money, no doubt.'

'Then he can fight us in court.'

'He doesn't show much remorse, does he? Maybe he's not quite right in the head. He could be suffering from shellshock?' suggested Connor.

'Unfortunately, I think he was always that way and I never really knew him,' admitted Ross.

'Then none of us did,' said Connor.

Ross gazed at the clusters of waterlilies on the billabong. Darcey's painting had never quite captured the essence of the scene and Ross now knew what was missing in the work. She'd made it too beautiful. Beneath the surface, creatures struggled to survive. The battle was different for everyone and everything but he was used to carrying his scars for the world to see. Concealing the fight to exist didn't make sense.

Ross wished that one of Alastair's books had survived. That they weren't all lost or destroyed. There was one on the plains where the buffalo ran and others unwittingly deposited like breadcrumbs across the breadth of his travels. If there had been a single remaining work left, he would have pitched it into the billabong to be eaten in the shallows. Darcey would like that.

The pain down Ross's arm was growing worse and he clutched at his chest as he fell to the ground. He felt Connor's arm about him, strong and tight.

'Ross, are you all right?'

Ross turned to him. 'I'm sorry for all of it.'

'Aye, right. The day you'll be sorry for everything you've done and said will be a poor day for the rest of us, for what example will we have to follow if Ross Grant turns out to be the same as the rest of us mere mortals? Now, let's get you indoors and out of the sun. You're not looking too well.'

'No, Connor. I want to be out here. You know how I love the bush.'

'Aye, no one could deny that. You've seen more of this country than most.' Connor propped Ross against the fence and sat next to him.

Ross stared out at the billabong and the camp straddling the far bank. 'I'm not at my best.' He tried to smile and winced instead, the absurdity of his comment not lost on either of them.

'You have two little bairns, I hear?'

'Twins, and Hugh's gone to war.' He clutched Connor's arm. 'We've had our differences, but can I ask you to stay on and take care of things until Hugh returns?'

'Aye, you can ask me, Ross, and I'll agree to it, for I figure I owe you and I'm far from being guilty of living a perfect life. But you're still capable of running Waybell and kicking that brother of yours off this land.'

The pain hit deeper. Ross shuddered and called out and Connor's arm was about him, asking again what was the matter. The Scotsman drew him to his chest. 'Ross, what are you doing, lad? Come back to me, boy.'

But Ross already knew he was moving in a different direction. He'd once been cheated of the life he'd craved and had deserted everyone. Now at the end, he thought of what he'd been through and done to himself, and the blessings that had been delivered so late in his life, and Ross knew that although it was his brother who had finally broken him, none of it mattered. For he'd loved and been loved, and now he was free.

'Stand fast, stand sure,' he whispered to his old friend.

Connor clasped his hand and held him as the world slipped away.

❧ Author's Note ❧

S*tone Country* is a work of fiction layered in historical fact, although at times I have applied my prerogative as author to alter some details to suit the narrative framework. The dialogue used is intended to reflect the attitude of the time, and may be confronting to some readers. The work is set when the White Australia policy effectively barred people of non-European descent from immigrating to Australia, specifically Chinese labourers, and at a time when much of the Northern Territory was still considered a frontier.

The novel's title refers to one of the main landforms in Kakadu National Park, the Arnhem Land plateau and escarpment complex, known as the stone country. I am indebted to Hamish Clark of Sugarbag Safaris for guiding me into this extraordinary area and for the early maps from the period he provided. It was quite something to stand atop rugged cliffs and to be able to match a 1920s map with the route taken by buffalo hunters of years past. I could clearly envisage Ross Grant riding towards the East Alligator River with young Don Hart.

Stone Country commences its story in South Australia, a natural beginning considering the history that links that state with the

Top End, which includes Adelaide as the starting point for arguably Australia's greatest inland explorer, the Scotsman John McDouall Stuart, Ross Grant's childhood hero. Undertaking research in this part of Australia has the advantage of side-trips to the Barossa Valley. Something I can highly recommend.

In 1863, that part of New South Wales to the north of South Australia was annexed to South Australia, by letters patent, as the 'Northern Territory of South Australia'. Land sales commenced on 1 March 1864 and speculators in Adelaide and London acquired most of it, sight unseen. The legislation did not consider the issue of land settlement or development, and for many decades thousands of acres were faced with absentee landlords, much like Morgan Grant's speculative ownership of Waybell Station. Properties faced distinctive problems: the treatment of Aboriginal workers and the general difficulties that came with managing large areas of land and the challenge of isolation, which made settlement problematic and affected the economic viability of businesses. In 1911 the Northern Territory was handed to the federal government and became a separate territory.

This work would not have been possible without the assistance of the Northern Territory Library located in Darwin. I spent a number of days searching through archives, poring over pastoral lease maps and was fortunate to have the expertise of former ranger Michael Barritt (Manager, Visitor Experience – Northern Territory Library), who also kindly took on the role of tour guide during my visit.

I must also thank those residents of Darwin, who on hearing the reason for my visit, kindly shared stories from their own family histories. The importance of oral history can never be underestimated. Maria's tale, that of a young woman sold into marriage, was based on a story told to me during my stay in Darwin. Around the turn of the century, the beautiful daughter of a Chinese shopkeeper (said to have either been located in Pine Creek or Katherine) was sold to the highest bidder. It is said that the couple enjoyed a long and happy marriage. Maria perhaps was not so fortunate.

Thank you to Beverley Cousins and Genevieve Buzo for their guidance in smoothing out the creases in the manuscript, the publishing, marketing, publicity and sales gurus at Penguin Random House, and Tara Wynne, for her friendship and advice.

Lastly, a big thank you to both booksellers and readers, who have had to wait a little longer for *Stone Country*.

As always, my family have supported my many hours glued to the chair!

I am indebted to many works and recommend a selection below for further reading:

Australia's Northern Capital: A short history of Darwin by David Carment; *Great Central State: The foundation of the Northern Territory* by Jack Cross; *A Stubborn City: Darwin 1911–1978* by Kathy De La Rue; *Report of the Acting Administrator for the Year Ended 30th June 1925 and 1926 (Northern Territory)*, the Parliament of the Commonwealth of Australia; *Felix Ernest Holmes: Darwin 1890–1930* by Bev Phelts; 'Sold and stolen: domestic "slaves" and the rhetoric of "protection" in Darwin and Singapore during the 1920s and 1930s', Claire Lowrie, University of Wollongong; *Riding the Wildman Plains: The letters and diaries of Tom Cole 1923–1943; Frontier Territory* by Glenville Pike; *Aboriginal Paintings at Ubirr and Nourlangie* by David M. Welch; *Kakadu People* by Sir Baldwin Spencer; *Healers of Arnhem Land* by John Cawte; *Kakadu National Park, Australia* by Ian Morris; *A History of Oenpelli* by Keith Cole; *Kakadu Homesteads Survey: final report on a survey of historic homesteads in Kakadu National Park* by Troppo Architects, 1991; *The Darwin Chinese: A study of assimilation* by C.B. Inglis; *Chinese Contribution to Early Darwin* by Charles See-Kee; *History of Buffalo in Australia: The Australian water buffalo manual* by Department of Primary Industries and Resources; *The Australian Buffalo* by Northern Territory Department of Primary Production, Technical Bulletin No. 62; *Australia's Buffalo Dilemma* by Tom L. McKnight; *Buffaloes: Adventures in Arnhem Land* by Carl Warburton; *The City of Adelaide: a thematic history* by McDougall & Vines Conservation and heritage consultants.

⤙ Reading Group Questions ⤚

1. Who is your favourite character and why?

2. Discuss how *Stone Country* explores rivalry, mateship, betrayal, the burden of duty, and the far-reaching ramifications of a loveless childhood.

3. Ross Grant is an unlikely hero, one who embodies the duality of human nature. In what ways is his personality affected by the limitations imposed on his life by both his family and his own poor decision-making?

4. Darcey and Maria are two very different women – but both are constrained by their gender and determined to make the best of their lives. Compare and contrast their similarities and differences.

5. Connor is the voice of reason in Ross's life and yet his interference, although well-intended, has far-reaching implications for Ross. Discuss how far a person should go to protect a friend, even if it's from themselves.

6. We're introduced to the hierarchy of a large cattle station in the Northern Territory in the 1900s. Compare and contrast the gender, class and race divides.

7. The beauty and harshness of the Australian landscape is an integral part of *Stone Country*. How well has the author succeeded in capturing both time and place in the novel?

Here's a sneak preview of Nicole Alexander's new novel

The Cedar Tree

In the spring of 1949, Stella O'Riain flees her home – a sheep property on the barren edge of the Strzelecki Desert. She leaves behind the graves of her husband Joe and her baby daughter.

With no money and limited options, Stella accepts her brother-in-law Harry's offer to live at the O'Riain cane farm in the Richmond Valley. There, she hopes to find answers to the questions that plague her about her marriage. However Harry refuses to discuss Joe or the family's secrets, even forbidding her to speak to the owner of the neighbouring property.

Nearly a century earlier in County Tipperary, cousins Brandon and Sean O'Riain also fled their homes – as wanted criminals. By 1867, they are working as cedar-cutters in New South Wales's lush green Richmond Valley.

But while Brandon embraces the opportunities this new country offers, Sean refuses to let go of the past. And one cousin is about to make a dangerous choice that will have devastating consequences down the generations . . .

COMING IN MARCH 2020

≪ Prologue ≫

Kirooma Station, far west New South Wales, 1949

S tella came from over the mountains. From a place battered by
the lash of the wind and buffeted by the lifting soil. It was a
snake-etched, empty environment; one stretched and hollowed out
by fragments of cultures that had once fought for its ownership, the
winners unaware that nature, not stubborn perseverance, would
decide their fates. White men had died traversing the interior tracks
that the black people called home. But in a place where fortitude
came second to knowledge, it was stupidity that kept most searching ever onwards for a portal further into the Great South Land.

Stella's homestead had faced north-east. It had stared defiantly from the New South Wales–South Australian border across
hundreds of kilometres to where people who were closer settled
lived underground and mined for pretty opals, and where great
pastoralists had once walked wagonloads of firm-packed wool bales
to the Darling River to be transported to market. There was water.
But they saw little of it. Most of what flowed beyond their grasp
terminated in shallow lakes and flood-outs in the northernmost
stretches of the Strzelecki Desert. It certainly wasn't all gibber
plains and sand dunes; there was some good country among the
useless. Stubby bushes stooped by nature sustained life, and among

the best of the acreage there were familiar trees, but it wasn't the promised land. In high summer when the westerlies arrived, there were days when Stella only had to open her mouth to taste salt on her tongue.

Her home of old was a space unlike any other. One littered with the echo of endless sighs that seemed to stretch far beyond the land that engulfed her married life. She had left a baby in that fierce land's grasp. One who might have survived, had circumstance and distance not prevented it. Her husband, Joseph, also remained there, buried deep in the red heart of their property where the dingoes and crows couldn't molest him. He belonged to that place. It had been his land, after all. Not once, not even at the very end, had she been unkind enough to tell him that the only thing he really possessed was a futile dream. Endings, no matter how painful, are no time for reproach. At least not of the verbal kind. Instead, the homestead haunted her that last day as she trailed through rooms, dragging furniture across floorboards, throwing clothes into suitcases, sorting through a life lived in the shadowlands. She was sure that the salty dunes edged a little nearer the day she drove away.

≪ Chapter 1 ≫

Richmond Valley, 1949

Now Stella was in this new place of waterways, crops, swampy lands and flood plains. Her eyes glazed over at the greenery, the brimming rivers and the concentration required for the undulating, twisting roads. She drove past fluffy trees with bushy crowns and papery bark and a sign that advertised the selling of tea-tree oil. She pressed the brake pedal and pulled the station wagon to the edge of the road, slowing to a stop. In the shade of a proud tree, she dug in the soil, squeezing the earth until it gummed together in her palms. She looked back towards the hills and the spring haze that blurred the scene in a whitish mist and breathed in hot, moist air. It was seven years since she'd left to go inland. Stella supposed the eastern coast hadn't changed much in her absence. She was the one altered. Her mind and body would forever remain braced for the dry, hot winds of the past, for the bulging dust storms that sought out man and beast, and the emptiness of that old life.

On her left was an expanse of tall, tropical grass. The fields of sugar cane that charted her course to the fork in the road were in various stages of growth. Some of the paddocks were cut off close to the ground. Other stands of cane had sent up new, bright green stalks. Green. The shade of life. The colour of most grasses and leaves, of some fruits, like limes and avocados, flavours she could barely recall. Stella stared at the simple cane shoots, and the strip of grass on the verge of the road, and considered the warp and weave of this new place.

She got back into the vehicle and checked the scratchy directions noted on the piece of paper sitting on the seat next to her, then looked back out the car window. Separated by a patch of burrs, two postboxes served as property signs. They were positioned on either side of the road just before it split into two. One of the letterboxes bore her married surname, O'Riain. The other had been vandalised, the words unreadable. In the rear-view mirror an indignant Watson stared back at her from his cage. The bird cocked his proud head sideways, his expressive sulphur-yellow crest rising in annoyance.

Her brother-in-law Harry had said that his house was less than two miles from the gravel road. Stella wished it were another twenty miles, or even thirty. Four days' driving had not lessened her unease. The car and trailer she towed jolted over a buckled ramp where a no-trespassing sign in red lettering hung at an angle. Stella drove past a turn-off that led to a double gate, behind which were what Stella guessed were the work sheds, while the road she followed ended directly at the front of the house. She followed the narrowing track and parked the station wagon to one side of the carport, near where a clothesline tilted ominously.

Stella carefully unclenched her hands from the steering wheel and wiped her palms across the skirt of her dress. To think she'd been married to Joe for seven years and only now was she visiting his family home.

'I'll be back for you,' she said to Watson, opening a window for him.

The bird averted his dark eyes in reply.

Dust flew from the rear of the vehicle as she opened the boot. The contents had shifted during the journey. Stella surveyed the assortment of belongings and then dragged out two suitcases. She ran her eyes over the remaining items and righted a large globe of the world, which had fallen on its side. She tucked her handbag under an arm and lifted the suitcases, setting her eyes squarely on the building before her. The sun-blistered walls of the old timber house were yellowish in colour. Someone had painted the gutters without sanding back the original shade and brown patches showed through a more recent coat of grey.

Stella swallowed, feeling the air catch in her throat, then she stepped up onto the open veranda and, placing the suitcases on the timber boards, knocked on the frame of the screen door. A sweetness hung in the air, reminding her of the caramel tart she used to make for Joe. She rapped on the door again, and when no one answered she started wandering along the length of the veranda.

'Stella?'

The voice was weak. Stella called out a response, her vocal cords scratchy through disuse after the long days of solo travel. She peered through each of the four gauze-covered windows, moving carefully so as not to trip on the buckled veranda that, like the house, was built flat on the ground. The wall was of tongue-and-groove pine like her old home and she ran her hand against the weathered timber until she came to the last window.

'Hello,' said a woman's voice.

Stella lifted a hand to her eyes. It was almost impossible to see anything through the flyscreen. 'Are you Ann?'

'You must be Stella.'

'Yes,' she replied.

'Let yourself in. My bedroom is at the end of the hallway.'

Stella returned to the front door. She propped it open with her foot and pushed the suitcases inside. The door closed loudly behind her. She was standing in a narrow passageway. Through an open door on her right was a kitchen with mint-coloured benchtops and wooden cupboards. From where she stood, every surface appeared to be covered with unwashed dishes, glasses and saucepans. Something crunched underfoot as Stella crossed the floor and entered the adjoining sitting room. It was in a similarly messy state. A trail of ants were making their way across the coffee table and up the side of a bottle of red cordial. Newspapers were scattered on the sofa and armchairs and an old roll-top desk and filing cabinets were crammed along a wall. She found herself hesitating, caught in the clutter of someone else's life.

The end of the sitting room led to another hallway. Stella walked its length slowly, studying the photographs that hung in a row, one by one. She recognised her brother-in-law Harry, and assumed the slight woman beside him was his wife Ann. She looked nice. Four children featured prominently. Three boys and a girl, the tallest boy dressed in a uniform. The other people were strangers, like most of her husband's family.

There were two doors on each side of the hallway and the last on the left was open.

'Hello?' called Stella.

'Come in.'

She entered tentatively. A woman was propped up in bed, a mass of pillows framing her. The sheet was moulded to her body so that her legs appeared long and skinny beneath the material. A table had been dragged to one side of the bed, and on it were magazines and books, a jug of water and a plate of uneaten, curling sandwiches. The bedroom was stuffy and smelt of stale air, and it was just as untidy as the rest of the house. Clothes were strewn across the floor while flies buzzed about a chair that had a sheet draped across it.

'So then, you're here. I'm Ann.' She smiled.

'Hello, Ann. I'm Stella.' The woman lying before her was fair-haired and pale-skinned, a frailer version of the person in the photographs. Stella guessed her to be in her mid-fifties, a good decade older than she was.

'It's nice to meet you,' said Ann. 'I can't believe that it's taken so long.'

Stella was unprepared for this moment. She knew that she

should be grateful. She had no other options, at least not ones that came with a home and employment of sorts, however these people were strangers and they must have wondered at her ready acceptance of their offer. They probably assumed she had nowhere else to go – which was true as far as her immediate future was concerned.

She brushed hair from her face in an effort to tidy it, recalling the sugary tea spilt on her dress, and ran a hand over the creases. The car had been her bed. It was four days since she'd showered. Cleanliness had been replaced by a terrible need for action, to pack her belongings, leave her home and simply drive. And now she was standing in her sister-in-law's bedroom, suffering the inspection of a woman she'd never met before.

'You're very Italian,' said Ann finally, as if she'd been searching for conversation in the absence of any help from Stella.

'That's because I am,' replied Stella, immediately wishing she'd not been so abrupt.

'Of course.' Ann smiled apologetically. 'I'm sorry about the state of the house. I've not been able to do anything since the accident. I don't know if Harry explained what happened.' She paused and, when Stella didn't interrupt, continued. 'I was on the ladder cleaning out the gutters. It was the simplest thing. One minute I was bucketing leaves, and the next I was backing away from one of those nasty black spiders. I woke up on the ground.' She gave a brief laugh. 'It was just like any ordinary day.'

'They always are,' said Stella, wincing at how formal she sounded. 'Quite ordinary.'

Ann stayed silently expectant, however Stella wasn't quite ready to reciprocate with her own story. She was still trying to make sense of the changes in her life.

Finally she asked, 'Where are you injured?'

'It's my lower back. The pain is excruciating. I've damaged three discs. If I lie still, it's not nearly half as bad. But I'm getting better. I couldn't move at all the first week. Now I can just manage to make the pot.' She glanced at the sheet-covered chair. 'Harry cut a hole in the upholstery and wedged a bowl in it. Sorry. Don't think I'm happy with the arrangement. I'm not used to living so basically.'

Stella thought of the walk to the long drop at Kirooma, with its plank of wood and three holes of different sizes. While Joe was out bush tending his sheep, living on silence and greasy mutton chops, a chamber pot had been a welcome alternative to the deep pits in the garden.

'It's been terribly hard on Harry,' Ann continued. 'It's harvest time here. The worst time to be laid up in bed.' Ann stopped again, as if she were waiting for Stella to reply.

Stella gave a slight smile, feeling foolish at her inability to chatter along.

'Well, you'll be wanting to settle in. You can take the first room on the left. It belonged to my eldest, Lyn, but she's long since married.'

Stella gave a grateful nod, both for the welcome and the lack of fuss. She supposed any queries regarding her own situation would come later – not that she had any plans that she could share, not yet. 'I don't want to impose, but I do have a few bits of furniture. Nothing much. A lamp and a table. A rug. Odds and ends. I can leave them in the car unless there's somewhere I can store them. And there's a cockatoo,' she added.

Ann pushed herself up a little higher in the bed, her already pale face turning white with the effort. 'A cockatoo.'

'I couldn't leave him behind.'

'I forgot. You've come straight from the property, haven't you? A long drive, I'd imagine.'

'I can leave the furniture in the car. It doesn't matter.'

'No. Don't do that. I'm pleased you've brought some things with you. It makes a person feel more at home. Anything in Lyn's room that you don't need you can put next door in Paddy's room. He's trying to be a banker in Sydney, much to his father's annoyance. He came home for a few months after he was demobbed, but he was too restless to stay.'

'It's just you and Harry, then?' queried Stella, pleased that she'd actually been capable of asking another question.

'Good heavens, no. The twins, Bill and John, still live with us. They work at the sugar mill and help out here when they can. They keep long hours during harvest season so you'll hardly see them. Sometimes they stay overnight in town. But if they intend on being home for dinner, they'll let you know.'

'Oh, dinner?' said Stella.

Ann sighed. 'I knew Harry wouldn't go into detail. I'm afraid you'll be doing more than just helping me until I'm up and about again. There's the house of course, which I'm sure is in a dreadful state. My boys have never been known for their cleaning abilities. The garden, like most, needs constant attention now we're heading into the hotter months, then there's clothes-washing and, of course, the meals. I should warn you, the three of them have large appetites. You'll have to keep an eye on the tea. We're lucky if we have enough to make it through each week. I thought they would have ended rationing by now.'

Cook, cleaner, carer. Ann was right. The extent of Stella's duties was more than she'd anticipated.

'Is that all right?' asked Ann.

'I wasn't expecting—'

'I'm sorry.' Ann drew up the sheet, fiddling with the top hem. 'Country homes. There's always so much to do.'

Although Stella hadn't considered her role beyond that of tending to Ann's needs, she realised that it was impractical of her to have believed that her tasks would have been limited to that of carer, and yet it irked her that Joe's family assumed that she'd be happy to do whatever was asked of her.

'You can put your bird on the rear veranda if you like.'

'Thank you, Ann, for having me here,' Stella said cordially.

'Keeping busy. That's the thing, Stella, during difficult times. It's always helped me. And I'm sorry – about what happened.'

'Thank you.'

'Now, you might empty my pot for me. The bathroom is just down the hall.'

Stella walked around the bed and, uncovering the chair, carried the pot out of the room, the flies trailing her. Harry had been remarkably plain in his speech across the telephone line when he'd told Stella of Ann's accident and offered her a bed in exchange for help in caring for his wife.

Perhaps she'd been a little too quick to accept.

Discover a
new favourite